The Best
AMERICAN
ESSAYS
2015

WITHDRAWN

D0958067

GUEST EDITORS OF
THE BEST AMERICAN ESSAYS

1986 ELIZABETH HARDWICK
1987 GAY TALESE
1988 ANNIE DILLARD
1989 GEOFFREY WOLFF
1990 JUSTIN KAPLAN
1991 JOYCE CAROL OATES
1992 SUSAN SONTAG
1993 JOSEPH EPSTEIN
1994 TRACY KIDDER
1995 JAMAICA KINCAID
1996 GEOFFREY C. WARD
1997 IAN FRAZIER
1998 CYNTHIA OZICK
1999 EDWARD HOAGLAND
2000 ALAN LIGHTMAN
2001 KATHLEEN NORRIS
2002 STEPHEN JAY GOULD
2003 ANNE FADIMAN
2004 LOUIS MENAND
2005 SUSAN ORLEAN
2006 LAUREN SLATER
2007 DAVID FOSTER WALLACE
2008 ADAM GOPNIK
2009 MARY OLIVER
2010 CHRISTOPHER HITCHENS
2011 EDWIDGE DANTICAT
2012 DAVID BROOKS
2013 CHERYL STRAYED
2014 JOHN JEREMIAH SULLIVAN
2015 ARIEL LEVY

The Best AMERICAN ESSAYS® 2015

Edited and with an Introduction
by ARIEL LEVY

Robert Atwan, Series Editor

A Mariner Original

HOUGHTON MIFFLIN HARCOURT

BOSTON • NEW YORK 2015

www.hmhco.com

ISSN 0888-3742
ISBN 978-0-544-56962-1

Printed in the United States of America
DOC 10 9 8 7 6 5 4 3 2 1

Contents

Foreword:
Of Essays and Essayists

WHEN I STARTED to write the first "Foreword" to this series, now in its thirtieth year, I remember thinking that it would be appropriate, perhaps necessary, to define what I meant by an essay. Here was a new series of books calling attention to a genre that at the time the literary world did not take very seriously. It was hard to forget that just a few years before we launched the series, America's most renowned essayist, E. B. White, acknowledged that "the essayist, unlike the novelist, the poet, and the playwright, must be content in his self-imposed role of second-class citizen." If, as White suggested, essays would not win anyone a Nobel Prize, how substandard were they? What exactly was the literary production that this new series would showcase and celebrate?

Thirty years later and I'm still asking myself that question. I think it's clear that the status of the essay has improved over that time (the longevity of this series being a part of the evidence), but a solid, tight definition of the genre featured thus far throughout thirty volumes continues to elude me. I would, of course, happily use another's definition if I could find one I thought satisfactory. With so many different types of essays being published year after year, it seems impossible to identify a few essential features that characterize the genre and encompass all its forms. But perhaps one way into the matter of definition is to ask not what essays *are* but what essayists *do*. What do they do differently from what the generally more respected writers in other genres do? And where else to begin but with Michel de Montaigne?

It's well known that the origin of the modern essay is usually traced to one writer who began composing odd prose pieces in the 1570s. At first he had no literary category to describe what he was doing, nor did he appear even to possess conventional rhetorical aims. In nearly all previous prose compositions, the act of writing remained in the background; Montaigne is perhaps the first to foreground the writing process. In his prose, he refused to adopt, as did his contemporaries, a professional, scholarly, clerical, or judicial authority. He allowed himself no authoritative posture —only that of being an author. As his pieces accumulated, Montaigne settled on the word *essai* to characterize his literary efforts.

The word was an ordinary term that at the time had no literary resonance. Like most common words, it carried a broad range of connotations. The etymology of *essai* can be traced to the late Latin *exagium*, which meant to weigh or a weight. By the fourth century the term had spread to the Romance languages with the additional and modern meaning of "to attempt" or "to try." (For a fascinating exploration of the word, see John Jeremiah Sullivan's introduction to *The Best American Essays 2014*.) Though we normally translate the title of Montaigne's book as *Essays*, suggesting only the genre, we should remember that in his time the term suggested no literary genre and would be read as "attempts" or "trials," or, since the verb *essayer* had a wide spectrum of synonyms, it could also suggest to sample, taste, practice, take a risk, to experiment, to improvise, to try out, to sound—and these are only a few ways we might understand the term. As Hugo Friedrich says in his splendid study of Montaigne's life and works, the word also implied modest beginnings and a learner's first attempts. The word *essay*, then, served as a caution not to take the work too seriously; these weren't, after all, airtight arguments or conclusive treatises but represented a unique style of prose with an apparently unfinished quality.

Montaigne deliberately pursued an anti-systematic and anti-rhetorical method of composition. He purposefully defied the formal conventions of classification, division, and logical progression that had long characterized serious prose. And he thus established an ironic authorial posture: the art of his essays would be grounded in the illusion of their artlessness. His essays would reflect the mind in process. The writer will not worry about main points and thesis statements, as digressions lead to further digressions and his thematic destination disappears. A practicing Catholic, he doesn't even try to avoid the intellectual mortal sin of inconsistency. For Montaigne, the essay essentially came to represent a compositional challenge to the established rhetorical order, as his fluid thoughts appear to be generated solely from the act of writing and not from a preconceived plan. From this brief description of Montaigne's method we can see how far first-year college writing courses, with their emphasis on clarity, coherence, and distinct rhetorical patterns, have distanced themselves from the original meaning of an essay.

Back in the 1930s, the multitalented J. B. Priestley succinctly and amusingly claimed that an essay is the kind of composition produced by an essayist. In that case, as so many writers have testified, including Virginia Woolf and E. B. White, Montaigne can be regarded as the quintessential essayist: skeptical, ironic, looking at a subject one way and then another while he forms a position that he will undoubtedly qualify, if not completely undermine. Many readers today seem to appreciate writers who aspire to be "subversive"—the word, like *disruptive*, has acquired a positive spin. But Montaigne perfected a manner of self-subversion, and therein lies much of the quality of his intellectual liveliness and enduring appeal, what Virginia Woolf called his "irrepressible vivacity." She cites his own description of his temperament: "bashful, insolent; chaste, lustful; prating, silent; laborious, delicate; ingenious, heavy; melancholic, pleasant; lying, true; knowing, ignorant; liberal, covetous, and prodigal."

Surely one of Montaigne's great achievements consists of the magical way he unites his unique compositional process with his infectious and mercurial personality. As he says in "Of Giving the Lie": "I have no more made my book than my book has made me —a book consubstantial with its author, concerned with my own self, an integral part of my life." He seems to want this notion of consubstantiality to be read as more than a metaphor. At least one of Montaigne's great students and supporters appeared to take him literally. In his brilliant essay on Montaigne, Emerson writes: "The sincerity and marrow of the man reaches to his sentences. I know not anywhere the book that seems less written. It is the language of conversation transferred to a book. Cut these words, and they would bleed; they are vascular and alive."

If the origin of the essay as a genre is French, the origin of the *essayist* is English. As Jean Starobinski, the author of what I consider the finest study of Montaigne (*Montaigne in Motion*), points out, *essayist* had a "pejorative nuance" when first used around the beginning of the seventeenth century. He cites the poet and dramatist Ben Jonson's complaint: "Mere essayists, a few loose sentences, and that's all!" So we are back to White's second-class citizens. From the experts of Montaigne's day to the specialists of ours—those whose work consists of original research, investigative fact-finding, and the formation of incontestable arguments—essays may seem slight and the essayist superficial. Known as an outstanding scholar, Starobinski admits that if someone declared him an essayist, he would feel "slightly hurt" and "take it as a reproach."

So the essayist appears to pursue a paradoxical career. The quintessential essayist parades an enormous ego and yet does so in a modest setting, that is, within a genre widely acknowledged to be unequal to fiction, poetry, and drama. E. B. White was very aware of this and felt the public somewhat justified in regarding the essay as "the last resort of the egoist," and said of himself, "I have always been aware that I am by nature self-absorbed and egoistical; to write of myself to the extent I have done indicates a too great attention to my own life, not enough to the lives of others." A few decades earlier, the *Saturday Review of Literature* critic Elizabeth Drew argued more positively for the essayist's ego, regarding the "pure" or "perfect" essayist—writers such as Montaigne, Lamb, and Hazlitt—as someone who possesses the "secret of the essayist," which she termed "creative egotism" as distinguished from a "trivial" egotism, which produces not great essays but recognizably mannered ones. Although she doesn't consider what I find paradoxical, Drew does recognize the peculiarity of major egos choosing to express themselves in a minor form. But it may be that the essay is the only form suitable for such expression.

You can teach someone many things about writing essays, but I wonder if you can teach anyone how to be an essayist. An essayist at heart, I mean. It may be that just as there are born poets and born storytellers, there are born essayists. This doesn't mean that they discover their genre early; in fact, I would guess that essayists recognize their special talents much later than do poets, novelists, and playwrights, a recognition that comes perhaps only after attempting the other genres. Then, too, there are the poets and novelists who also excel at essays and whose work frequently winds up in these books. That is why the series is called *The Best American*

Essays and not *The Best American Essayists.* But that is a discussion for another time.

The Best American Essays features a selection of the year's outstanding essays, essays of literary achievement that show an awareness of craft and forcefulness of thought. Hundreds of essays are gathered annually from a wide assortment of national and regional publications. These essays are then screened, and approximately one hundred are turned over to a distinguished guest editor, who may add a few personal discoveries and who makes the final selections. The list of notable essays appearing in the back of the book is drawn from a final comprehensive list that includes not only all of the essays submitted to the guest editor but also many that were not submitted.

To qualify for the volume, the essay must be a work of respectable literary quality, intended as a fully developed, independent essay on a subject of general interest (not specialized scholarship), originally written in English (or translated by the author) for publication in an American periodical during the calendar year. Today's essay is a highly flexible and shifting form, however, so these criteria are not carved in stone.

Magazine editors who want to be sure their contributors will be considered each year should submit issues or subscriptions to The Best American Essays, Houghton Mifflin Harcourt, 222 Berkeley Street, Boston, MA 02116. Writers and editors are welcome to submit published essays from any American periodical for consideration; unpublished work does not qualify for the series and cannot be reviewed or evaluated. Also ineligible are essays that have been published in book form—such as a contribution to a collection—but have never appeared in a periodical. All submissions must be directly from the publication and not in manuscript or printout format. Editors of online magazines and literary bloggers should not assume that appropriate work will be seen; they are invited to submit printed copies of the essays to the address above. Please note: because of the increasing number of submissions from online sources, material that does not include a full citation (name of publication, date, author contact information, etc.) will no longer be considered.

As always, I appreciate all the assistance I regularly receive from my editor, Nicole Angeloro. I was fortunate that Liz Duvall once again handled production. I appreciate, too, the assistance of Megan Wilson, Mary Dalton-Hoffman, and Carla Gray. It was a pleasure to work this year with Ariel Levy, who has put together an impressive collection of essays that vividly shows why the genre is so difficult to define. Readers will find here an engaging diversity of moods, voices, stances, and tones, but all with a unifying spirit that reflects the special qualities of her own essays—the seamless dialogue of intimacy and ideas, the creative convergence of public issues and personal identity.

R.A.

Introduction

THE PROBLEM WITH ideas is that you can't decide to have them.

Certain kinds of nonfiction can be made to happen. The writer who is diligent, observant, and inquisitive enough can always find a story: you read the paper, you watch the world, you ask enough questions, and sooner or later, there it is. You have to write it, of course, but it exists with or without you. There are decisions to be made—how best to unfurl the information, what to prioritize, whose perspective to privilege. But you do not have to invent the story, you just have to tell it. I'm not saying it's easy. I'm just saying it can be done.

An essay is another matter. Because whatever its narrative shape, an essay must have an idea as its beating heart. And ideas come to you on their own terms. Searching for an idea is like resolving to have a dream.

At least that's been my experience as a writer. Once in a while —a very extended while—an idea is there in my head, ready to become an essay, and I feel lucky and elated. (So long as I have a pen in my purse, that is. "I am always disturbed," as the composer Igor Stravinsky said of his ideas for musical compositions, "if they come to my ear when my pencil is missing and I am obliged to keep them in my memory." If he was forced to wait too long to write down his idea, Stravinsky went on, "I am in danger of losing the freshness of first contact and I will have difficulty in recapturing its attractiveness.") For me, writing an essay is more pleasurable than any other kind of writing. Usually producing prose is like swimming: a test of will and discipline and fitness that feels good after you've finished doing it. But writing an essay is like catching a wave.

That ideas come as they please is just one of the challenges of writing essays, of course. To catch a wave, you need skill and nerve, not just moving water. As anyone can tell you who has paddled belly-down on a surfboard—frantic and futile as a windup tub toy pulled out of the bath—it is by no means a given that you'll be able to stand up and ride just because the perfect wave comes along. It takes practice and finesse and, not least of all, courage. Because falling off can make you look foolish, and it can hurt. Crafting a piece of writing around an idea you think is worthwhile —an idea you suspect is an insight—requires real audacity. It is an act of daring.

The pleasure of *reading* essays is that you don't have to wait for the waves. (And you don't have to paddle out and get dragged under and bonked in the face with your surfboard over and over until you're dizzy and bedraggled and enraged—which may have happened to me once or thrice.) You just lie back on your towel and gaze out toward the horizon.

There goes Roger Angell, whizzing across the sea! I am no less impressed that he can write an essay as brilliant as "This Old Man" at ninety-three years of age than I would be if I saw him shredding a ten-foot wave—when, as he is the first to admit, "the lower-middle sector of my spine twists and jogs like a Connecticut country road, thanks to a herniated disk seven or eight years ago. This has cost me two or three inches of height, transforming me from Gary Cooper to Geppetto." Angell's accomplishment here is significant: he has managed to turn kvetching about aging into a page-turner. (As he quite accurately puts it, "I am a world-class complainer.") Ultimately, though, his essay isn't stunning because he wrote it in his tenth decade; it's just an astoundingly wonderful piece of writing. "'How great you're looking! Wow, tell me your secret!' they kindly cry when they happen upon me crossing the street or exiting a dinghy or departing an X-ray room," he writes, "while the little balloon over their heads reads 'Holy shit—he's still vertical!'" But it's not all funny. Looming over the essay is the "oceanic force and mystery" of loss. Angell's oldest daughter, Callie, took her own life. He has outlived most of his friends and contemporaries. Angell's wife of forty-eight years, Carol, died in 2012, and he still hears her voice in his head. Propelling the reader from Angell's first sentence to his last is an insight we are desperate to follow until it crashes on the sand: the amazing thing about getting old, Angell tells us, is that the "accruing weight of these departures doesn't bury us, and that even the pain of an almost unbearable loss gives way quite quickly to something more distant but still stubbornly gleaming."

Aging was a big topic in the essays submitted this year, possibly because the baby boomers are doing so much of it. Mark Jacobson, a champion word surfer, has the insight that becoming an *alte kaker* is no different from becoming middle-aged when you're accustomed to being a young adult, or from turning into a young adult when you've just gotten the hang of hormone-riddled adolescence. At sixty-five, "ear hair and all, I remain resolutely myself. I am the same me from my baby pictures, the same me who got laid for the first time in the bushes behind the high school field in Queens, the same me who drove a taxi through Harlem during the Frank Lucas days, the same me my children recognize as their father, the same me I was yesterday, except only more so by virtue of surviving yet another spin of the earth upon its axis. I was at the beginning again," Jacobson writes. "A Magellan of me."

Those are the ideas and words of two men who have been writing for a long time, and it's great fun sitting on the shore watching the pros do what they've been practicing for decades. But it's joyous in a different way to see someone who's just starting out get it right. That's how I felt reading Kelly Sundberg's elegant, haunting "It Will Look Like a Sunset." The insight she gives us is that domestic violence happens "so slowly, then so fast." (Which is to say that it is not as inconceivable as we—I—might imagine.) She spent years married to someone she found impressive and beautiful: "When our elderly neighbor developed dementia and one night thought a boy was hiding under her bed, Caleb stayed with her. When the child of an administrative assistant in Caleb's department needed a heart transplant, Caleb went to the assistant's house and helped him put down wood floors in his basement to create a playroom for the little boy." Violence enters their life in little flashes—forgivable, far apart. "First he pushed me against a wall. It was two more years before he hit me, and another year after that before he hit me again." Along the way, there was the creation of a home, the birth of a child, the invention of a shared adult life. And Sundberg takes us inside it. We are with her, in the texture of her days, in the sparkling intimacy of her early relationship with a young man who lived in a cabin in the woods that he built with his own hands. We experience her isolation when they move to be near his parents, and her disbelief as her only friend, the father of her child, becomes increasingly dangerous.

Her idea—like Angell's and Jacobson's and all the writers' ideas in this book—teaches us something, offers us a new way of thinking about a subject we may imagine we already understand. But her writing also lets us *feel* what it is like to be her. (An essay need not be in the first person, of course, and not all of these are. In Malcolm Gladwell's "The Crooked Ladder," there is no "I"; the writer's presence is never acknowledged in the writing. But we feel him there all the same—his intellect and his empathy. His idea is enlightening, but it's his writing that makes us experience it as truth.)

For me, reading the essays in this anthology was as satisfying and invigorating as glimpsing a school of dolphins rippling in and out of the water: a privilege.

ARIEL LEVY

The Best
AMERICAN
ESSAYS
2015

HILTON ALS

Islands

FROM *Transition*

*Written on the occasion of Peter Doig's exhibition
at the Montreal Museum of Fine Arts*

for Peter

I AM WRITING this some time after standing at the edge of the
bay for the first time. The bay's edge runs parallel to the water,
from east to west in a not-at-all-straight line. For students of master
prints and drawings, a line occurring in nature is the original mark
or beginning, inspiring artists from Da Vinci to Picasso and one
or two hundred others to wonder how to approximate that line's
naturalness on the page, in an artificial medium, just as I am trying to use another artificial medium—prose—to describe what I
see: the water's edge, little white pebbles embedded in light brown
sand at the lip, sand that turns brown and then browner as baby
waves wash up and over a little sandy beach like the one I stood
on this evening. There was a moon, not full and not at all poetical;
on the surface of the water, a small craft hobbled back and forth
on the black bay water, like a legless man rocking back and forth
on an expanse of black. I could not find irony in anything I saw.
There was a bit of moon in the night sky. It killed me. That sky's
largeness and generosity reminded me of how pitiful I can feel
on islands, where one's ideas about the place amount to so much
sentimental or ideological bullshit next to shoeless island dwellers
with rust-colored heels tramping through pig shit putting pigs to
bed, or other island dwellers sitting, legs spread, on a concrete
step leading to a little tin-roofed house, a house with one or two

rooms and black people coupling and talking their coupling in a bedroom in that house, maybe under a window crammed with stars. I like it here. I stay on this island on weekends, when I visit a friend who lives here, a friend I love like no other. It's far north of the island my family came from originally, which is smaller, mean, and turned in on itself, like an evil-smelling root. Looking down at the black wavelets in the black night bay—the patterns were visible to me because of that piece of moon—I could not help but think of lines—lines made in nature, and then lines on a canvas or in a drawing, and how those lines were not really very different from lines of writing brought together to describe sensations such as the love I feel on this island with its bay, and my friend, whom I love like no other.

Earlier in the day, my friend and I came down to the bay with a picnic. After a while, my companion rolled his trouser cuffs up; he walked to the water's edge and then put his feet in the water. I did not join him. In my mind's eye I could see his flat, skeletal feet in clear bay water and suddenly I felt such sadness: he could walk away from me at any moment, walk across the water like Jesus or Robinson Crusoe and set up shop on another island, with some other island dweller. Love can make you feel as though you're shipwrecked; love can make you feel as lonely as an island. Watching my friend standing in the bay water, I wanted to call out to him: Come back! Come back! But he had not left. And yet I feared he would, leaving me behind with all that love and potential and bay water.

The ripples, not waves, made by the turn of the water near my feet at the edge of the night bay sounded like a dog's tongue lapping in a bowl half-filled with water, or perhaps the waves lapping sounded like two human tongues meeting inside mouths joined together less out of comfort than boredom, saying, We might as well, what else is there for us on this island but the tedium of being ourselves alone, our jawbones snap into place as we stretch our mouths open, not to accept one another but to accept the hope that can sometimes happen between two people sitting on a bed in a house on an island, let's call it Barbados, in 1970 or 1971, years before I stood at the wide-open mouth of the bay.

I am not predisposed to the tenets of geography. East and west remain, for me, abstractions that my mind and body cannot make real, since east and west do not relate to the experience of where I am standing in my mind just now, which is near a bay on another island looking into water as if I have a right to it; Marianne Moore said that. In any case, I don't have a right to anything, certainly not an island, which cannot be owned, its citizens can only lease it. Islands belong to themselves. In any case. But I cleave to knowing my friend's island as a way of protecting myself against the memory of other islands I had no choice but to visit at one time or another, like Barbados, which has bays, too. When I am not standing at the edge of the bay on this northern island, I live on another island— Manhattan. Unlike other islands, Manhattan is not a cloud dump. That's how Elizabeth Bishop described Crusoe's Caribbean island —as a "sort of cloud dump"—in her brilliant 1971 poem "Crusoe in England." She goes on:

> Was that why it rained so much?
> And why sometimes the whole place hissed?

Manhattan hisses—with savagery. It's an island of bodies while other islands steam with the hissing of volcanoes—volcanoes that dare you to forget that some islands came into being because of volcanic eruptions or tectonic shifts. But no matter how islands like Barbados and Trinidad, say, came to be formed, you can feel them percolating beneath your feet as you walk to market, or up to the graveyard, or on your way to meet a lover. They bubble with impermanence. The whole thing might sink in a minute just as volcanoes erupt in a minute, and it's that potential impermanence, I think, that contributes to an island's lonely feel, even in Manhattan, where you have to fight to be alone even if you're lonely.

Standing at the edge of the bay, which is a body of water that's connected to an ocean or a sea, and formed by an inlet of land —standing by the edge of the bay for the first time, I didn't want to think about all I'd left behind in Manhattan, which is to say I didn't want to think about my life without my true friend, he whom I love like no other and who introduced me to that northern bay in the first place. To think about my life in the city would be like creating an island that excluded him—an island composed of streets that don't lead to the edge of a bay but end in rivers, and not to get all Langston Hughes about it, but my whole life I have known rivers but not bays, and not love, not like this. My friend's love can feel like the best part of islands and its various intensities, its occasional lushness and aridity, colors that hurt your eyes and skin, smells—peppers, onions, frangipani—that can hurt your skin, too, while shattering any idea you might have had about your own originality: the smells and colors on certain islands in the Caribbean, say, are you and you are the smells and colors because for the most part island life is small and intense and no one who lives there or spends any time in that part of the world escapes being absorbed in the din of its colors, the orchestra of its smells, the horizon line where sea and sky meet and go on and on, seemingly forever.

I want to go on with my friend forever, not least because he wants to know who I am; he wants to see me, and that includes knowing something about my past, and that past includes, of course, my first experiences on islands. He wants to connect my past of water and tectonic shifts with his island, and the bay. One memory: my younger brother and I were sent to visit our mother's enormous family in 1970 or 1971, when we were around ten and eight, respectively. Being sent away on summer holiday meant leaving behind our social lives in Brooklyn, where we grew up, and where pebbles were embedded in concrete and streetlights relieved the darkness and one would see and smell, on summer nights, acrid children in striped T-shirts, musty earth in vacant lots, rusting car parts in vacant lots, older children sitting in those non-automotive cars smoking cigarettes and pinching the small nipples on small-tittied girls whose long legs in their Bermuda shorts or denim cutoffs were like osprey legs in that they would have trod delicately through bay water, had there been any as lapidary as the bay water edging toward my feet moments before I recalled visiting Barbados as a child, which was not the great adventure some parents, like my own, expect their children to have, especially if those parents are interested in geography and are familiar with the terrain they are sending their children off to see, partially in the hope that their past experience will make their children, whom they cannot see, behave in a way that is responsible to the landscape that the parents themselves used to have their wildest dreams of escape on, but won't admit to, needing to believe in the fiction of family, of geography, in order to maintain some sense of who they are. The mind unfamiliar with geography does not know how to define any one place. That summer in Barbados: I could only make sense of it through the character of the people, various someones I could touch or sit with at the foot of a stunted coconut tree, people who smelled of themselves, their island. Nevertheless, the homesickness my brother and I felt in Barbados (our first long trip away from everything) could not be assuaged by anything, nor was it in the least modified by knowing one another. Our loneliness cast us further apart than we had ever been and could ever be again. We were guests, charges, therefore our behavior had to contain a certain forced humility. This further emphasized our separateness. The only way we could be in the least bold was to reject one another. We refused to share any experience and agree on its value. The dust on the road rising and settling on concrete walls, on the fronts of houses and in our hair, did not affect us the same. When we had to accompany one of our mother's relatives to market to buy blowfish, or pork for stew, or something equally foreign, one of us resolutely "liked" this experience while the other did not. Until we arrived in Barbados, my brother and I had wanted to be as much like one another as two people can be. In Barbados, one thing in particular was different: my brother did not dream of one of our older male cousins swallowing my tongue whole and then spitting it out on a plate, then commanding me to lick my own tongue up, which I couldn't, being tongueless. In short, my brother abandoned me to myself on that island, he who knew what an island was, as though I did not, starting and staring at the water. At home, our mother and sisters had protected our natural timidity. On this trip to that place neither of us could ever call home, my brother had to be as different from me as he could allow. He became less timid and more afraid to be thought unconventional. On that island—where blue, really violet-colored seawater stretched to points east, west, north, and south, points I had seen written in various books but could not make any sense of—he became what he is now: mindful of the fact that he cannot look his girlish brother in the eye. Before Barbados, I had never seen so many black people who disliked one another, or who did not have photographs in their homes. The people we saw quarreled with one another in the streets, in front of their homes. They kicked skinny dogs that hung around their yards with heads bowed; the dogs took as much hurt as those hurt people took from one another. Their fucking sounded like hurt, too. The fucking my brother and I heard those people do occurred after lunch, after they had eaten their strange food and the sun was so hot it was ugly. My brother and I sat not-together on opposite sides of whatever house we were staying in, listening to their bodies breed more misery. There was nothing else for those people to do in that place except dissect one another in the cruelest language imaginable, and breed more people who would behave the same way everyone else did. My brother's hairline hair was a dark blond that was nearly the color of the sand shifting beneath my feet at the mouth of the bay I stood at so many years later. In Barbados, my brother wanted to join that community of men who talked their sex as much as they performed it. At least in Barbados, his thinking went, he would be recognized as a male (and overvalued as such), not just as the brother or son of so many girls (in Brooklyn we lived with our four sisters, our mother, and Mother's mother), girls who talked and talked to men as if they weren't there. Late into our stay, my brother invited two girls into our aunt's home, where we were staying. My brother invited these two girls in when my aunt was out being unkind to people. I can recall the two young girls looking as thin and vulnerable as my brother and I must have looked then. My brother demanded that I lie on top of one of the girls as he lay on top of the other, on the floor. He wanted me to be less the girl I had become and more of the boy he was inventing himself as, right before my very eyes. I stood over the girl my brother had chosen for me as my brother lay on top of the other girl, both of us writhing in imitation of all we had ever heard other men say to women, listening outside their bedroom windows. The young girl lying beneath me wore a green school uniform and a brown beret. I stood over her for what felt like forever, as forever as standing at the edge of the bay felt, years later. No words came out of my mouth as I lay on top of the young girl not speaking, not daring to move, since what I wanted, she wanted, which was a fatter, bigger, larger tongue that would swallow her own whole, just as I began to be afraid of this: that my brother would never leave the family we were born into, doing everything, including fucking, just as they all have, and perhaps always will. The only photographs I took back from Barbados that summer were photographs of the young girl I could not kiss, photographs I took moments after our non-exchange, since I couldn't really touch her, she being myself. Once the photographs were developed and installed in my mother's photograph album, I could not write this girl's name on the back of the image. I never looked at them again. Labeling photographs was a habit I had developed in Brooklyn, where the people I lived with or my parents' relatives kept photographs of relatives from Barbados they had never met, keepsakes that didn't mean a thing. They kept those passport-size portraits taken in a photographer's studio, against backgrounds meant to resemble small churches, or a bamboo grove, in plastic binders whose covers showed brightly colored flowers in 3-D, or bay water at midnight, with boats on it. The photographs were arranged by my mother in a haphazard way; she was the least sentimental person I have ever known. I wrote the names of the people I could identify on the surface of the pictures my mother had collected because I feared, somehow, that unless I did, everyone connected to my family would be forgotten, long before I began to want to forget them. There was one photograph my mother owned that never ceased to interest me, though. It was oval-shaped and framed in fake gold leaf. Originally, the frame and the image it contained had belonged to my grandmother—my father's mother. The image was of my grandmother's nephew, after whom I was named. *Hilton Rolston* was the name written in faint black script at the bottom of the photograph. In it, one could see his full lips and straight black hair parted in the middle. One could also see his wing collar, tie, and jacket with fairly wide lapels. It was taken sometime in the 1890s, just before Hilton Rolston left Barbados to pan for gold in California nearly sixty years after the gold rush had taken place. I don't think he knew where he was going, except toward a dream. He was pretty. Perhaps going to California and dying in the gold rush that kept never happening for him was a way to be himself, far from the horror of feigned intimacy that defines family life in Barbados, like most other places. I don't know a thing about him except what my grandmother told me. Hilton's portrait is one of the few things she brought with her when she emigrated from Barbados to Brooklyn—that and another large painted photograph, of my grandmother with her father and brother, that was destroyed, along with everything else she owned, in a fire in a house she had bought for her children long before I came along. My mother was given Hilton as a gift, shortly after his namesake was born. In that portrait of Hilton, he appears to be more dead than alive, even though he was photographed and painted when he was alive. The photograph is a memento mori, really, which is a quality that all painted photographs share. And it is what I might have looked like—another memento mori—had I been photographed recently, and the photograph had been painted over, standing at the edge of the bay.

ROGER ANGELL

This Old Man

FROM *The New Yorker*

CHECK ME OUT. The top two knuckles of my left hand look as if I'd been worked over by the KGB. No, it's more as if I'd been a catcher for the Hall of Fame pitcher Candy Cummings, the inventor of the curveball, who retired from the game in 1877. To put this another way, if I pointed that hand at you like a pistol and fired at your nose, the bullet would nail you in the left knee. Arthritis.

Now, still facing you, if I cover my left, or better, eye with one hand, what I see is a blurry encircling version of the ceiling and floor and walls or windows to our right and left but no sign of your face or head: nothing in the middle. But cheer up: if I reverse things and cover my right eye, there you are, back again. If I take my hand away and look at you with both eyes, the empty hole disappears and you're in 3-D, and actually looking pretty terrific today. Macular degeneration.

I'm ninety-three, and I'm feeling great. Well, pretty great, unless I've forgotten to take a couple of Tylenols in the past four or five hours, in which case I've begun to feel some jagged little pains shooting down my left forearm and into the base of the thumb. Shingles, in 1996, with resultant nerve damage.

Like many men and women my age, I get around with a couple of arterial stents that keep my heart chunking. I also sport a minute plastic seashell that clamps shut a congenital hole in my heart, discovered in my early eighties. The surgeon at Mass General who fixed up this PFO (a patent foramen ovale—I love to say it) was a Mexican-born character actor in beads and clogs, and a fervent admirer of Derek Jeter. Counting this procedure and the stents, plus a passing balloon angioplasty and two or three false alarms, I've become sort of a table potato, unalarmed by the X-ray cameras swooping eerily about just above my naked body in a darkened and icy operating room; there's also a little TV screen up there that presents my heart as a pendant ragbag attached to tacky ribbons of veins and arteries. But never mind. Nowadays I pop a pink beta-blocker and a white statin at breakfast, along with several lesser pills, and head off to my human-wreckage gym, and it's been a couple of years since the last showing.

My left knee is thicker but shakier than my right. I messed it up playing football, eons ago, but can't remember what went wrong there more recently. I had a date to have the joint replaced by a famous knee man (he's listed in the Metropolitan Opera program as a major supporter) but changed course at the last moment, opting elsewhere for injections of synthetic frog hair or rooster combs or something, which magically took away the pain. I walk around with a cane now when outdoors—"Stop *brandishing!*" I hear my wife, Carol, admonishing—which gives me a nice little edge when hailing cabs.

The lower-middle sector of my spine twists and jogs like a Connecticut country road, thanks to a herniated disk seven or eight years ago. This has cost me two or three inches of height, transforming me from Gary Cooper to Geppetto. After days spent groaning on the floor, I received a blessed epidural, ending the ordeal. "You can sit up now," the doctor said, whisking off his shower cap. "Listen, do you know who Dominic Chianese is?"

"Isn't that Uncle Junior?" I said, confused. "You know—from *The Sopranos?*"

"Yes," he said. "He and I play in a mandolin quartet every Wednesday night at the Hotel Edison. Do you think you could help us get a listing in the front of *The New Yorker?*"

I've endured a few knocks but missed worse. I know how lucky I am, and secretly tap wood, greet the day, and grab a sneaky pleasure from my survival at long odds. The pains and insults are bearable. My conversation may be full of holes and pauses, but I've learned to dispatch a private Apache scout ahead into the next sentence, the one coming up, to see if there are any vacant names or verbs in the landscape up there. If he sends back a warning, I'll pause meaningfully, duh, until something else comes to mind.

On the other hand, I've not yet forgotten Keats or Dick Cheney or what's waiting for me at the dry cleaner's today. As of right now, I'm not Christopher Hitchens or Tony Judt or Nora Ephron; I'm not dead and not yet mindless in a reliable upstate facility. Decline and disaster impend, but my thoughts don't linger there. It shouldn't surprise me if at this time next week I'm surrounded by family, gathered on short notice—they're sad and shocked but also a little pissed off to be here—to help decide, after what's happened, what's to be done with me now. It must be this hovering knowledge, that two-ton safe swaying on a frayed rope just over my head, that makes everyone so glad to see me again. "How great you're looking! Wow, tell me your secret!" they kindly cry when they happen upon me crossing the street or exiting a dinghy or departing an X-ray room, while the little balloon over their heads reads, "Holy shit—he's still vertical!"

Let's move on. A smooth fox terrier of ours named Harry was full of surprises. Wildly sociable, like others of his breed, he grew a fraction more reserved in maturity, and learned to cultivate a separate wagging acquaintance with each fresh visitor or old pal he came upon in the living room. If friends had come for dinner, he'd arise from an evening nap and leisurely tour the table in imitation of a three-star headwaiter: Everything O.K. here? Is there anything we could bring you? How was the crème brûlée? Terriers aren't water dogs, but Harry enjoyed kayaking in Maine, sitting like a figurehead between my knees for an hour or more and scoping out the passing cormorant or yachtsman. Back in the city, he established his personality and dashing good looks on the neighborhood to the extent that a local artist executed a striking head-on portrait in pointillist oils, based on a snapshot of him she'd sneaked in Central Park. Harry took his leave (another surprise) on a June afternoon three years ago, a few days after his eighth birthday. Alone in our fifth-floor apartment, as was usual during working hours, he became unhinged by a noisy thunderstorm and went out a front window left a quarter open on a muggy day. I knew him well and could summon up his feelings during the brief moments of that leap: the welcome coolness of rain on his muzzle and shoulders, the excitement of air and space around his outstretched body.

Here in my tenth decade, I can testify that the downside of great age is the room it provides for rotten news. Living long means enough already. When Harry died, Carol and I couldn't stop weeping; we sat in the bathroom with his retrieved body on a mat between us, the light-brown patches on his back and the near-black of his ears still darkened by the rain, and passed a Kleenex box back and forth between us. Not all the tears were for him. Two months earlier, a beautiful daughter of mine, my oldest child, had ended her life, and the oceanic force and mystery of that event had not left full space for tears. Now we could cry without reserve, weep together for Harry and Callie and ourselves. Harry cut us loose.

A few notes about age is my aim here, but a little more about loss is inevitable. "Most of the people my age is dead. You could look it up" was the way Casey Stengel put it. He was seventy-five at the time, and contemporary social scientists might prefer Casey's line delivered at eighty-five now, for accuracy, but the point remains. We geezers carry about a bulging directory of dead husbands or wives, children, parents, lovers, brothers and sisters, dentists and shrinks, office sidekicks, summer neighbors, classmates, and bosses, all once entirely familiar to us and seen as part of the safe landscape of the day. It's no wonder we're a bit bent. The surprise, for me, is that the accruing weight of these departures doesn't bury us, and that even the pain of an almost unbearable loss gives way quite quickly to something more distant but still stubbornly gleaming. The dead have departed, but gestures and glances and tones of voice of theirs, even scraps of clothing—that pale-yellow Saks scarf—reappear unexpectedly, along with accompanying touches of sweetness or irritation.

Our dead are almost beyond counting and we want to herd them along, pen them up somewhere in order to keep them straight. I like to think of mine as fellow voyagers crowded aboard the *Île de France* (the idea is swiped from *Outward Bound*). Here's my father, still handsome in his tuxedo, lighting a Lucky Strike. There's Ted Smith, about to name-drop his Gloucester hometown again. Here comes Slim Aarons. Here's Esther Mae Counts, from fourth grade: hi, Esther Mae. There's Gardner—with Cecille Shawn, for some reason. Here's Ted Yates. Anna Hamburger. Colba F. Gucker, better known as Chief. Bob Ascheim. Victor Pritchett—and Dorothy. Henry Allen. Bart Giamatti. My elder old-maid cousin Jean Webster and her unexpected, late-arriving Brit husband, Capel Hanbury. Kitty Stableford. Dan Quisenberry. Nancy Field. Freddy

Alexandre. I look around for others and at times can almost produce someone at will. Callie returns, via a phone call. "Dad?" It's her, all right, her voice affectionately rising at the end—"Da-ad?" —but sounding a bit impatient this time. She's in a hurry. And now Harold Eads. Toni Robin. Dick Salmon, his face bright red with laughter. Edith Oliver. Sue Dawson. Herb Mitgang. Coop. Tudie. Elwood Carter.

These names are best kept in mind rather than boxed and put away somewhere. Old letters are engrossing but feel historic in numbers, photo albums delightful but with a glum after-kick like a chocolate caramel. Home movies are killers: Zeke, a long-gone Lab, alive again, rushing from right to left with a tennis ball in his mouth; my sister Nancy, stunning at seventeen, smoking a lipstick-stained cigarette aboard *Astrid*, with the breeze stirring her tied-up brown hair; my mother laughing and ducking out of the picture again, waving her hands in front of her face in embarrassment —she's about thirty-five. Me sitting cross-legged under a Ping-Pong table, at eleven. Take us away.

My list of names is banal but astounding, and it's barely a fraction, the ones that slip into view in the first minute or two. Anyone over sixty knows this; my list is only longer. I don't go there often, but once I start, the battalion of the dead is on duty, alertly waiting. Why do they sustain me so, cheer me up, remind me of life? I don't understand this. Why am I not endlessly grieving?

What I've come to count on is the white-coated attendant of memory, silently here again to deliver dabs from the laboratory dish of me. In the days before Carol died, twenty months ago, she lay semiconscious in bed at home, alternating periods of faint or imperceptible breathing with deep, shuddering catch-up breaths. Then, in a delicate gesture, she would run the pointed tip of her tongue lightly around the upper curve of her teeth. She repeated this pattern again and again. I've forgotten, perhaps mercifully, much of what happened in that last week and the weeks after, but this recurs.

Carol is around still, but less reliably. For almost a year, I would wake up from another late-afternoon mini-nap in the same living-room chair, and in the instants before clarity would sense her sitting in her own chair, just opposite. Not a ghost but a presence, alive as before and in the same instant gone again. This happened often, and I almost came to count on it, knowing that it wouldn't last. Then it stopped.

People my age and younger friends as well seem able to recall entire tapestries of childhood, and swatches from their children's early lives as well: conversations, exact meals, birthday parties, illnesses, picnics, vacation B and B's, trips to the ballet, the time when . . . I can't do this and it eats at me, but then, without announcement or connection, something turns up. I am walking on Ludlow Lane, in Snedens, with my two young daughters, years ago on a summer morning. I'm in my late thirties; they're about nine and six, and I'm complaining about the steep little stretch of road between us and our house, just up the hill. Maybe I'm getting old, I offer. Then I say that one day I'll be really old and they'll have to hold me up. I imitate an old man mumbling nonsense and start to walk with wobbly legs. Callie and Alice scream with laughter and hold me up, one on each side. When I stop, they ask for more, and we do this over and over.

I'm leaving out a lot, I see. My work—I'm still working, or sort of. Reading. The collapsing, grossly insistent world. Stuff I get excited about or depressed about all the time. Dailiness—but how can I explain this one? Perhaps with a blog recently posted on Facebook by a woman I know who lives in Australia. "Good Lord, we've run out of nutmeg!" it began. "How in the world did that ever happen?" Dozens of days are like that with me lately.

Intimates and my family—mine not very near me now but always on call, always with me. My children Alice and John Henry and my daughter-in-law Alice—yes, another one—and my granddaughters Laura and Lily and Clara, who together and separately were as steely and resplendent as a company of Marines on the day we buried Carol. And on other days and in other ways as well. Laura, for example, who will appear almost overnight, on demand, to drive me and my dog and my stuff five hundred miles Down East, then does it again, backward, later in the summer. Hours of talk and sleep (mine, not hers) and renewal—the abandoned mills at Lawrence, Mass., Cat Mousam Road, the Narramissic River still there —plus a couple of nights together, with the summer candles again.

Friends in great numbers now, taking me to dinner or cooking in for me. (One afternoon I found a freshly roasted chicken sitting outside my front door; two hours later another one appeared in the same spot.) Friends inviting me to the opera, or to Fairway on Sunday morning, or to dine with their kids at the East Side Deli, or to a wedding at the Rockbound Chapel, or bringing in ice cream to share at my place while we catch another Yankees game. They saved my life. In the first summer after Carol had gone, a man I'd known slightly and pleasantly for decades listened while I talked about my changed routines and my doctors and dog walkers and the magazine. I paused for a moment, and he said, "Plus you have us."

Another message—also brief, also breathtaking—came on an earlier afternoon at my longtime therapist's, at a time when I felt I'd lost almost everything. "I don't know how I'm going to get through this," I said at last.

A silence, then: "Neither do I. But you will."

I am a world-class complainer but find palpable joy arriving with my evening Dewar's, from Robinson Cano between pitches, from the first pages once again of *Appointment in Samarra* or the last lines of the Elizabeth Bishop poem called "Poem." From the briefest strains of Handel or Roy Orbison, or Dennis Brain playing the early bars of his stunning Mozart horn concertos. (This Angel recording may have been one of the first things Carol and I acquired just after our marriage, and I hear it playing on a sunny Saturday morning in our Ninety-Fourth Street walkup.) Also the recalled faces and then the names of Jean Dixon or Roscoe Karns or Porter Hall or Brad Dourif in another Netflix rerun. Chloë Sevigny in *Trees Lounge*. Gail Collins on a good day. Family ice skating up near Harlem in the 1980s, with the park employees, high on youth or weed, looping past us backward to show their smiles.

Recent and not-so-recent surveys (including the six-decades-long Grant Study of the lives of some 1940s Harvard graduates) confirm that a majority of us people over seventy-five keep surprising ourselves with happiness. Put me on that list. Our children are adults now and mostly gone off, and let's hope full of their own lives. We've outgrown our ambitions. If our wives or husbands are still with us, we sense a trickle of contentment flowing from the reliable springs of routine, affection in long silences, calm within the light boredom of well-worn friends, retold stories, and mossy opinions. Also the distant whoosh of a surfaced porpoise outside our night windows.

We elders—what kind of a handle is this, anyway, halfway between a tree and an eel?—we elders have learned a thing or two, including invisibility. Here I am in a conversation with some trusty friends—old friends but actually not all that old: they're in their sixties—and we're finishing the wine and in serious converse about global warming in Nyack or Virginia Woolf the cross-dresser. There's a pause, and I chime in with a couple of sentences. The others look at me politely, then resume the talk exactly at the point where they've just left it. What? Hello? Didn't I just say something? Have I left the room? Have I experienced what neurologists call a TIA—a transient ischemic attack? I didn't expect to take over the chat but did await a word or two of response. Not tonight, though. (Women I know say that this began to happen to them when they passed fifty.) When I mention the phenomenon to anyone around my age, I get back nods and smiles. Yes, we're invisible. Honored, respected, even loved, but not quite worth listening to anymore. You've had your turn, Pops; now it's ours.

I've been asking myself why I don't think about my approaching visitor, death. He was often on my mind thirty or forty years ago, I believe, though more of a stranger. Death terrified me then, because I had so many engagements. The enforced opposite—no dinner dates or coming attractions, no urgent business, no fun, no calls, no errands, no returned words or touches—left a blank that I could not light or furnish: a condition I recognized from childhood bad dreams and sudden awakenings. Well, not yet, not soon, or probably not, I would console myself, and that welcome but then tediously repeated postponement felt in time less like a threat than like a family obligation—tea with Aunt Molly in Montclair, someday soon but not now. Death, meanwhile, was constantly onstage or changing costume for his next engagement—as Bergman's thick-faced chess player; as the medieval night rider in a hoodie; as Woody Allen's awkward visitor half falling into the room as he enters through the window; as W. C. Fields's man in the bright nightgown—and in my mind had gone from specter to a waiting second-level celebrity on the Letterman show. Or almost. Some people I knew seemed to have lost all fear when dying and awaited the end with a certain impatience. "I'm tired of lying here," said one. "Why is this taking so long?" asked another. Death will get it on with me eventually, and stay much too long, and though I'm in no hurry about the meeting, I feel I know him almost too well by now.

A weariness about death exists in me and in us all in another way as well, though we scarcely notice it. We have become tireless voyeurs of death: he is on the morning news and the evening news and on the breaking, middle-of-the-day news as well—not the celebrity death, I mean, but the everyone-else death. A roadside accident figure, covered with a sheet. A dead family, removed from a ramshackle faraway building pocked and torn by bullets. The transportation dead. The dead in floods and hurricanes and tsunamis, in numbers called "tolls." The military dead, presented in silence on your home screen, looking youthful and well combed. The enemy war dead or rediscovered war dead, in higher figures. Appalling and dulling totals not just from this year's war but from the ones before that, and the ones way back that some of us still around may have also attended. All the dead from wars and natural events and school shootings and street crimes and domestic crimes that each of us has once again escaped and felt terrible about and plans to go and leave wreaths or paper flowers at the site of. There's never anything new about death, to be sure, except its improved publicity. At second hand we have become death's expert witnesses; we know more about death than morticians, feel as much at home with it as those poor bygone schlunks trying to survive a continent-ravaging, low-digit-century epidemic. Death sucks but, enh—click the channel.

I get along. Now and then it comes to me that I appear to have more energy and hope than some of my coevals, but I take no credit for this. I don't belong to a book club or a bridge club; I'm not taking up Mandarin or practicing the viola. In a sporadic effort to keep my brain from moldering, I've begun to memorize shorter poems—by Auden, Donne, Ogden Nash, and more—which I recite to myself some nights while walking my dog, Harry's successor fox terrier, Andy. I've also become a blogger, and enjoy the ease and freedom of the form: it's a bit like making a paper airplane and then watching it take wing below your window. But shouldn't I have something more scholarly or complex than this put away by now—late paragraphs of accomplishments, good works, some weightier op cits? I'm afraid not. The thoughts of age are short, short thoughts. I don't read scripture and cling to no life precepts, except perhaps to Walter Cronkite's rules for old men, which he did not deliver over the air: Never trust a fart. Never pass up a drink. Never ignore an erection.

I count on jokes, even jokes about death.

> TEACHER: Good morning, class. This is the first day of school and we're going to introduce ourselves. I'll call on you, one by one, and you can tell us your name and maybe what your dad or your mom does for a living. You, please, over at this end.
>
> SMALL BOY: My name is Irving and my dad is a mechanic.
>
> TEACHER: A mechanic! Thank you, Irving. Next?
>
> SMALL GIRL: My name is Emma and my mom is a lawyer.
>
> TEACHER: How nice for you, Emma! Next?
>
> SECOND SMALL BOY: My name is Luke and my dad is dead.
>
> TEACHER: Oh, Luke, how sad for you. We're all very sorry about that, aren't we, class? Luke, do you think you could tell us what Dad did before he died?
>
> LUKE (seizes his throat): He went "N'gungghhh!"

Not bad—I'm told that fourth graders really go for this one. Let's try another.

A man and his wife tried and tried to have a baby, but without success. Years went by and they went on trying, but no luck. They liked each other, so the work was always a pleasure, but they grew a bit sad along the way. Finally she got pregnant, was very careful, and gave birth to a beautiful eight-pound-two-ounce baby boy. The couple were beside themselves with happiness. At the hospital that night, she told her husband to stop by the local newspaper and arrange for a birth announcement, to tell all their friends the good news. First thing next morning, she asked if he'd done the errand.

"Yes, I did," he said, "but I had no idea those little notices in the paper were so expensive."

"Expensive?" she said. "How much was it?"

"It was eight hundred and thirty-seven dollars. I have the receipt."

"Eight hundred and thirty-seven dollars!" she cried. "But that's impossible. You must have made some mistake. Tell me exactly what happened."

"There was a young lady behind a counter at the paper, who

gave me the form to fill out," he said. "I put in your name and my name and little Teddy's name and weight, and when we'd be home again and, you know, ready to see friends. I handed it back to her and she counted up the words and said, 'How many insertions?' I said twice a week for fourteen years, and she gave me the bill. O.K.?"

I heard this tale more than fifty years ago, when my first wife, Evelyn, and I were invited to tea by a rather elegant older couple who were new to our little Rockland County community. They were in their seventies at least, and very welcoming, and it was just the four of us. We barely knew them, and I was surprised when he turned and asked her to tell us the joke about the couple trying to have a baby. "Oh, no," she said, "they wouldn't want to hear that."

"Oh, come on, dear—they'll love it," he said, smiling at her. I groaned inwardly and was preparing a forced smile while she started off shyly, but then, of course, the four of us fell over laughing together.

That night Evelyn said, "Did you see Keith's face while Edie was telling that story? Did you see hers? Do you think it's possible that they're still—you know, still doing it?"

"Yes, I did—yes, I do," I said. "I was thinking exactly the same thing. They're amazing."

This was news back then, but probably shouldn't be by now. I remember a passage I came upon years later, in an op-ed piece in the *Times*, written by a man who'd just lost his wife. "We slept naked in the same bed for forty years," it went. There was also my splendid colleague Bob Bingham, dying in his late fifties, who was asked by a friend what he'd missed or would do differently if given the chance. He thought for an instant and said, "More venery."

More venery. More love; more closeness; more sex and romance. Bring it back, no matter what, no matter how old we are. This fervent cry of ours has been certified by Simone de Beauvoir and Alice Munro and Laurence Olivier and any number of remarried or recoupled ancient classmates of ours. Laurence Olivier? I'm thinking of what he says somewhere in an interview: "Inside, we're all seventeen, with red lips."

This is a dodgy subject, coming as it does here from a recent widower, and I will risk a further breach of code and add that this was something that Carol and I now and then idly discussed. We didn't quite see the point of memorial fidelity. In our view, the departed spouse—we always thought it would be me—wouldn't be around anymore but knew or had known that he or she was loved forever. Please go ahead, then, sweetheart—don't miss a moment. Carol said this last: "If you haven't found someone else by a year after I'm gone I'll come back and haunt you."

Getting old is the second-biggest surprise of my life, but the first, by a mile, is our unceasing need for deep attachment and intimate love. We oldies yearn daily and hourly for conversation and a renewed domesticity, for company at the movies or while visiting a museum, for someone close by in the car when coming home at night. This is why we throng Match.com and OkCupid in such numbers—but not just for this, surely. Rowing in Eden (in Emily Dickinson's words: "Rowing in Eden— / Ah—the sea") isn't reserved for the lithe and young, the dating or the hooked-up or the just lavishly married, or even for couples in the middle-aged mixed-doubles semifinals, thank God. No personal confession or revelation impends here, but these feelings in old folks are widely treated like a raunchy secret. The invisibility factor—you've had your turn—is back at it again. But I believe that everyone in the world wants to be with someone else tonight, together in the dark, with the sweet warmth of a hip or a foot or a bare expanse of shoulder within reach. Those of us who have lost that, whatever our age, never lose the longing: just look at our faces. If it returns, we seize upon it avidly, stunned and altered again.

Nothing is easy at this age, and first meetings for old lovers can be a high-risk venture. Reticence and awkwardness slip into the room. Also happiness. A wealthy old widower I knew married a nurse he met while in the hospital, but had trouble remembering her name afterward. He called her "kid." An eighty-plus, twice-widowed lady I'd once known found still another love, a frail but vibrant Midwest professor, now close to ninety, and the pair got in two or three happy years together before he died as well. When she called his children and arranged to pick up her things at his house, she found every possession of hers lined up outside the front door.

But to hell with them and with all that, O.K.? Here's to you, old dears. You got this right, every one of you. Hook, line, and sinker; never mind the why or wherefore; somewhere in the night; love me forever, or at least until next week. For us and for anyone this unsettles, anyone who's younger and still squirms at the vision of an old couple embracing, I'd offer John Updike's "Sex or death: you take your pick"—a line that appears (in a slightly different form) in a late story of his, "Playing with Dynamite."

This is a great question, an excellent insurance plan choice, I mean. I think it's in the Affordable Care Act somewhere. Take it from us, who know about the emptiness of loss and are still cruising along here feeling lucky and not yet entirely alone.

KENDRA ATLEEWORK

Charade

FROM *Hayden's Ferry Review*

WHEN IT RAINED in Swall Meadows, Elizabeth and I took to the street. The best rains fell at night in the autumn, out of clouds resting on the side of Wheeler Crest, fat and freezing. They rolled down the mountain, swallowing my house and the surrounding blue spruce, the skeletons of silver poplars, peaks bristled by evergreens. By November snow had reached the ridge, and the air was tangible, flavored with frost and the slow death of plants and birds. In the evenings came the smell of smoke, the metallic ping of my father's ax against knotty wood.

The street that leads from my house to Elizabeth's, gravelly and tilting to the south, is lined with dusty pines and mailboxes. Swall Meadows is high desert. The few deciduous trees that survive the dry summers lose their leaves and spend winter growing naked, branches freezing and snapping off, one by one.

Water comes to our region three times a year. First are hot summer thunderstorms that draw steam from the mesas in the valley below. Next is autumn rain, gentle, resigned to an approaching freeze, hardened almost to ice but falling softly, melting into skin or the knit of a sweatshirt. Finally there is winter, when a flat plane of snow, sharpened by nights of wind, crusts over the mountainside and around the dead willow groves that encircle Swall Meadows.

Autumn I remember best, when Elizabeth and I were sixteen. It was then that we walked. Each night when the rain fell we crept out Elizabeth's ragged screen door. Swall Meadows has no streetlights, and we could see no more than twenty feet ahead. When the clouds settled they blocked out my house, higher up the flank of Wheeler Crest. Headlights never appeared. In the nearest town, thirty minutes from home, was a two-screen movie theater, two coffee shops, the high school. But that was all very far away. If the neighbors looked out their windows on those autumn nights, they would have seen two tall girls, walking slowly.

When I was a child, before I knew Elizabeth, the house where she would someday move with her father, Russell, was a bad place. The man who lived there owned a white wolf that battered its body against the screen door. The man left suddenly without explanation, and Elizabeth and Russell took his place, fleeing an eviction in the town. For a few years Elizabeth and I had been reading *Calvin and Hobbes* comics together behind our choir folders and hiding in the locker room during PE. When she moved to Swall Meadows, isolation made us the focal point of each other's lives.

For Russell, the move made sense. Rent was cheap in Swall, and he was still able to work as a cabinetmaker for new apartment complexes in town. The neighborhood placed him four hours from the nearest city. In Sparks, Nevada, Russell could gamble and visit the Wild Horse Resort, the corners of his suitcase lined stealthily with condoms—we found them accidentally, snooping in the hotel room, when he let us come along on one of his trips.

Elizabeth's house was small and flat and always dirty. Outside, white Christmas lights shone year round, illuminating a plastic baby skeleton that hung from a tree in the front yard, a relic from a past Halloween. Inside, Russell decorated with mirrors, antique paintings, old army knives—one designed for killing, curved in such a way that suction would not trap it in the body, meaning it could be removed and plunged in again and again. Most of the light fixtures were broken and without bulbs. The kitchen floor left bare feet tacky with food scraps and dirt tracked in by Sara, the German shepherd. The windows were always closed, and the furniture and carpet took on the smell of steak and sawdust. I spent most of my time in this house.

During the autumn when we were sixteen, the neighbors who drove Elizabeth and me to and from school turned up the heaters in their Hondas. The Hydes tried to make us talk. The O'Brians, who owned a sailboat in San Diego, listened to classic rock on KRHV and left us to stare out the windows at the bitterbrush and the frozen surface of Crowley Lake.

On each November day, the neighbors dropped us at our respective houses after school. Both were on Mountain View Drive, hers slightly south, mine higher up against the incline of Wheeler Crest. For a few hours I would sit on the floor in front of the neglected fireplace, waiting for Elizabeth's text message.

sleepover bears?

I could picture Russell bent over his workbench in the garage, his hands cold, scraping a knuckle. When the sun fell behind the mountain and the light dropped, he would amble inside for his first bottle of wine, Elizabeth waiting in the kitchen doorway.

"How was school?" Russell would ask, rinsing a dirty glass.

"Fine."

"Sleepover bears again?"

Russell called me "Kendra Bear." Elizabeth was "Boo Boo Bear." He could not acknowledge that his daughter was a woman, who had sex with men and kept her life a secret. Her mother lived in Palm Springs, makeup tattooed on her face, and Elizabeth hated both of them more deeply than a child can hate.

It took ten minutes to reach Elizabeth's door if I ran down Mountain View Drive as fast as I could. The thinning soles of my Converse slid on pavement that had been sloughing into dirt for decades. My nose turned pink and my eyes watered from the cold, my black sweatshirt too thin for autumn. Pressed into the flank of the mountain, Swall Meadows sits in chilly, sharp-shadowed light once the sun sets. For a few hours after evening comes to our neighborhood, the valley below still glows golden.

We spent most nights on the floor of Elizabeth's living room. I had a bed at my house, but my room was dark and empty in those days, haunted, I knew, by a specter named Victor and his little sister, who turned off my lamp without warning. Each evening Elizabeth and I stoked the fire heavily before falling asleep. Inevitably it died, and we woke, shivering under holey baby blankets dotted with wood chips tracked around by the guinea pig, Hitler. He lived wild under the stove, and he had his name because Elizabeth loved terrible things.

That autumn Elizabeth almost never came to my house. When she did she left her Converse (matching mine) in the mudroom while we sat on my mother's bed. My mother asked polite questions, thoughtful questions. But Elizabeth was uncomfortable and I was uncomfortable for her. I looked at the two most important women in my life, and I knew I could only be with them apart.

On November 17 my mother was diagnosed with terminal cancer. I gave my junior anatomy class a presentation on the disease, and I got a good grade. Metastatic cholangiocarcinoma (pronounced as naturally as my name) attacks the bile ducts of the liver, beginning as an autoimmune disease which, in 10 percent of cases, changes. It turns from preparing your three children for the inevitability of your liver transplant to the inevitability of your very near death. It turns from buying rubber livers that grow when put in water, and making jokes about motorcycle riders without helmets (won't they make good donors for Mom), and it turns metastatic. Metastatic means the cancer has already spread to the lymph nodes by the time you take your family to the Mayo Clinic in Jacksonville, Florida, to eat Thanksgiving dinner at a twenty-four-hour diner. The specialists cry when they give you your prognosis, because what goes to the lymph nodes spreads to the rest of the body, and what you get is a tumor on the abdomen that makes you look five months pregnant, according to my mother, and still I can't look at babies. Life expectancy upon diagnosis is three months. My mother lived for four.

The months passed and Elizabeth learned these facts with me. But she was sixteen and she didn't know what to do about them. She knew enough to defend me from our Spanish class, when it was over and the teacher asked her, "What do we say to Kendra?"

She told them to leave me alone. That they should not mention God, or his plan. She understood enough to attend the memorial at the United Methodist Church. I sat in the first pew with my family, next to my crying, balding cousin who had removed his bandanna in public for the first time; I watched Elizabeth come in late with Russell, picking through the legs of the congregation, looking for a seat, and I felt a kind of comfort. But this was as involved as Elizabeth could become.

And so we spent our time together beneath the low ceiling of her house, and Russell flipped cauliflower in a wrought-iron pan.

Russell wore work boots and jeans with small holes nicked in the denim, and he left dishes gray with lard on the counter for days. He was a wonderful cook. Whenever I stepped into the warm, dirty kitchen, Russell poked me in my skinny ribs and asked, "What does Kendra Bear want for dinner?"

We ate with Russell on the stained living-room couch. Spinach salad and stir-fried shrimp, garlic pasta. *The Count of Monte Cristo,*

Six Feet Under, or *Lord of the Rings* played on the television. For a while it was *Pirates of the Caribbean,* over and over. Russell tossed his boots into the hall and stretched his feet in their yellowed socks beneath the coffee table.

"Boo Boo Bear, pour me another glass of wine."

Eventually the bottle of Cabernet was empty and the black woodstove began choking smoke into the living room. We waited for Russell to fall asleep, and once he was drowsing, Brie and cracker crumbs smeared into his work sweatshirt, we tiptoed past him.

In half-sleep, Russell's face was slack. His cheeks sagged, and the rolls of his neck were gray and unshaven. In the dark hall there was a picture of Russell at twenty, handsome and thin in high-waisted jeans. He was standing in a barn, hand resting on a horse's back, a saddle at his feet. Russell-thirty-years-before stared into the camera with a half-smile, and his face was like Elizabeth's—curly black eyelashes, small nose, mouth like a rosebud. That night, as he sputtered and snorted in the smoky living room, I looked at the picture and did not understand.

By late autumn of the year I was sixteen, my mother weighed eighty pounds. For long months she grew thinner; her pain intensified. I carried her, one arm behind her back and the other under her knees, and I could feel her spine through blue pajamas dotted with tiny roses. I placed her on an overturned bucket in the shower, so she could sit beneath the spray. Her ankles were bone under loosening skin. I helped her to the bed she shared with my father and held a squirt bottle to her mouth so she could drink. I kissed the sweat on her forehead.

She told me, *"Te amo."*

A few months before, she was beautiful—you could still see it in flashes. Her hair was thick and blondish, and her body was round in some places and slender in others. Her hands, always cold, held pens and typed and cooked scrambled eggs. Her eyes were blue and her heels were narrow. She looked a lot like me.

Elizabeth's roof felt very low on those autumn nights, as the rain hit the sheet metal and the clouds heaved over the mountaintop, moving south. We crept down the hall to Russell's bathroom, the darkest room in the house, which we were both afraid to enter alone. It was windowless, a huge mirror reflecting the jumble of the closet. The shower was a cavern walled in dark stone. When I spent the night I washed my hair, nervous beneath a torrent of hot well water, watchful of shadows blurred by the slimy plastic curtain. I dried myself, the dark mouth of the shower gaping behind me in the mirror.

Our fear of this bathroom began early that autumn. Elizabeth called me one evening, when October had yellowed the aspens outside her window.

"There was a little girl in the shower."

I was sitting in my bedroom when she called, back to my locked door, staring at the floor-length black curtains I bought at Kmart for ten dollars.

"I saw her in the mirror." Elizabeth relied on sharp and sometimes cruel humor. She was not dramatic and she was never publicly afraid or weak. "Her throat was slit. She was looking at me."

"Did you tell Russell?"

"He'll say I'm dropping acid." I pictured her in her room alone, listening to her father's bed creak on the other side of the wall. "Do you believe me?"

I did. I never saw the little dead girl, even though sometimes I wanted to; I would gaze into the mirror until the darkness of the shower distorted.

"Jesus fuck. I'm never going back in there alone."

I promised she wouldn't have to.

Thus began the showers with the door cracked, at six o'clock before school, whispering, one rocking on the shaggy carpet while the other washed quickly. We chose our clothes—red pistols on a black tank top, a pewter belt buckle in the shape of a skull—and waited for whatever neighbor had been saddled with driving us over black ice, between mountain ranges, through the gorge.

Every morning in my house, my brother and sister fought as they ate cereal and gathered little bags of trail mix for lunch, then waited in the mudroom to be picked up. Sometimes my father was awake. Other times he was with my mother. Once she woke with a red rash covering her back, but most mornings she slept late, against the rasp of the oxygen tank.

Elizabeth and I had a memory of Halloween, a few weeks before my mother made the long drive to the city for tests, when we only suspected something was wrong. On a clear cold night before much snow had gathered, we put on costumes and ran beneath sharp autumn stars between my house and hers. And because it was Halloween, and my mother had thrown a party for the few kids of Swall Meadows, this time we weren't strange.

We sang while we ran from house to house, down Mountain View Drive, on the scavenger hunt my mother had planned. We searched for items she printed on lists—toenail clippings from the neighbors, hair from my black cat Helena, an apple from the orchard. And from Elizabeth's house, the last stop on the hunt, a piece of kibble from Sara's bowl.

Elizabeth and I shouted, out of tune, running ahead of the other kids. We sang songs by our favorite band, My Chemical Romance—we were in love with the singer, white makeup spread over his face, who screamed and trembled in music videos, glowering at the camera beneath a lop of black hair—and finished the chorus of the best song together.

So long, and goodnight; so long and goodnight!

When the hunt was over, my mother gathered everyone in the living room and pulled out her camera. In the photographs Elizabeth and I are surrounded by neighbor kids, mostly Tiggers and fairies. There is pride in my face, for the completeness of the costume, the long black veil stitched together from scraps. We stand apart from the group slightly, leaning into each other, smiling.

We spent the year with books, taking turns reading aloud while the other sewed or painted with the oils we saved up for. Our pictures were misshapen and artless. Her favorite, a distorted woman sitting at a piano, hung over her bedroom window. The woman was naked except for her hair, which was long and black like Elizabeth's.

One of our books was *Dracula.*

"Denn die Toten reiten schnell," she read one afternoon while I sewed stringy black hairs onto the head of a doll I was making. The doll's name was Victoria and she had a scar of a seam running vertically through her face, mismatched buttons for eyes. Her limbs were long and her mouth was wide and jagged. I tattooed her name onto her back and gave her dress a black satin bow.

"What does it mean?"

"For the dead travel fast."

We pierced our ears until they prickled with metal, punching new holes after school, dipping the needle in rubbing alcohol and holding each other's hair out of the way—a stinging, a *pop-pop* as the point broke the skin. We filled the holes with fake diamonds, red and black.

In front of the bathroom mirror, we painted our faces with white makeup, eyeliner, lipstick the color of old blood. At sixteen, we decayed. Our skin gathered in the asthmatic carpet of the bathroom. We left pieces of our bodies in the dark corners of my house on the afternoons we ventured there, eyelashes drifting in the shadows between rafters on the redwood ceiling, floating away from us, only to grow back. We crumbled under a light snow on Mountain View Drive, when the sky was huge and gray above Wheeler Crest. We fell apart in the halls of our tiny high school, where our lockers were pocked with bullet-hole stickers and the roof caved in every winter from the weight of snow.

I went around in a black Hello Kitty T-shirt that read *Lost in Wonderland.* My belt shed metal spikes the janitor found under desks after class, empty pyramids with barbs that dug into the plastic. Teachers with intuition let me sit in the back and deconstruct my mechanical pencil.

In school we were a half-presence. We didn't do homework. We memorized Edgar Allan Poe's "The Raven," filled notebooks with sketches, drew on our bodies and clothing with Sharpie—lyrics, complex roses, women with wings. We jabbed pencils through denim and ripped holes in our jeans. Elizabeth, who had to conceal even pierced ears from Russell, shredded her pants in two-inch increments, exposing strips of pale flesh from ankle to thigh. I walked in front of her, hiding her, when we came through the front door after school.

We filled in class assignments with clues to our lives. A teacher told us to keep a journal, to log the songs that defined us. I recorded my favorite: "It's Not a Fashion Statement, It's a Fucking Deathwish."

You get what everyone else gets, the singer growls, *you get a lifetime.*

Standing at the mirror on autumn nights, the slippery skin of our arms touching, we could hear the rain. Elizabeth wore black feathered wings. She painted a slice across her throat. Outside our faces might smear, but we were not alone or lonely. We could almost feel our pulses slow slightly, our skin cool, our limbs stiffen. We were ready.

We left the house while Russell slept. Sara whimpered, then hushed at Elizabeth's arched eyebrow. Once outside, we walked.

The rain fell on our bodies, chilling us through black sweatshirts with enormous hoods that hid our faces so well in class. In the morning when the darkness cleared and the sun shone in our eyes, we would wake with clean skin, ribs rising and falling, and we would remember these nights when we shivered together in the coming winter.

Elizabeth almost escaped. Under her window that looked over the mountain, with nothing and no one for hundreds of miles, she tried and she failed. While Russell slumped on the sofa in front of a cooking show, Elizabeth missed the radial artery. Kneeling on the floor, Seether playing quietly on the stereo, she looked out the window and she waited, but it never came. She lived, her life would go on; she would find the drugs so prevalent in small towns, she would drop out of school. I would get used to eating lunch by myself, in the dark hall by the band room where we once sat together, throwing a sticky eyeball at the wall and watching it roll to the floor.

I knew, to her, life seemed very long.

On winter nights, while Elizabeth's skin healed to pink shiny scars, I returned to my silent house, the lights already off and my father asleep. The counter was clustered with uneaten lasagna and unwatered lilies, a thousand condolences from neighbors who tried with a new desperation to talk to me in the car. They wondered at my charade, the romance of what had taken my mother away, painted over my lips, over my eyes. With makeup gone I was undeniably warm and living, and I shook with the realization that perhaps we were not as beautiful as we were permanent.

ISAIAH BERLIN

A Message to the Twenty-First Century

FROM *The New York Review of Books*

On November 25, 1994, Isaiah Berlin accepted the honorary degree of Doctor of Laws at the University of Toronto. He prepared the following "short credo," as he called it in a letter to a friend, for the ceremony, at which it was read on his behalf. Twenty years later, on October 23, 2014, The New York Review of Books *printed Berlin's remarks for the first time. For more on Isaiah Berlin, please see the Contributors' Notes.*

"IT WAS THE best of times, it was the worst of times." With these words Dickens began his famous novel *A Tale of Two Cities.* But this cannot, alas, be said about our own terrible century. Men have for millennia destroyed each other, but the deeds of Attila the Hun, Genghis Khan, Napoleon (who introduced mass killings in war), even the Armenian massacres, pale into insignificance before the Russian Revolution and its aftermath: the oppression, torture, murder which can be laid at the doors of Lenin, Stalin, Hitler, Mao, Pol Pot, and the systematic falsification of information which prevented knowledge of these horrors for years—these are unparalleled. They were not natural disasters but preventable human crimes, and whatever those who believe in historical determinism may think, they could have been averted.

I speak with particular feeling, for I am a very old man, and I have lived through almost the entire century. My life has been peaceful and secure, and I feel almost ashamed of this in view of what has happened to so many other human beings. I am not a historian, and so I cannot speak with authority on the causes of these horrors. Yet perhaps I can try.

They were, in my view, not caused by the ordinary negative human sentiments, as Spinoza called them—fear, greed, tribal hatreds, jealousy, love of power—though of course these have played their wicked part. They have been caused, in our time, by ideas; or rather, by one particular idea. It is paradoxical that Karl Marx, who played down the importance of ideas in comparison with impersonal social and economic forces, should, by his writings, have caused the transformation of the twentieth century, both in the direction of what he wanted and, by reaction, against it. The German poet Heine, in one of his famous writings, told us not to underestimate the quiet philosopher sitting in his study; if Kant had not undone theology, he declared, Robespierre might not have cut off the head of the king of France.

He predicted that the armed disciples of the German philosophers—Fichte, Schelling, and the other fathers of German nationalism—would one day destroy the great monuments of Western Europe in a wave of fanatical destruction before which the French Revolution would seem child's play. This may have been unfair to the German metaphysicians, yet Heine's central idea seems to me valid: in a debased form, the Nazi ideology did have roots in German anti-Enlightenment thought. There are men who will kill and maim with a tranquil conscience under the influence of the words and writings of some of those who are certain that they know perfection can be reached.

Let me explain. If you are truly convinced that there is some solution to all human problems, that one can conceive an ideal society which men can reach if only they do what is necessary to attain it, then you and your followers must believe that no price can be too high to pay in order to open the gates of such a paradise. Only the stupid and malevolent will resist once certain simple truths are put to them. Those who resist must be persuaded; if they cannot be persuaded, laws must be passed to restrain them; if that does not work, then coercion, if need be violence, will inevitably have to be used— if necessary, terror, slaughter. Lenin believed this after reading *Das Kapital*, and consistently taught that if a just, peaceful, happy, free, virtuous society could be created by the means he advocated, then the end justified any methods that needed to be used, literally any.

The root conviction which underlies this is that the central questions of human life, individual or social, have one true answer which can be discovered. It can and must be implemented, and those who have found it are the leaders whose word is law. The idea that to all genuine questions there can be only one true answer is a very old philosophical notion. The great Athenian philosophers, Jews and Christians, the thinkers of the Renaissance and the Paris of Louis XIV, the French radical reformers of the eighteenth century, the revolutionaries of the nineteenth—however much they differed about what the answer was or how to discover it (and bloody wars were fought over this)—were all convinced that they knew the answer, and that only human vice and stupidity could obstruct its realization.

This is the idea of which I spoke, and what I wish to tell you is that it is false. Not only because the solutions given by different schools of social thought differ, and none can be demonstrated by rational methods—but for an even deeper reason. The central values by which most men have lived, in a great many lands at a great many times—these values, almost if not entirely universal, are not always harmonious with each other. Some are, some are not. Men have always craved for liberty, security, equality, happiness, justice, knowledge, and so on. But complete liberty is not compatible with complete equality—if men were wholly free, the wolves would be free to eat the sheep. Perfect equality means that human liberties must be restrained so that the ablest and the most gifted are not permitted to advance beyond those who would inevitably lose if there were competition. Security, and indeed freedoms, cannot be preserved if freedom to subvert them is permitted. Indeed, not everyone seeks security or peace, otherwise some would not have sought glory in battle or in dangerous sports.

Justice has always been a human ideal, but it is not fully compatible with mercy. Creative imagination and spontaneity, splendid in themselves, cannot be fully reconciled with the need for planning, organization, careful and responsible calculation. Knowledge, the pursuit of truth—the noblest of aims—cannot be fully reconciled with the happiness or the freedom that men desire, for even if I know that I have some incurable disease this will not make me happier or freer. I must always choose: between peace and excitement, or knowledge and blissful ignorance. And so on.

So what is to be done to restrain the champions, sometimes very fanatical, of one or other of these values, each of whom tends to trample upon the rest, as the great tyrants of the twentieth century have trampled on the life, liberty, and human rights of millions because their eyes were fixed upon some ultimate golden future?

I am afraid I have no dramatic answer to offer: only that if these ultimate human values by which we live are to be pursued, then compromises, trade-offs, arrangements have to be made if the worst is not to happen. So much liberty for so much equality, so much individual self-expression for so much security, so much justice for so much compassion. My point is that some values clash: the ends pursued by human beings are all generated by our common nature, but their pursuit has to be to some degree controlled —liberty and the pursuit of happiness, I repeat, may not be fully compatible with each other, nor are liberty, equality, and fraternity.

So we must weigh and measure, bargain, compromise, and prevent the crushing of one form of life by its rivals. I know only too well that this is not a flag under which idealistic and enthusiastic young men and women may wish to march—it seems too tame, too reasonable, too bourgeois, it does not engage the generous emotions. But you must believe me, one cannot have everything one wants—not only in practice, but even in theory. The denial of this, the search for a single, overarching ideal because it is the one and only true one for humanity, invariably leads to coercion. And then to destruction, blood—eggs are broken, but the omelet is not in sight, there is only an infinite number of eggs, human lives, ready for the breaking. And in the end the passionate idealists forget the omelet and just go on breaking eggs.

I am glad to note that toward the end of my long life some realization of this is beginning to dawn. Rationality, tolerance, rare enough in human history, are not despised. Liberal democracy, despite everything, despite the greatest modern scourge of fanatical, fundamentalist nationalism, is spreading. Great tyrannies are in ruins, or will be—even in China the day is not too distant. I am glad that you to whom I speak will see the twenty-first century, which I feel sure can be only a better time for mankind than my terrible century has been. I congratulate you on your good fortune; I regret that I shall not see this brighter future, which I am convinced is coming. With all the gloom that I have been spreading, I am glad to end on an optimistic note. There really are good reasons to think that it is justified.

SVEN BIRKERTS

Strange Days

FROM *Lapham's Quarterly*

THINGS HAVE GOTTEN quiet these days, in a way they haven't for a long time. It's strange, like at some point there was another hand closing over my hand on the lever, pulling back to slow it all down—if not everywhere then at least here, in my place on the couch in the sunroom at the far back of the house, where everything has been set up to accommodate me. Extra pillows, bottles of water, the stage set for recuperation. All of a sudden, I am more still in myself than I can remember being in a very long time, so still that I can now just sit and watch the slow smooth sliding of the shadow through the room, which for extended moments I think of not as a gradual increase of dark but rather as an ebbing away of the light, a sensation like something being gently lifted, gently peeled back . . .

. . . *extended moments*—because those are what I have now, day after day, the succession of them marking the path back to being fully mobile, fully able, but on the way I have these near silences, the house ticking faintly on its old beams, the soft blurry purr of the refrigerator, little swirls of water through the pipes. How the feel of time changes when all the terms are altered. What on most days had moved with an almost hectic momentum, an ill-choreographed succession of one thing after another, one day just halted, causing the hours to then pool up behind it: the afternoon immobilized, with almost nothing to mark the change or confirm that this is not the world paralyzed into still life.

One day, another day, each day there when I open my eyes like something uncrated and laid out on all sides—to be assembled, no directions given, except of course that one thing will always follow another. You set the spoon down onto the lap tray and then ask yourself, *What next?* And if you are reflective, since you have the time, you think, *How right that there is always a next thing.* But you could also just sit and stare. It pulls at you, almost a challenge, a temptation: *What if?* What if I did nothing now but look here in front of me at the vase of these flowers, tulips, delivered at the door days ago (an event!), with a card from a former student— consider them, how they've started to droop on their stems, the petals losing that first waxy shine, the way they seem to measure the time in the room, and so it's not so odd that I would think of the line from Keats, the urn, the "foster child of silence and slow time," the reminder, there—and here—that in back of the obvi- ous pulse that marks the outer day are these other measures, like the measure of the afternoon light on these tulips, and past them —out the big window—that faint but incessant twitching of the new leaves in the aspen.

Convalescence—means exactly what? I look it up. *Con-* + *valescere:* "altogether grow strong." Gain health—simple enough. I am gain- ing back my health after a surgery, the right hip replaced, because finally there could be no more waiting. Everything hurt, I heard myself crackling like wicker with every movement I made. I was going up the stairs on all fours, like a dog. It was time. The opera- tion was decided, scheduled. It would require deep anesthesia, the implanting of a titanium part, and then a designated period of recovery, a month or more of seriously curbed activity, daily pain- killers, exercises to reinstate movements . . .

Three dots here, ellipsis, and in fact they are the punctuation proper to this whole surgery, and often enough apt to the convales- cence as well—representing the sensation, at times drug-related, of a moment prolonging itself, taking on no defining inflection, connecting to the next moment only because the next moment is there to be connected *to*.

Everything was explained to me. I was told, step by step, what would happen. But the experience—from the morning of my go- ing in for the surgery on—has been nothing like what I had come to imagine. I did not have the terms, the real terms. I could pic- ture all of the separate components of what would happen, but I had no way of putting them together into anything that matched what I then went through. Not that I went through anything beyond what had been described—no part of that had been exaggerated or understated. But how can you warn a person about actual physical sensations, or about time, how it changes? Weeks before I went in I could already see myself there on the couch, set up with occupations; I could put myself in the room, tally up the hours of the day when my wife, Lynn, would be away working and I would be alone. I pictured with great accuracy the downstairs where I'm now confined—the couch set up on risers in the sunroom, bookcase right there in arm's reach, the big dining-room table where I would spread my papers out, that whole afternoon atmosphere of a still life inhabited. But I featured the passing of hours without accounting for how they would feel. I had forgotten the great lesson of Thomas Mann's *The Magic Mountain,* a novel I had lost myself in in my twenties. I had not remembered (because I had never really known) that illness—or in my case, waiting to gain back health—rearranges the world.

I think right back to the start of the strangeness, to the business of being *out,* being under, that step in the process that they explain so matter-of-factly, almost in passing. "After the anesthesia is administered," the doctors say, as if they were setting out the simple schedule: "And in the morning, after breakfast . . ." I hardly gave it any thought either, at least in the weeks before the operation. But as the day neared, I began to realize what was involved, that I would be lowered down very close to the root of consciousness. The thought of it—the dread—was there with me all the night before. It was not dread of the surgery, the *cutting into*—though of course that was also on my mind—but the dread of the total blackout, the erasure. That an IV chemical would so deaden me to the world that I would not know that my thigh was being opened along a seam, that a major piece of metal (I had seen and handled the implant at a mandatory pre-op meeting) was being inserted . . . The idea gave me a pit in the stomach.

At the same time, though, it also pulled me, it fascinated. I have to say that images of such oblivion have always found their way into my fantasy life, I'm not even sure why. I know I have always been hyperattuned to those moments in movies when a character is rendered unconscious, after which—always—comes the briefest pause, a single beat or two of cinematic nothingness. And then the eyes snap open. He or she is in a hospital bed, being tended to, and everything that had happened before is erased by the image of white sheets and restorative sunlight streaming in through the window. That beat or two of nothingness is so powerful, that pocket of timelessness between A and B . . . Such unconsciousness suggests to me the possibility of some complete existential reset.

So it happened—just as I had been told it would. I was in the room, alert through the IV hookup for the anesthetic. The anesthesiologist said I would be awake as I was wheeled into surgery, that there would be more drug given through a ventilator. But that's where it all stops. I remember no wheeling, and I remember no sudden heaviness or drowsiness, no slipping away. I remember nothing. One minute I was on my back wearing a hospital johnny, the very next I was in recovery, by merest increments becoming aware that something important had happened to me, while still swimming in a pleasant chemical stupor . . .

In a sense, the last few weeks have been a continuation of that indeterminate state—the world drawing back, though really, I know, it is the self that has pulled away; the terms of attention completely altered, and all actions affected by that alteration. Is this what old age will be? I have to wonder. I study the changes. I, who have never taken pills of any kind, vitamins included, now find myself every morning laying out—and *taking pleasure* in doing so—a lovely long row of differently sized and colored shapes on a placemat in front of me. I've watched my parents doing this for years, but now I finally understand. Though the most minor sort of doing, this is, health matters aside, one distinct and symbolic gesture, a token ordering applied to what is now understood to be a vast undivided expanse of time.

The days—mornings and then long afternoons . . . People ask, "How do you pass the time?" and though I usually answer glibly in the moment, I find myself getting stuck on the question when I'm alone. The words make less and less sense as I consider. The idea that there is this great intangible entity that we are all of us—the convalescing ones maybe particularly—passing through or in some way channeling through ourselves, and that this entity is somehow singular, as in *the* time. I know it's a casual figure of speech, not a reasoned proposition, but all the more reason to ponder it. For it is in terms of the assumed and collectively accepted logic of such phrases that we live and take our basic bearings. "How do you pass the time?" suggests the basic model of existence, in which living a life is seen on the one hand as traversing an unspecified span of time—marked out in years—and on the other as moving through the natural cycle of hours, from dawn to dusk. Time, then, is understood to be a medium one negotiates. And in this respect, how *do* I pass the time? Well, I suppose that I pass it in various ways —reading, writing notes, napping, taking walks, eating . . . And as it happens, each of these things gives me a different feeling about time. There is the sense of distended pause that I have when I am sitting in place, thinking or writing; and there is the more marked-off, syncopated rhythm of mailboxes and driveways and birds fluttering up into the trees when I go walking. And the almost otherworldly silence that comes over me in these rooms, when I just sit at the table and let the gaze pan from the corner all the way across —taking in the framed photos of the kids on top of the shelf, the bowl of stones gathered on the Truro beaches, the clay pitcher borrowed straight from a Morandi canvas, and then the big mirror on the far wall, which holds these same objects captive in its smooth silver depth. Mirrors create silence, I think. I make a note. Other afternoons I have that feeling that is like floating slowly through the air sometimes when I close my eyes and just listen to the sounds around me. These—and so many others—are the ways I *pass* the time, or ways that the time passes through me. They are also the different ways I am, and now I have to wonder what time even has to do with it.

The drugs, the painkillers, though mild in their effect, do make a difference. They introduce a set of new variations into the old picture. I take the little yellow pills at given intervals and I have quickly come to know their working. Though the time of the day might flow in these different ways, the cycle of medications sketches over that flow a grid of definite expectations, and these delineate the day, much as do meals, appointed times for exercises . . . I know that after just four hours, the effect of the little pill will start to wear off. I will feel heavier, more aware of the sore part of my body; I will notice, too, an unpleasant, edgy, gnawing sensation, and when this arrives the mind begins to cast around for relief. Too early for the pill—so says the plan—though I'm not above negotiating with myself, and at times I nearly capitulate. I invent a reason why this occasion, now, is a special case—but no, the logic of the slippery slope most always prevails, and I go looking for distraction instead. I decide to shave, and then arrange those CDs; I do a crossword and read for a bit. And what a sense of virtue I have after I have held out like this, resisted jumping the gun, when I can hold that merest dot of a thing on the tongue for a moment before washing it down. I do love the feeling, once it's taken, that the cavalry is on the way. Just knowing *that* is a pill's worth of ease.

And yes, as promised, there comes the moment when that craving edge drops away and the dull sense of the body fades. The body, I am suddenly aware, is fine. What I know is that I now have one especially good hour, a shiny hour, when I can park myself in comfort on the couch, blankets around my feet, warm light on just over my right shoulder. I can read, focus, or—better—write. My thoughts and words feel more synchronous; they have a capacity that they don't necessarily always have for darting this way and that, taking little runs at things. I'm not sure how to describe it, this sense that the leash has gained some extra bit of elasticity, my slightly increased confidence that if I push this way or that way the phrases will be there.

And so I write, I try to write. Which is to say I enter into yet another relation to time. The one that is finally the best, the most gratifying of all. For though I can have this special merged sense for short intervals when I read—or certainly did in the past, before so much distraction supervened—it is really only when I am putting thoughts and impulses into words, when I am attuned to whatever is just then the right rhythm of expression, the live cadence, that I feel all sense of lapsing time fall away. Except I don't feel it fall away, it just *does*. It's as if I have, for a moment, broken out of the shell of that constant awareness, am free to take a look around.

This fine state does not last, of course. But it has not been *so* much of a change of state that it brings a crash after—nothing like that. Just a fading, an ebbing, the mind no longer quite so intent on muscling around. I feel the shift come in the language first —using words gets just that slight degree less pleasurable, and with that the first crack opens and the old sense of time comes leaking back in. Just that little bit, but it's enough.

The convalescence is not at all times solitary, of course. The long afternoon eventually ends, and Lynn comes home from work and brings the world in the door with her—a feeling of different activity, an agenda for cooking and eating, bits of news and stories from her day. That mood that was many moods, but also all just the self in a room for hours and hours, dissolves. Now there is talk. Music. I sit on a high stool in the kitchen and busy myself peeling carrots or dicing an onion. It is not an easy or immediate transition. The long afternoon is become all bright lights, radio music. Lynn gives her account, but she also asks for mine. Which can be vexing. I have to figure out how to translate what has been a long and largely unmarked procession of thoughts and fancies into a narrative that somehow signifies. How to create the context and make the bridge; how to bring across the rhythm and duration of all that sitting and looking? Yes, *duration* is the right word here. How do I bring some essence of that state over into what feels like a completely differently structured kind of time?

In the presence of another—even if the other is in the next room and otherwise occupied—the reality of the solitude pulls away, just as in the heart of the solitude that other reality takes on a character of unlikeliness.

Finally, of course, there is the night. It has become unfamiliar and phantasmal during this period—and for this I blame the discomfort, the drugs, the new sleeping arrangement in our daughter's old room. I can almost feel the different layers opening out one from the other, depending on the hour. Sleep, usually so ordinary, has become a kind of voyaging. I prepare for this even before I switch off the light. So many phases, intervals. At different points I feel myself come awake. Sometimes I look at my watch, press the tiny button and see the hour light up—but in that moment my location on that grid connects with very little. I will have far more connection when the first birds start up, which they always do right at the touch of the first faint trace of light. Their warbling is a fantastic thing to listen to. What an indescribable state to be in, lying there, adrift, slightly awake, but merged enough in sleep that the bird sounds can somehow blend with the meander of thoughts and images in my head.

The layers of the night are in fact the layers of the self; they offer the most random unfolding of the accumulations of experience—everything that happened and mattered and lapsed away as the next new thing claimed the attention. There is no way to guess what will suddenly surface in those hours. At times I need only to call to mind a specific person, place, or event and the images will rear up, imbued with a kind of radiance of meaningfulness—as if this moment of return had been the point all along. And then, granted a single flash of what I know is the extent of the past, I think, *There will never be time enough.* How to reckon it all? Right then I understand, as if I truly had forgotten, why we will always need art. Writing. The slow and greedy embrace of language.

Where else but in the dead of night do we encounter the extent of it all? Life—the sport of insomniacs. Because the soul needs the arching vastness of the night as well as the edgy hovering that sleeplessness delivers. It needs long unsettled hours in which to lay out the strands, one after the next, and then follow them out, letting the memories and meanings overlap and crosshatch until the full force of the uncanny comes sweeping in.

Awake in the dark, I engage with that other time—not the time of the sink's faucet dripping or the blue jays tyrannizing the yard but the long-term tangle of meanings and connections. This is a different world, not so often present to me in the light. Lying there, eyes open, I will feel that great swinging shift, foreground to background. The day world is obliterated: I find myself, as I did the other night, for no clear reason thinking of my old school friend Mark—of him, but really of his parents—how friendly they were: they would greet me so warmly every time I came by. On my back, eyes now closed again, I fix them with such a clarity, a distinctness, that it shocks me—after all, it's been forty years. I'm wondering, almost anxious, did I give any like response back then to their kindness and interest? I'm wondering, too, if they are still alive. I try to imagine what they might be like if they are (and why not, I ask, *my* parents are alive)—and then sensations, little details, arrive: like Mark's father's peculiar bent-back thumb, and his mother's amazing involvement with her cats, her way of whispering to them, fussing with them, even as she was talking to us, remembering along with that the looks Mark would give me as we walked out of the kitchen and headed to his room, the flick of the brows that said, "If only you knew" . . . All this so starkly real to me at three or four o'clock in the morning.

I've taken a pain pill. I'm lying here waiting to see if I can settle back into sleep. But now I have these people, and there is so much to remember about them. I realize I never gave them the thought they deserve. But have I given *anything* that thought? Because if there is so much here to do with these two people, what must there be of all the rest? I test myself. I cast around, I pick someone else, the manager of a bookstore where I once worked. And again, just like with Mark's parents, I find the images—so clear—and then the layers. How quickly and smoothly they lift off, one from the next, until I am in a state of excited distress, thinking of the complete impossibility of bringing back what needs to be brought back. But it *does* need to be—otherwise all these things are just left for dead. Proust, that cork-lined room, it all makes sense. What could be more worthy, and rewarding, I think, than to give over the second half of life to the recovery of the first?

Later, again, sleep—unsettling dreams; I'm with odd groups of others and we are all together caught up in premises that defy any summary, that make sense only in the dream, and even then only just. As the eye converts one thing into another, instantly—pile of rags to sleeping dog—so the mind makes its little scenes from the random images thrown up by the psyche.

The bird sounds wake me. I move the curtain by my head and see the faint light over the yards . . .

The convalescence—which is what I call it when talking to others, never to myself—has been its own period, distinct from all other periods, an island I will always remember having been marooned on. There will be times, I know already, when I'll find myself craving the intensity of so much uninterrupted self, for such looking and thinking. Don't we turn back with some nostalgia to those sickbed days from childhood? Not just because we were cared for, indulged, but also because of how in that widening eye of time the blankets became entire landscapes, and great cloud caravans moved so slowly outside the window.

But it's coming to an end, this interlude—I feel health gaining on me. There are a thousand little signs, from increased appetite to greater ease in making simple movements to, alas, less patience with the kind of daydreamy looking. Those lazy, horizontal meanderings, though I still indulge, are more and more trumped by the itch to be up and *doing* something. Another walk! I get my crutch —aware as I pick it up that soon I won't be needing it—and make my way up the street. It feels good, the spring air, so much activity I can hardly take it all in—from the neighbor up on the hill bending over his hedge clippers to the two squirrels winding in some strange figure eights around the trunk of the maple, and all that song coming down from the branches and wires.

The crutch tip makes a satisfying punctuation, feels almost like I'm saying *now, now, now* . . .

TIFFANY BRIERE

Vision

FROM *Tin House*

1.

FOR THREE NIGHTS my mother hasn't slept. Since her cousin died, his spirit has visited her each night, for hours at a time. He appears from the waist up on the north wall of her bedroom, facing her directly, blinking but not speaking. He doesn't frighten her; on the contrary, she hopes that one of these nights he will claim her, escort her to the other side, where he now resides. She prepares me for this possibility.

My mother suffers from more than one autoimmune disease. The pain—which plagues her joints and shoots throughout her back and legs—has outwitted medical intervention. When I hold her hand (its appearance is that of a claw, palm curled inward, digits at odd angles, the whole hand functioning as a single unit) I feel clusters of marbles all along her knuckles. To hold her hand is to let it rest in mine as I rub my thumb across her paper-thin skin. Her back painfully hunched, she walks only to get from one chair to another, her legs giving in to spasms.

We share an apartment, and on the morning after the third visitation, I make her a cup of tea, strong and sweet. I find her sitting up in bed, more distracted and distant than usual. When I hand her the tea, she looks at me with the kind of adoring expression you give a child who has done something unexpected and delightful. I bring my daughter into the room, and for the rest of the day we engage my mother with nursery rhymes, picture books, and puzzles.

In the evening my husband returns from work at the pharmaceutical company where he is a biologist. He brings my mother another cup of tea, chamomile, then sprawls across her bed to ask about her day.

No one has ever spoken to my husband about visions or the ubiquity of the dead. He is of German descent, not West Indian, but over time he's learned that this intimacy with the dead—for him, unimaginable and unreal—is woven into the fabric of my family. He's a scientist for a reason, drawn to black-and-white explanations of the world. But there, in my mother's bed, he holds her hand, willing to consider all things possible.

2.

I'm an undergraduate conducting research in a neurophysiology lab. We study diabetes and epilepsy in rodents, diseases we induce with drugs that kill off the pancreas and alter the brain's chemistry.

On this day I'm decapitating rats. "Rapid decap" is the preferred method. I use a rudimentary guillotine. I position the rat with one hand and bring down the angled blade with the other. The rats protest little. By this point they are obese and lethargic, side effects of the drugs. Their tails are thick and limp. They are soaked in their own urine, and the sugar they leak fills the small procedure room with a sweet, clingy odor. When the blade returns to its resting place, there is a satisfactory click that I feel rather than hear. I move quickly to isolate the brain and preserve its tissue. This is done with forceps, a process of removing skin and skull to expose the chestnutlike organ within. I discard the bodies in a red biohazard bag. Still innervated with electrical impulse, the bodies twitch, causing the bag to shape-shift, to crackle intermittently.

I'm not alone. There is a graduate student helping me, and if not for his presence, I may faint. I'm not cut out for this work, but this realization is years down the road. Now I'm the sole undergrad in a lab full of grad students, and I have something to prove.

The grad student is a muscular redhead with the neck of a football player and hazel eyes. He teaches the practical section of the physiology course I'm taking, and a group of us girls comment on his appearance: his long, curly hair tied down with a bandanna; his wholesome overalls; his rugged, midwestern good looks. The other girls are jealous of the long hours the grad student and I spend alone in the lab, the longer hours we spend at bars and on golf courses.

I'm isolating a brain, facing away from the grad student, when I feel a hand on my back. Fingers graze my skin, a firm palm presses against my shoulder blade. I take a deep breath and close my eyes, savoring the seconds that compromise the integrity of the organ I'm harvesting. I've anticipated this moment: the grad student and I acting on—in the midst of this gruesome study—our attraction for each other. He has seen me struggling with the day's work, and this hand on my back is a release. When I turn around, I'm ready for whatever he has in mind.

But he's across the room. And it's clear from his posture, the way he's settled in his chair, that he hasn't been on his feet for some time. The hand on my back remains a moment longer before setting me free. It will visit me again at dawn on the day of my wedding and at one astonishing moment on the morning I give birth.

What does the hand hope to show me? That is always the question. My unlikely career path? My growing anxiety over its moral implications? The grotesque nature of the work I do?

Or perhaps it hopes to reassure me, to gesture to this grad student—this gentle, enthusiastic man—whom, sooner than I could ever imagine, I will wed.

3.

My parents don't save photographs. There are very few from their childhoods—my father's in Guyana, my mother's in Jamaica. They don't believe, as I do, in the value of mementos. What they have, what they cling to, are stories that always begin with the words *Back home.*

Three of my grandparents die before I'm born. The fourth, my maternal grandmother, at the end of her life, is locked away in religion. By the time I meet her, she is residing in the Jamaican countryside, at my uncle's house, and I am permitted to speak to her through a gate and only for a few minutes. A few years later, she too passes away.

I've been raised with the belief that the deceased are always with us, that their presence can be felt. Through stories, I have come to know my ancestors. In my dreams, they are very much alive. There are many guiding forces in life, many ways, genetic and otherwise, in which the past adheres to the present.

My paternal grandmother had a tattoo on her right arm, a mark placed on indentured servants who were shipped from India to work the sugarcane fields in Guyana. The tattoo was her name in Hindi. To me she is a mystery, a black-and-white photograph that I had to borrow from an aunt. My grandmother was "coolie," as the Guyanese say, East Indian. She wore saris and bangles and parted her hair down the middle to sweep it back in a low bun. I have her eyes.

Now when I see my own arm, the tattoo that on my eighteenth birthday marked my freedom, I think only of the tattoo that marked her servitude. Through this ink, I feel the connectivity of flesh.

4.

I'm a child, impressionable, and my mother's explanations of the world are bigger than skyscrapers and dinosaurs. She says that our ancestors are always with us, that our dead relatives inhabit our lives. They are disappointed when I misbehave, pleased when I'm obedient. I can speak to them, aloud or silently, and·they will hear me. Eternity, she says, is fluid.

I'm haunted by her words, never quite able to behave naturally because of this omniscient audience. My mother says I shouldn't feel disconnected from the dead but, rather, bound to them. She says the fabric of humanity is ancient and unfathomable. She says life is infinite and eternal. She says when I meet my ancestors, I will recognize their faces and know them by name.

In other words, heaven is family.

5.

I take a secretarial job at a hospital to make money while I'm in college. I'm assigned to the hematology-oncology floor. On heme-onc, patients are given private rooms and have access to services not offered on other floors: aromatherapy, yoga, and massage. Some days a pianist plays in the lounge; other days a clown goes room to room.

I'm one of the weekend secretaries. I sit at the nurses' station and handle admissions and discharges, relay orders, answer phones, and man the call box. When patients have requests, they press their call button and talk to me through the intercom. When the request is simple, I don't bother the nurses. I bring the pitcher of ice chips, the blanket, or the menu. In their rooms you're pulled into the patients' worlds—children's drawings and get-well cards, headscarves and earrings, self-help books and classical music.

On heme-onc you see the same patients again and again. A complication—such as a fever, an infection, a spike or drop in blood count—and they're admitted to our floor. The emergency department calls up and lets me know a familiar patient is returning, and I make sure that the room has been cleaned and the television is functional. The family members turn the corner before the stretcher, and you see that their shoulders are heavy with portable radios, books, photographs, and linens from home.

The nurses all want the leukemics. They negotiate over acute and chronic myeloids. They say *my patient* and *my leukemic* and trade assignments as if they are baseball cards. *I'll give you Cunningham for Howard, Chakrabarti for Williams.* They maneuver for the ones who are young and very sick, because everyone loves a fighter.

No one, however, wants the anemics.

The sickle-cell anemics are what the doctors call "frequent flyers." Their multivolume charts are heavy, wrapped tight with thick rubber bands. When their nurses aren't looking, one has sex with her brother-in-law and another sneaks whiskey from a mouthwash bottle. And because I'm young like them and black like them, they let me in on their secrets.

We get a frequent flyer, a thirtysomething sickle-cell patient, admitted with a port-a-cath infection, the result of injecting heroin through the direct line to his heart. He's lost most of his legs— both are amputated above the knee—and he's scheduled to lose more.

He calls the nurses' station and tells me to come. The volume on his television is turned up high, and there are clothes all over the floor. He is jaundiced, but because his skin is dark, I can tell this only from looking at his eyes, which are yellow where they should be white. He's sitting up in bed, basketball shorts covering what's left of his legs. Like my mother, pain transforms him. He tells me he could strangle someone, that he was promised his morphine an hour ago. *C'mon man, c'mon man,* he says. He tells me that I better find his nurse and drag her in here. He's bare-chested and sweaty, and when he pounds his thighs with his fists, he wants to see me jump. He wants to fill the room with the scent and heat of pain, so that it's no longer his alone.

A few hours later, when he's comfortable and feeling more like himself, he shows me a school photo of one of his sons. The backdrop is autumnal and artificial, meant to evoke harvest.

He talks to me about this son and the others, about the sports they play, their report cards, and their talents. His boys, I've been told, haven't inherited his disease.

I don't interrupt him. I don't return to the nurses' station, where the intercom is ringing. I listen quietly as he describes his family, witnessing a different transformation now: from condition to man.

6.

At Yale, genetics becomes my religion. I'm a graduate student, studying kidney disease in lower organisms, namely mice and fish. Ash Wednesday arrives and my forehead is a blank canvas. My father, a devout Catholic, reminds me of the importance of going to mass. My uncle, one of my father's many brothers, is an atheist and a professor. I remember him teasing: *What if your land of milk and honey is right here?*

What attracts me to genetics isn't purely the validation of thought or the process of discovery but, rather, what it symbolizes. Our genomes contain our complete ancestral history, a record of where we've been. The history of our evolution has been transcribed and it lives in every one of our cells. And perhaps more inspiring than this record are the vast open regions that represent where we, as a species, have yet to go. These regions are wide open, ready to be filled with fortitude and endurance.

Genetics, like storytelling, is a search for core truths, for what informs the human condition. At its best, it tells an artful story, a narrative meant to inspire and enrich our lives. But it also invokes the worst about living: misfortune, pain, and truncation.

The genetic code is a language, written in a four-letter alphabet. I spend hours at the computer, interpreting its narrative. I read in one gene the story of an ancestor, common to both man and fish, an ancestor of the sea from which man descended. I read in another gene our similarity to other unlikely species—fish and dogs, rats and mice—similarities that make them suitable models for studying human disease. I read in a third gene our connection to chimpanzees: beyond both species having nurturing relationships and problem-solving abilities, we share somewhere near 98 percent of the same genetic material. The blueprints that govern us are nearly identical.

And it's this that preoccupies me: the connectivity of all living things, past and present. What is passed on? Is this record all that remains after we're gone, or is there something more?

And can a single narrative—one single truth—encompass all the forces at work in our lives?

7.

On a Tuesday morning, my father goes to work. He arrives, as he always does, on the E train, which has a stop in the concourse beneath his building. He goes up to the trading floor, boots the computers, and heads to his office in the next building.

He is many floors above the city when a loud seismic boom draws people away from their desks and into doorways. He makes his way to a window of his office building and sees that the adjacent building, its twin, is swaying.

He doesn't know what has happened, but thinking only of the chaos and traffic that will ensue, he and a friend ignore the order to stay put and make the decision to leave. Outside he watches an airplane disappear inside a tower of steel. Around him, clusters of people are—as he is—hands-over-mouth transfixed, stunned and silent. He sees bodies fall from the sky, and he and his friend run, until they find themselves on a train and headed off the island.

At home, my father frets over the welfare of the children who were in the building that morning, at the on-site day-care facility. When he finds out that all of them—more than forty infants and toddlers—made it out alive, his body absorbs the news, releasing tension in the small muscles of his neck. He retreats to the den, draws the curtains, and curls up in the loam of quilts and sheets, further blanketed by the glow of the television. Two days later, he has a stroke.

On my wedding day, my father and I are in the back of the limo, waiting for the ceremony to begin. The night before was the first time he'd seen my mother since their divorce. He doted on her all night, bringing her drinks from the hotel bar and whispering in her ear. He is remarried, but when my mother is in the room, no one else exists.

Outside, a storm rages. Wind shakes the limo. My father tells me he's seen the face of God. I ask him to tell me another story. I ask him not to say anything that will make me cry. God's face, he tells me, is round and full of magnificent, soothing light. He says he spoke to God, that he bargained for his life, offering up his service and devotion, his cigarettes and his alcohol, in exchange for the chance to walk me down the aisle. This is the closest he has ever come to expressing his love.

There are forces at work on my father, forces that are slowly exposing his fragile nucleus. Terror, disease, heartbreak. I have seen him lose everything that matters to him, including my mother. I have seen him kiss the dead. I have yet to see him cry.

He made his deal with God after suffering a massive heart attack, years before the towers and the stroke. The night before his open-heart surgery, he spoke of his father, who was fifty-four when he died—same age as my father at the time—from complications during surgery.

The vision came to my father while he was on the operating table. As I sat in the waiting room, I couldn't help but picture him, somewhere beyond the electrified doors, lying there in a cavernous operating theater. I imagined him in his most vulnerable state: his chest cracked wide open, God and steel rebuilding him.

8.

I harvest organs. I'm taught different methods of immobilization. Cervical dislocation—the pinning of a mouse across its shoulder blades followed by a quick yank of its tail—is one I won't try.

Ether doesn't require any manipulation of the mouse, but it has been deemed unsafe for researchers. Ketamine is what we use in our lab.

There is a sweet spot in the belly where the needle slides in smoothly, at an angle that doesn't hit an organ and cause the mouse to buck. When the ketamine is successfully administered, the mouse tumbles out of your hand, staggering in the first minutes before falling still on its side or belly, its inhalations sharp and pronounced. When you hit the sweet spot, it's a good omen.

Once the animal is sedated, there is nothing you can't do to it. I study cystic disease, and because the mouse has been engineered, I hope to find cysts on its kidneys and liver. I pin the mouse, belly up, to the Styrofoam board I use for my dissections. With forceps, I pinch the loose skin below the abdomen, pull it up into a tent, and reach for my scissors.

I cut from the groin to the neck, across the shoulders, then hip to hip, so the final product is an incision in the shape of the letter *I*. The body speaks indisputable truths. To examine the workings of a body is to experience the logic, the divine order, of nature. When the flaps of skin are pinned down, you have a window into the animal, its mechanics more intricate, more intelligent—yet cruder and messier, so more difficult to appreciate—than the clean, articulated movements behind the face of a watch.

I perform harvests, not surgeries, and at some point during the removal of organs the mouse will die. I have performed countless harvests alone, but it's much easier when someone stands over your shoulder, someone interested and experienced, his or her excitement contagious, so much so your nerves masquerade as anticipation. You peel away layers of fat and see what you have, the person beside you—hand on your back—rooting for cysts.

9.

God is taking my mother in pieces.

First her kidneys, now her eyes—her organs are failing her. She loses perspective, colors, and words on the page. It seems to happen overnight: one morning I discover her left eye has drifted off-center. I'm suddenly aware of the shape of her eyeball, elliptical and oblong, the distinct pointedness of the pupil. I no longer know how to look her in the eye. I have a choice: stare into the eye that is dying or the one that still has life.

With the loss of her vision, her prayers increase in frequency, and I buy her a large-print Bible in the hopes it will sustain her. She doesn't want anyone operating on her eyes. She says, in the strange and beautiful way she has of phrasing things, that she had always thought her eyes would outlive her.

She talks at great length about her childhood and tells stories I've never heard. She misses her parents, her father more so, and when she says that all she wants is to see him again, I can't know for certain which world she'd prefer to see him in.

Several times in my life, a deceased relative has visited me in a dream. I remind my mother of one of these times, of one particular dream:

> It's my wedding day. It looks and feels like the wedding day of my memory, except that in this version there is no turbulent weather; the mansion's French doors are wide open, and long, white drapes billow in the breeze. As I walk from room to room, I'm met by family.
>
> I enter a room, and there before me are my maternal grandparents, who died long ago. My grandmother is in a white dress, my grandfather in a white suit and fedora. And though I never met my grandfather, I recognize him. He says, *Tell your mother I am proud of her.*

Upon waking from this dream, I phoned my mother to relay his message. As I described the details, she cried. When she was calmer, she told me that it was her father's birthday.

My mother hears the end of this story now as if for the first time. For a short while she feels the presence of her father, and there is distance between her and her suffering. In the following days her prayers maintain their frequency, but now they are inflected with hope.

She decides to fight for her vision. While she prays to retain what's left of her sight, she seeks out doctors who hope to save her eyes with surgery. This is her treatment plan: God and medicine.

10.

On a Saturday afternoon, I'm sitting on the living room floor reading, my daughter napping nearby, when I feel the hand on my back. My husband is behind me on the sofa. But he's not within arm's reach, and the hand remains as I stare upon my husband's face.

When I tell my husband that the hand has visited me again, when I describe again the sensation of the palm and the articulated digits, he listens. He doesn't try to explain it away, to interject with a scientific explanation that would undermine its significance to me. The hand is a gift, a force that solidifies moments, that suggests I pause and take inventory. My husband accepts it for what it is: a piece of the larger narrative of my life. He knows that my understanding of this world comes a sliver at a time, in fragments and not as a whole.

At the opposite end of our apartment, my mother is resting. She's in her bedroom, as she tends to be, behind a closed door. She's able to sleep once again; the spirit of her cousin no longer visits her. There are nights when he comes to her in dreams, but for the most part he's gone. And though his spirit has never spoken to her, this vision was an answer to her prayers. Someone has heard her call for death and responded: *Soon, soon.*

JUSTIN CRONIN

My Daughter and God

FROM *Narrative*

FOUR YEARS AGO, driving home from picking up our twelve-year-old daughter from summer camp, my wife reached into her purse for a tissue and lost control of the car. This occurred on a stretch of Interstate 10 between Houston and San Antonio, near the town of Gonzales. The accident occurred as many do: a moment of distraction, a small mistake, and suddenly everything is up for grabs. My wife and daughter were in the midst of a minor argument over my daughter's need to blow her nose. During high-pollen season, she is a perennial sniffer, and the sound drives my wife crazy. *Get a Kleenex,* Leslie said, *for God's sake,* and when Iris, out of laziness or exhaustion or the mild day-to-day defiance of all teenagers, refused to do so, my wife reached for her purse, inadvertently turning the wheel to the left.

In the case of some vehicles, the mistake might have been rectified, but not in the case of my wife's—a top-heavy SUV with jacked-up suspension. When she realized her error, she overcorrected to the right, then again to the left, the car swerving violently. They were on a bridge that passed above a gully: on either side, nothing but gravity and forty vertical feet of air. That they would hit the guardrail was now inevitable. In moments of acute stress, time seems to slow. The name for this is *tachypsychia,* from the Greek *tach,* meaning "speed," and *psych,* meaning "mind." Thus, despite the chaos and panic of these moments, my wife had time to form a thought: *I have killed my daughter.*

This didn't happen, although the accident was far from over. The car did not break through the guardrail but ricocheted back onto the highway, spinning in a one-eighty before flopping onto its side in a powdery explosion of airbags. It struck another vehicle, driven by a pastor and his wife on their way home from Sunday lunch, though my wife has no memory of this. For what seemed like hours the car traveled in this manner, then gravity took hold once more. Like a whale breaching the surface, it lifted off the roadway, turned belly-up, and crashed down onto its roof. The back half of the car compacted like an accordion: steel crushing, glass bursting, my daughter's belongings—clothes, shoes, books, an expensive violin—exploding onto the highway. Other cars whizzed past, narrowly missing them. A final jolt, the car rolled again, and it came to a halt, facing forward, resting on its wheels.

As my wife tells it, the next moment was very nearly comic. She and my daughter looked at each other. The car had been utterly obliterated, but there was no blood, no pain, no evidence of bodily injury to either of them. "We've been in an accident," my wife robotically observed.

My daughter looked down at her hand. "I am holding my phone," she said—as, indeed, she somehow still was. "Do you want me to call 911?"

There was no need. Though in the midst of things the two of them had felt alone in the universe, the accident had occurred in the presence of a dozen other vehicles, all of which had now stopped and disgorged their occupants, who were racing to the scene. A semi moved in behind them to block the highway. By this time my wife's understanding of events had widened only to the extent that she was aware that she had created a great deal of inconvenience for other people. She was apologizing to everyone, mistaking their amazement for anger. Everybody had expected them to be dead, not sitting upright in their destroyed vehicle, neither one of them with so much as a hair out of place. Some began to weep; others had the urge to touch them. The cops arrived, a fire truck, an ambulance. While my wife and daughter were checked out by an EMT, onlookers organized a posse to prowl the highway for my daughter's belongings. Because my wife and daughter no longer had a car to put them into, a woman offered to bring the items to our house; she was headed for Houston to visit her son and was pulling a trailer of furniture. The EMT was as baffled as everybody else. "Nobody walks away from something like this," he said.

*

I was to learn of these events several hours later, when my wife phoned me. I was in the grocery store with our six-year-old son, and when I saw my wife's number my first thought was that she was calling to tell me she was running late, because she always is.

"Okay," I said, not bothering to say hello, "where are you?"

Thus her first tender steps into explaining what had occurred. An accident, she said. A kind of a big fender-bender, really. Nobody hurt, but the car was out of commission; I'd need to come get them.

I wasn't nice about this. Part of the dynamic in our marriage is the unstated fact that I am a better driver than my wife. I have never been in an accident; my one and only speeding ticket was issued when the first George Bush was president. About every two years my wife does something careless in a parking lot that costs a lot of money, and she has received so many tickets that she has been forced to retake driver's education—and those are just the tickets I know about. The rules of modern marriage do not include confiscating your wife's car keys, but more than once I have considered doing this.

"A fender-bender," I repeated. *Christ almighty, this again.* "How bad is it?"

"Everybody's fine. You don't have to worry."

"I get that. You said that already." I was in the cereal aisle; my son was bugging me to buy a box of something much too sweet. I tossed it into the cart.

"What about the car?"

"Um, it kind of . . . rolled."

I imagined a Labrador retriever lazily rotating onto his back in front of the fireplace. "I don't understand what you're telling me."

"It's okay, really," my wife said.

"Do you mean it rolled *over?*"

"It happened kind of fast. Totally no big deal, though."

It sounded like a huge deal. "Let me see if I have this right. You were driving and the car rolled over."

"Iris wouldn't blow her nose. I was getting her a Kleenex. You know how she is. The doctors say she's absolutely fine."

"What doctors?" It was becoming clear that she was in a state of shock. "Where are you?"

"At the hospital. It's very small. I'm not even sure you'd call it a hospital. Everybody's been so nice."

And so on. By the time the call ended, I had some idea of the seriousness, though not completely. Gonzales was three hours away. I abandoned my grocery cart, raced home, got on the phone, found somebody to look after our son, and got in my car. Several more calls followed, each adding a piece to the puzzle, until I was able to conclude that my wife and daughter were alive but should be dead. I *knew* this, but I didn't *feel* it. For the moment I was locked into the project of retrieving them from the small town where they'd been stranded. It was after ten o'clock when I pulled into the driveway of Gonzales Memorial Hospital, a modern building the size of a suburban dental office. I did not see my wife, who was standing at the edge of the parking lot, looking out over the empty fields behind it. I raced inside, and there was Iris. She was slender and tan from a month in the Texas sunshine, and wearing a yellow T-shirt dress. She had never looked more beautiful, and it was this beauty that brought home the magnitude of events. I threw my arms around her, tears rising in my throat; I had never been so happy to see anybody in my life. When I asked her where her mother was, she said she didn't know; one of the nurses directed us outside. I found myself unable to take a hand off my daughter; some part of me needed constant reassurance of her existence. I saw my wife standing at the edge of the lot, facing away. I called her name, she turned, and the two of us headed toward her.

As my wife tells the story, this was the moment when, as the saying goes, she got God. Once the two of them had been discharged, my wife had stepped outside to call me with this news. But the signal quality was poor, and she abandoned the attempt. I'd be along soon enough.

She found herself, then, standing alone in the Texas night. I do not recall if the weather was clear, but I'd like to think it was, all those fat stars shining down. My wife had been raised Missouri Synod Lutheran, but a series of intertribal squabbles had soured her parents on the whole thing, and apart from weddings and funerals, she hadn't set foot in a church for years. Yet the outdoor cathedral of a starry Texas night is as good a place as any to communicate with the Almighty, which she commenced to do. In the hours since the accident, as the adrenaline cleared, her recollection of events had led her to a calculus that rewrote everything she thought she knew about the world. Until that night, her vision of a universal deity had been basically impersonal. God, in her mind, was simply too busy to take an interest in individual human affairs. The universe possessed a moral shape, but events were haphazard, unguided by providence. Now, as she contemplated the accident, mentally listing the many ways that she and our daughter should have died and yet did not, she decided this was wrong. Of course God paid attention. Only the intercession of a divine hand could explain such a colossal streak of luck. Likewise did the accident become in her mind a product of celestial design. It was a message; it meant something. She had been placed in a circumstance in which a mother's greatest fear was about to be realized, then yanked from the brink. Her future emerged in her mind as something given back to her—it was as if she and our daughter had been killed on the highway and then restored to life—and like all supplicants in the wilderness, she asked God what her purpose was, why he'd returned her to the world.

That was the moment when Iris and I emerged from the building and called her name, giving her the answer.

Until that night we were a family that had lived an entirely secular existence. This wasn't planned; things simply happened that way. My religious background was different from my wife's, but only by degree. I was raised in the Catholic Church, but its messages were delivered to me in a lethargic and off-key manner that failed to gain much traction. My father did not attend mass—I was led to believe this had something to do with the trauma of his attending Catholic grade school—and my mother, who dutifully took my sister and me to church every Sunday, did not receive communion. Why this should be so I never thought to ask. Always she met us at the rear of the church so that we could make a quick exit "to avoid the traffic." (There was no traffic.) We never attended a church picnic or drank coffee in the basement after mass or went to Bible study; we socialized with no other families in the parish. Religion was never discussed over the dinner table or anyplace else. I went to just enough Sunday school to meet the minimum requirements for first communion, but because I went to a private school with afternoon activities, I could not attend confirmation class. My mother struck a deal with the priest. If I met with him for a couple of hours to discuss religious matters, I could be confirmed. I had no idea why I was doing any of this or what it meant, only that I needed to select a new name, taken from the saints. I chose Cornelius, not because I knew who he was but because that was the name of my favorite character in *Planet of the Apes.*

Within a couple of years I was off to boarding school, and my life as a Roman Catholic, nominal as it was, came to an end. During a difficult period in my midtwenties, I briefly flirted with church attendance, thinking it might offer me some comfort and direction, but I found it just as stultifying and embarrassing as I always had, full of weird sexual obsessions, exclusionary politics, and a deep love of hocus-pocus, overlaid with a doctrine of obedience that was complete anathema to my newly independent self. If asked, I would have said that I believed in God—one never really loses those mental contours once they're established—but that organized religious practice struck me as completely infantile. When my wife and I were married, a set of odd circumstances led us to choose an Anglican priest to officiate, but this was a decision we regretted, and when our daughter was born, the subject of baptism never came up. Essentially, we viewed ourselves as too smart for religion. I'll put it another way. Religion was for people who wanted to stay children all their lives. We didn't. We were the grown-ups.

In the aftermath of the accident, and the event that I now think of as "the revelation of the parking lot," all this went out the window. I was not half as sure as my wife that God had interceded; I'm a skeptic and always will be. But it was also the case that I was due for a course correction. In my midforties, I had yet to have anything truly bad happen to me. The opposite was true: I'd done tremendously well. At the university where I taught, I'd just been promoted to full professor. A trilogy of novels I had begun writing on a lark had been purchased for scads of money. We'd just bought a new house we loved, and my daughter had been admitted to a terrific school, where she'd be starting in the fall. My children were happy and healthy, and my newfound financial success had allowed my wife to quit her stressful job as a high school teacher to look after our family and pursue her interests. It had been a long, hard climb, but we'd made it—more than made it—and I spent a great deal of time patting myself on the back for this success. I'd gone out hunting and brought back a mammoth. Everything was right as rain.

In hindsight, this self-congratulatory belief in my ability to chart my own destiny was patently ridiculous. Worldly things are worldly things; two bad seconds on the highway can take them all away, and sooner or later something's going to come along that does just that.

Once you have it, this information is unignorable, and it seems to me that you can do one of two things with it. You can decide that life doesn't make sense, or you can decide that it does. In version one, the universe is a stone-cold place. Life is a series of accumulations—friends, lovers, children, memories, the contents of your 401(k)—followed by a rapid casting off (i.e., you die). Your wife is just somebody you met at a party; your children are biological accretions of yourself; your affection for them is nothing more than a bit of well-engineered firmware to guarantee the perpetuation of the species. All pleasures are sensory, since nothing goes deeper than the senses, and pain, whether psychological or physical, is meaningless bad news you can only endure till it's over.

Version two assumes that life, with all its vicissitudes, possesses an organized pattern of meaning. Grief means something, joy means something, love means something. This meaning isn't always obvious and is sometimes maddeningly elusive; had my wife and daughter been killed that afternoon on the highway, I would have been hard-pressed to take solace in religion's customary clichés. (It is likely that the only thing that would have prevented me from committing suicide, apart from my own physical cowardice, would have been my son, into whom I would have poured all my love and sorrow.) But it's there if you look for it, and the willingness to search—whether this search finds expression in religious ritual or attentive care for one's children or a long run through falling autumn leaves—is what is meant, I think, by faith.

But herein lies the problem: we don't generally come to these things on our own. Somebody has to lay the groundwork, and the best way to accomplish this is with a story, since that's how children learn most things. My Catholic upbringing was halfhearted and unfocused, but it made an impression. At any time during my thirty-year exile from organized religion, I could have stepped into a Sunday mass and recited the entire liturgy by heart. For better or worse, my God was a Catholic God, the God of smells and bells and the BVM and the saints and all the rest, and I didn't have to build this symbolic narrative on my own. My wife is much the same; I have no doubt that the image of the merciful deity she addressed in the parking lot came straight off a stained-glass window, circa 1975. Yet out of arrogance or laziness or the shallow notion that modern, freethinking parents ought to allow children to decide these things for themselves, we'd given our daughter none of it. We'd left her in the dark forest of her own mind, and what she'd concluded was that there was no God at all.

This came about in the aftermath of our move to Texas—a very churchy place. My daughter was entering the first grade; my son was still being hauled around in a basket. Houston is a sophisticated and diverse city, with great food, interesting architecture, and a vivid cultural life, but the suburbs are the suburbs, and the neighborhood where we settled was straight out of Betty Friedan's famous complaint: horseshoe streets of more or less identical one-story, 2,500-square-foot houses, built on reclaimed ranchland in the 1960s. A neighborhood of 2.4 children per household, fathers who raced off to work each morning before the dew had dried, moms who pushed their kids around in strollers and passed out snacks at soccer games and volunteered at the local elementary school. We were, after ten years living in a dicey urban neighborhood in Philadelphia, eager for something a little calmer, more controlled, and we'd chosen the house in a hurry, not realizing what we were getting into. Among our first visitors was an older woman from down the block. She presented us with a plate of brownies and proceeded to list the denominational affiliations of each of our neighbors. I was, to put it mildly, pretty weirded-out. I counted about a dozen churches within just a few miles of my house—Baptist, Methodist, Presbyterian, United Church of Christ —and all of them were *huge*. People talked about Jesus as if he were sitting in their living room, flipping through a magazine; nearly every day I saw a car with a bumper sticker that read, *Warning: In case of Rapture, this car will be unmanned.* Stapled to the local religious culture was a socially conservative brand of politics I found abhorrent. To hear homosexuality described as an "abomination" felt like I'd parachuted into the Middle Ages. I couldn't argue with my neighbors' devotion to their offspring—the neighborhood revolved around children—but it seemed to me that Jesus Christ, whoever he was, had been pretty clear on the subject of loving everybody.

This was the current my daughter swam in every day at school. Not many months had passed before one of her friends, the daughter of evangelicals, expressed concern that Iris was going to hell. Those were the words she used: "I don't want you to go to hell, Iris." The girl in question was adorable, with ringlets of dark hair, perfect manners, and lovely, doting parents. No doubt she thought she was doing Iris a kindness when she urged her to attend church with her family to avoid this awful fate. But that wasn't how I saw the situation. I dropped to a defensive crouch and came out swinging. "Tell her that hell's a fairy tale," I said. "Tell her to leave you alone."

The better choice would have been to offer her a more positive, less punishing view of creation—less hell, more heaven—and over time my wife and I tried to do just that. But when you're seven years old, "love your neighbor as yourself" sounds a lot like "don't forget to brush your teeth"—words to live by but hardly a description of humanity's place in the cosmos. As the playground evangelism continued, so did my daughter's contempt, and why wouldn't it? She'd learned it from me. I don't recall when she announced she was an atheist. All I remember was that she did this from the back seat of the car, sitting in a booster chair.

After the accident, my daughter spent the better part of a week in her closet. From time to time I'd stop by and say, "Are you still in there?" Or "Hey, it's Daddy, how's it going?" Or "Let me know if you need anything."

"All good!" she said. "Thanks!"

There were things to sort out: an insurance claim to file, a replacement vehicle to acquire, arrangements to make for our summer vacation, for which we'd be leaving in two weeks. My wife and I were badly shaken. We had entered a new state: we were a family that had been nearly annihilated. Every few hours one of us would burst into tears. Genesis 2:24 speaks of spouses "cleaving" to each other, and that was what we did: we cleaved. We badly wanted to comfort our daughter, but she had made herself completely unreachable. Of course she'd be confused and angry; in a careless moment, her mother had nearly killed her. But when we probed her on the matter, she insisted this wasn't so. Everything was peachy, she said. She just liked it in the closet. No worries, she'd be along soon.

A day later we received a phone call from the pastor whose car my wife's had struck. At first I thought he was calling to get my insurance information, which I apologetically offered. He explained that the damage was minor, nothing even worth fixing, and that he had called to see if my wife and daughter were all right. Perfectly, I said, omitting my daughter's temporary residence among her shirts and pants, and thanked him profusely.

"It's a miracle," he said. "I saw the whole thing. Nobody should have survived."

He wasn't the first to say this. The *M*-word was bandied about freely by virtually everyone we knew. The following afternoon we were visited by the woman who had collected Iris's belongings: two cardboard boxes of books and clothes covered with highway grime and shards of glass, a suitcase that looked like it had been run over, and her violin, which had escaped its launch into the gulley unharmed. We chatted in the living room, replaying events. Like the pastor, she seemed a little dazed. When the conversation reached a resting place, she explained that she couldn't leave until she'd seen Iris.

"Give me just a sec," my wife said.

A minute later she appeared with our daughter. The woman rose from her chair, stepped toward Iris, and wrapped her in a hug. This display made my daughter visibly uncomfortable, as it would anyone. Why was this stranger hugging her? The woman's face was full of inexpressible emotion; her eyes filmed with tears. My daughter endured her embrace as long as she could, then backed away.

"God protected you. You know that, don't you?"

My daughter's eyes darted around warily. "I guess."

"You're going to have a wonderful life. I just know it."

We exchanged email addresses, knowing we would never use them, and said our goodbyes in the yard. When we returned to the house, Iris was still standing at the base of the stairs. I had never seen her look so freaked-out.

"God had nothing to do with it," she said. "So don't ask me to say he did." And with that she headed back upstairs to her closet.

The psychologist, whom Iris nicknamed "Dr. Cuckoo," told us not to worry. Iris was a levelheaded girl; hiding in the closet was a perfectly natural response to such a trauma. The best thing, she said, was to give our daughter space. She'd talk about it when the time was right.

I doubted this. Levelheaded, yes, but that was the problem.

Doing a double gainer with a twist at 70 miles an hour, without so much as dropping your iPhone, was nothing that the rational mind could parse on its own. The psychologist also didn't know my daughter like I did. Iris can be the most stubborn person on earth. This is one of her cardinal virtues when, for instance, she has a test and two papers due on the same day. She'll stay up till 3:00 A.M. no matter how many times we tell her to go to bed, and get A's on all three, proving herself right in the end. But she can also hold a grudge like nobody I've ever met, and a grudge with the cosmos is no simple matter. How do you forgive the world for being godless? When she declared her atheism from the booster seat, I'd thought two things. First, *How cute! The world's only atheist who eats from the kids' menu!* I couldn't have been more charmed if she'd said she'd been reading Schopenhauer. The second thing was, *This can't last.* How could a girl who still believed in the tooth fairy fail to come around to the idea of a cosmic protector? And yet she didn't. Her atheism had hardened to such a degree that any mention of spiritual matters made her snort milk out her nose. By inserting nothing in its stead, we had inadvertently given her the belief that she was the author of her own fate, and my wife's newfound faith in a God-watched universe was as much a betrayal as crashing their car into the guardrail over a minor argument. It was a philosophical reversal my daughter couldn't process, and it left her feeling utterly alone.

My wife and I felt perfectly awful. In due course our daughter emerged, with one condition: she didn't want to discuss the accident. Not then, not ever. This seemed unhealthy, but you can't make a twelve-year-old girl talk about something she doesn't want to. We left for Cape Cod, where we'd rented a house for the month of July. I'd just turned in a manuscript to my editor and under ordinary circumstances would have been looking forward to the time away, but the trip seemed like too much data. Everyone was antsy and out of sorts, and the weather was horrible. The only person who enjoyed himself was our son, who was too young to comprehend the scope of events and was happy drawing pictures all day.

The school year resumed, and with it life's ordinary rhythms. My wife began looking around for a church to attend. To say this was a sore spot with Iris would be a gross understatement. She hated the idea and said so. "Fine with me," she said, "if you want to get all Jesus-y. Just leave me out of it."

It didn't happen right away. God may have shown his face to my wife in the parking lot, but he'd failed to share his address. We were stymied by the things we always had been: our jaundiced view of organized religion, the conservative social politics of most mainline denominations, the discomfiting business of praying aloud in the presence of people we didn't know. And what, exactly, did we believe? Faith asks for a belief in God, which we had; religion asks for more, a great deal of it literal. Christian ritual was the most familiar, but neither of us believed that the Bible was the word of God or that Jesus Christ was a supernatural being who walked on water when he wasn't turning it into wine. Certainly somebody by that name had existed; he'd gotten a lot of ink. He'd done and said some remarkable stuff, scared the living shit out of an imperial authority, and given humanity two thousand years' worth of things to think about. But the son of God? Really? That Jesus was no more or less divine than the rest of us seemed to me the core of his message.

We wanted something, but we didn't know what. Something with a little grace, a bit of wonder, the feeling of taking a few minutes out of each week to acknowledge how fortunate we were. We decided to give Unitarianism a shot. From the website, it seemed safe enough. Over loud objections, we made Iris come with us. The service was overseen by two ministers, a married couple, who took turns speaking from the altar, which seemed about as holy as the podium in a college classroom. After the hokey business of lighting the lamp, they droned on for half an hour about the importance of friendship. There were almost no kids in the congregation, or even anybody close to our age. It was a sea of white-haired heads. After the service, everyone lingered in the lobby over coffee and stale cookies, but we beat a hasty retreat.

"Well, that was awkward," Iris said.

It was. It had felt like sitting in the audience at a talk show. We tried a few more times, but our interest flagged. When, on the fourth Sunday, Iris found me making French toast in the kitchen in my bathrobe and asked why we weren't going, I told her that I guessed church wasn't for us after all.

"Thank God," she said, and laughed.

In the end, as in the scriptures, it was a child who led us. To our surprise, our son, Tuck, had become a secret Episcopalian. His school is affiliated with an Episcopal parish, and students attend chapel once a week. We'd always assumed this was the sort of wishy-washy, nondenominational fare most places dish out, but we were wrong. One day, apropos of nothing, as I was driving him home from school, he announced that he believed in Jesus.

"Really?" I said. "When did that happen?"

"I don't know," he said, and shrugged. "It just makes sense to me. Pastor Lisa's nice. We should go sometime."

"To church, you mean?"

"Sure," he said. "I think that would be great."

Just like that, the matter was settled. We now go every week—the three of us. St. Stephen's is located in a diverse neighborhood in Houston, and much of the congregation is gay or lesbian. There are protocols, but very loose ones, and the church has open communion and a terrific choir. Pastor Lisa is a woman in her fifties with a gray pageboy who wears blue jeans and Birkenstocks under her robe and gives a hug that feels like falling into bed. She knows I was raised Catholic, and she laughed when I told her that I didn't mind that she "got some of the words wrong." I have my doubts, as always, but it seems like a fine church to have them in. My son finds some of the service boring, as all children do, but he likes communion, which he calls his "force field for the week." He has asked to be baptized next fall.

Will Iris be there? I hope so. But it's her choice. She has yet to go with us. I know this makes her sad, and it makes me sad, too. It's the first thing the three of us have ever done without her.

Three years after the accident, in spring 2012, I failed a blood test at my annual physical, then failed a biopsy and found myself, two months shy of my fiftieth birthday, facing a surgery that would tell me if I was going to see my children grow up. Two of my doctors assured me this would happen; a third said maybe not. We were spending the summer on Cape Cod, where we'd bought a house, and in late July my wife and I flew back to Texas for my operation. When I awoke in the recovery room, my wife was standing over me, smiling. I was so dopey with painkillers that focusing on her face felt like trying to carry a piano up the stairs. "It's over," she said. "The margins were clear. You're going to be okay."

Two days after my surgery, I was instructed to walk. This

sounded impossible, but I was determined. With my wife holding my arm, I shuffled up and down the hall of the ward, gritting my teeth against the discomfort of the catheter, which was the weirdest thing I'd ever felt. The last two months had pummeled me to psychological pieces, but the worst was over. Once again the car had rolled and we had walked away.

From the far end of the hall, a woman was approaching. Like a pair of ocean liners, we headed toward each other in slow motion. She was very thin and wearing a silk robe; like me, she was pulling an IV stand. Some greeting was called for, and she was the first to speak.

"May I give you something?"

We were within just a few feet of each other, and I saw what the situation was. Her body was leaving her; death was in her face.

"Of course."

She gestured downward, indicating the pockets of her robe. "Pick one."

I chose the left. With an uncertain hand she withdrew a wad of white cotton, tied with a bow. She placed it in my hand. It was an angel, made from a dish towel. To this she'd affixed a heart-shaped piece of laminated paper printed with these words from the Book of Numbers:

> The Lord bless and keep you;
> The Lord make his face shine upon you,
> And be gracious to you;
> May the Lord lift up His countenance upon you;
> And give you peace.

When I first learned about my illness, a very smart man told me that I should select an object. It could be anything, he said. A piece of jewelry. A spoon. A rock. Since I was a writer, maybe something to do with writing, such as a pen. It didn't matter what it was. When I was afraid, he said, and thinking that I was going to die, I should take that object in my hand and put my fear inside it.

Wise as his counsel was, I'd never managed to do this. I'd tried one thing and then another. Nothing had felt right. This did. Not just right: miraculous.

"Bless you," I said.

Two weeks later I returned to the Cape to complete my recovery. There wasn't much I could do, but I was glad to be there. A few days before my diagnosis, I had bought a ten-year-old Audi convertible and shipped it north. Iris had just gotten her learner's permit, and after a week of lounging around the house, I asked her if she'd take me for a drive. The day was sunny and hot. We put the top down and sped north, bisecting the peninsula on a rolling, two-lane road. From the passenger seat, I watched my daughter drive. In the past year a startling change had occurred. Iris wasn't a kid anymore. She was taller than my wife, with a full, womanly shape. Her facial features had organized into mature proportions. Her hair, a honeyed red, swept away from her face in a stylish arc. She could have been mistaken for a college student, and often was. But the difference was more than physical; to look at my daughter was to know that she was somebody with a private, inner existence. She was standing at the edge of life; everything was ahead of her. All she had to do was let it come.

"How's it feel?" I asked. She had perfect motorist's manners: hands at ten and two, shoulders pressed back, eyes on the road. She was wearing large tortoiseshell sunglasses that would have been perfectly at home on Audrey Hepburn's face.

"Okay."

"Not scary?"

She shrugged. "Maybe a little."

Our destination was a beach on the Cape's north side, called Sandy Neck. From there, on the clearest days, you can see all the way from Plymouth to Provincetown. We parked and got out of the car and walked to the little platform built to take in the view. I knew we couldn't stay long; even standing was an effort.

"I'm sorry if I scared you," I said.

Iris was looking away. "You didn't. Not really."

"Well, *I* was scared. I'm glad you weren't."

She thought a moment. "That's the thing. I knew I should have been. But I wasn't. I actually feel kind of guilty about that."

"There's no reason you should."

"It's just . . ." She hunted for the words. "I don't know. You're *you*. I just can't imagine you not being okay."

She was wrong. Someday I wouldn't be. Time and chance would do its work, as it does for all of us. But she didn't need to hear that from me on a sunny summer day.

"Do you remember the accident?" I asked.

She laughed, a little nervously. "Well, duh."

"I've always wondered. What were you doing in the closet?"

"Not much. Mostly watching *Project Runway* on my laptop."

"And being mad at us."

She shrugged. "That whole God thing really pissed me off. I mean, you guys can believe whatever you want. I just wanted Mom to feel the same way I did."

"How did you feel?"

She didn't answer right away. Boats were creeping across the horizon.

"Abandoned."

We were silent for a time. I had a sudden vision of myself as old —an old man, being taken to the beach by his grown daughter. The dunes, the ocean, the rocky margin where they met—all would be the same, unchanged since I was boy. It was a sad thought, but it also made me happy in a way that seemed new. These things were years away, and with any luck, I would be around to see them.

"Are you doing all right? Do you need to go back?"

I nodded. "Probably I should get off my feet."

We returned to the car. Three steps ahead of me, Iris moved to the passenger side, opened the door, and got in.

"What are you doing?" I asked.

She looked around. "Oh, right," she said, and laughed. "I'm the driver, aren't I?"

She was sixteen years old. I hoped someday she'd remember how it felt, how invincible, how alive. I'd heard it said that one tenth of parenting is making mistakes; the other nine are prayer and letting go.

"Yes," I said. "You are."

MEGHAN DAUM

Difference Maker

FROM *The New Yorker*

THE FIRST CHILD whose life I tried to make a difference in was Maricela. She was twelve years old and in the sixth grade at a middle school in the San Gabriel Valley, about a half hour's drive from my house, near downtown Los Angeles. We'd been matched by the Big Brothers Big Sisters organization, which put us in a "school-based program." This meant that Maricela would be excused from class twice a month in order to meet with me in an empty classroom. On our first visit, I brought art supplies—glue and glitter and stencils you could use to draw different types of horses. I hadn't been told much about Maricela, only that she had a lot of younger siblings and often got lost in the shuffle at home. She spent most of our first meeting skulking around in the doorway, calling out to friends who were playing kickball in the courtyard. I sat at a desk tracing glittery horses, telling myself she'd come to me when she was ready.

Several months later, it was determined that Maricela saw me largely as a way to get out of class and therefore needed "different kinds of supports." I was transferred to a Big Brothers Big Sisters community-based program to work with fifteen-year-old Kaylee. She had requested a Big Sister, writing on her application that she needed "guidance in life." I found out that Kaylee had mentors from several volunteer organizations. Each had an area of expertise: help with college applications and financial aid, help finding a summer job, help with "girl empowerment." Nearly every time I asked her if she'd been to a particular place—to the science center or the art museum or the Staples Center to see an L.A. Sparks women's basketball game—she told me that another mentor had taken her. So we often wound up going to the mall.

I was thirty-five years old when I worked with Maricela and thirty-six when I met Kaylee. I came to see these years as the beginning of the second act of my adult life. If the first act—college through age thirty-four or so—had been mostly taken up by delirious career ambition and almost compulsive moving among houses and apartments and regions of the country, the second was mostly about appreciating the value of staying put. I'd bought a house in a city that was feeling more and more like home. And though I could well imagine being talked out of my single life and getting married if the right person and circumstances came along—in fact, I met my eventual husband around the time I was matched with Kaylee—one thing that seemed increasingly unlikely to budge was my lack of desire to have children. After more than a decade of being told that I'd wake up one morning at age thirty or thirty-three —or, God forbid, forty—to the ear-splitting peals of my biological clock, I would still look at a woman pushing a stroller and feel no envy at all, only relief that I wasn't her.

I was willing to concede that I was possibly in denial. All the things people say to people like me were things I'd said to myself countless times. If I found the right partner, maybe I'd want a child because I'd want it *with him.* If I went to therapy to deal with whatever neuroses could be blamed on my own upbringing, maybe I'd trust myself not to repeat my childhood's more negative aspects. If I understood that you don't necessarily have to like other children in order to be devoted to your own (as it happens, this was my parents' stock phrase: "We don't like other children, we just like you"), I would stop taking my aversion to kids kicking airplane seats as a sign that I should never have any myself. After all, only a very small percentage of women genuinely feel that motherhood isn't for them. Was I really that exceptional? And if I was, why did I have names picked out for the children I didn't want?

For all this, I had reasons. They ran the gamut from "Don't want to be pregnant" to "Don't want to make someone deal with me when I'm dying." (And, for the record, I've never met a woman of any age and any level of inclination to have children who doesn't have names picked out.) Chief among them was my belief that I'd be a bad mother. Not in the Joan Crawford mode but in the mode of parents you sometimes see who obviously love their kids but clearly do not love their own lives. For every way I could imagine being a good mother, I could imagine ten ways that I'd botch the job irredeemably.

More than that, I simply felt no calling to be a parent. As a role, as *my* role, it felt inauthentic. It felt like not what I was supposed to be doing with my life. My contribution to society was not about contributing more people to it but, rather, about doing something for the ones who were already here. Ones like Maricela and Kaylee. I liked the idea of taking the extra time I had because I wasn't busy raising my own child and using it to help them. It also helped that if anyone, upon learning my feelings about having children, lobbed the predictable "selfish" grenade, I could casually let them know that I was doing my part to shape and enrich the next generation.

When Kaylee graduated from high school and went to college, I didn't take on a new mentee. The reason I gave the volunteer coordinator was that my life had got busier and more complicated. This was true. I had got married at thirty-nine, my mother had died shortly thereafter following a brutal illness, and I'd finally managed, after years of troubling inertia, to publish a new book. More true, though, was that being a Big Sister seemed almost categorically to call for activities that I normally avoided. I'd grown fond of Kaylee. Beneath her taciturn aloofness was an intuitive kindness. When I bawled my eyes out at the end of the movie *Charlotte's Web,* she kindly passed me tissues from her purse. But I had also come to believe that whatever satisfactions were to be gleaned from youth outreach did not offset the soul-numbing torpor of the Beverly Center parking garage on a Saturday afternoon.

When my husband and I married, we both saw ourselves as ambivalent about having children. Since then, aside from a brief interlude of semi-willingness, my ambivalence had slid into something more like opposition. Meanwhile, my husband's ambivalence had slid into abstract desire. A marriage counselor would surely advise a couple in such a situation to discuss the issue seriously and thoroughly, but, wrenching as it was not to be able to make my husband happy in this regard, it seemed to me that there was nothing to discuss. I didn't want to be a mother; it was as simple as that. And as if to prove that my reasons weren't shallow or rooted in some deep-seated antipathy toward kids, I decided to return to kid-related do-goodism. This time, though, I would not be going to the mall or buying useless art supplies. I would not stumble through the motions of being a role model. Instead I would go where I was really needed, where the mall was beside the point. So I became a court-appointed advocate for children in the foster-care system. It was there that I met Matthew.

There is very little that I am permitted to reveal about Matthew, starting with his name, which is not Matthew, as Maricela's is not Maricela and Kaylee's is not Kaylee. I cannot provide a physical description, but for the sake of giving you something to hold on to I'm going to say he's African American, knobby-kneed, and slightly nearsighted, and had just turned twelve years old when I met him. I cannot tell you about his parents or what they did to land their son in the child-welfare system, but I can say that it's about as horrific as anything you can imagine. They were permanently out of the picture, as were any number of others who'd tried at times to take their place. Matthew lived in an institutional group home with about seventy-five other kids. He'd lived in quite a few of these places over the years, and, bleak as they were, they'd come to represent familiar interstices between the preadoptive placements that he inevitably sabotaged by acting out as soon as he began to get comfortable. Like many foster kids, he felt safer in institutions than in anything resembling a family setting.

Court-appointed advocacy is a national program designed to facilitate communication among social workers, lawyers, judges, and others in particularly complicated foster-care cases. The advocate's job is to fit together the often disparate pieces of information about a child's situation and create a coherent narrative for the judge. This narrative takes the form of written reports submitted to the court and is supplemented with actual appearances in court, where the advocate can address the judge directly. Sometimes the information is simple: this child wants to play baseball but needs transportation to the practices and the games. Sometimes it's gothic: this child is being locked in her bedroom by her foster mother because she's become violent and some glitch in the insurance plan has temporarily stopped coverage of her antipsychotic medication. Though advocates are encouraged to develop a relationship with the children they work with, they are not mentors as much as investigators.

I'd been told that Matthew's problems were neither as simple as needing a ride to baseball practice nor as dire as being locked in his bedroom. During our first visit, he told me that what he wanted most was for me to take him to McDonald's. (The Happy Meal, it turns out, is the meal of choice for the unhappiest kids in the world.) But I wasn't allowed to take him off the grounds of the group home, so we sat in the dining hall and hobbled through a conversation about what my role as his advocate amounted to. (He already knew; he'd had one before.) In my training sessions, I'd learned that it was a good idea to bring a game or a toy. After much deliberation, I had settled on a pack of cards that asked hundreds of "Would you rather" questions: "Would you rather be invisible or able to read minds?"; "Would you rather be able to stop time or fly?" Matthew's enthusiasm for this activity was tepid at best, and when I got to questions like "Would you rather go to an amusement park or a family reunion?" and "Would you rather be scolded by your teacher or by your parents?" I shivered at my stupidity for not having vetted them ahead of time.

"We don't have to play with these," I said.

"Uh-huh," Matthew said. This turned out to be his standard response to just about everything. It was delivered in the same tone regardless of context, a tone of impatience mixed with indifference—the tone people use when they're waiting for the other person to stop talking.

The next time I saw him, I was allowed to take him out. I suggested that we go to the zoo or to the automotive museum, but he said he wanted to go shopping at Target. For his recent birthday he'd received gift cards from his social worker and also from his behavioral specialist at the group home. He seemed upbeat, counting and recounting the cash in his pocket (he received a small weekly allowance from the group home) and adding it to the sum total of his gift cards, which included a card worth \$25 that I'd picked up at the advocacy office. He wanted something digital, preferably an MP3 player. The only thing in his price range was a Kindle. I tried to explain the concept of saving up a little while longer, but he insisted that he wanted the Kindle, even after

I reminded him that he'd said he didn't like to read and that he would still have to pay for things to put on the Kindle. He took it to the checkout counter, where he was $25 short anyway. The cashier explained that there were taxes. Also, it appeared that one of his gift cards had been partly spent. Matthew cast his eyes downward. He wouldn't look at me or at anyone, and I couldn't tell if he was going to cry or fly into a rage. There was a line of people behind us, so I lent him $25 on the condition that he pay me back in installments.

"Do you know what installments are?" I asked.

"No."

"It's when you give or pay something back in small increments."

I knew he didn't know what *increments* meant, but I couldn't think of another word.

"So now you haven't just gone shopping—you've learned something, too!" I said.

Once we were back in the car, I found a piece of paper, tore it in half, and wrote out two copies of an IOU, which we both signed. Matthew seemed pleased by this and ran his index finger along the perimeter of the Kindle box as though he'd finally got his hands on a long-coveted item. I gave him command of the radio, and as he flipped from one Auto-Tuned remix to the next I found myself basking in the ecstatic glow of altruism. When I dropped him off at the group home, the promissory note tucked in his Target shopping bag along with the Kindle and the greasy cardboard plate that held the giant pretzel I'd also bought him, I felt useful. I felt proud.

It had been a long time between accomplishments. At least, it had become hard to identify them, as most of my goals for any given day or week took the form of tasks, mundane and otherwise, to be dreaded and then either crossed off a list or postponed indefinitely (*meet article deadline, get shirts from dry cleaner, start writing new book*). Little seemed to warrant any special pride. And though I wanted to believe that I was just bored, the truth was that the decision not to have children was like a slow drip of guilt into my veins.

My husband was patient and funny and smart. In other words, outstanding dad material. Wasting such material seemed like an unpardonable crime. Besides, I've always believed that it is not possible to fall in love with someone without picturing what it might be like to combine your genetic goods. It's almost an aspect of courtship, this vision of what your nose might look like smashed up against your loved one's eyes, this imaginary cubist rendering of the things you hate most about yourself offset by the things you adore most in the other person. And a little over a year after we married, this curiosity, combined with the dumb luck of finding and buying an elegant, underpriced, much-too-large-for-us house in a foreclosure sale, had proved sufficient cause for switching to the leave-it-to-fate method of birth control. Soon enough, I'd found myself pregnant.

It was as if the house itself had impregnated me, as if it had said, "I have three bedrooms and there are only two of you; what's wrong with this picture?" For eight weeks I hung in a nervous limbo, thinking my life was about to become either unfathomably enriched or permanently ruined. Then I had a miscarriage. I was forty-one, so it was not exactly unexpected. And though there had been nothing enriching about my brief pregnancy, which continued to harass my hormones well after vacating the premises, I was left with something that in a certain way felt worse than permanent ruin. I was left with permanent doubt.

My husband was happy about the pregnancy and sad about the miscarriage. I was less sad about the miscarriage, though I undertook to convince myself otherwise by trying to get pregnant again. After three months of dizzying cognitive dissonance, I walked into the guest room that my husband used as an office and allowed myself to say, for once and for all, that I didn't want a baby. I'd thought I could talk myself into it, but those talks had failed.

As I was saying all this, I was lying on the cheap platform bed we'd bought in anticipation of a steady flow of out-of-town company. The curtains were lifting gently in the breeze. Outside, there was bougainvillea, along with bees and hummingbirds and mourning doves. There was a grassy lawn where the dog rolled around scratching its back, and a big table on the deck where friends sat on weekends eating grilled salmon and drinking wine and complaining about things they knew were a privilege to complain about (the cost of real estate, the noise of leaf blowers, the overratedness of the work of more successful peers). And as I lay on that bed it occurred to me, terrifyingly, that all of it might not be enough. Maybe such pleasures, while pleasurable enough, were merely trimmings on a nonexistent tree. Maybe nothing—not a baby or the lack of a baby, not a beautiful house, not rewarding work—was ever going to make us anything other than the chronically dissatisfied, perpetual second-guessers we already were.

"I'm sorry," I said. I meant this a million times over. To this day, there is nothing I've ever been sorrier about than my inability to make my husband a father.

"It's O.K.," he said.

Except it wasn't, really. From that moment on, a third party was introduced into our marriage. It was not a corporal party but an amorphous one, a ghoulish presence that functioned as both cause and effect of the absence of a child. It had even, in the back of my mind, come to have a name. It was the Central Sadness. It collected around our marriage like soft, stinky moss. It rooted our arguments and dampened our good times. It taunted us from the sidelines of our social life (the barbecues with toddlers underfoot; a friend's child interrupting conversations midsentence; the clubby comparing of notes about Ritalin and dance lessons and college tuition, which prompted us to feign interest lest we come across like overgrown children ourselves). It haunted our sex life. Not since I was a teenager (a virginal one at that) had I been so afraid of getting pregnant. I wondered then if our marriage was on life support, if at any moment one of us was going to realize that the humane thing to do would be to call it even and call it a day.

Compared with this existential torment, foster-care advocacy was almost comforting. Though it was certainly more demanding than Big Brothers Big Sisters, I found it considerably easier—or at least more straightforward than traditional mentoring. For one thing, advocating for a foster kid mostly required dealing with adults. It meant talking to lawyers about potential adoptive placements and meeting with school administrators about Matthew's disciplinary issues and sitting around the courthouse all day when there was a hearing. Despite the mournful quality of it all, I found not just gratification but actual enjoyment in my efforts to help. I liked spending hours on the phone with my supervisor, a more seasoned advocate, lamenting the labyrinthine bureaucracy of the child-welfare system. I liked sitting around the tiny attorneys' lounge outside the courtroom, where there was always a plate of stale supermarket pastries next to the coffeemaker and clusters of lawyers grumbling about the judge, their clients, the whole hopeless gestalt. I was moved by the family dramas playing out in the courthouse waiting areas. Everywhere there were children with women —relatives, neighbors, foster mothers—who had taken custody of them. Occasionally there would be a physical altercation and an officer would have to intervene. The courthouse was its own little planet of grimness and dysfunction. By contrast, I felt bright and capable.

Matthew was smart in the way a lot of longtime foster kids are smart. He was a quick and reasonably accurate judge of character, and as soon as he determined that someone was not a threat he began the process of figuring out what the person could do for him. As much of a downer as this behavior could be for people with romantic ideas of helping troubled kids, it was a perfectly understandable survival mechanism, and I grew to respect it. Much of the work I did for Matthew took place behind the scenes. I made sure that his highly competent, crushingly overworked lawyer knew what his less competent, also crushingly overworked social worker was doing. Working with an education attorney, I got Matthew out of his raucous, overcrowded public school and into a calmer learning environment. But though Matthew was vaguely aware of my efforts, what he seemed to most appreciate was my ability to transport him to places like Target and GameStop. In turn, I grudgingly appreciated his GPS-like knowledge of any such place within a twenty-mile radius of wherever he happened to be at any given time. Not that we didn't have our teachable moments. One afternoon, after taking Matthew out for giant burritos, I gave my leftovers to a homeless man sleeping in the alley near the restaurant. At first Matthew was confused about why anyone would do such a thing, but as we continued down the street he said he wanted to give his food away, too, so we turned around and walked back toward the man. Matthew was shy about approaching him, even whispering that he'd changed his mind. But after he set his food on the sidewalk and skittered away, his look of surprised delight suggested that he'd momentarily stepped into a different life, one in which charity was something he could provide as well as receive.

Still, I knew better than to think I was a major role model. I certainly wasn't a mother figure. I was more like a random port in the unrelenting storm that was his life. And that was enough.

Matthew's lot was so bad that it could be improved, albeit triflingly, with one minipizza at a food court. A kid with higher expectations would have been more than I could handle.

By then more than a year had passed since my miscarriage and my subsequent declaration that I did not want to have a child. Though my husband had been supportive and accepting, he now began to say out loud again that he wanted to be someone's father —or at least that he might not be O.K. with never being someone's father. He wanted to use what he knew about the world to help someone find his or her own way through it. He wanted "someone to hang out with" when he got older. He didn't necessarily need the baby- or toddler-rearing experience. He didn't need the kid to look like him or be the same race. When I asked if he'd consider mentoring or even being an advocate, he said he wasn't sure that would be enough.

The seeds of a potential compromise were planted. Maybe we could take in, or even adopt, a foster child. This would be a child old enough that we might actually qualify as young or average-age parents rather than ones of "advanced age." (If I adopted a ten-year-old at forty-three, it would be the equivalent of having had him at the eminently reasonable age of thirty-three.)

We knew that any child we took in would surely need intensive therapy. He would have demons and heartbreaking baggage. But we would find the needle in the haystack, the kid who dreamed of being an only child in a quiet, book-filled house. I probably wouldn't be a great mother, but my standards would be so different from those set by the child-welfare system that it wouldn't matter if I dreaded birthday parties or resorted to store-bought Halloween costumes.

I knew that this was 90 percent bullshit. I knew that it wasn't O.K. to be a mediocre parent just because you'd adopted the child out of foster care. A few times my husband and I scrolled through online photo listings of available children in California, but we might as well have been looking at personal ads from a faraway land that no one ever traveled to. There were three-year-olds with cerebral palsy on ventilators, huge sibling groups who spoke no English, kids who "struggle with handling conflict appropriately." Occasionally there would be some bright-eyed six-or seven-year-old who you could tell was going to be O.K., who had the great fortune of being able to turn the world on with his smile. So as the Central

Sadness throbbed around our marriage, threatening to turn even the most quotidian moments, like the sight of a neighbor tossing a ball around with his kid in the yard, into an occasion for bickering or sulking, the foster-child option placated us with the illusion that all doors were not yet closed.

One day, while my nerves swung on a wider-than-usual pendulum between empathy for Matthew and despondency over my marriage, I decided to call a foster and adoption agency. Actually I asked my husband to call. I'd been told in my training that advocates are not supposed to get involved with fostering children, even those who have nothing to do with their advocacy. Matthew was not allowed to go to my house or even to meet my husband or any of my friends. I didn't want to do anything that might be construed as a conflict of interest. When my husband and I arrived at an orientation meeting, I signed in using his last name, something I'd never done before.

"I've got to be incognito," I said, rather dramatically. "Let's not draw attention to ourselves."

Each of us was asked to say why we were there. When our turn came, my husband spoke briefly about how we were exploring things in a very preliminary way. Then I spoke about how I was ambivalent about children but that this potentially seemed like a good thing to do. I then proceeded to dominate the rest of the meeting. I acted as if I were back in advocacy training. I raised my hand to ask overly technical questions about things like the Indian Child Welfare Act and the Adoptions and Safe Families Act and throw around their acronyms as if everyone knew what they meant. I asked what the chances of getting adopted were for a twelve-year-old who had flunked out of several placements.

"Maybe this isn't the right setting for these questions," my husband whispered.

As the meeting wrapped up, the woman from the agency announced that the next step was to fill out an application and then attend a series of training sessions. After that, she said, prospective parents who passed their home studies could be matched with a child at any time and be on their way to adoption.

Her words were like ice against my spine.

"We're not at that point!" I said to my husband. "Not remotely close."

I suggested that he apply to be a mentor for "transitional-age youth," kids who are aging out of the system but still need help figuring out the basics of life. He filled out a form, with the slightly bewildered resignation of someone agreeing to repair something he hadn't noticed was broken. The woman from the agency said she'd call him about volunteer opportunities. She never did.

A phrase you frequently hear in the foster-care world is that a child has "experienced a lot of loss." It comes up in the blurbs accompanying the photo listings. *Jamal has experienced a lot of loss but knows the right family is out there. Clarissa is working through her losses and learning to have a more positive attitude.* These appear to be references to the original loss of being taken away from the biological family, but often they mean that the child has got close to being adopted but that things haven't worked out. With Matthew, I suspected that the trauma of being removed from his biological parents had been dwarfed by the cumulative implosions of the placements that followed. He seemed to know that he'd lost his temper too many times or let himself lapse into behavior that frightened people. But when I asked about this, which I did only once or twice, he tended to offer some rote excuse on behalf of the estranged parents, which he'd probably heard from his social workers. He'd say that they lacked the resources to sufficiently meet his needs. He'd say that they didn't have the skills to handle a kid like him.

About eight months into my work with Matthew, a couple who had been visiting him at the group home and later hosted him at their home on weekends decided not to pursue adoption after all. He'd been hopeful about the placement, and when I saw him a few days after things fell through, I found him pacing around his cinder-block dormitory like a nervous animal. The prospective mom had given him a used MP3 player, perhaps as a parting gift, but the group-home staff had locked it up for some kind of disciplinary reason. He sat down on a bench outside the dormitory with his Kindle, bending the plastic until pieces began breaking off.

"I know what a huge bummer this is," I said. "I'm really sorry."

"I don't care," he said.

Every possible response seemed inadequate, maybe even capable of doing long-term damage.

"I know you probably do care," I said finally. "But sometimes we care so much about stuff that it's easier to pretend for a while that we don't care at all."

The temperature was in the high nineties; the choke of autumn in Southern California was in full, scorching force. The Kindle was practically melting into soft, curling shards as Matthew tore it apart. I thought about the $23 he still owed me for it and wondered which was worse, letting him destroy it or lecturing him about how money and the stuff it buys aren't disposable. Both tactics seemed fairly useless, but the latter seemed almost like a joke. The kid's whole life was disposable. Like most foster kids, he kept many of his things in a plastic garbage bag so he could grab and go as needed.

Through angry tears, Matthew declared that he was never going back inside the dormitory and would sleep on the lawn until he could live in a real home. He said that he'd got mad at the prospective mom for not buying him something he wanted but that he hadn't done anything too bad. He said he'd kicked over some chairs but they weren't broken or anything. He just wanted another chance but they wouldn't give him one and it wasn't fair. After a while, I suggested that he put his feelings in writing, a suggestion that was based less on his own predilections than on what I would do in his situation, but it was all I could think of.

"Let's go inside and get a piece of paper," I said. "And you write down what you want and how you feel."

He agreed, which surprised me. We went inside and into his room, where blue industrial carpet covered the floor and a low-slung twin bed was draped with a thin blue blanket. He got out a spiral-bound notebook and lay on the floor on his stomach, legs spread slightly and elbows propped up as he began to write. He looked more like a normal kid than I'd ever seen him. I left him and headed down to the common room, where about six boys, some of them older and as tall as men, were sprawled in front of a loud television. I asked a staff member where the bathroom was, and without looking up, she directed me down a corridor that ran through an adjacent dormitory.

I passed another common room, filled with younger children. They were seated at a long table set for dinner and they squirmed in their chairs and fiddled with their utensils. One kid shouted above the others and held a basket of breadsticks over his head so that no one could reach them. I slowed down as I passed the entryway. It had been a while since I'd looked through the state photo listings, but seeing the small, open faces, the feet that barely touched the floor, the institutional food heaped onto institutional plates, I was reminded of the tiny spark of hope those listings had given me and the few occasions when the conversation with my husband about adopting from foster care didn't necessarily feel like bullshit or a pacifier but, rather, like a viable antidote to the Central Sadness.

I returned to Matthew's room. He was sitting on the bed, reading over his statement. He handed me the notebook.

I want to live with —— and ——. I'm sorry I got mad. If you give me another chance I promise I'll never get mad again.

"Will you give that to them?" Matthew asked me.

"If I can," I said, even though the decision had been made. Later I realized that telling Matthew to write that note was the cruelest thing I could have done to him.

There are times when I harbor a secret fantasy that one day my husband will get a call from a person claiming to be his son or his daughter. Ideally, this person will be in his or her late teens or early twenties, the product of some brief fling or one-night stand during the Clinton administration. My husband will be shocked, of course, and probably in denial, and then suddenly his face will blanch and his jaw will grow slack. He will hang up the phone and tell me the news and I will also be shocked. Eventually, though, we'll both be thrilled. This new relation will breeze in and out of our lives like a sort of extreme niece or nephew. We'll dispense advice and keep photos on the fridge but, having never got into the dirty details of actual child-rearing, take neither credit nor blame for the final results.

I thought I'd undertaken volunteer work with kids because I was, above all, a realist. I thought it showed the depth of my understanding of my own psyche. I thought it was a way of turning my limitations, specifically my reluctance to have children, into new and useful possibilities. I thought the thing I felt most guilty about could be turned into a force for good. But now I know that I was under the sway of my own complicated form of baby craziness. Wary as I've always been of our culture's reflexive idealization—even obsessive sanctification—of the bond between parent and child, it seems that I fell for another kind of myth. I fell for the myth of the village. I fell for the idea that nurture from a loving adoptive community could erase or at least heal the abuses of horrible natural parents.

I'd also tricked myself into believing that trying to help these kids would put the Central Sadness on permanent hiatus, that my husband and I could find peace (not just peace but real fulfillment) in our life together. Instead we continued to puzzle over the same unanswerable questions. Were we sad because we lacked some essential element of lifetime partnership, such as a child or an agreement about wanting or not wanting one, or because life is just sad sometimes—maybe even a lot of the time? Or perhaps it wasn't even sadness we were feeling but simply the dull ache of aging. Maybe children don't save their parents from this ache as much as distract from it. And maybe creating a diversion from aging is in fact much of the point of parenting.

Matthew got transferred to a new group home shortly after he turned thirteen. It was practically indistinguishable from the old one. I took him to Target to spend a $25 gift card I'd mailed him for his birthday, but like the other times, when we reached the front of the checkout line the cashier said there wasn't enough left on the card. Matthew claimed it was defective. On the conveyor belt sat several bags of chips, a package of cookies, and boxes of macaroni and cheese that he wanted to keep in the kitchen at the group home. I pulled out my credit card and paid. I knew he was lying and I told him so. He said he wasn't. He said no one ever believed him. He said he had nothing, that no one cared about him or ever did anything for him. He said no one ever gave him a chance or cut him a break. He said everyone in his life was useless.

We got in the car and he ate his chips as we drove in silence. When I pulled up to the entrance of the group home, he gathered his loot without looking at me.

"Happy birthday," I said.

"Uh-huh," he said.

Back at home, my husband and I sat down to dinner around our usual time of eight-thirty. We looked through the magazines that had come in the mail. The evening air was still cool, but the daylight was beginning to linger. Soon it would be summer. Friends would start coming over to eat on the deck. After that it would be fall and then what passes for winter. I would continue to work with Matthew, and he would grow older in his group home while I grew older in my too-big-for-us house. My husband would make peace with the way things had turned out—except in those moments when he didn't have peace, which, of course, come around for everyone. Our lives would remain our own. Whether that was fundamentally sad or fundamentally exquisite, we'd probably never be certain. But if there's anything Matthew taught me, it's that having certainty about your life is a great luxury.

ANTHONY DOERR

Thing with Feathers That Perches in the Soul

FROM *Granta*

1. The House

I AM DRIVING my twin sons home from flag football practice. It's September, it hasn't rained in two months, and seemingly half of the state of Idaho is on fire. For a week the sky has been an upturned bowl the color of putty, the clouds indistinguishable from haze, enough smoke in the air that we taste it in our food, in our throats, in our sleep. But tonight, for some reason, as we pass St. Luke's Hospital, something in the sky gives way, and a breathtaking orange light cascades across the trees, the road, the windshield. We turn onto Fort Street, the road frosted with smoldering, feverish light, and just before the stoplight on Fifth, in a grassy lot, I notice, perhaps for the first time, a little house.

It's a log cabin with a swaybacked roof and a low door, like a cottage for gnomes. A little brick chimney sticks out of its shingles. Three enamel signs stand on the south side; a stone bench hunkers on the north.

It's old. It's tiny. It seems almost to tremble in the strange, volcanic light. I have passed this house, I'm guessing, three thousand times. I have jogged past it, biked past it, driven past it. Every election for the last twelve years I voted in a theater lobby three hundred yards from it.

And yet I've never really seen it before.

2. *Jerry*

A week later I'm standing outside the little house with a City Parks employee named Jerry. A plaque above the door reads THIS CABIN WAS THE FIRST HOME IN BOISE TO SHELTER WOMEN AND CHILDREN. The outer walls are striped with cracked chinking and smudged with exhaust. The ratcheting powerheads of sprinklers spatter its back with each pass. An empty green bottle of something called Übermonster Energy Brew has rolled up against its north wall.

Jerry has to try three keys before he manages to push open the front door.

Inside, it's full of old leaves and hung with the pennants of cobwebs. Little fissures of light show through the paneling.

No furniture. It smells like old paint. Through the dirty steel mesh bolted over a window I can watch cars barrel past on Fort, sedans and Suburbans and pickups, maybe every third one piloted by a sunglasses-wearing mom, a kid or two or three belted into the back seat. Any minute my own wife, ferrying my own kids to school, will come charging past.

"How many people ask to come in here to look at this?" I ask Jerry.

"In four years," he says, "you're the first."

3. *Boise Before Boise*

Take away the Capitol building, the Hoff building, the US Bank building. Take away all eighteen Starbucks, all twenty-nine playgrounds, all ten thousand streetlights. Take away the parking garages, Guido's Pizza, the green belt, the fire hydrants, the cheat grass, the bridges.

It's 1863 in the newly christened Idaho Territory and we're downtown. There are rocks. Magpies. The canvases of a dozen infantry tents flutter beside a cobble-bottomed creek.

Into this rides a man named John.

John has a gnarly, foot-long beard, a wagon full of tools, and a girl back in Colorado. Born in Ireland, he has sailed around the globe; he's been to London, to Calcutta, around Cape Horn; he has heard the *whump* of Russian artillery, saw men die, won a medal.

For years he was a sailor. Now he's a prospector.

He's something else, too. He's in love.

John stops at the tents and asks the infantrymen who they are, where he is, what they call this place.

Camp Boise, they say. Boise Barracks. Fort Boise.

John unpacks his wagon. To his south a green river slides along. To his north the shadows of clouds drag over foothills. All this time he's thinking of Mary.

Mary is seventeen years old. Big-nosed, wavy-haired, as Irish as he is. Good with a needle, good at seeing into people, too. Her eyes, curiously, are like the eyes of a grandmother. As if, though she's half his age, she knows more about the world than he does. She, too, has seen a measure of the planet: born in Cork County, sent to the New World at age nine, enrolled at a convent school in New Orleans, married a man in Philadelphia at age fifteen. Gave birth to a girl. That marriage caved in, God knows why, and Mary found John in Louisville, or John found Mary, and they got married and rode two thousand miles west into the unknown, into Colorado, and now he's here, another thousand miles farther on, in this place that is not yet a place, to look for gold.

John is almost forty years old. Try for a moment to imagine all the places he might have slept: hammocks, shanties, wickiups made of willows, the lurching holds of ships, the cold ruts of the Oregon Trail. Curled on his side next to a mountain stream with his mules hobbled and elk bugling and wolves singing and the great swarming arm of the Milky Way draped over them all.

John rolls away rocks, uproots sage. Cottonwoods are bunched along the river, plenty of them. They're lousy with caterpillars, but they're lightweight, and they're close. He cuts his logs and drags them to a flat area beside the creek and uses the blade of a broadax to wrestle their crooked shapes into straight lines.

A simple rectangle in the sand. Three feet high, then four, then five. Into the spaces between he jams clay and leaves and sticks. He leaves two low doors and two windows to cover—for now—with paper. Later, maybe, he can put in real window glass, if window glass ever makes it all the way out here along two thousand miles of ruts and raids and storm.

If he's lucky. If this place is lucky.

He starts on the roof. Mary is coming from Colorado in a train of fourteen wagons. Already she could be pregnant. Already she could be close.

He fashions wooden pins for door hinges. He installs a stove. He nails fabric to the insides of the walls. Just get here, Mary. Get here before winter.

4. Hope

Three hundred yards from the spot where John O'Farrell raised what would become the first family home in Boise, my wife and I used to pick up drugs from a fertility clinic. We wanted to start a family, but we weren't getting pregnant. Month after month. We went through the expected stuff: tests, doubt, despair. Then I got a chance to move from Boise to work at Princeton University for a year.

Then we got pregnant.

Then we found out it was twins.

Hope, wrote Emily Dickinson, *is the thing with feathers—*

> That perches in the soul—
> And sings the tune without words—
> and never stops—at all.

All autumn in New Jersey we worried the pregnancy wouldn't last, biology wouldn't work, the fetuses wouldn't hang on. But they did.

When my wife went home early to Idaho for Christmas, I stood in our rented New Jersey apartment, in the shadowless gray light of a snowstorm, and let myself believe for the first time that it was actually going to happen, that in a couple of months we would open the squeaky back door and carry in two babies.

The apartment's walls were blank, its stairs were steep. It was not, I realized, ready. Was not a home.

Who hasn't prepared a welcome? Set flowers on a nightstand for a returning hospital patient? Festooned a living room for a returning soldier? Stocked a refrigerator, washed a car, laid out towels? All of this is a kind of hope, a tune without words. Hope that the beloved will arrive safely, that the beloved will feel beloved.

I stood in that little apartment in 2003 thinking of my wife, of the two unknown quantities siphoning nutrients out of her day and night. How she never complained. How she ate Fruit Roll-Ups by the dozen because they were the only food that didn't make her feel sick. Then I drove alone to a shopping mall, not something I've done before or since, and bought foot-high fabric-covered letters—A, B, and C—and a night-light shaped like a star and something called a Graco Pack 'n Play Playard and set it up and then stayed up till midnight trying to figure out how to fold and zip it back inside the bag it came in.

When you prepare a welcome, you prepare yourself. You prepare for the moment the beloved arrives, the moment you say, *I understand you've come a long way, I understand you're taking the larger risk with your life.*

You say, *Here. This might be humble, this might not be the place you know. This might not be everything you dreamed of. But it's something you can call home.*

5. *Questions*

Mary O'Farrell leaves Colorado in the summer of 1863. Lincoln is president; the Emancipation Proclamation is five months old. Across the country, in South Carolina, Union batteries are bombarding Fort Sumter and they won't let up for two years. On the long road north, does she remember what it was like to be a nine-year-old girl and leave her home in Ireland? Does she remember the birds she saw at sea, and the light heaving on the immense fields of the Atlantic? Does she hear in her memory the Latin of Irish priests; the Gaelic of her parents; the terror when she showed up for her first day of school in New Orleans, and heard those accents, and saw faces that were utterly different from every face she had known before? Does she think of her first husband, and their first night together, and does she ponder the circumstances under which she—a sixteen-year-old with a newborn daughter—left him? Does she think of that decision as a failure? Or as an exercise of courage? And was it that same courage that kept her from turning back when she saw the storm-racked brow of the Rockies for the first time, and is it courage that keeps her going now, Pike's Peak at her back, her daughter at her knees, very possibly a new, second child growing in her uterus, the wagon pressing into newer, rawer country, the bench bouncing, wheels groaning—courage that keeps her from weeping at the falling darkness and the creaking trees and the unfettered miles of sage?

It takes Mary four months and four days to reach Fort Boise. Here there are no telegrams, no grocery stores, no pharmacies. There aren't even bricks.

On legs weary from the road she walks into the little house John has built for her. Stands on the dirt floor. Sees the light trapped in its paper-covered windows.

John stops beside her, or in front of her, or behind her.

How many thousands of questions must have been coursing through that little space at that moment?

Is it good enough, does she like it, did I make it all right?

Where will I cook, where will we sleep, where will I give birth?

Will I find gold and will winter be awful and how will I feed us?

Have we finally come far enough to stop moving?

6. Home

Whatever magic John threads into the walls of their house, it works. Fort Boise survives the winter; the O'Farrells survive the winter. John embarks upon a remodel: he replaces the gable ends with board-and-batten siding; he cuts shingles for a proper roof.

Around them civilization mushrooms. By the time the O'Farrell cabin is a year old, Boise has a population of 1,658. There are now sixty buildings, nine general stores, five saloons, three doctors, and two breweries.

John buys wallpaper to cover the interior planking. He builds a fireplace from bricks.

Meanwhile, Mary does not need a fertility clinic. In the years after she arrives in Idaho, she gives birth to six more kids. She loses three. She also adopts seven children.

Their home is two hundred square feet, smaller than my bedroom. There are no *SpongeBob* reruns to put on when the kids get too loud. No pizzerias to call when she can't think of what to cook; there is no telephone, no freezer, no electricity. No internal plumbing. No premoistened baby wipes.

But it's fallacy to imagine Mary O'Farrell's years in that tiny house as unrelenting hardship. Her life was almost certainly full of laughter; without question it was full of noise and energy and sunlight. One day she convinces two passing priests to start holding Catholic mass in her house, and they celebrate Sundays there for four consecutive years.

By 1868, Boise boasts four hundred buildings. Ads in the *Tri-Weekly Statesman* from that year offer coral earrings and eighteen-carat-gold ladies' watches and English saucepans and hydraulic nozzles and twenty-four-hour physicians' prescriptions. A stage line boasts that it can bring a person to San Francisco in four days.

This is no longer a place of single men: by the end of that year, Boise has two hundred children in four different schools.

Eventually John shifts from the unpredictability of crawling into mining tunnels to the rituals of farming: a more sunlit profession. Soon enough he starts construction on a colonial revival at Fourth and Franklin, a real house, made of bricks.

But before it's done, before they move in, John rides to a store downtown and buys panes of glass and carries them home and fits them into strips of wood and builds real French windows for his wife, so she can sit inside their cabin and look out, so the same golden sunshine of a summer evening that every person who has ever lived in this valley knows can fall through the glass and set parallelograms of light onto the floor.

7. *Probably I'm Wrong About a Lot of This*

Maybe John O'Farrell had some help raising the walls of his cabin. Maybe Mary hated it when she first saw it. Maybe they weren't devoted to each other the way I want to believe they were; maybe I'm trying to fashion a love story out of cobwebs and ghosts.

But listen: to live for a minimum of seven years with a minimum of seven kids in two hundred square feet with no toilet paper or Netflix or Xanax requires a certain kind of imperturbability. To adopt seven kids; to not give out when snow is sifting through cracks in the chinking; to not lose your mind when a baby is feverish and screeching and a toddler is tugging your skirts and the hair-dryer wind of August is blowing 110-degree heat under your door and the mass production of electric refrigerators is still fifty-five years away—something has to hold you together through all that.

It has to be love, doesn't it? In however many of its infinite permutations?

John and Mary are married for thirty-seven years. They live to see a capitol dome raised and streetcars glide up and down the streets. Out in the world, Coca-Cola and motion pictures and vacuum cleaners are invented.

On May 13, 1900, the page 8 "Local Brevities" section of the *Idaho Daily Statesman* includes the following items:

The rainfall during the 36 hours preceding 5 o'clock last evening was 1.72 inches.

The May term of the supreme court will begin tomorrow.

Mrs. John O'Farrell is lying at death's door. The physicians have given up all hope.

The second stanza of Emily Dickinson's poem reads like this:

> And sweetest—in the gale—is heard;
> And sore must be the storm—
> That could abash the little bird
> That kept so many warm—

Sore must be the storm indeed. John outlives Mary by only a few months. According to his obituary,

Mr. O'Farrell was one of the pioneers of Idaho, having come to this section in the early sixties. He was well and favorably known throughout Idaho and the northwest.

And then there's this:

Mr. O'Farrell's wife died last spring and he never recovered from the blow.

8. What Lasts

Through the decades the house John built for Mary has been softened by lawn sprinklers and hammered by sun. The cottonwood it was built from makes a weak and spongy lumber, nonresistant to decay, prone to warping, and to keep the house from collapsing,

Boiseans have had to come together every few decades and retell its story. In the early 1910s, the Daughters of the American Revolution collected $173 to move and reroof it; in the 1950s a dance was held to raise funds; seven hundred people showed up. And at the turn of the last century, folks who live in the houses around the O'Farrell cabin raised $52,000 to help the architect Charles Hummel repair the logs, doors, windows, and roof.

And so it stands, 150 years old, the same age as the city it helped establish.

As unassuming as Boise itself. Invisible to most of us. The first family home in our city. On a given night John might have lain in here on a home-made cot dreaming of his years at sea, Anatolia, cannon fire, the churning Pacific; four or five or six or seven kids might have been hip-to-hip under quilts, breathing in unison, their exhalations showing in the cold; owls would have been hunting in the gulches and dogs barking in town; Mary might have been sitting up, hands in her lap, drowsing, watching stars rotate past her new windows. Out the door was Boise: place of salmon, place of gold, place to buy supper and a saddle and have the doctor stitch you up before heading back out to try to wrench another quarter ounce of metal from the hills.

Fifteen decades have passed. It's late September now, and smoke from a dozen fires still hangs in the valley, hazing everything, as I drive to a windowless gray warehouse not too far from the O'Farrell cabin. Inside, stored in an amber-colored gloom, are rows of fifteen-foot-high shelves loaded with artifacts. There's Native American basketry in here and antique typewriters and a covered wagon, and Nazi daggers, and scary-looking foot-powered dental equipment probably eighty years old. There are prisoners' manacles and nineteenth-century wedding gowns and optometry kits and opium scrapers brought to Idaho by Chinese miners who have been dead for more than a century.

From the arcane depths of these shelves a curatorial registrar for the Idaho State Historical Museum named Sarah retrieves four items and lays them out on white Ethafoam.

A miner's pick. A long metal spike called a miner's candlestick. A tin lantern. And an ornate wooden candlestick painted white and gold.

Each is inscribed with a little black number and looped with a paper tag. Each, Sarah tells me, belonged to the O'Farrells.

Did Mary carry this lantern into town on some winter night? Did her adopted sons carry the candlestick during mass, sheltering its flame with one hand, like the altar boys I knew in childhood? How many times did John swing this pick, hoping to feed his family, hoping to strike gold? ·

All four objects sit mute in front of me—points of light dredged out of the shadows, incapable of testimony.

What lasts? Is there anything you've made in your life that will still be here 150 years from now? Is there anything on your shelves that will be tagged and numbered and kept in a warehouse like this?

What does not last, if they are not retold, are the stories. Stories need to be resurrected, revivified, reimagined; otherwise they get bundled with us into our graves: a hundred thousand of them going into the ground every hour.

Or maybe they float a while, suspended in the places we used to be, waiting, hidden in plain sight, until a day when the sky breaks and the lights come on and the right person is passing by.

Outside the warehouse, the air seems smokier than before. The sky glows an apocalyptic yellow. Beneath a locust tree at the edge of the parking lot, doves hop from foot to foot. My hands tremble on the steering wheel. I start the engine, but for a long minute I cannot drive.

It's not that the stuff is still here. It's not that the house still stands. It's that someone keeps the stuff on shelves. It's that someone keeps the house standing.

MALCOLM GLADWELL

The Crooked Ladder

FROM *The New Yorker*

IN 1964 THE anthropologist Francis Ianni was introduced to a man in a congressional waiting room. His name was Philip Alcamo. People called him Uncle Phil, and he was, in the words of the person who made the introduction, "a business leader from New York City and an outstanding Italian American." Uncle Phil was in his early sixties, twenty years older than Ianni. He was wealthy and charming and told Runyonesque stories about the many characters he knew from the old neighborhood, in Brooklyn. The two became friends. "He spoke the lobbyist's language, but with a genial disdain for Washington manners and morals," Ianni later wrote. "He was always very good in those peculiar Washington conversations in which people try to convince each other how much they really know about what is going on in the government, because he generally did know."

Ianni was by nature an adventurous man. He had two pet wolves, called Remus and Romulus. He once drove his young family from Addis Ababa to Nairobi in a Volkswagen microbus. ("I cannot tell you how many times we broke down," his son Juan recalls. "I remember my father fixing the generator by moonlight, and the nuts and bolts falling into the sand.") Uncle Phil fascinated him. At dinners and social functions, Ianni met the other families in the business syndicate whose interests Uncle Phil represented in Washington—the Tuccis, the Salemis, and, at the heart of the organization, the Lupollos. When Ianni moved to New York to take a position at Columbia University, he asked Uncle Phil if he could write about the Lupollo clan. Phil was "neither surprised nor distressed," Ianni recounted, but advised him that he should "tell each member of the family what I was about *only* when it was necessary to ask questions or seek specific pieces of information." And for the next three years he watched and learned—all of which he memorably described in his 1972 book, *A Family Business: Kinship and Social Control in Organized Crime.*

The Lupollos were not really called the Lupollos, of course; nor was Uncle Phil really named Philip Alcamo. Ianni changed names and identifying details in his published work. The patriarch of the Lupollo clan he called Giuseppe. Giuseppe was born in the 1870s in the Corleone district of western Sicily. He came to New York in 1902, with his wife and their two young sons, and settled in Little Italy. He imported olive oil and ran an "Italian bank," which was used for loan-sharking operations. When a loan could not be repaid, he would take an equity stake in his debtor's business. He started a gambling operation and moved into bootlegging; during Prohibition, the business branched out into trucking, garbage collection, food products, and real estate. He recruited close relatives to help him build his businesses—first his wife's cousin Cosimo Salemi, then his son, Joe, then his daughter-in-law's brother, Phil Alcamo, and then the husband of his granddaughter, Pete Tucci. "From all accounts, he was a patriarch, at once kindly and domineering," Ianni wrote of Giuseppe. "Within the family, all important decisions were reserved for him . . . Outside of the family, he was feared and respected." The family moved from Little Italy to a row house in Brooklyn, and from there—one by one—to Queens and Long Island, as its enterprise grew to encompass eleven businesses totaling tens of millions of dollars in assets.

A Family Business was the real-life version of *The Godfather,* the movie adaptation of which was released the same year. But Ianni's portrait was markedly different from the romanticized accounts of Mafia life that have subsequently dominated popular culture. There were no blood oaths in Ianni's account, or national commissions or dark conspiracies. There was no splashy gunplay. No one downed sambuca shots at Jilly's, on West Fifty-Second Street, with Frank Sinatra. The Lupollos lived modestly. Ianni gives little evidence, in fact, that the four families had any grand criminal ambitions beyond the illicit operations they ran out of storefronts in Brooklyn. Instead, from Giuseppe's earliest days in Little Italy, the Lupollo clan was engaged in a quiet and determined push toward respectability.

By 1970, Ianni calculated, there were forty-two fourth-generation members of the Lupollo-Salemi-Alcamo-Tucci family—of which only four were involved in the family's crime businesses. The rest were firmly planted in the American upper middle class. A handful of the younger members of that generation were in private schools or in college. One was married to a judge's son, another to a dentist. One was completing a master's degree in psychology; another was a member of the English department at a liberal arts college. There were several lawyers, a physician, and a stockbroker. Uncle Phil's son Basil was an accountant, who lived on an estate in the posh Old Westbury section of Long Island's North Shore. "His daughter rides and shows her own horses," Ianni wrote, "and his son has some reputation as an up-and-coming young yachtsman." Uncle Phil, meanwhile, lived in Manhattan, collected art, and frequented the opera. "The Lupollos love to tell of old Giuseppe's wife Annunziata visiting Phil's apartment," Ianni wrote. "Her comment on the lavish collection of paintings was '*manga nu Santa*' ('not even one saint's picture')."

The moral of the *Godfather* movies was that the Corleone family, conceived in crime, could never escape it. "Just when I thought I was out," Michael Corleone says, "they pull me back in." The moral of *A Family Business* was the opposite: that for the Lupollos and the Tuccis and the Salemis and the Alcamos—and, by extension, many other families just like them—crime was the means by which a group of immigrants could transcend their humble origins. It was, as the sociologist James O'Kane put it, the "crooked ladder" of social mobility.

Six decades ago Robert K. Merton argued that there was a series of ways in which Americans responded to the extraordinary cultural emphasis that their society placed on getting ahead. The most common was "conformity": accept the social goal (the American dream) and also accept the means by which it should be pursued (work hard and obey the law). The second strategy was "ritualism": accept the means (work hard and obey the law) but reject the goal. That's the approach of the Quakers or the Amish or of any other religious group that substitutes its own moral agenda for that of the broader society. There was also "retreatism" and "rebellion" —rejecting both the goal and the means. It was the fourth adaptation, however, that Merton found most interesting: "innovation."

Many Americans—particularly those at the bottom of the heap—believed passionately in the promise of the American dream. They didn't want to bury themselves in ritualism or retreatism. But they couldn't conform: the kinds of institutions that would reward hard work and promote advancement were closed to them. So what did they do? They innovated: they found alternative ways of pursuing the American dream. They climbed the crooked ladder.

All three of the great waves of nineteenth- and early-twentieth-century European immigrants to America innovated. Irish gangsters dominated organized crime in the urban Northeast in the mid- to late nineteenth century, followed by the Jewish gangsters —Meyer Lansky, Arnold Rothstein, and Dutch Schultz, among others. Then it was the Italians' turn. They were among the poorest and the least skilled of the immigrants of that era. Crime was one of the few options available for advancement. The point of the crooked-ladder argument and *A Family Business* was that criminal activity, under those circumstances, was not rebellion; it wasn't a rejection of legitimate society. It was an attempt to join in.

When Ianni's book came out, there was widespread speculation among Mafia experts about who the Lupollos really were. One guess was that they were descendants of the crime family originally founded by Giuseppe Morello and Ignazio (Lupo) Saietta in the early 1900s. (Lupo plus Morello equals Lupollo.) If that is the case, then the origins of the Lupollos were distinctly unsavory. Morello and Saietta were members of the Black Hand, the name given to bands of southern Italian immigrants who engaged in crude acts of extortion—threatening merchants with bodily injury if protection money wasn't paid. Saietta was thought to be responsible for ordering as many as sixty murders; people in Little Italy, it was said, would cross themselves at the mention of his name.

During Prohibition, the Lupollo gang moved into bootlegging. The vehicles that were used in the liquor trade became the basis for a trucking business. Gambling money went to family bankers, who directed the funds to Brooklyn Eagle Realty and other legal investments. "After the money from gambling is 'cleansed' by reinvestment in legal activities," Ianni wrote, "the profit is then reinvested in loan-sharking."

Ianni didn't romanticize what he saw. He didn't pretend that the crooked ladder was the principal means of economic mobility in America, or the most efficient. It was simply a fact of American life. He saw the pattern being repeated in New York City during the 1970s, as the city's demographics changed. The Lupollos' gambling operations in Harlem had been taken over by African Americans. In Brooklyn, the family had been forced to enter into a franchise arrangement with blacks and Puerto Ricans, limiting themselves to providing capital and arranging for police protection. "Things here in Brooklyn aren't good for us now," Uncle Phil told Ianni. "We're moving out, and they're moving in. I guess it's their turn now." In the early seventies, Ianni recruited eight black and Puerto Rican ex-cons—all of whom had gone to prison for organized crime activities—to be his field assistants, and they came back with a picture of organized crime in Harlem that looked a lot like what had been going on in Little Italy seventy years earlier, only with drugs, rather than bootleg alcohol, as the currency of innovation. The newcomers, he predicted, would climb the ladder to respectability just as their predecessors had done. "It was toward the end of the Lupollo study that I became convinced that organized crime was a functional part of the American social system and should be viewed as one end of a continuum of business enterprises with legitimate business at the other end," Ianni wrote. Fast-forward two generations and, with any luck, the grandchildren of the loan sharks and the street thugs would be riding horses in Old Westbury. It had happened before. Wouldn't it happen again?

This is one of the questions at the heart of the sociologist Alice Goffman's extraordinary new book, *On the Run: Fugitive Life in an American City.* The story she tells, however, is very different.

When Goffman was a sophomore at the University of Pennsylvania, she began tutoring an African American high school student named Aisha, who lived in a low-income neighborhood that she calls 6th Street, not far from campus. (Goffman, like Ianni, altered names and details.) Through Aisha she met a group of part-time crack dealers and was soon drawn into their world. She asked them if she could follow them around and write about their lives. They agreed. She had taken an apartment close by and lived in the neighborhood for the next six years, profiling the lives of people who, in many ways, were the modern-day equivalents of old Giuseppe Lupollo, in his earliest days on the streets of Little Italy.

At the center of Goffman's story are two close friends, Mike and Chuck. Mike's mother worked two and sometimes three jobs, which meant that he was well-off by the standards of the neighborhood. His mother's house was immaculate. Chuck was a senior in high school when he and Goffman met. He had two younger brothers, Reggie and Tim, both of whom were devoted to him. Chuck had a harder time of it; he lived in the basement of his family's derelict row house, where, Goffman writes, "sometimes the rats bit him, but at least he had his own space."

Goffman immersed herself in the 6th Street community. Her school friends dropped away. Chuck and Mike—and occasionally another friend of theirs, Steven—eventually moved in with her, sleeping on two couches in the living room. She lived through a war between her friends on 6th Street and the "4th Street Boys." One day Mike came home with seven bullet holes in the side of his car. ("We hid it in a shed so the cops wouldn't see," she writes.) Goffman, Mike, and Chuck would text one another every half hour, to make sure each was still alive:

You good?
Yeah.
Okay.

Chuck did not survive the gang war. At the end of the book, Goffman attaches a fifty-page "Methodological Note," in which she describes the night that he was shot in the head outside a Chinese restaurant. The passages are devastating. She came running to the hospital room where his body lay. "I cried to him and told him that I loved him," she writes. Then Chuck's girlfriend, Tanesha, and his friend Alex arrived. "Tanesha was talking to him and telling Alex and me what she saw: how he moved his arm because he was fighting, he always was a fighter; how she had followed the ambulance here. How could he leave her and leave his girls? She noticed that his body was beginning to grow stiff." Tanesha began to cry softly. "You are my baby," she said. "Why did you leave me?" Finally, gathered around Chuck's bed, Goffman writes,

we talked about bringing Reggie home from county jail on a funeral furlough. I said that if Reggie came home, all he was gonna do was go shoot someone, and Alex said, "Please—somebody gon' die regardless," and Mike nodded his head in agreement, and Tanesha too. Alex counted one, two, three, four with his fingers. The number of people who would die.

Chuck and Mike were criminals: they were complicit in the barbarism of the drug trade. But in the Mertonian sense, they were also innovators. Goffman describes how they craved success in mainstream society. They tried to get an education and legitimate jobs, only to find themselves thwarted. Selling crack was a business they entered into only because they believed that all other doors were closed to them. In Chuck's case, his mother had a serious crack habit. He began dealing at thirteen in order to buy food for the family and to "regulate" his mother's addiction; if he was her supplier, he figured, she wouldn't have to turn tricks or sell household possessions to pay for drugs. Chuck's criminal activities were an attempt to bring some degree of normalcy to his family.

The problem was that on 6th Street crime didn't pay. Often Chuck and Mike had no drugs to sell: "their supplier had gotten arrested or was simply unavailable, or the money they owed this 'connect' had been seized from their pockets by the police during a stop and search." And if they did have drugs, the odds of evading arrest were small. The police saturated 6th Street. Each day Goffman saw the officers stop young men on the streets, search cars, and make arrests. In her first eighteen months of following Mike and Chuck, she writes:

> I watched the police break down doors, search houses and question, arrest, or chase people through houses fifty-two times. Nine times, police helicopters circled overhead and beamed searchlights onto local streets. I noted blocks taped off and traffic redirected as police searched for evidence . . . seventeen times. Fourteen times during my first eighteen months of near daily observation, I watched the police punch, choke, kick, stomp on, or beat young men with their nightsticks.

Years later, when Chuck went through his high school yearbook with Goffman, he identified almost half the boys in his freshman class as currently in jail or prison. Between the ages of twenty-two and twenty-seven, Mike had spent three and a half years behind bars. He was on probation or parole for 87 weeks of the 139 weeks that he was out of prison, and made 51 court appearances.

The police buried the local male population under a blizzard of arrest warrants: some were "body" warrants for suspected crimes, but most were bench and technical warrants for failure to appear in court or to pay court fees, or for violations of probation or parole. Getting out from under the weight of warrants was so difficult that many young men in the neighborhood lived their lives as fugitives. Mike spent a total of thirty-five weeks on the run, steering clear of friends and loved ones, moving around by night. The young men of the neighborhood avoided hospitals, because police officers congregate there, running checks on those seeking treatment for injuries. Instead they turned to a haphazard black market for their medical care. The police would set up a tripod camera outside funerals, to record the associates of young men murdered on the streets. The local police, the ATF, the FBI, and the U.S. Marshals Service all had special warrant units, using computer-mapping software, cell-phone tracking, and intelligence from every conceivable database: Social Security records, court records, hospital admission records, electricity and gas bills, and employment records. "You hear them coming, that's it, you gone," Chuck tells his little brother. "Period. 'Cause whoever they looking for, even if it's not you, nine times out of ten they'll probably book you." Goffman sometimes saw young children playing the age-old game of cops and robbers in the street, only the child acting the part of the robber wouldn't even bother to run away:

> I saw children give up running and simply stick their hands behind their back, as if in handcuffs; push their body up against a car without being asked; or lie flat on the ground and put their hands over their head. The children yelled, "I'm going to lock you up! I'm going to lock you up, and you ain't never coming home!" I once saw a six-year-old pull another child's pants down to do a "cavity search."

When read alongside Ianni, what is striking about Goffman's book is not the cultural difference between being an Italian thug in the early part of the twentieth century and being an African American thug today. It's the role of law enforcement in each era. Chuck's high school education ended prematurely after he was convicted of aggravated assault in a schoolyard fight. Another boy called Chuck's mother a crack whore, and he pushed his antagonist's face into the snow. In a previous generation, this dispute would not have ended up in the legal system. Until the 1970s, outstanding warrants in the city of Philadelphia were handled by a two-man team, who would sit in an office during the evening hours and make telephone calls to the homes of people on their list. Anyone stopped by the police could show a fake ID. Today there are computers and sometimes even fingerprint machines in squad cars. Between 1960 and 2000, the ratio of police officers to Philadelphia residents rose by almost 70 percent.

In the previous era, according to Goffman, the police "turned a fairly blind eye" to prostitution, drug dealing, and gambling in poor black neighborhoods. But in the late 1980s, she writes, "corruption seems to have been largely eliminated as a general practice, at least in the sense of people working at the lower levels of the drug trade paying the police to leave them in peace."

The Lupollos, of course, routinely paid the police to leave them in peace, as did the other crime families of their day. They got the benefit of law enforcement's "blind eye." Ianni observed that in Giuseppe's lifetime, "no immediate member of the Lupollo clan had ever been arrested." Uncle Phil hung out in Washington, in a blue suit. "I have met judges, commissioners, members of federal regulatory bodies, and congressmen socially when I have been with Phil Alcamo," Ianni wrote. At such meetings, "Phil openly discusses the needs of the family where government is concerned and often asks for advice or favors. He also suggests favorable business investments or land-purchase opportunities and will 'put someone in touch with someone who can do something for them.'" Apparently no one in Washington during that period found anything unusual about a Mafia capo openly discussing "the needs of the family where government is concerned" and suggesting "favorable business investments" for the politicians and regulators whom he was lobbying.

The Federal Witness Protection Program did not yet exist; federal wiretaps weren't admissible in court. Only the FBI was properly equipped to tackle organized crime, and under J. Edgar Hoover the Bureau saw targeting communism and political subversion as its primary mandate. "As late as 1959, the FBI's New York field office had only 10 agents assigned to organized crime compared to over one hundred and forty agents pursuing a dwindling population of Communists," the attorney C. Alexander Hortis writes, in *The Mob and the City.* In the unlikely event that a mobster was arrested, Hortis points out, he could expect to walk. Between 1960 and 1970, 44 percent of indictments of organized crime figures in courts around New York City were dismissed before trial. In that same ten-year period, 536 mobsters were arrested on felony charges, but only 37 ended up in prison.

Hortis retells the story of the famous Apalachin incident, in

1957, when several dozen mobsters from around the country gathered at the upstate New York property of Joseph Barbara, Sr., for a weekend retreat. The get-together was broken up by the police. Some of the mobsters ran into the surrounding woods—and the resulting arrests led to congressional hearings and headlines. How did this happen? By chance, a detective ran into Barbara's son at a local motel and eavesdropped on his conversation. He drove by the Barbara estate, saw lots of fancy cars, ran their plates, and called in reinforcements. The subsequent grand jury investigation, Hortis says, was a "farce." One mobster claimed that he had dropped in while on an olive oil sales trip. Another said that he had had car trouble. A third said that he had heard there was free food. Twenty mobsters were convicted on conspiracy charges, and all twenty convictions were reversed on appeal.

That's why the crooked ladder worked as well as it did. The granddaughter could end up riding horses because the law—whether from indifference, incompetence, or corruption—left her gangster grandfather alone.

The idea that in the course of a few generations the gangster can give way to an equestrian is perhaps the hardest part of the innovation argument to accept. We have become convinced of the opposite trajectory: the benign low-level drug dealer becomes the malignant distributor and then the brutal drug lord. The blanket policing imposed on 6th Street is justified by the idea that, left unchecked, Mike and Chuck will get worse. Their delinquency will metastasize. The crooked-ladder theorists looked at the Mafia's evolution during the course of the twentieth century, however, and reached the opposite conclusion: that over time, the criminal vocation was inevitably domesticated.

One of the dominant organized crime figures on Long Island during the 1970s and '80s was a former garment manufacturer named Salvatore Avellino, and Avellino's story is an example of the crooked ladder in action. It is a good bet that Ianni's Lupollos dealt with Avellino, because they were in the garbage business and Avellino was the king of "carting" (as it was known). He was the de facto head of a trade association called the Private Sanitation Industry Association; it represented a cluster of small, family-owned carting companies that picked up commercial and residential garbage in Nassau and Suffolk Counties. Each carter paid membership dues to the PSI, a portion of which Avellino dutifully passed on to the Lucchese and Gambino crime families.

Avellino was a gangster. He would burn the trucks of those who crossed him. He eventually went to prison for his role in assassinating two carters who refused to play along with the PSI. But in other ways Avellino didn't behave like a thug at all. He worked largely by persuasion and charisma. As the economist Peter Reuter observes in his history of the Long Island carting wars, Avellino's mission was to rationalize the industry, to enforce what was called a "property rights" system among the carters. Individual firms were allowed to compete for new customers. But once a carter won a customer, he "owned" that business; the function of Avellino's PSI was to make sure that no one else poached that customer. Avellino was essentially acting as an agent for the garbage collectors of Long Island, inserting himself between his membership and the marketplace the way a Hollywood agent inserts himself between the pool of actors and the studios.

Ordinary thieves act covertly. They hide their identity from the person whose money they are taking. Avellino did the opposite. He ran a public organization. The ordinary thief is outside the legitimate economy. Avellino was integrated into the legitimate economy. When it came to his PSI members, Avellino acted not as a predator but as a benefactor. By Reuter's estimates, Avellino's cartel enabled PSI members to charge their commercial customers 50 percent more than would otherwise have been possible.

On one federal wiretap, Avellino was recorded speaking about a PSI carter named Freddy, who, Avellino says, drove up to his house in a brand-new Mercedes, "the fifty-thousand-dollar one." Avellino goes on: "So I walked out. It was a Sunday morning and I said, 'Congratulations, beautiful, beautiful.' He says, 'I just wanted you to see it, 'cause this is thanks to you and to PSI that I bought this car.'"

In his economic analysis, Reuter marvels at how scrupulously Avellino defended the interests of his carters. Avellino allowed the bulk of that 50 percent margin to go to the carters and the unions —not to the Luccheses and the Gambinos. Reuter reports, with similar incredulity, about Avellino's personal business dealings. He ran a carting company of his own, but as he expanded his business —buying up routes from other companies—he never demanded discounts. Here was the representative of a major crime family, and he paid retail. "Ya see, out here, Frank, in Nassau, Suffolk County . . . we don't shake anybody down, we don't steal anybody's work, we don't steal it to sell it back to them," Avellino says in another of the wiretaps. "Whenever I got a spot back for a guy because somebody took it, never was a price put on it, because if it was his to begin with and he was part of the club and he was payin' every three months, then he got it back for nothin', because that was supposed to be the idea."

This restraint was, in fact, characteristic of the late-stage mobster. James Jacobs, a New York University law professor who was involved in anti-Mafia efforts in New York during the 1980s, points out that the Mafia had every opportunity to take over the entire carting industry in the New York region—just as they could easily have monopolized any of the other industries in which they played a role. Instead they stayed in the background, content to be the middlemen. At New York's Fulton Fish Market, one of the largest such markets in the country, the Mob policed the cartel and controlled parking—a crucial amenity in a business where time is of the essence and prompt delivery of fresh fish translates to higher profits. What did they charge for a full day's parking? Twelve dollars. And when the Mob-controlled cartel was finally rooted out, how much did fish prices decline at the Fulton Fish Market? Two percent.

In the mid-eighties, when Jacobs worked for the Organized Crime Task Force in New York, trying to rid the construction industry of racketeering, he said that the task force's efforts "had no interest from the builders and the employers." Those immediately involved in the business rather liked having the Mafia around as a referee, because it proved to be such a reasonable business partner. "This was a system that worked for everybody, except maybe the *New York Times*," Jacobs said dryly.

"This is one of the most interesting things about the Mafia," Jacobs went on. "They did business and cooperated. They weren't trying to smash everybody. They created these alliances and maintained these equilibriums . . . You'd think that they would keep expanding their reach."

They didn't, though, because they didn't think of themselves as ordinary criminals. That was for their fathers and grandfathers, who murderously roamed the streets of New York. Avellino wanted to be in the open, not in the shadows. He wanted to be integrated into the real world, not isolated from it. The PSI was a sloppy, occasionally lethal, but nonetheless purposeful dress rehearsal for legitimacy. That was Merton's and Ianni's point. The gangster, left to his own devices, grows up and goes away. A generation ago we permitted that evolution. We don't anymore. Old Giuseppe Lupollo was given that opportunity; Mike and Chuck were not.

"The pioneers of American capitalism were not graduated from Harvard's School of Business Administration," the sociologist Daniel Bell wrote, fifty years ago, in a passage that could easily serve as Goffman's epilogue:

> The early settlers and founding fathers, as well as those who "won the West" and built up cattle, mining and other fortunes, often did so by shady speculations and a not inconsiderable amount of violence. They ignored, circumvented, or stretched the law when it stood in the way of America's destiny and their own—or were themselves the law when it served their purposes. This has not prevented them and their descendants from feeling proper moral outrage when, under the changed circumstances of the crowded urban environments, latecomers pursued equally ruthless tactics.

MARK JACOBSON

65

FROM *New York*

THROUGHOUT MY LIFE, there has always been a number that sounded old. When I was sixteen, it was twenty-seven; at twenty-nine, it was forty-two; at thirty-eight, it was fifty-two. At sixty-five, however, it was sixty-five.

After all, sixty-five is a longtime bullet-point mile marker along the Interstate of American Life, the product of uncounted hours of congressional backroom dealing and insurance-company probability charts. Sixty-five is when you're supposed to retire, put your feet up, smell the roses, to bask in the glow of a well-spent life in the land of the fee. This lovely neo-utopian vision has largely been replaced by the ethic of work-work-work until you drop, but sixty-five still remains the top of the stretch, where, like a creaky claiming horse in the sixth race at Aqueduct, you're supposed to be turning for home.

For me, sixty-five was an onset of pure panic, an ingress of cold claustrophobia. My father died when he was seventy-five, but he was sick. Years of kidney dialysis and he keels over from a heart attack. My mother made it to eighty-four, full speed ahead to the last breath. If the DNA holds up, that gives me another nineteen years, but what's nineteen years? Only yesterday I was twenty-six, a strapping Icarus, soaring on the drunken tailwind of my own infinity. Or was that last week?

Time! Marches On!

You know where it's going. Shortly following my sixty-fifth birthday, I decided to tidy up my "home office." A little fall cleaning, so to speak. Under a pile of carefully curated possessions (you couldn't quite throw out a collection of vomit bags snatched from the seat pockets of such regional carriers as Cebu Pacific, Biman Bangladesh, and Air Namibia, could you?), I found a forgotten piece of correspondence from Beth David Cemetery, which is where several dozen of my relatives, the ones who managed to escape the Nazis, lie in eternal rest just over the city line in Elmont, Long Island. Dated December 27, 1999, and signed by "Warren Rosen, Vice President," the letter advised me of the "following burial reservations: Mark Jacobson . . . Plot 101, Grave #8."

It was Mom's work, no doubt. Child of the Depression, she was always such a planner.

Old. I was having a problem accommodating myself within the format. Until quite recently the main boon of growing old appeared to be not dying young, not perishing when I got this scar across the right side of my face, not being blown up in Vietnam, not going through the windshield after hitting that black-ice spot on Highway 117 in New Mexico. When I was growing up, it was always easy to recognize the old. They were the dry and brittle-boned, the silver-eyed and liver-spotted, sitting on woven plastic beach chairs beneath buzzing fluorescent lights on the porches of decaying hotels before coke money, haute deco, and LeBron James's talents came to South Beach. If these predeceased had anything more on their minds than lining up for tomorrow's early-bird special, who cared? Old people were all basically the same, weren't they? Like, you know, old. On the verge of joining the shadowy ranks of these tattered sticks, I was seized by a hitherto unfelt fear. Back in the day of Youth, us hippies would sit around reading the Walter Evans-Wentz edition of *The Tibetan Book of the Dead* (none of that rationalist Robert Thurman stuff for us), digging on the Roger Corman spook-house descriptions of the blood-drinking "Wrathful Deities" encountered by all nobly born so-and-so's on their trip through Bardo to the next womb door. How fun it was to learn that these beasts were nothing but "projections" of the harrowed human mind, no more genuine than the "Atomic Man" we used to mock at Hubert's Museum and Flea Circus on Forty-Second Street.

Now, however, standing at the mouth not of a passage between lives but rather to the end of this one was to feel the hot, seething, very real breath of the health-care monster upon your face. If the Greeks had Charon, boatman across the River Styx, we have a recorded message saying "Death will not end your financial obligation." There are a lot of levels to beat in life's endgame. Dodge cancer and here comes Alzheimer's, nature's payback for living too long. If *Alien* was once a scary movie, now it was *Amour.*

"Beats the alternative"; that's what you're supposed to say about getting old. Yet a strange thing was happening. As I trod ever deeper into the outer ring of oldness, my fears, nightmares I've nurtured the bulk of my life, began to lighten. I began to look upon my venerability not as a state preferable only to death but rather as an opportunity of a lifetime.

This new paradigm took hold as a scattershot succession of time-specific mini-epiphanies. One of these realizations came while thumbing through a book titled *A History of Old Age.* In addition to detailing Aristotle's distaste for the aged, whom he thought to be excessively pessimistic, malicious, and small-minded owing to their extended interface with life's grinding "disappointments," *A History of Old Age* featured a number of Enlightenment-era drawings titled "The Stages of Man's Life from the Cradle to the Grave."

In this scheme, life is depicted as an eternal staircase; the steps ascend, reach a topmost platform, then go down. The traveler begins on the ground floor as "a lamb-like innocent," then climbs upward, each step signifying a ten-year interval. The "eagle-like" twenties lead to the "bull-like" thirties, nearing the apex in the forties, when "nought his courage quails but lion-like, by force prevails." (A companion chart notes a woman's peak to be thirty, when she is said to be a "crown to her husband.") From this upper perch, it is all downhill, through the grasping, Scrooge-like sixties; the languorous, ineffectual seventies; and ending in the largely symbolic "one-hundredth year," when, "tho' sick of life, the grave we fear." In a French version of "The Stages," called "Le Jugement Universel," the final downward phases are known as *l'âge de décadence* and *l'âge décrépit.*

Probably even Anna Karina in *Vivre Sa Vie* couldn't make *l'âge décrépit* sound sexy, but it was no great task to create a personalized, modern-age version of "The Stages." A pattern of whiplash upheaval emerged. I was born in 1948; my "lamb-like innocence" was spent learning how to be a Cold War kid, schooled in the nuances of 1950s preteen reality, *Have Gun—Will Travel* and *Gun-*

smoke on the tube every Saturday night. Then, just as I mastered my kidlike state, becoming a King of Kids, the rug was pulled out. Without warning I was thrust into a hormone-laced universe of spouting pubic hair and the Rolling Stones. It was back to square one, a whole new playing field to navigate. The ensuing "eagle-like" adolescent-cum-teen quake lasted through the lionization-canonization-commodification of youth culture during the 1960s and early '70s, during which time I would grow to become an exemplar, warts-and-all specimen of my burgeoning bunch, who were on the cover of *Time* magazine every other week. This period also ended with unprecognitioned abruptness when I became a husband, a father, and a simulacrum of a grown-up. It was one more Sisyphean moment, a brand-new rock of unknown size and density to roll up the hill. This was the structure, a repeating push-pull of stasis and change requiring periodic recalibration of self.

So here I am, again, in this as-yet-uncharted territory, working through the break-in period. It isn't that I'm any further from *l'âge décrépit*. With my silver hair (better than none!), I still look the part. I continue to rack up the requisite litany of pre–*alter kaker* woes: the lower back, the plantar fasciitis, the floaters in the right eye. An arthritic right shoulder has joined the left in the crosshairs of the surgeon's hungry arthroscope. Plenty of my parts are out of warranty, or close. My whole corpus delicti could go at any minute. It is just that as an old man, I am new, as fresh to the scene as when I turned into a teen on the 7 train, riding into the Village to see Muddy Waters for the first time at the Café Au Go-Go on Bleecker Street.

That was the real epiphany, what I told myself when I looked into the mirror this very morning—that, ear hair and all, I remain resolutely myself. I am the same me from my baby pictures, the same me who got laid for the first time in the bushes behind the high school field in Queens, the same me who drove a taxi through Harlem during the Frank Lucas days, the same me my children recognize as their father, the same me I was yesterday, except only more so by virtue of surviving yet another spin of the earth upon its axis. I was at the beginning again, stepping off into one more blank space of the Whitmanesque cosmos, a Magellan of me.

*

I mention the above because even if there is nothing new about getting old, it is always good to beat the traffic. As we speak, more people are growing longer in the tooth than at any time in the history of the species. I'm talking about my generation, the one that claimed to want to die before it got old, one more bit of moldy bravado only Keith Moon was bonkers enough to make good on. Every day ten thousand fellow Americans I might have shared a joint with in a freshman dorm join me here on the downside of the stairway to heaven and/or hell. I am in just the first wave of the so-called baby boomers to line up at the cashier's window. The tide will be coming in until 2029, 70 million souls all told, enough to bankrupt a hundred Obamacares. And take it from me, if other generations might have been willing to quietly fade to black, it is going to take a way bigger hook to get the Boom Krewe off the stage.

That's because we're special. We always have been, in our endlessly self-reverential way. There was no such thing as youth until we came with the invincible troika of sex, drugs, and rock and roll. Likewise, when we got around to the procreating, there had never been such babies as the ones we whelped. These were the most loved, most written about, best-equipped babies in history. So it makes sense that even if Adam, the first man, was supposed to have lived to nine hundred, no one has ever really been old, not the way we will be old.

Expect a whole industry of sunset-themed books, blogs, and consoling lectures, even if a certain proportion of this Last Days rhetoric will be couched in terms of the so-called Apocalypse and other cable TV favorites. Some riffs on the topic are bound to be more annoying than others. Not so long ago I saw a video of former *New York Times* columnist Anna Quindlen on Huff/Post50 (the flagship outlet for the Net's elder-chic sector) explaining the instant she knew it was better to be old than young. "When I finally nailed a headstand," she said. She probably had the "physical acumen" to do it when she was younger, but it was "the confidence" of old age that made this late-inning feat possible, said Quindlen.

It is a given: if my big-ass generation is doing anything, it must be the thing to do. Like Diana Nyad swimming 103 miles from Cuba, hardly a day goes by without a story detailing the spectacular exploits of the advanced in age. After all, anyone can be cool and powerful in their twenties. To be cool and powerful in your sixties and beyond—that's the real rabbit in the hat. The way things are going, it won't be long before boomer bloggers proclaim death to be hipper than life.

Sixty-five might be the new forty-five, but what I want to ask the boys at Herbalife is how much omega-3 you have to guzzle before two hundred becomes the new one hundred. One oft-cited study in the chronicle of boomer aging is the so-called U-shaped happiness curve, the theory that human contentment peaks primarily in the early, preadolescent years and again in old age. The stuff in the middle, the muck of everyday life—that's flyover country, easily edited from the highlight reel. For a society with a dense streak of Spielbergian desperation to link the mystical innocence of childhood and the wonderment of the wrinkled and wise, this proprietary attitude toward the possession of happiness fits like a Frye boot.

The vicissitudes of getting old often dominate the conversation among my co-ageist buddies around the virtual communal kitchen table, which is pretty ridiculous, since the majority of us are still wearing (far more expensive) facsimiles of the sneakers and jeans we did when we were seventeen. My father was no fashion plate, but when he went to work, he put on a coat and tie. He looked his age. Then again, he was raised before the invention of television and never made more than $25,000 in any calendar year. Nowadays you can direct a dozen blockbusters and sell a million computers and never once take off that boyish puce-colored baseball cap. Such are the perks when you're brought up in the time that affords the greatest economic and social latitude in American history, are possessed of society's sanctioned skin color, and went to the best schools, even if you only used to get juiced in them.

Here are some of the things nice modern people talk about when they talk about getting old: (a) the nature of regret and whether it is too late or worth it to set things right; (b) fears of irrelevance; (c) what's worse, dying too soon or living too long —and, of course, the money and the pain. Pain more than money. These bummers fight it out with any number of more copacetic, if possibly rationalized, koans (dialogue quoted verbatim) like (a) "to be older frees you from the suffocating anxieties and conventions of youth," (b) "to be older is to be better at integrating the interior and exterior worlds," and (c) "to be older is to be empowered to simply not give a fuck at any given moment." Bo Diddley's classic exhortation about having "a tombstone hand and a graveyard mind / I'm just twenty-two and I don't mind dying" still sounded good. But no one I talk to, whatever their personal history or current circumstances, says they would have signed up for Achilles' choice of living fast, dying young, and leaving a beautiful corpse.

A recurring trope in these discussions is the eternal love-hate relationship every modern generation maintains with its successor, i.e., "da youth." The prevailing view was that if once upon a time old people seemed the same, now it was the young who presented themselves as an indistinct mass. Who were these invaders, this interchangeable gaggle of screen-addicted, brand-worshipping solipsists who filled every bar and hoarded all the good body parts? Sure, they got laid a lot, but how was it possible for a seemingly intelligent twenty-four-year-old to rack up hundreds of thousands in college debt yet know nearly nothing of the world prior to the year 2000?

"They don't know anything" pretty much summed up the position. The Internet, the supposed information superhighway, was actually a giant forgetting machine. If you were of a certain age, you had to watch what you said around the young. Bringing up bulwarks of the personal universe, names like Lenny Bruce or even Miles Davis, was to risk a soul-deadening reply of "Who?" It was the same for every other person, place, or thing, from Michelangelo Antonioni to Pol Pot. Huge swaths of twentieth-century cultural literacy—my century!—were being removed from public consciousness. The shock lay in the speed and the casual know-nothingness of the deletion. It felt deliberate, one more Illuminati plot.

It was out of this well-chewed bleat that I came upon one more useful insight into the post-sixty-five life. This arrived via email from Carl Gettleman, once of Fresh Meadows, Queens, now of Santa Monica, California. One of the worst things about getting older is that people you know and love begin to die at a more rapid rate. A few years ago, Budd Schulberg, then in his early nineties, offered to give me his address book. "It is of no use to me," said the author of *On the Waterfront* and *What Makes Sammy Run?* "Everyone in it is dead." But it also works the other way, since the longer you live, the longer you get to keep treasured friends, and I've known Carl Gettleman for more than fifty years now.

We went to Francis Lewis High School together; Carl was one

of those happy little junior beatniks who accompanied the fifteen-year-old me to drink our first cups of coffee at Café Figaro on Macdougal Street. Then we lost touch for decades, only to find each other through the hitherto unimagined magick of Facebook, a generational irony we received in pothead stride. Gettleman figured to be a whiz on this geezer topic not only because he was the only member of our 1966 graduating class to major in philosophy at Columbia, reading Kierkegaard as the NYPD stormed Hamilton Hall, but also because he is the son of the late Estelle Getty, a onetime Fresh Meadows Community Theatre performer who from 1985 to 1992 played Bea Arthur's mother on *Golden Girls,* therefore defining a certain kind of oldness for untold millions of TV viewers.

"Memory is editing and reediting the narrative of our lives, both consciously and unconsciously," Gettleman wrote of the vast capacity of human beings to lie to themselves. This was the "liberating urgency of old age and knowing we're on the way out." Truth, such as it was, was now available because "we finally realize that the world no longer belongs to us."

It seemed a very small and self-evident thing, the notion that "the world no longer belongs to us," that it was only by being on the outside looking in that a clearer picture could be seen. I mean, is it really any business of mine what a twenty-five-year-old knows and doesn't know? Probably this cache-emptying is an evolutionary imperative, because with all the supposedly hallowed crap floating around in my brain, it is like an episode of *Hoarders.* Besides, where I'm going, it is better to travel light. Triage is the order of the day, with excess baggage thrown overboard. This is the chore: what to keep and what to leave. Like everything, it is a negotiation.

It is a matter of family evolution, the tangle of helices that link me to both forebears and offspring. In the house where I grew up in the 1950s and early '60s, boundaries were well defined. My sister and I were the kids, the parents were the parents. They provided, we didn't screw up, and occasionally there would be a car trip to some place historical like Gettysburg, Pennsylvania—four days in the Plymouth sitting on your hands and looking for cheap gas. As far as the famous Generation Gap went, it wasn't so much a divide as two gravitationally aligned alternative universes. They were from the Depression, the War, and old Williamsburg. I was from Elvis, the Beatles, and the Bomb. The night they bought their first portable record player, they sat in the living room relaxing to Maurice Chevalier. I was in my room, head pressed to the transistor radio, listening to Murray the K's reportage on how Jackie Wilson got shot by his girlfriend in the hallway of his building on Fifty-Seventh Street. It was true we didn't talk much, but there wasn't all that much to talk about.

This didn't mean there weren't valuable lessons to be learned from my father. Battle of the Bulge veteran, lifelong New Yorker, homeowner, he worked hard and deployed a mordant sense of humor. He was resolutely a man of his times, a quality I have come to treasure as what might be called Wisdom, the supposed cardinal virtue of the old.

Once I derided Wisdom as nothing but the gummy verbiage Polonius tried to lay on the head of Laertes. Now I despair over what thoughts of value I might be able to impart to my own children. After all, our house is very different from the one in which I grew up. We never shut up, and the separation between us has never been especially well delineated. Even though each of the kids would eventually get his or her own room, we could often be found piled on top of each other like a litter of cats. We continue to listen to a lot of the same music, even the new stuff, and talk more with each other in a single night than I did with my parents in a month. Once we took a trip around the world, staying in crappy hippie hotels all the way; I wrote a book about it, alternating chapters with my eldest daughter, who described the entire country of India as a living hell. Most people thought her sections, written at age seventeen, were better than mine. There was a kind of haphazard democracy to us, a vague division of labor and authority that we generally took for granted.

I never thought much about this structure, loose as it was, until quite recently, around the time my then-twenty-six-year-old youngest daughter, after four years of college in Indiana, a job in Philly, and a stint in Bed-Stuy, moved back into our house. For me, such a move would have been akin to placing a gun to my head, but that was then and now is now. When I was twenty-six, living on St. Marks Place, the rent was $168 a month. The same apartment now probably goes for $168 a square foot. With the job market slow for experts in the hermeneutics of Michel Foucault, slack must be cut. It seemed a boon, getting extra time with *die Kinder*. Still, with my twenty-three-year-old son already in residence, that made the better part of a hat trick.

The arrangement was less than smooth. Things like waking up in the morning to find those familiar dirty dishes in the sink were particularly vexing. It was no problem for me to slip into the dismaying role of the ticked-off, hectoring dad. According to any system of "stages," wasn't all that supposed to be over long ago?

Eventually we worked much of it out because we realized that we were both in motion, me to oldness, she to wherever she was going. We engaged in several encounters concerning our transitioning Weltanschauungs. Instead of grumping about how everything is derivative, my daughter said, I should examine modernity as a series of Venn diagrams, ever-shifting spheres, floating balloons of self-defining identities, separate yet fungible. What was necessary was to look for those areas of coincidence, where the circles overlap. It was in those zones that we could make common cause. It was probably a rap she learned sitting around in some crusty punk squat, but in a world where those ubiquitous screens are actually NSA panopticons, it sounded good. So we sat down and watched six straight episodes of *The X-Files*.

One conversation during this period stands out. It was a few months after she'd moved back, right before I turned sixty-five. I'd just pitched a TV show, receiving the inevitable pass. The thirty-year-old executive, who looked at my partner and myself as a pair of Willy Lomanish narrative peddlers who had washed up like graying hairballs on his sleek desktop, listened to our spiel and pronounced it "too optimistic." This was a new one. Hollywood is like Eskimos and snow—they've got a million ways to say no. For a century they peddle fake uplift, the bogus happy ending, and now everything is supposed to be so bleak.

My daughter, who knows far more about current television than I ever will, explained it all to me.

"Things are shitty," she said. "The politics are shitty. The economy is shitty. You can't even lie about it anymore."

Did she really believe this?

Yeah, she did.

"Shitty," I wrote on my pad, a useful note for further TV pitches.

Later I felt like weeping. It was no fun to hear my own daughter characterize her world in such a dystopic fashion. What do you do to help someone you love in such a situation? It was time for the voice of experience to step forward. It was time for Wisdom, the font of accumulated knowledge, the voice of experience. In this I cannot say I stepped to the plate. The future was the best I had to offer. That was the extent of my wisdom: Wait. It will seem better in the morning.

A few months later she informed us she would be moving out. It wouldn't be easy because she is easily made homesick, but for the present time she regarded Chicago as a better place to be than Brooklyn. Sure, it won't be New York, city of the collective soul, but you could get a share for $350. Life is full of passages, and it was time to move on.

As a very young man, fancying myself a budding filmmaker of rare potential, I thought I had all the time in the world. Orson Welles didn't make *Citizen Kane* until he was twenty-five. I hadn't even turned twenty. Today I note that Robert Bresson directed *L'Argent* when he was eighty-two, which gives me a whole decade and a half to work up to it, provided I learn French in the meantime. This is one more game I play on the approach to sixty-six (the number of a once-endless highway, you may recall, that used to wind from Oklahoma City, oh so pretty, on through Flagstaff, Arizona, and don't forget Winona, except it doesn't anymore).

This isn't to say I am not serious about the future. In fact, I've never been so excited about my prospects. Unshackled from infinity, with a mind thankfully still fueled by a not-inconsiderable trove of accessible empiricism, I feel as creative as ever, brimming with new ideas. Whether this newfound clarity is a result of something growing together at long last or a chunk of gray matter falling off like a rusted lug nut, it's different up there. I can feel it. Time may be short, but in this job, you learn to produce on a deadline.

Years ago, in a last gasp of heroic ethnobotanical exploration, I ingested a fair amount of ayahuasca, the so-called Vine of the Soul, which transported me from a small apartment on East Seventh Street to the Amazon jungle, where all time dissolved and I was faced with the ineffable assumption that the world had gone on for billions of years before my birth and would continue for billions more after my death. The concept left me clutching my frayed ego like an airplane-seat cushion in a stormy sea. But not anymore. Rather, it seems an ultimate freedom, to glimpse a vision of the vaunted self in the rearview mirror, my atoms redispersed to the ceaseless continuum that is the true beauty of things.

Longevity has its place, but those nineteen years referenced at the top of this tome now sound like a reasonable deal. If a bus with my name comes around the corner tomorrow, so be it. For a schmo born into a lower-middle-class, second-generation immigrant family, eater of pastrami, fan of the Ramones, I preemptively declare my life a success.

The other day, after the requisite period of denial, I got my half-price MetroCard. It goes with my senior citizen movie tickets, although I've been getting into multiplexes cheap for some time (twenty-year-old cashiers rarely think someone would claim to be older than he is). After years of lying to get the "child price" during my early teens, I delight in the symmetry of the subterfuge. Indeed, I've gone underground, invisible to most people I pass on the street or stand next to on the subway. It is good for picking up dialogue. Get caught eavesdropping and no one cares. You're just old, and all old people are the same, aren't they?

So it goes. Last week, on the theory that everyone should at least try to die laughing, I drove by Emmons Avenue in Sheepshead Bay, where my late friend George Schultz ran his comedy club, Pip's. The place was replaced by an all-you-can-eat sushi joint, but the vibe remained. Once a roommate of Lenny Bruce and Jacob Cohen (aka Rodney Dangerfield), George was called the Ear because he could always tell what was funny and what was not. Comics like Richard Lewis and the recently deceased David Brenner would journey out to the Bay on the old D train, which Lewis called a "bad neighborhood on wheels," and go through their routines for George, joke by joke.

"Funny . . . not funny," the Ear would croak, the late-afternoon light playing across his rubbery face as he sat slouched in the empty club in his green terry-cloth robe.

George lived in the apartment above Pip's with his two sons, then in their early twenties. "Look at these young Warren Beattys . . . steaming hot Warren Beattys," he'd say, in a rare moment of *kvell.* "I let them stay here, but I don't let them see me naked. It is the old ass. Way of all flesh. They don't need to see the old ass. Let them live a little."

That was George's Wisdom: the old ass.

I try to follow his dictum, hiding the wrinkly bottom from da youth whenever they're around. Today's modern world is full of technological flimflammery, subject to every manner of visual and structural manipulation, capable of convincing anyone of anything. But the old ass is analog, it cannot be Photoshopped; its impression is indelible. It is truth. And recently I've noticed that the children have turned a tad more solicitous. When I come in the room, they actually look up, ask me how I'm doing, offer to bring me a glass of water. They even look worried sometimes. I like this and am milking it for all it's worth. Just when they think I'm laid low, I pop out again, like the guy in the hockey mask. Good to keep them, and everyone else, on their toes. Still, there's no doubt about it. Things have changed.

MARGO JEFFERSON

Scenes from a Life in Negroland

FROM *Guernica*

I.

ARE WE RICH?

Mother raises those plucked, deep-toned eyebrows that did such excellent expressive work for women in the 1950s. Lift the penciled arch by three to four millimeters for bemused doubt, blatant disdain, or disapproval just playful enough to lure the speaker into more error. Mother's lips form a small, cool smile that mirrors her eyebrow arch. She places a small, emphatic space between each word: *Are. We. Rich?* Then she adds, with a hint of weariness, *Why do you ask?*

I ask because I had been told that day. *Your family must be rich.* A schoolmate had told me and I'd faltered, with no answer, flattered and ashamed to be. We were supposed to eschew petty snobberies at the University of Chicago Laboratory School: intellectual superiority was our task. Other fathers were doctors. Other mothers dressed well and drove stylish cars. Wondering what had stirred that question left me anxious and a little queasy.

Mother says, *We are not rich. And it's impolite to ask anyone that question. Remember that. If you're asked again, you should just say, "We're comfortable."* I take her words in and push on, because my classmate had asked a second question.

Are we upper class?

Mother's eyebrows settle now. She sits back in the den chair and pauses for effect. I am about to receive general instruction in the liturgies of race and class.

We're considered upper-class Negroes and upper-middle-class Americans,

Mother says. *But of course most people would like to consider us Just More Negroes.*

II.

Ginny asked me if we know their janitor, Mr. Johnson. She thinks he lives near us. Ginny had spoken of him so affectionately I longed to say I knew our janitor as well and that he liked me as much as Mr. Johnson seemed to like her. She had rights of intimacy with her janitor that I lacked.

It's a big neighborhood, Mother says. *Why would we know her janitor? White people think Negroes all know each other, and they always want you to know their janitor. Do they want to know our laundryman?*

That would be Wally, a smiling, big-shouldered white man who delivered crisply wrapped shirts and cheerful greetings to our back door every week.

Good morning, Mrs. Jefferson, he'd say. *Morning, doctor. Hello, girls.*

Hello, Wally, we'd chime back from the breakfast table. Then one afternoon I was in the kitchen with Mother doing something minor and domestic like helping unpack groceries, when she said slowly, not looking at me: *I saw Wally at Sears today. I was looking at vacuum cleaners. And I looked up and saw him*—here she paused for a moment of Rodgers and Hammerstein irony—*across a crowded room. He was turning his head away, hoping he wouldn't have to speak. Wally the laundryman was trying to cut me.* She made a small *hmmm* sound, a sound of futile disdain. *I don't even shop at Sears except for appliances.*

Langston Hughes said, *Humor is laughing at what you haven't got when you ought to have it*—the right, in this case, to snub or choose to speak kindly to your laundryman in a store where he must shop for clothes and you shop only for appliances.

Still, Wally went on delivering laundry with cheerful deference, and we responded with cool civility. Was there no Negro laundry to do Daddy's shirts as well or better? Our milkman was a Negro. So was our janitor, our plumber, our carpenter, our upholsterer, our caterer, and our seamstress. Though I don't remember all their names, I know their affect was restful. Comfortable.

If perchance a Negro employee did his work in a sloppy or sullen way (and it did happen), Mother and Daddy had two responses.

One was a period wisecrack along the lines of "Well, some of us *are* lazy, quiet as it's kept." *Humor is laughing at what you haven't got when you ought to have it:* in this case a spotless race reputation.

The second was somber and ominously layered: Some Negroes would rather work for white people. They don't resent their status in the same way.

Let's unpack that. Let's say you are a Negro cleaning woman, on your knees at this minute, scrubbing the bathtub with its extremely visible ring of body dirt, because whoever bathed last night thought, *How nice. I don't have to clean the tub because Cleo/Melba/ Mrs. Jenkins comes tomorrow!* Tub done, you check behind the toilet (a washcloth has definitely fallen back there); the towels are scrunched, not hung on the racks, and you've just come from the children's bedroom where sheets will have to be untangled and almost throttled into shape before they can be sorted for the wash. Cleo/Melba/Mrs. Jenkins will do that.

Would you rather look at the people you do all that for and think, *If the future of this country is anything like its past, I will never be able to have what these white people have,* or would you rather look at them and think, *Well, if I'd had the chance to get an education like Dr. and Mrs. Jefferson did, if I hadn't had to start doing housework at fifteen to help my family out when we moved up here from Mississippi, then maybe I could be where they are.*

Whose privilege would you find more bearable?

Who are "you"? How does your sociological vita—race or ethnicity, class, gender, family history—affect your answer?

Whoever you are, reader, please understand this: never did my parents, my sister, or I leave a dirty bathtub for Mrs. Blake to clean. (My sister and I called her Mrs. Blake. Mother called her Blake.) She was broad, not fat. She had very short, very straightened hair that she patted flat and put behind her ears. When it got humid in the basement, where the washer and dryer were, or in the room where she ironed clothes, short pieces of hair would defy hot comb and oil to stick up. My sister and I never made direct fun of her hair—Mother would have punished our rudeness—but we did find many occasions to mock Negro hair that blatantly defied rehabilitation. We used hot combs and oil, but more discreetly. And our hair was longer.

Mrs. B's voice was southern South Side: leisurely and nasal. Now that I've given my adult attention to the classic blues singers, I can say she had the weighted country diction of Ma Rainey and the short nasal tones of Sippie Wallace. Vowels rubbed down, end-word consonants dropped or muffled.

Mother made clear that we were never to leave our beds unmade when Mrs. Blake was coming. She was not there to pick up after us. When we were old enough, we stripped our own beds each week and folded the linen before putting it in the hamper for her to remove and wash.

Mother's paternal grandmother, great-aunt, and aunt had been in service, so she was sensitive to inappropriate childish presumption.

Mrs. Blake ate her lunch (a hot lunch which Mother made from dinner leftovers) in the kitchen. When her day was done, Mr. Blake and their daughters drove to our house. He sent his daughters to the front door to pick her up. They had the same initials we did. Mildred and Diane. Margo and Denise. Mother brought us to the front door to exchange hellos with them. Sometimes Mrs. Blake left carrying one or two bags of neatly folded clothes. What did Mildred and Diane think as they unfolded, studied, and fit themselves into our used ensembles and separates?

III.

Do we have Indian blood? I ask.

Why do you want to know? Mother answers.

I want to know because I've spent two weeks as a Potawatami tribe member at the Palos Park summer camp in the Forest Preserves of Cook County, Illinois, being led down foot- and bridle paths, sharing space with deer, birds, amphibians, and small mammals, wearing moccasins and woven feathered headbands at nighttime campfires.

According to an official history of Palos Park Village, Indians "roamed the hills" there in the eighteenth century, along with French explorers, traders, and soldiers, but the first white man to "settle" Palos was James Paddock, in 1834. Now, some 120 years later, Denise and Margo Jefferson have become two of the first Negro girls to attend the Palos Park camp alongside the descendants of white settlers.

And one of those descendants had asked if I had Indian blood.

When I said I didn't know whether I did or not, she scanned my face and said, *You must. Ask your mother when she comes to pick you up.*

On the last day of camp the little descendant stood beside me as Mother emerged from her car. Cotton piqué rose-and-white-striped dress. Light brown skin. A Claudette Colbert cap of dark hair. Beneath her black sunglasses a hooked nose asserted itself. The little descendant turned to me, nodded, and whispered, *I told you you have Indian blood. Ask your mother on the way home.*

Why should this be information I'm denied? It would be exciting to be something other than just Negro. I wait till we get home, till Denise and I have made our way through talk of cabin mates and counselors, hikes and canoe trips, through the success, achieved once more, by our normality. Then I ask my question and Mother sighs.

Yee-sss (drawn out to telegraph reluctance), *we do have some Indian blood. But I get so tired of Negroes always talking about their Indian blood. And so tired of white people always asking about it.* Here was an unexpected similarity between Negroes and whites: the slightly desperate need to believe we had Indian blood, or at least recreational kinship rights.

And the next summer a full-blooded Indian comes to camp. Denise and I take her up, enjoying her sweet manner and her dark, shining waist-length braids. Mysteriously, on the last day, no one arrives to take her home. We volunteer our mother.

Lanova gets into the back seat with us and tells Mother where she lives. The three of us grow quiet as Mother drives, drives, and drives. Finally we arrive at a shabby group of apartment buildings. No trees, no trimmed shrubbery. We don't hug, but we say goodbye till next summer. Lanova gets out of the car, turns, and walks toward one of the big ugly housing project buildings. She has on a rust-colored shirt and the same jeans she's worn every day at camp. Mother starts the car and speeds away. None of us says anything about Lanova. *Do you know what tribe she really belonged to?* I ask Denise that night when we're alone in our room. She doesn't answer.

The next summer no recognizable Indian appears at Palos Park. Another Negro does, though. Ronnie arrives a few days after the rest of the campers. He's in my age group, he's a little bit chubby, and he wears glasses, though not as thick as mine. He's definitely browner than I am, by several shades. He's dark brown. I notice how carefully his blue jean cuffs are rolled—folded up and ironed

—and how just-from-the-package his navy and white T-shirt looks with its crisp, three-button collar. I know he has bad hair because it's been shaved so close to his scalp.

At the end of the week my counselor takes me aside. Can I help Ronnie fit in better, she wants to know, can I talk to him? Everyone is still calling him the New Kid. I'm mortified. I hate it when I'm supposed to be enjoying myself and Race singles me out for special chores. I will, I tell her, making myself sound agreeable. And I do. I can see the two of us even now, Ronnie and me, making trite, labored conversation. Neither of us smiling.

After that he leaves my memory. We had no more encounters. But here's something I still want to know: Why wasn't Phillip asked to talk to Ronnie? Because Phillip was a Negro, too, Phillip was the other Negro at camp and he was a boy; he should have been asked to talk to Ronnie. Phillip was my friend; our parents were close friends. Phillip had Negro hair, but it was curly-frizzy hair no one would mind touching. Phillip had pale olive skin and crisp, neatly tailored features.

Phillip should have been asked to talk to Ronnie! I exclaim when I tell the story to a white friend fifty-eight years later.

The counselors didn't read Phillip as Negro, my white friend answers. She's seen a picture of us standing with our mothers in Washington Park. *Phillip settled into the landscape of whiteness.*

Yes. Of course. We map it out. The counselors might have thought Phillip was half white: his mother was clearly a Negro, but his father was often taken for a white man. Even if they'd only seen his mother, they would have decided that it was more appropriate, that Ronnie would be more comfortable talking to someone who looked more like him.

I feel a surge of grief when I think of Ronnie. And inside that grief is guilt, because I looked down on him, and shame, because "looked down on him" is accurate but not sufficient.

I dreaded him.

IV.

We thought of ourselves as the Third Race, poised between the masses of Negroes and all classes of Caucasians. Like the Third Eye, the Third Race possessed a wisdom, intuition, and enlightened knowledge the other two races lacked. Its members had education, ambition, sophistication, and standardized verbal dexterity.

—If, as was said, too many of us ached, longed, strove to be be be be White White White White WHITE;

—If (as was said) many of us boasted overmuch of the blood *des blancs* which for centuries had found blatant or surreptitious ways to flow, course, and trickle tepidly through our veins;

—If we placed too high a value on the looks, manners, and morals of the Anglo-Saxon . . .

. . . white people did too. They wanted to believe they were the best any civilization could produce. They wanted to be white just as much as we did. They worked just as hard at it. They failed just as often. But they could pass so no one objected.

V.

In Negroland, nothing highlighted our privilege more than the threat to it. Inside the race we were the self-designated aristocrats, educated, affluent, accomplished; to Caucasians we were oddities, underdogs, and interlopers. White people who, like us, had manners, money, and education . . . But wait . . . "like us" is presumptuous for the 1950s. Liberal whites who saw that we, too, had manners, money, and education lamented our caste disadvantage. Other whites preferred not to see us in the private schools and public spaces of their choice. They had ready a bevy of slights: from skeptics, the surprised glance and spare greeting; from waverers, the pleasantry, eyes averted; from disdainers, the direct cut. Caucasians with materially less than we had license from Caucasians with more than they to subvert or attack our privilege.

Caucasian privilege lounged and sauntered, draped itself casually about, turned vigilant and commanding, then cunning and devious. We marveled at its tonal range, its variety, its largesse in letting its most humble share the pleasures of caste with its mighty. We knew what was expected of us. Negro privilege had to be circumspect: impeccable but not arrogant; confident yet obliging; dignified, not intrusive.

Early summer, 1956.
Two Negro parents and two Negro daughters stand at a hotel

desk in Atlantic City. This is the last stop on their road trip after Montreal, Quebec City, and New York: the plan is to lounge on the beach and stroll the boardwalk. It's midday, and guests saunter through the lobby in resort wear. The Caucasian clerk in his brown uniform studies the reservation book, looking puzzled as he traces the list with his finger.

You said Mr. and Mrs. Jefferson. . .

Dr. and Mrs. Jefferson, says my father.

The clerk turns the page, studies the list again, running his eyes and his index finger slowly up and down. Just before he turns it back again, he stops.

Oh, here you are, doc. The hotel is so crowded this week. We had to change your room.

Trailing my sister and me, our parents follow the uniformed bellboy into the elevator. It stops a few floors up, they get out, he leads them to the end of a long hall then around a corner, unlocks the door, and puts their suitcases just inside a small room, leading into another small room. We're looking out on a parking lot.

When the bellboy leaves, my father goes into the larger small room without saying anything. My sister and I had stopped talking when the clerk's finger reached the bottom of the first page.

Unpack your towels and swimsuits, our mother orders. *Read or play quietly till we go to the beach.* She follows my father into the other room and shuts the door.

We unpack quickly so she won't be annoyed when she comes back. Just what is going on? All the other hotels had our reservations. Our mother has said that a lot of white people don't like to call Negroes "doctor."

At the beach the girls settle on their new beach towels and fondle the sand. Dr. and Mrs. Jefferson sit on their own blanket talking in low voices. My mother never swims, but my father loves to. Today, though, he takes us to the water's edge and watches us go in and come out.

It's getting cooler, it's late afternoon: time to fold the towels neatly, put them in the beach bag, and return to the hotel. *Take your baths,* Mother says, but only after she has taken a hotel facecloth and soap bar to the lines on the bottom of the tub that don't wash away.

Where are we going for dinner? I ask. *What should we wear?*

We're eating here, Mother answers.

We want to eat in the hotel dining room.

We're ordering room service and eating here, Mother says in her implacable voice. *And we're leaving tomorrow.*

Denise speaks up for us both.

We just got here. We didn't get to stay long at the beach. Why can't we eat in the hotel dining room?

We resent the bad mood that has come over our parents. We want the beach and we want the boardwalk we've been promised since the trip began.

Mother pauses, then addresses us and herself. *This is a prejudiced place. What kind of service would we get in that restaurant? Look at these shabby rooms. Pretending they couldn't find the reservation. We're leaving tomorrow. And your father will tell them why.*

My father has not smiled since the four of us walked into the lobby and stood at the desk waiting as the clerk turned us into Mr. and Mrs. Negro Nobody with their Negro children from somewhere in Niggerland.

The next morning Denise and I are told to sit on the lobby couch while our parents check out; we don't hear what our father says, if he says anything.

We drive back to Chicago, an American family returning home from the kind of vacation successful American families have. We'd stayed at the Statler Hilton in New York and eaten in their restaurant. We'd pummeled and pounced on the bolsters of the Château Frontenac in Quebec. When Daddy asked strangers in Montreal for directions, their answers were always accurate and polite. Only Atlantic City went wrong. In the car our parents reproach themselves for not doing more research, consulting friends on the East Coast before taking the risk.

Such treatment encouraged privileged Negroes to see our privilege as hard-won and politically righteous, a boon to the race, a source of compensatory pride, an example of what might be achieved. Back in the privacy of an all-Negro world, Negro privilege could lounge and saunter, too, show off its accoutrements and lay down the law. Regularly denounce Caucasians, whose behavior toward us, and all dark-skinned people, proved they did not morally deserve *their* privilege. We had the moral advantage; they had the assault weapons of "great civilization" and "triumphant history." Ceaselessly we chronicled our people's achievements. Ceaselessly we denounced our people's failures.

Too many of us just aren't trying. No ambition. No interest in education. You don't have to turn your neighborhood into a slum just because you're poor. Negroes like that made it hard for the rest of us. They held us back. We got punished for their bad behavior.

1956, a month after our trip.

Professionals and small businessmen live on one end of our block. A cabdriver and his wife, a nurse, live at the midpoint next door to us. I play often with their daughter Shirley. At the other end of the block is Betty Ann, somebody's daughter, we don't know whose. She has lots of short braids on her head, fastened with red, yellow, and green plastic barrettes. She wears red nail polish and keeps it on till it's nothing but tiny chips. I beg to be allowed to wear red nail polish outside, and not just when I dress up in Mother's old clothes. *No,* comes the answer, *red nail polish on children is cheap.*

In the summer Betty Ann saunters up and down the block letting the backs of her shoes flap against her heels. When she finds something ridiculous she folds her arms and goes *oooo-oooo-OOO, Uh-un-UNNHH.* When she laughs she bends over at the waist and shuffles her feet. Denise and I start to do this at home. *Where did you pick that up?* our mother asks. *Don't collapse all over yourself when you laugh.*

One afternoon we see Betty Ann playing double Dutch with two girls we've never met. They laugh a lot and say *Girrlll . . .* Then they start to turn the ropes.

Betty Ann's the jumper. She leans in, arms bent, fists balled, gauging her point of entry. Turn slap turn slap turn slap and there she goes! Her knees pump, her feet quick-slap the ground, parrying the ropes till, fleet of foot and neat, she jumps out. Rapt and envious, we watch them take turns. Betty Ann doesn't come down to play jacks with us or borrow Denise's bike. She and her friends laugh and eat candy and jump double Dutch. After a week of this we stroll down the block hoping they'll ask us to join. After a few days they do. Denise isn't good but she's not bad: she swings correctly and manages a few solid intervals before the ropes catch her. My swinging isn't fast or steady enough, and the ropes reject my anxious feet in seconds. By the time I clamor for a third try, Betty Ann and her friends say no.

It's not the no I remember; it's their snickering scorn. I'm used to being the youngest and clumsiest when I play with Denise's friends, but if one of them mocks or reproves me, another pets me to make up for it. If they act too badly, their mothers intervene. Or Denise does, and after a short quarrel and apology they resume play.

Not now. Betty Ann's *Ooo ooh ooooo, Uh-un-unhhhh* is definitive. Denise raises her voice: *We have to go home now.* Betty Ann and her friends laugh a little harder. Denise sets a slow pace, as if we're leaving by choice. My father and uncle are waiting in front of the apartment: they've heard the laughter and looked down the block to see us in shamed, haughty retreat. I bask in their sympathy.

Over dinner the adults concur: we will never play with Betty Ann again. *She and her friends are loud and coarse. They envy you girls.*

Of course they envy us. Now I remember, now I can repeat to myself all the things I've heard my parents say about Betty Ann. *Where are her mother and father? What kind of work do they do? Have you noticed how unkempt their end of the block looks?*

We moved to this neighborhood just five years ago, my father says gravely. *We may need to move again, soon.*

PHILIP KENNICOTT

Smuggler

FROM *Virginia Quarterly Review*

"Then what are you complaining about?"
"About hypocrisy. About lies. About misrepresentation. About
that smuggler's behavior to which you drive the uranist."
—André Gide, *Corydon*, Fourth Dialogue

1.

I REMEMBER MY first kiss with absolute clarity. I was reading on a
black chaise longue, upholstered with shiny velour, and it was right
after dinner, the hour of freedom before I was obliged to begin my
homework. I was sixteen.

It must have been early autumn or late spring, because I know
I was in school at the time, and the sun was still out. I was shocked
and thrilled by it, and reading that passage, from a novel by Hermann Hesse, made the book feel intensely real, fusing Hesse's
imaginary world with the physical object I was holding in my
hands. I looked down at it, and back at the words on the page,
and then around the room, which was empty, and I felt a keen and
deep sense of discovery and shame. Something new had entered
my life, undetected by anyone else, delivered safely and surrepti-
tiously to me alone. To borrow an idea from André Gide, I had
become a smuggler.

It wasn't, of course, the first kiss I had encountered in a book.
But this was the first kiss between two boys, characters in *Beneath
the Wheel*, a short, sad novel about a sensitive student who gains
admission to an elite school but then fails, quickly and inexorably,

after he becomes entwined in friendship with a reckless, poetic classmate. I was stunned by their encounter—which most readers, and almost certainly Hesse himself, would have assigned to that liminal stage of adolescence before boys turn definitively to heterosexual interests. For me, however, it was the first evidence that I wasn't entirely alone in my own desires. It made my loneliness seem more present to me, more intelligible and tangible, and something that could be named. Even more shocking was the innocence with which Hesse presented it:

> An adult witnessing this little scene might have derived a quiet joy from it, from the tenderly inept shyness and the earnestness of these two narrow faces, both of them handsome, promising, boyish yet marked half with childish grace and half with shy yet attractive adolescent defiance.

Certainly no adult I knew would have derived anything like joy from this little scene—far from it. Where I grew up, a decaying Rust Belt city in upstate New York, there was no tradition of schoolboy romance, at least none that had made it to my public high school, where the hierarchies were rigid, the social categories inviolable, the avenues for sexual expression strictly and collectively policed by adults and youth alike. These were the early days of Ronald Reagan's presidency, when recent gains in visibility and political legitimacy for gay rights were being vigorously countered by a newly resurgent cultural conservatism. The adults in my world, had they witnessed two lonely young boys reach out to each other in passionate friendship, would have thrashed them before committing them to the counsel of religion or psychiatry.

But the discovery of that kiss changed me. Reading, which had seemed a retreat from the world, was suddenly more vital, dangerous, and necessary. If before I had read haphazardly, bouncing from adventure to history to novels and the classics, now I read with focus and determination. For the next five years, I sought to expand and open the tiny fissure that had been created by that kiss. Suddenly, after years of feeling almost entirely disconnected from the sexual world, my reading was finally spurred both by curiosity and Eros.

From an oppressive theological academy in southern Germany, where students struggled to learn Latin, Greek, and Hebrew, to the rooftops of Paris during the final days of Adolf Hitler's occupation, I sought in books the company of poets and scholars, hoodlums and thieves, tormented aristocrats bouncing around the spas and casinos of Europe, expat Americans slumming it in the City of Light, an introspective Roman emperor lamenting a lost boyfriend, and a middle-aged author at the height of his powers and the brink of exhaustion. These were the worlds, and the men, presented by Gide, Jean Cocteau, Oscar Wilde, Jean Genet, James Baldwin, Thomas Mann, and Robert Musil, to name only those whose writing has lingered with me. Some of these authors were linked by ties of friendship. Some of them were themselves more or less openly homosexual, others ambiguous or fluid in their desires, and others, by all evidence, bisexual or primarily heterosexual. It would be too much to say their work formed a canon of gay literature—but for those who sought such a canon, their work was about all one could find.

And yet, in retrospect, and after rereading many of those books more than thirty years later, I'm astonished by how sad, furtive, and destructive an image of sexuality they presented. Today we have an insipid idea of literature as self-discovery, and a reflexive conviction that young people—especially those struggling with identity or prejudice—need role models. But these books contained no role models at all, and they depicted self-discovery as a cataclysmic severance from society. The price of survival, for the self-aware homosexual, was a complete inversion of values, dislocation, wandering, and rebellion. One of the few traditions you were allowed to keep was misogyny. And most of the men represented in these books were not willing to pay the heavy price of rebellion and were, to appropriate Hesse's phrase, ground beneath the wheel.

The value of these books wasn't anything wholesome they contained, or any moral instruction they offered. Rather, it was the process of finding them, the thrill of reading them, the way the books themselves, like the men they depicted, detached you from the familiar moral landscape. They gave a name to the palpable, physical loneliness of sexual solitude, but they also greatly increased your intellectual and emotional solitude. Until very recently, the canon of literature for a gay kid was discovered entirely alone, by threads of connection that linked authors from intertwined demimondes. It was smuggling, but also scavenging. There was no Internet, no "customers who bought this item also bought," no helpful librarians steeped in the discourse of tolerance and diversity, and certainly no one in the adult world who could be trusted to give advice and advance the project of limning this still mostly forbidden body of work.

The pleasure of finding new access to these worlds was almost always punctured by the bleakness of the books themselves. One of the two boys who kissed in that Hesse novel eventually came apart at the seams, lapsed into nervous exhaustion, and then one afternoon, after too much beer, he stumbled or willingly slid into a slow-moving river, where his body was found, like Ophelia's, floating serenely and beautiful in the chilly waters. Hesse would blame poor Hans's collapse on the severity of his education and a lamentable disconnection from nature, friendship, and congenial social structures. But surely that kiss, and that friendship with a wayward poet, had something to do with it. As Hans is broken to pieces, he remembers that kiss, a sign that at some level Hesse felt it must be punished.

Hans was relatively lucky, dispensed with chaste, poetic discretion, like the lover in a song cycle by Franz Schubert or Robert Schumann. Other boys who found themselves enmeshed in the milieu of homoerotic desire were raped, bullied, or killed, or lapsed into madness, disease, or criminality. They were disposable or interchangeable, the objects of pederastic fixation or the instrumental playthings of adult characters going through aesthetic, moral, or existential crises. Even the survivors face, at the end of these novels, the bleakest of futures: isolation, wandering, and a perverse form of aging in which the loss of youth is never compensated with wisdom.

One doesn't expect novelists to give us happy endings. But looking back on many of the books I read during my age of smuggling, I'm profoundly disturbed by what I now recognize as their deeply entrenched homophobia. I wonder if it took a toll on me, if what seemed a process of self-liberation was inseparable from infection with the insecurities, evasions, and hypocrisy stamped into gay identity during the painful, formative decades of its nascence in the last century. I wonder how these books will survive, and in what form: historical documents, symptoms of an ugly era, cris de coeur of men (mostly men) who had made it only a few steps along the long road to true equality? Will we condescend to them, and treat their anguish with polite, clinical detachment? I hesitate to say that these books formed me, because that suggests too simplistic a connection between literature and character. But I can't be the only gay man in middle age who now wonders if what seemed a gift at the time—the discovery of a literature of same-sex desire just respectable enough to circulate without suspicion—was in fact more toxic than a youth of that era could ever have anticipated.

2.

Before the mid-1990s, when the Internet began to collapse the distinction between cities, suburbs, and everywhere else, books were the most reliable access to the larger world, and the only access to books was the bookstore or the library. The physical fact of a book was both a curse and a blessing. It made reading a potentially dangerous act if you were reading the wrong things, and of course one had to physically find and possess the book. But the mere fact of *being* a book, the fact that someone had published the words and they were circulating in the world, gave a book the presumption of respectability, especially if it was deemed "literature." There were, of course, bad or dangerous books in the world—and self-appointed guardians who sought to suppress and destroy them—but decent people assumed that these were safely contained within universities.

I borrowed my copy of Hesse's *Beneath the Wheel* from the library, so I can't be sure whether it contained any of the small clues that led to other like-minded books. At least one copy I have found in a used bookstore does have an invaluable signpost on the back cover: "Along with Heinrich Mann's *The Blue Angel*, Emil Strauss's *Friend Death*, and Robert Musil's *Young Törless*, all of which came out in the same period, it belongs to the genre of school novels." Perhaps that's what prompted me to read Musil's far more complicated, beautifully written, and excruciating schoolboy saga. Hans, shy, studious, and trusting, led me to Törless, a bolder, meaner, more dangerous boy.

Other threads of connection came from the introductions, afterwords, footnotes, and the solicitations to buy other books found just inside the back cover. When I first started reading independently of classroom assignments and the usual boy's diet of Rudyard Kipling, Jonathan Swift, Alexandre Dumas, and Jules Verne— reading without guidance and with all the odd detours and byways of an autodidact—I devised a three-part test for choosing a new volume: first, a book had to have a black or orange spine, then the colors of Penguin Classics, which someone had assured me was a reliable brand; second, I had to be able to finish the book within a few days, lest I waste the opportunity of my weekly visit to the bookstore; and third, I had to be hooked by the narrative within one or two pages. That is certainly what led me, by chance, to Cocteau's *Les Enfants Terribles,* a rather slight and pretentious novel of incestuous infatuation, gender slippage, homoerotic desire, and surreal distortions of time and space. I knew nothing of Cocteau but was intrigued by one of his line drawings on the cover, which showed two androgynous teenagers, and a summary which assured it was about a boy named Paul, who worshipped a fellow student.

I still have that copy of Cocteau. In the back there was yet more treasure, a whole page devoted to advertising the novels of Gide (*The Immoralist* is described as "the story of man's rebellion against social and sexual conformity") and another to Genet (*The Thief's Journal* is "a voyage of discovery beyond all moral laws; the expression of a philosophy of perverted vice, the working out of an aesthetic degradation"). These little précis were themselves a guide to the coded language—"illicit, corruption, hedonism"—that often, though not infallibly, led to other enticing books. And yet one might follow these little broken twigs and crushed leaves only to end up in the frustrating world of mere decadence, Wagnerian salons, undirected voluptuousness, the enervating eccentricities of Joris-Karl Huysmans or the chaste, coy allusions to vice in Wilde.

Finally, there were a handful of narratives that had successfully transitioned into open and public respectability, even if always slightly tainted by scandal. If the local theater company still performed Wilde's *The Importance of Being Earnest,* who could fault a boy for reading *The Picture of Dorian Gray?* Conveniently, a 1982 Bantam Classics edition contained both, and also the play *Salomé.* Wilde's novel was a skein of brilliant banter stretched over a rather silly, Gothic tale, and the hiding-in-plain-sight of its homoeroticism was deeply unfulfilling. Even then, too scared to openly acknowledge my own feelings, I found Wilde's obfuscations embarrassing. More powerful than anything in the highly contrived and overwrought games of *Dorian* was a passing moment in *Salomé* when the Page of Herodias obliquely confesses his love for the Young Syrian, who has committed suicide in disgust at Salomé's licentious display. "He has killed himself," the boy laments, "the man who was my friend! I gave him a little box of perfumes and earrings wrought in silver, and now he has killed himself." It was these moments that slipped through, sudden intimations of honest feeling, which made plowing through Wilde's self-indulgence worth the effort.

Then there was the most holy and terrifying of all the publicly respectable representations of homosexual desire, Mann's *Death in Venice,* which might even be found in one's parents' library, the danger of its sexuality safely ossified inside the imposing façade of its reputation. A boy who read *Death in Venice* wasn't slavering over a beautiful Polish adolescent in a sailor's suit, he was climbing a mountain of sorts, proving his devotion to culture.

But a boy who read *Death in Venice* was receiving a very strange moral and sentimental education. Great love was somehow linked to intellectual crisis, a symptom of mental exhaustion. It was entirely inward and unrequited, and it was likely triggered by some dislocation of the self from familiar surroundings, to travel, new sights and smells, and hot climates. It was unsettling and isolating, and drove one to humiliating vanities and abject voyeurism. Like so much of what one found in Wilde (perfumed and swaddled in cant), Gide (transplanted to the colonial realms of North Africa, where bourgeois morality was suspended), or Genet (floating freely in the postwar wreckage and flotsam of values, ideals, and norms), *Death in Venice* also required a young reader to locate himself somewhere on the inexorable axis of pederastic desire.

In retrospect I understand that this fixation on older men who suddenly have their worlds shattered by the brilliant beauty of a young man or adolescent was an intentional, even ironic repurposing of the classical approbation of Platonic pederasty. It allowed the "uranist"—to use the pejorative Victorian term for a homosexual—to broach, tentatively and under the cover of a venerable and respected literary tradition, the broader subject of same-sex desire. While for some, especially Gide, pederasty was the ideal, for others it may have been a gateway to discussing desire among men of relatively equal age and status, what we now think of as being gay. But as an eighteen-year-old reader, I had no interest in being on the receiving end of the attentions of older men; and as a middle-aged man, no interest in children.

The dynamics of the pederastic dyad—like so many narratives

of colonialism—also meant that in most cases the boy was silent, seemingly without an intellectual or moral life. He was pure object, pure receptivity, unprotesting, perfect and perfectly silent in his beauty. When Benjamin Britten composed his last opera, based on Mann's novella, the youth is portrayed by a dancer, voiceless in a world of singing, present only as an ideal body moving in space. In Gide's *Immoralist,* the boys of Algeria (and Italy and France) are interchangeable, lost in the torrents of monologue from the narrator, Michel, who wants us to believe that they are mere instruments in his long, agonizing process of self-discovery and liberation. In Genet's *Funeral Rites,* a frequently pornographic novel of sexual violence among the partisans and collaborators of Paris during the liberation, the narrator/author even attempts to make a virtue of the interchangeability of his young objects of desire: "The characters in my books all resemble each other," he says. He's right, and he amplifies their sameness by suppressing or eliding their personalities, dropping identifying names or pronouns as he shifts between their individual stories, often reducing them to anonymous body parts.

By reducing boys and young men to ciphers, the narrative space becomes open for untrammeled displays of solipsism, narcissism, self-pity, and of course self-justification. These books, written over a period of decades, by authors of vastly different temperaments and sexualities, are surprisingly alike in this claustrophobia of desire and subjugation of the other. Indeed, the psychological violence done to the male object of desire is often worse in authors who didn't manifest any particular personal interest in same-sex desire. For example, in Musil's *Confusions of Young Törless,* a gentle and slightly effeminate boy named Basini becomes a tool for the social, intellectual, and emotional advancement of three classmates who are all, presumably, destined to get married and lead entirely heterosexual lives. One student uses Basini to learn how to exercise power and manipulate people in preparation for a life of public accomplishment; another tortures him to test his confused spiritual theories, a stew of supposedly Eastern mysticism; and Törless turns to him, and turns on him, simply to feel something, to sense his presence and power in the world, to add to the stockroom of his mind and soul.

We are led to believe that this last form of manipulation is, in its effect on poor Basini, the cruelest. Later in the book, when Musil offers us the classic irony of the bildungsroman—the guarantee that everything that has happened was just a phase, a way station on the path of authorial evolution—he explains why Törless "never felt remorse" for what he did to Basini:

> For the only real interest [that "aesthetically inclined intellectuals" like the older Törless] feel is concentrated on the growth of their own soul, or personality, or whatever one may call the thing within us that every now and then increases by the addition of some idea picked up between the lines of a book, or which speaks to us in the silent language of a painting[,] the thing that every now and then awakens when some solitary, wayward tune floats past us and away, away into the distance, whence with alien movements tugs at the thin scarlet thread of our blood—the thing that is never there when we are writing minutes, building machines, going to the circus, or following any of the hundreds of other similar occupations.

The conquest of beautiful boys, whether a hallowed tradition of all-male schools or the vestigial remnant of classical poetry, is simply another way to add to one's fund of poetic and emotional knowledge, like going to the symphony. Today we might be blunter: to refine his aesthetic sensibility, Törless participated in the rape, torture, humiliation, and emotional abuse of a gay kid.

And he did it in a confined space. It is a recurring theme (and perhaps cliché) of many of these novels that homoerotic desire must be bounded within narrow spaces, dark rooms, private attics, as if the breach in conventional morality opened by same-sex desire demands careful, diligent, and architectural containment. The boys who beat and sodomize Basini do it in a secret space in the attic above their prep school. Throughout much of Cocteau's *Les Enfants Terribles,* two siblings inhabit a darkly enchanted room, bickering and berating each other as they attempt to displace unrequited or forbidden desires onto acceptable alternatives. Cocteau helpfully gives us a sketch of this room—a few wispy lines that suggest something that Henri Matisse might have painted —with two beds, parallel to each other, as if in a hospital ward. Sickness, of course, is ever-present throughout almost all of these novels as well: the cholera that kills Aschenbach in *Death in Venice,* the tuberculosis which Michel overcomes and to which his hapless wife succumbs in *The Immoralist,* and the pallor, ennui, listlessness, and fevers of Cocteau. James Baldwin's *Giovanni's Room,* a later, more deeply ambivalent contribution to this canon of illness and enclosure, takes its name from the cramped, cluttered *chambre de bonne* that contains this desire, with the narrator keenly aware that if what happens there—a passionate relationship between a young American man in Paris and his Italian boyfriend—escapes that space, the world of possibilities for gay men would explode. But floods of booze, perhaps alcoholism, and an almost suicidal emotional frailty haunt this space, too.

Often it is the author's relation to these dark spaces that gives us our only reliable sense of how he envisioned the historical trajectory of being gay. In Cocteau's novel, the room becomes a ship, or a portal, transporting the youth into the larger world of adult desires. The lines are fluid, but there is a possibility of connection between the perfervid world of contained sexuality and the larger universe of sanctioned desires. In Baldwin, the young Italian proposes the two men keep their room as a space apart, a refuge for secret assignations, even as his American lover prepares to reunite with his fiancée and return to a life of normative sexuality. They could continue their relationship privately, on the side, a quiet compromise between two sexual realms. But Musil's attic, essentially a torture chamber, is a much more desperate space, a permanent ghetto for illicit desire.

Even those among these books that were self-consciously written to advance the cause of gay men, to make their anguish more comprehensible to a reflexively hostile straight audience, leave almost no room—no space—for many openly gay readers. The parallels with colonial discourse are troubling: the colonized "other," the homosexual making his appeal to straight society, must in turn pass on the violence and colonize and suppress yet weaker or more marginal figures on the spectrum of sexuality. Thus in the last of Gide's daring dialogues in defense of homosexuality, first published piecemeal, then together commercially as *Corydon* in 1924 —a tedious book full of pseudoscience and speculative extensions of Darwinian theory—the narrator contemptuously dismisses the unmanly homosexual: "If you please, we'll leave the inverts aside for now. The trouble is that ill-informed people confuse them with normal homosexuals. And you understand, I hope, what I mean by 'inverts.' After all, heterosexuality too includes certain degenerates, people who are sick and obsessed."

Along with the effeminate, the old and the aging are also beneath contempt. The casual scorn in Mann's novella for an older man whom Aschenbach encounters on his passage to Venice is almost as horrifying as the sexual abuse and mental torture of young Basini in Musil's novel. Among gay men, Mann's painted clown is one of the most unsettling figures in literature, a "young-old man" whom Mann calls a "repulsive sight." He apes the manners and dress of youth but has false teeth and bad makeup, luridly colored clothing, and a rakish hat, and is desperately trying to run with a younger crowd of men: "He was an old man, beyond a doubt, with wrinkles and crow's feet round eyes and mouth; the dull carmine of the cheeks was rouge, the brown hair a wig." Mann's writing rises to a suspiciously incandescent brilliance in his descriptions of this supposedly loathsome figure. For reasons entirely unnecessary to the plot or development of his central characters, Baldwin resurrects Mann's grotesquerie, in a phantasmagorical scene that describes an encounter between his young American protagonist and a nameless old "queen" who approaches him in a bar:

> The face was white and thoroughly bloodless with some kind of foundation cream; it stank of powder and a gardenia-like perfume. The shirt, open coquettishly to the navel, revealed a hairless chest and a silver crucifix; the shirt was covered with paper-thin wafers, red and green and orange and yellow and blue, which stormed in the light and made one feel that the mummy might, at any moment, disappear in flame.

This is the future to which the narrator—and by extension the reader if he is a gay man—is condemned. Unless, of course, he succumbs to disease or addiction. At best there is a retreat from society, perhaps to someplace where the economic differential between the Western pederast and the colonized boy makes an endless string of anonymous liaisons economically feasible. Violent death is the worst of the escapes. Not content with merely parodying older gay men, Baldwin must also murder them. In a scene that does gratuitous violence to the basic voice and continuity of the book, the narrator imagines in intimate detail events he has not actually witnessed: the murder of a flamboyant bar owner who sexually harasses and extorts the young Giovanni (by this point betrayed, abandoned, and reduced to what is, in effect, prostitution). The murder happens behind closed doors, safely contained in a room filled with "silks, colors, perfumes."

3.

If I remember with absolute clarity the first same-sex kiss I encountered in literature, I don't remember very well when my interest in specifically homoerotic narrative began to wane. But again, thanks to the physicality of the book, I have an archaeology more reliable than memory. As a young reader, I was in the habit of writing the date when I finished a book on the inside front cover, and so I know that sometime shortly before I turned twenty-one, my passion for dark tales of unrequited desire, sexual manipulation, and destructive Nietzschean paroxysms of self-transcendence peaked, then flagged. That was also the same time that I came out to friends and family, which was prompted by the complete loss of hope that a long and unrequited love for a classmate might be returned. Logic suggests that these events were related, that the collapse of romantic illusions and the subsequent initiation of an actual erotic life with real, living people dulled the allure of Wilde, Gide, Mann, and the other authors who were loosely in their various orbits.

It happened this way: For several years I had been drawn to a young man who seemed to me curiously like Hans from Hesse's novel. Physically, at least, they were alike: "Deep-set, uneasy eyes glowed dimly in his handsome and delicate face; fine wrinkles, signs of troubled thinking, twitched on his forehead, and his thin, emaciated arms and hands hung at his side with the weary gracefulness reminiscent of a figure by Botticelli." But in every other way my beloved was an invention. I projected onto him an elaborate but entirely imaginary psychology, which I now suspect was cobbled together from bits and pieces of the books I had been reading. He was sad, silent, and doomed, like Hans, but also cold, remote, and severe, like Törless, cruelly beautiful like all the interchangeable sailors and hoodlums in Genet, but also intellectual, suffering, and mystically connected to dark truths from which I was excluded. When I recklessly confessed my love to him—how long I had nurtured it and how complex, beautiful, and poetic it was—he responded not with anger or disgust but impatience: "You can't put all this on me."

He was right. It took me only a few days to realize it intellectually, a few weeks to begin accepting it emotionally, and a few years not to feel fear and shame in his presence. He had recognized in an instant that what I had felt for years, rather like Swann for Odette, had nothing to do with him. It wasn't even love, properly speaking. I can't claim that it was all clear to me at the time, that I was conscious of any connection between what I had read and the excruciating dead end of my own fantasy life. I make these connections in retrospect. But the realization that I would never be with him because he didn't in fact exist—not in the way I imagined him —must have soured me on the literature of longing, torment, and convoluted desire. And the challenge and excitement of negotiating a genuine erotic life rendered so much of what I had found in these books painfully dated and irrelevant.

I want to be rigorously honest about my feelings for this literature, whether it distorted my sense of self and even, perhaps, corrupted my imagination. The safe thing to say is that I can't possibly find an answer to that, not simply because memory is unreliable, but because we never know whether books implant things in us or merely confirm what is already there. In *Young Törless,* Musil proposes the idea that the great literature of Johann Wolfgang von Goethe, Friedrich Schiller, and William Shakespeare is essentially a transitional crutch for young minds, a mental prosthesis or substitute identity during the formlessness of adolescence: "These associations originating outside, and these borrowed emotions, carry young people over the dangerously soft spiritual ground of the years in which they need to be of some significance to themselves and nevertheless are still too incomplete to have any real significance."

It's important to divorce the question of how these books may have influenced me from the malicious accusations of corruption that have dogged gay fiction from the beginning. In the course of our reading lives, we will devour dozens, perhaps hundreds, of crude, scabrous, violent books, with no discernible impact on our moral constitution. And homosexual writers certainly didn't invent the general connection between sexuality and illness, or the thin line between passion and violence, or sadism and masochism, or the sexual exploitation of the young or defenseless. And the mere mention of same-sex desire is still seen in too many places around the world today as inherently destructive to young minds. Gide's Corydon decried the illogic of this a century ago: "And if, in spite of advice, invitations, provocations of all kinds, he should manifest a homosexual tendency, you immediately blame his reading or some other influence (and you argue in the same way for an entire nation, an entire people); it has to be an acquired taste, you insist; he must have been taught it; you refuse to admit that he might have invented it all by himself."

And I want to register an important caveat about the literature of same-sex desire: it is not limited to the books I read, the authors I encountered, or the tropes that now seem to me so sad and destructive. In 1928, E. M. Forster wrote a short story called "Arthur Snatchfold" that wasn't published until 1972, two years after the author's death. In it, an older man, Sir Richard Conway, respectable in all ways, visits the country estate of a business acquaintance, where he has a quick, early-morning sexual encounter with a young deliveryman in a field near the house. Later, as Sir Richard chats with his host at their club in London, he learns that the liaison was seen by a policeman, the young man was arrested, and the authorities sent him to prison. To his great relief, Sir Richard also learns that he himself is safe from discovery, that the "other man" was never identified, and despite great pressure on the working-class man to incriminate his upper-class partner, he refused to do so.

"He [the deliveryman] was instantly removed from the court and as he went he shouted back at us—you'll never credit this —that if he and the old grandfather didn't mind it why should anyone else," says Sir Richard's host, fatuously indignant about the whole affair. Sir Richard, ashamed and sad but trapped in the armor of his social position, does the only thing he can: "Taking a notebook from his pocket, he wrote down the name of his lover, yes, his lover who was going to prison to save him, in order that he might not forget it." It isn't a great story, but it is an important moment in the evolution of an idea of loyalty and honor within the emerging category of homosexual identity. I didn't discover it until years after it might have done me some good.

Forster's story is exceptional because only one man is punished, and he is given a voice—and a final, clear, unequivocal protest against the injustice. The other man escapes, but into shame, guilt, and self-recrimination. And yet it is the escapee who takes up the pen and begins to write. We might say of Sir Richard what we often say of our parents as we come to peace with them: he did the best he could. And for all the internalized homophobia of the authors I began reading more than thirty years ago, I would say the same thing. They did the best they could. They certainly did far more than privately inscribe a name in a book. I can't honestly say that I would have had even Sir Richard's limited courage in 1928.

But Forster's story, which he didn't dare publish while he was alive, is the exception, not the rule. It is painful to read the bulk of this early canon, and it will only become more and more painful, as gay subcultures dissolve and the bourgeois respectability that so many of these authors abandoned yet craved becomes the norm. In Genet, marriage between two men was the ultimate profanation, one of the strongest inversions of value the author could muster to scandalize his audience and delight his rebellious readers. The image of same-sex marriage was purely explosive, a strategy for blasting apart the hypocrisy and pretentions of traditional morality. Today it is becoming commonplace.

I wonder if these books will survive like the literature of abolition, such as Harriet Beecher Stowe's *Uncle Tom's Cabin*—marginal, dated, remembered as important for its earnest, sentimental ambition but also a catalogue of stereotypes. Or if they will be mostly forgotten, like the nineteenth-century literature of aesthetic perversity and decadence that many of these authors so deeply admired. Will Gide and Genet be as obscure to readers as Huysmans and the Comte de Lautréamont (Isidore-Lucien Ducasse)?

I hope not, and not least because they mattered to me, and helped forge a common language of reference among many gay men of my generation. I hope they survive for the many poignant epitaphs they contain, grave markers for the men who were used, abused, and banished from their pages. Let me write them down in my notebook, so I don't forget their names: Hans, who loved Hermann; Basini, who loved Törless; the Page of Herodias, who loved the Young Syrian; Giovanni, who loved David; and all the rest, unnamed, often with no voice, but not forgotten.

TIM KREIDER

A Man and His Cat

FROM *The New York Times*

I LIVED WITH the same cat for nineteen years—by far the longest relationship of my adult life. Under common law, this cat was my wife. I fell asleep at night with the warm, pleasant weight of the cat on my chest. The first thing I saw on most mornings was the foreshortened paw of the cat retreating slowly from my face and her baleful crescent glare informing me that it was Cat Food Time. As I often told her, in a mellow, resonant, Barry White voice, "There is no *luuve* . . . like the *luuve* that exists . . . between a man . . . and his cat."

The cat was jealous of my attention; she liked to sit on whatever I was reading, walked back and forth and back and forth in front of my laptop's screen while I worked, and unsubtly interpolated herself between me and any woman I may have had over. She and my ex Kati Jo, who was temperamentally not dissimilar to the cat, instantly sized each other up as enemies. When I was physically intimate with a woman, the cat did not discreetly absent herself but sat on the edge of the bed with her back to me, facing rather pointedly away from the scene of debauch, quietly exuding disapproval, like your grandmother's ghost.

I realize that people who talk at length about their pets are tedious at best, and often pitiful or repulsive. They post photos of their pets online, tell little stories about them, speak to them in disturbing falsettos, dress them in elaborate costumes and carry them around in handbags and BabyBjorns, have professional portraits taken of them and retouched to look like Old Master oil paintings. When people over the age of ten invite you to a cat birthday party or a funeral for a dog, you need to execute a very deft etiquette maneuver, the equivalent of an Immelmann turn or triple axel, in order to decline without acknowledging that they are, in this area, insane.

This is especially true of childless people, like me, who tend to become emotionally overinvested in their animals and to dote on them in a way that gives onlookers the creeps. Often the pet seems to be a surrogate child, a desperate focus or joint project for a relationship that's lost any other raison d'être, like becoming insufferable foodies or getting heavily into cosplay. When such couples finally have a child their cats or dogs are often bewildered to find themselves unceremoniously demoted to the status of pet; instead of licking the dinner plates clean and piling into bed with Mommy and Daddy, they're given bowls of actual dog food and tied to a metal stake in a circle of dirt.

I looked up how much Americans spend on pets annually and have concluded that you do not want to know. I could tell you what I spent on my own cat's special kidney health cat food and kidney and thyroid medication, and periodic blood tests that cost $300 and always came back normal, but I never calculated my own annual spending, lest I be forced to confront some uncomfortable facts about me. What our mass spending on products to pamper animals who seem happiest while rolling in feces or eating the guts out of rodents—who don't, in fact, seem significantly less happy if they lose half their limbs—tells us about ourselves as a nation is probably also something we don't want to know. But it occurs to me that it may be symptomatic of the same chronic deprivation as are the billion-dollar industries in romance novels and porn.

I've speculated that people have a certain reservoir of affection that they need to express, and in the absence of any more appropriate object—a child or a lover, a parent or a friend—they will lavish that same devotion on a pug or a Manx or a cockatiel, even on something neurologically incapable of reciprocating that emotion, like a monitor lizard or a day trader or an aloe plant. Konrad Lorenz confirms this suspicion in his book *On Aggression,* in which he describes how, in the absence of the appropriate triggering stimulus for an instinct, the threshold of stimulus for that instinct is gradually lowered; for instance, a male dove deprived of female doves will attempt to initiate mating with a stuffed pigeon, a rolled-up cloth, or any vaguely bird-shaped object, and eventually with an empty corner of its cage.

Although I can clearly see this syndrome as pathological in others, I was its medical textbook illustration, the Elephant Man of the condition. I did not post photographs of my cat online or talk about her to people who couldn't be expected to care, but at home, alone with the cat, I behaved like some sort of deranged arch-fop. I made up dozens of nonsensical names for the cat over the years—the Quetzal, Quetzal Marie, Mrs. Quetzal Marie the Cat, the Inquetzulous Q'ang Marie. There was a litany I recited aloud to her every morning, a sort of daily exhortation that began, "Who knows, Miss Cat, what fantastical adventures the two of us will have today?" I had a song I sang to her when I was about to vacuum, a brassy Vegas showstopper called "That Thing You Hate (Is Happening Again)." We collaborated on my foot-pedal pump organ to produce the Hideous Cat Music, in which she walked back and forth at her discretion on the keyboard while I worked the pedals. The Hideous Cat Music resembled the work of the Hungarian composer György Ligeti, with aleatory passages and unnervingly sustained tone clusters.

I never meant to become this person. My own cat turned up as a stray at my cabin on the Chesapeake Bay when I was sitting out on the deck eating leftover crabs. She was only a couple of months old then, small enough that my friend Kevin could fit her whole head in his mouth. She appeared from underneath the porch, piteously mewling, and I gave her some cold white crab meat. I did not know then that feeding a stray cat is effectively adopting that cat.

For a few weeks I was in denial about having a cat. My life at that time was not structured to accommodate the responsibility of returning home once every twenty-four hours to feed an animal. I posted fliers in the post office and grocery store with a drawing of the cat, hoping its owner would reclaim it. It seems significant in retrospect that I never entertained the possibility of taking the cat to the pound.

When I left for a long weekend for a wedding in another state, my friend Gabe explained to me that the cat clearly belonged to me now. I protested. This was a strictly temporary situation until I could locate a new home for the cat, I explained. I was not going to turn into some Cat Guy.

"How would you feel," he asked me, "if you were to get home from this weekend and that cat was gone?"

I moaned and writhed in the passenger seat.

"You're Cat Guy," he said in disgust.

It's amusing now to remember the strict limits I'd originally intended to place on the cat. One of the boundaries I meant to set was that the cat would not be allowed upstairs, where I slept. That edict was short-lived. It was not long before I became wounded when the cat declined to sleep with me.

"You're in *love* with that cat!" my then-girlfriend Margot once accused me. To be fair, she was a very attractive cat. People would comment on it. My friend Ken described her as "a supermodel cat," with green eyes dramatically outlined in what he called "cat mascara" and bright pink "nose leather." Her fur, even at age nineteen, was rich and soft and pleasant to touch.

Biologists call cats "exploitive captives," an evocative phrase that might be used to describe a lot of relationships, not all of them interspecies. I made the mistake, early on, of feeding the cat first thing in the morning, forgetting that the cat could control when I woke up—by meowing politely, sitting on my chest and staring at me, nudging me insistently with her face, or placing a single claw on my lip. She refused to drink water from a bowl, coveting what she believed was the superior-quality water I drank from a glass. I attempted to demonstrate to the cat that the water we drank was the very same water by pouring it from my glass into her bowl right in front of her, but she was utterly unmoved, like a birther being shown Obama's long-form Hawaiian birth certificate. In the end I gave in and began serving her water in a glass tumbler, which she had to stick her whole face into to drink from.

Sometimes it would strike me that *an animal was living in my house,* and it seemed as surreal as if I had a raccoon or a kinkajou running loose in my house. Yet that animal and I learned, on some level, to understand each other. Although I loved to bury my nose in her fur when she came in from a winter day and inhale deeply of the Coldcat Smell, the cat did not like this one bit, and fled. For a while I would chase her around the house, yelling, "Gimme a little whiff!" and she would hide behind the couch from my hateful touch. Eventually I realized that this was wrong of me. I would instead let her in and pretend to have no interest whatsoever in smelling her, and after not more than a minute or so the cat would approach me and design to be smelled. I should really be no less impressed by this accord than if I'd successfully communicated with a Papuan tribesman or decoded a message from the stars.

Whenever I felt embarrassed about factoring a house pet's desires into major life decisions, some grown-up-sounding part of me told myself, *It's just a cat.* It's generally believed that animals lack what we call consciousness, although we can't quite agree on what exactly this is, and how we can pretend to any certainty about what goes on in an animal's head has never been made clear to me. To anyone who has spent time with an animal, the notion that they have no interior lives seems so counterintuitive, such an obdurate denial of the empathetically self-evident, as to be almost psychotic. I suspect that some of those same psychological mechanisms must have allowed people to rationalize owning other people.

Another part of me, perhaps more sentimental but also more truthful, had to acknowledge that the cat was undeniably another being in the world, experiencing her one chance at being alive, as I was. It always amused me to hit or elongate the word *you* in speaking to the cat, as in, "*Yooouu* would probably *like* that!" because it was funny—and funny often means disquieting and true —to remind myself that there really was another ego in the room with me, with her own likes and dislikes and idiosyncrasies and exasperatingly wrongheaded notions about whose water is better. It did not seem to me like an insoluble epistemological mystery to divine what the cat would like when I woke up and saw her face two inches from mine and the Tentative Paw slowly withdrawing from my lip.

I admit that loving a cat is a lot less complicated than loving a human being. Because animals can't ruin our fantasies about them by talking, they're even more helplessly susceptible to our projections than other humans. Though of course there's a good deal of naked projection and self-delusion involved in loving other human beings, too.

I once read in a book about feng shui that keeping a pet can maintain the chi of your house or apartment when you're not there; the very presence of an animal enlivens and charges the space. Although I suspect feng shui is high-end hooey, I learned when my cat was temporarily put up elsewhere that a house without a cat in it feels very different from a house with one. It feels truly empty, dead. Those moments gave me some foreboding of how my life would feel after she was gone.

We don't know what goes on inside an animal's head; we may doubt whether they have anything we'd call consciousness, and we can't know how much they understand or what their emotions feel like. I will never know what, if anything, the cat thought of me. But I can tell you this: a man who is in a room with a cat—whatever else we might say about that man—is not alone.

KATE LEBO

The Loudproof Room

FROM *New England Review*

An Earmoir

I WAS BORN with a strawberry hemangioma splashed over the bottom half of my right ear and two inches down my neck. The sort of red that has purple trapped inside it. A swollen, shocking hue. For the first year, I had no hair to disguise it. The sight of me made strangers uncomfortable.

My birthmark was so red and angry and I cried so murderously when my parents bathed it that it became, as I grew, the explanation for a lot of things. Why I was teased in school, why I cried easily. Why I couldn't hear conversational tones out of my right ear.

By the time I was ten the skin faded to a mottle of mostly normal-looking tissue. It looks enough like a burn scar that no one asks what happened. Mostly I forget it's there. When a new friend asks me, "What's up with your ear?" I need a second to remember what she's talking about. My father and I were in a motorcycle accident when I was five, I say. It tore my ear half off. When she looks sorry for asking, I tell her I was born this way. Which isn't exactly the truth. If it was, I'd still have a stoplight for an ear.

Until my family began to comment on how deaf I was—when my back was to them I didn't respond to direct questions, didn't know they were being asked—I didn't know my hearing was going. I'd gotten so used to having a half-deaf ear that it didn't occur to me the aural slips I'd been experiencing might be the fault of the other ear, the good one going bad. I booked an appointment in the otolaryngology department at the city's biggest hospital. The nurse who took my vitals said "You're the youngest person I've talked to all day" in a way that was supposed to make me feel better but didn't.

Dehiscence is a word botanists use to describe a flower bud that's about to burst into bloom.

Otolaryngologists use *dehiscence* to describe two spots in my skull, one over each superior canal of my hearing organs, that have thinned to two tiny gaps. The gaps leak sound waves into my body and allow body noises to echo too loudly in my ears. To diagnose me, the doctor asked if I could hear myself blink. Yes, I said. Can you hear your heels when you walk? Yes. He rapped a tuning fork on my ankle. Can you hear that? No. That's a good thing, he said.

My pulse, my flexing knees, my neck bones as I turn my head on the pillow, my teeth as they crunch into chips—all these sounds are louder than the conversation of the person sitting next to me. Now I understood why I could sing on key but never hold a tune: when I make a melody with my body, it mutes the music that's outside my skull.

The doctor said my superior-canal dehiscence could be cured with minor surgery that involved a night in the ICU. That doesn't sound like minor surgery, I said. Nothing to worry about, he said. When would you like to schedule your pre-op? I wouldn't, I said.

The next doctor I visited was the teacher of the first doctor. He was cautious, patient, uneager to cut me open. I liked him immediately. He said my condition represented "multiple pathologies" —a stiff stapes bone, a collapsed eardrum, dehiscence, possibly something else. My symptoms muddle the identity of each individual malady. What mattered, what wasn't a mystery: I had significant hearing loss in both ears. We decided to try hearing aids first. If they worked, I would wear them the rest of my life.

I preferred this decision. It is reversible. You see, half sensibility has benefits. Not knowing what I'm missing can be a different kind of knowing.

Open the Window

My friend, I'll call him Carl, was born with one ear. Once, while sleeping with his hearing side buried in the pillow, he slept through the burglary of his home. Just woke up the next day to find his guitar, stereo, and TV missing from the living room.

Hearing aids augment hearing organs, they don't replace them, so they can't help Carl's condition. When we talk about this, we have to face each other and position ourselves a bit to the right so we can speak into each other's left ears.

I have another friend whose son is functionally deaf. When he doesn't wear hearing aids he retreats into his own world, she says. Though he's fluent with sign language—communication isn't the issue—he's distant, hard to reach in a way that he isn't when the world can get at him through an amplifier.

In my semi-sentient state I'm a champion sleeper, a binge reader. The world is easy to tune out when its volume is low to begin with. What I miss in overheard bons mots I make up for in dreams, I tell myself. I'm sincere, but I'm lying. It's a pain in the ass to ask *What?* all the time. Often I only pretend to know what people are saying. This feels easier than repetition.

Nearly as often, a few beats after nodding my assent, I figure out what the hell it is I've just agreed to.

When I used a hearing aid for the first time, I finally understood what my friend meant: it's like someone has taken the wrapping off the world, and I'm in it, closer and more profoundly immersed than I thought possible. What I hear is so mundane: footsteps, conversations at reception, an intercom, air conditioning. It feels like I've dipped my head into a public pool—I'm in this water, making these noises, soft within a busyness. This is beyond healing.

My audiologist says that when people go too long without hearing a certain frequency, the ear can forget how to hear it, that mechanical augmentation can't navigate that "dead zone." She uses the word *forget*, implying that cochlea have memories, that those memories are refreshed by the nerve signals a sound wave sets off in the hair cells. I imagine there's a more specific, scientific word to describe what's actually happening, but after panicking over the other doctor's medical jargon, I think the precise word will obscure the diagnosis. When my new otolaryngologist says everyone's ear has three windows and that at least one of those windows must be closed to maintain balance and prevent vertigo, he turns my eardrum into a breezy little house. I'm grateful to him for speaking my language.

The Skin of the Line

Difficulty creates sensitivity. If a hearing test asks me to listen and repeat words, I will score higher than a person with normal hearing.

In conversation, this sensitivity is an inept but beautiful translator. "Messing with my students" becomes "wisteria in tents." A "reef of dead metaphors" becomes a raft of them. "*The Skin of a Lion*" (an Ondaatje novel) is "the skin of the line" and "a silk lawn." I hear them almost simultaneously, the fantastic phrase bursting through the door just ahead of the intended one. These interpretations don't decode the meaning of the intended phrase, but they do create new phrases whose strangeness invites me to interpret them figuratively. When the misheard accompanies the heard, a conversation about classroom manners can shelter an encampment of flowering vines.

Through poetry writing, I attuned my eye and ear to these mishearings and came to love how the actual phrase, which is often prosaic but easy to interpret, echoes under the figurative magic of the misheard phrase. In other words, the poet gives us a surprising turn of phrase whose resemblance to cliché helps us interpret it. I might write "I pay my hills" instead of "I pay my bills" because the word *bills* is expected. With "pay my hills," I have the figurative riches of what paying a hill might mean while the reader and I hear "pay my bills" underneath. If the phrase were to go the other way around, I would hear *bills* but never think of *hills*. In a way, it's the best of both worlds—surprising language that echoes on multiple levels and is coupled to an interpretive strategy. The sense within nonsense that keeps a line lively.

A Private Volume

Hearing aids are just amplifiers. After a year of wearing one, I think of mine as a jealous speaker. It doesn't like talking to other speakers. It needs distance from sound makers to maintain a clear, intelligible tone.

In the car with my music turned up, the hearing aid crackles, a delicate plasticky sound that wraps the beat in subtle static. On long drives I store my hearing aid in the center console and *always* forget it there. Panic when I touch my empty right ear. The aid is dime-sized. It costs more than my car.

If I whistle, a high note triggers feedback. A harmony that pierces my sinuses and jaw, trills down my spine. My voice was already the loudest thing in my head. Now I'm a chorus only I can hear.

When a man cups my face with his hand and kisses me, the gentle pressure of his fingers against my ear sets the speaker off. His face is so close I'm sure he hears the screeching, but he's oblivious. While he lunges for the light switch I rip the hearing aid out, hide it in my purse.

Because everything within my body is louder than it should be, a symptom hearing aids can't mute, eating provides a kind of privacy. A bag of chips, a bowl of cereal, a crisp apple—I enter them like private rooms. Loudproof. The easiest pleasure comes from surrendering to the noise and giving up on any other experience I might have had while eating. This makes it difficult to eat during dinner parties, difficult to speak during family supper. If my plate is clean, I haven't been listening.

Hearing aids make this symptom worse, delivering deafness via meaningless crunching. They do this constantly, with smaller noises, in less irritating but more insidious ways. What sounded like clarity when I first tried them is, I know now, just the volume turned up. On everything. This lack of focus is disturbing. What I'm missing now isn't conversation. It's the impossible quality of natural sound and the ear's ability to create foreground and background, to cut static. To tune into my beloved's voice as he speaks from across the divide of a table, the dinner in front of me cooling with every word.

The Loudproof Room

I am tired of leaning closer, of watching faces for meaning. Though it sparks an easy intimacy with conversation partners. Though it is, by now, integral to the way I interpret and how I am perceived.

I want to hear.

If surgery goes well, a stapedotomy will restore 90 percent of normal hearing range without cutting me open. The deeper cut, the one I'm avoiding, would have addressed the dehiscence. I'll preserve those holes and keep my internal chorus.

My desire to hear has been rivaled, for years, by a fear of losing my sensibility. It is a part of myself that only I understand. My secret. Plus a deeper, colder fear: of going deaf altogether. A slipped knife, a wrong cut.

Disability can create sensibility. My disability is invisible, my limitations are aesthetic. They make art and they make mistakes, reminding me constantly that the way I sense and experience the world is different. At a slight angle, as Forster said of Cavafy. Which is a reminder that difference isn't unique to me. That's why listening creates a conversation. That's how reading creates a poem. It's terrifying to lose your senses. Then, sometimes, it's a pleasure.

JOHN REED

My Grandma the Poisoner

FROM *Vice*

WHEN I WAS four or five, sometimes I'd walk into my grandmother's bedroom to find her weeping. She'd be sitting on the
side of the bed, going through boxes of tissues. I don't believe this
was a side of herself she shared with other people; she may have
felt we had a cosmic bond because I had her father's name as my
middle name and his fair features. She was crying for Martha, her
daughter, who died of melanoma at the age of twenty-eight. Ten
years later, after Norman—her youngest child, my uncle—died,
also at twenty-eight, she would weep for him.

People were always dying around Grandma—her children, her
husbands, her boyfriend—so her lifelong state of grief was understandable. To see her sunken in her high and soft bed, enshrouded
in the darkness of the attic and surrounded by the skin-and-spit
smell of old age, was to know that mothers don't get what they
deserve. Today, when I think back on it, I don't wonder whether
Grandma got what she deserved as a mother; I wonder whether
she got what she deserved as a murderer.

A few months ago I loaded the wife and kids into the car and
went out to visit Grandma. I hadn't seen her in more than a year
and a half, and in that time she had moved from her house to an
assisted-living place to another assisted-living place. There was no
good excuse for my lapse—I guess I couldn't quite deal with the
way we'd left her house. A catastrophe. Full of stuff. The buyers
said they'd take care of it, and they did; they tore the whole thing
down. My brother had a friend from the neighborhood (out on
Long Island, aka Lawng Islund) who said it was the scandal of the
year.

That house, where I spent so much of my childhood visiting Grandma, was disgusting. In the late 1990s, my brother and I dedicated three days to cleaning it up. Joe, my grandmother's last boyfriend, had died, and his stuff was there. He was one of five dead people whose stuff was there, was everywhere. My aunt's stuff, my uncle's stuff, my grandfather's stuff, and Grandma's second husband's stuff filled, I'd estimate, about half the total volume of the house. Driver's licenses and important papers and half-finished projects and mementos like the rusted bolts my uncle Norman, on his diving trips, had dragged out of sunken wrecks. In the basement library we uncovered a vial of red viscous fluid. The vial, sealed with a hard wax or plastic, was hand-blown and quite beautiful, and the box was neatly jointed hardwood. We thought the thing might be valuable. It could have been old—we weren't sure. So we tried to sell it to an East Village curiosity shop, which advised that we dispose of it via the Poison Control Center.

In the basement's woodshop we found a sprinkling of half-melted heroin spoons (Grandma had let some pretty questionable characters crash with her), and in the backyard we found a big black garbage bag full of dead animals. You could tell it was animals from the outside of the bag; you could see the shapes of the corpses. We both peeked in but were so quick about it that all we confirmed was the presence of dead bodies, not what kind. My brother says he saw turtles, which seems likely, since my mother had owned half a dozen turtles that all perished in a sudden, inexplicable cataclysm. I saw an owl, which is less likely but also possible, since there are owls on Long Island. Most likely, we decided, the bag was full of cats and raccoons, which were always getting into Grandma's garbage. She'd yell at them from the back porch. The last time I saw the bag it was on the lawn waiting for the trash pickup. In the shining black plastic you could still see the rounded shapes of haunches.

In that house, even the stuff worth keeping was depressing. Once-beautiful oak rocking chairs and cherrywood secretary desks had been covered with white porch paint. Bookshelves were lined with mouse-eaten library castoffs. The carpets were thriving with mold. Dishes were stained or flecked with dried food. The toilets were full, unflushed, and dusted with baby powder. Grandma would say not flushing saved money, but really, she just wanted to remind you that everything was about saving money.

In Grandma's defense, she came to consciousness during the Great Depression and never mentally left the era. When the economy turned sour, in the 1990s and 2000s, she would point out the cultural similarities, laying it all out: during times of scarcity there's a turn to mystical thinking, self-help, and the occult, she'd tell us. I have no doubt that she was right. Even in her old age, she was insightful and informed. She'd rattle around her disgusting house with public radio blaring in every room. She knew everything, for instance that prune juice could be employed as hair dye (to this day her hair is prune-brown). She had heard a dentist advise on NPR that it was very important to rinse your mouth out with water and to floss, even if you didn't have a chance to brush your teeth, and as of this writing she's ninety-four and still has all her teeth in her head. Only now they're all loose. Her whole jaw looks like it's loose in her mouth.

When we went to visit her at the assisted-living place, I fixed her hearing aids, and my wife went out to get some adult diapers. Grandma barely knows who I am, and when I asked her about her children, she didn't remember Martha at all. I hadn't exactly missed her during those months of not visiting, so I didn't expect the visit to upset me. But Grandma not knowing Martha's name, Grandma lying in bed sucking on her unmoored jaw, Grandma with all of her teeth about to fall out—I almost lost it. The kids sat there, unblinking, their mouths hanging open in stupefied horror. For them, the last year has been a tour of deathbeds: Gigipop. Poppa. Abuelita. Granmaman. And now Grandma. It was obvious—she was next.

They managed to buck up when Grandma asked them to sing. They knew some German songs from school, and she joined in. She said that when she sings she returns to her childhood. She lives in it, she said, like it's the present moment. And maybe in her mind, when she sings, her childhood is still there—but I don't think there's much else there. Sometimes she points to her head and jokes about her "forgettery."

It's strange to see a parental figure get like that. As a kid I'd stay at Grandma's house so my too-young parents could get a break, often for weeks at a time. She'd tell me that Jews invent things, that Jews don't drink, that Jews are smart because the philosophy of the Jews values thinking, and that I'm not supposed to call them Jews. She would say, "Even when we argue, you have a good mind." When I announced my engagement to a Gentile, Grandma dropped to her knees and begged me not to get married in a church. The wedding took place on a tennis court, and Grandma was the belle of the ball, flirting with my wife's uncles, who were twenty years younger than she was. Grandma was always a good time, but when she wasn't the host, wasn't responsible for the food, it was like a weight was lifted from her, like she could really be free.

Grandma's expertise in nutrition dates back to the sixties. By the mid seventies, she had written several self-published mimeographed books on nutritional intake and vitamins. Around then or possibly earlier, I think, she started to poison people.

I can't pin down exactly what she did with what ingredients. I can't even be sure that she really did the things I think she did. All I have, really, are pieces of circumstantial evidence and hunches that have coalesced over the years. In my narrative of suspicions, she preferred to use vitamin A (which can cause sleepiness, blurred vision, and nausea, among other things), then she used laxatives, and then, as she got older and lazier, she moved on to prescription drugs.

Grandma never cooked the same thing twice, and her creations were greasy beyond belief and usually really weird. For example: chicken baked with apricots and canned tomatoes, or mixed-up ground meats with prunes, or pickled things. She was infamous at the local grocery store. They saved the shark livers for her.

In later years her meals featured courses of ready-made, or nearly ready-made, food, and eventually that became her favored methodology. She had this effective strategy of finding the food you loved most, buying it in ridiculous amounts, and feeding it to you unrelentingly. You'd eat it—the imported Jarlsberg, the ice cream. And you'd pass out on the couch, or on the train back to the city. Of course, the longer you stayed with Grandma, the more likely it was that something bad would happen to you. If you visited her for a week, you'd suffer from the shits, you'd be exhausted, and your vision would start to blur.

At first my mother was the only one who'd refuse to eat Grandma's food, and I thought she was being paranoid. Then I started noticing that every time I went to Grandma's, I'd pass out on the couch or on the train on the way back to the city. When I stopped eating Grandma's food, my brother thought I was paranoid. But I stopped passing out, and pretty soon he stopped eating Grandma's food, too.

But here's the thing: you don't want to believe your grandmother is poisoning you. You know that she loves you—there's no doubt of that—and she's so marvelously grandmotherly and charming. And you know that she would never want to poison you. So despite your better judgment, you eat the food until you've passed out so many times that you can't keep doubting yourself. Eventually we would arrive for holidays at Grandma's with groceries and takeout, and she'd seem relieved that we wouldn't let her touch our plates. By then her eyesight was starting to go, so she wouldn't notice the layer of crystalline powder atop that fancy lox she was giving you.

So the question became, how did we explain to guests, outsiders, that they shouldn't eat Grandma's food? One time, maybe on Passover, my brother brought his new girlfriend, an actress. Grandma had promised not to prepare anything, and it seemed she'd kept her word, so we didn't mention the poisoning thing to the girlfriend, but after we'd eaten lunch, Grandma came out of the kitchen with these oatmeal raisin cookies that looked terrible. They were bulbous, like the baking soda had gone haywire. My brother's girlfriend ate two of them, maybe out of politeness. We looked on, aghast. She had a rehearsal in the city, but she passed out on the couch and missed it.

So why would Grandma poison us? Well, for some time my mother has postulated that Grandma has Munchausen syndrome by proxy, a condition that causes caregivers to poison or injure their charges. Me? I'm sure that Grandma wasn't trying to hurt anyone. If she slipped you a Mickey it was because she didn't want you to leave—she loved to make people miss their train. "Stay the night, stay the night," she'd coo.

Other times Grandma's concerns seemed more practical. My mother, when she moved back to Grandma's for a brief time, had many pets—turtles, dogs, hamsters, cats—that successively took ill and died. And there was Joe, the ex-paratrooper who was Grandma's last boyfriend. He got into the habit of blowing his pension checks in Atlantic City and mooching off Grandma until the next check arrived. Then he got a broken leg and we got all these hysterical calls from Grandma saying she was forced to wait on him hand and foot—and then he was dead.

And what would Grandma say? Well, even if she was inclined or in a condition to tell me why she did what she did, I don't think she'd be able to. She's always been a mystery, even to herself. There's this story she would tell: when she was a very young girl, a boy tried to kiss her in a closet, so she shoved him away and ran home and cried and cried. "Why, Grandma?" we would ask her. "Because," she would say, "I was in love with him!"

Grandma's father was an older man, tall and handsome, a widower who had been an equestrian back in Russia. Her mother was seventeen when she married him. The couple had four daughters and one boy, who died very young. When the Depression hit, the father was called in to the office of the Brooklyn factory where he worked as a foreman: they had no choice; they would have to let him go. He begged for a job, any job, to support his family, which was how he became a "fireman," shoveling coal into a furnace. An explosion, a backfire, I think it's called, injured him badly, and he didn't come home. He disappeared. Three weeks after the accident, my grandmother went out to talk to a man who was sitting on the stoop across from their house. His face was covered in bandages. She asked why he hadn't come home, and he said, "I was afraid you wouldn't love me anymore." He was scarred for the rest of his life. I never met my great-grandfather Benjamin, my namesake.

Grandma's first husband, Irving—she was married to him through the fifties and sixties—was adored by everyone, just like her father. He was in business with some Italians, which is one way to describe his trade. After twenty years of marriage, she divorced him, and it wasn't until much later that I got the inkling it might have been because Irving had a frightening side.

In 1982, when he was seventy years old, Irving was in a car accident. He drove his Cadillac off the highway. He might have fallen asleep, or it might have been the fault of the screwdriver that was discovered in the steering column. His head was smashed up in the wreck, but he was a tough old Jew, and after four years he woke up and spent ten more fighting his paralysis before dying in his late eighties. Meanwhile his money became the object of a convoluted lawsuit that resulted in Irving's business partners and second wife (who cared for him) getting most of his fortune. Throughout all that, Grandma would bemoan the fact that she'd left Irving. She'd say, "The kinds of things he did all day, you can't come home and be Mr. Nice Guy, no way."

Martha, Grandma's oldest child and my aunt, got cancer in her twenties. Grandma cared for her. Martha's disease might have killed her, but . . . well, I don't know. Aaron, Grandma's second husband, also died of cancer back in the 1970s. He was deaf, he hated television, and he yelled at children—Grandma said that she married him because "he was the only one who would have me." He smoked pipes. After his first operation, for throat cancer, he played Ping-Pong with me; he seemed happy and was less of a monster. He took up gardening. But no matter how much he ate, he kept losing weight and withered away. Or . . . Again, it could have just been the cancer.

Next up in the funerary procession was Norman, Grandma's youngest child and only son. So let's talk about him: Norman was a piece of shit. He was only eight years older than I was, and he tortured me when I was a kid. He had the most hideous laugh, like a pig squealing. Not a happy pig. Like a pig in pain. He'd threaten me with knives and steal and break my things. He'd try to convince me that he was going to kidnap me in the middle of the night and sell me to "the Arabs." Maybe all that was because he was envious of me; he was chunky and Jewish-looking, so Grandma, with her blue eyes and blond hair, found him repellent. In sharp contrast to Norman, the fleshy failure, I was a natural athlete with Gentile features and therefore her favorite. Once I saw Grandma punish Norman by standing him in front of the open stove, turning up the broiler flames, and threatening to burn off his dick. He was maybe twelve at the time. She'd also cook him huge plates of food and offer them to him. He'd say no because he didn't want to get any fatter, but she'd keep pushing the food under his chin until he finally ate—and then berate him for being so fat.

Norman liked weapons. He collected things that killed, like crossbows and axes, and everyone was terrified of him. He would sometimes storm around the house with a bowie knife or machete, and the rest of us would cower in our rooms. When I was maybe seven, he covered my arm in methane and set it on fire, just to show me how powerful methane was and how lighting it wouldn't hurt me. It's true that I didn't feel any pain, though it did burn all the hair off my arm. Another time, when I was visiting Long Island as a teenager, a bunch of other kids tackled me and kicked me over and over. My mother thought Norman had sent them.

Should I mention that he was a genius? He was; he could do anything. When I was eight, he walked me to Canal Street, just a few blocks from where I lived in Tribeca, to show me how he could buy computer parts and assemble a working machine in an afternoon, which he did.

In the late eighties, when he was twenty-eight, Norman was still living with Grandma, but he was kind of figuring things out: he had lost weight, he had a girlfriend, and he was thinking about some kind of career in computers, "networked computers," as they called what would become the Internet back then. He was way into scuba diving, too. He would sleep underwater in the tub with his equipment on, and sometimes he'd rent a boat and dive down to some wreck and take photos.

The day of the accident, he was scheduled to go out on a rented boat, but Grandma didn't want him to go—she always complained about how expensive it was—so she slipped him something. I think. He was feeling pretty out of it that morning; he thought maybe he was sick. His partner persuaded him to go out anyway, and then there was a problem with the configuration of Norman's equipment when he was underwater. Maybe it was a malfunction, or maybe it was his own fault; he had customized all his gear (because he was a genius). His diving partner swam to the surface alone, instead of sharing his tank with Norman in a "buddy-system" ascent. We don't know exactly why Norman stayed down there. It might have been that he thought he didn't have enough oxygen to attempt a "controlled emergency" ascent, which is when you exhale all the way up. Or it might have been that he was entangled in the U-boat wreck he and his partner were investigating. Or he might have just been too out of it to save himself. There are these flags that divers can fire up toward the surface to alert the rescue diver, who's supposed to be ready to go on the deck of the boat, and Norman did send up his flag. But this was Long Island, where rules about keeping rescue divers on boats aren't taken too seriously, and Norman died down there, watching that fucking flag wave.

Then there was my wife's miscarriage. Funny thing about that. Or not "funny," I guess, but I forgot about it until I decided to write this story and I was going over some old notes. When we announced my wife's pregnancy, Grandma freaked out about how there'd be another mouth to feed and we couldn't afford it. We visited her just before my wife miscarried, and even though my wife knew to stay away from her food, everyone slips up a little from time to time. And, well . . . it was late in the pregnancy for a miscarriage. And the dates line up. But it could be a coincidence.

Later, when we did have a child, Grandma came over to celebrate, bearing a present for the baby: a pair of medical scissors— sharp, pointed, big medical scissors. On another visit she brought us beets she had bought. I was like, "Grandma, why are you giving me fifteen cans of beets?" She had recipes, beets this and beets that, and lots and lots of them included sunflower seeds, too. She was enormously proud of one invention: beet-and-sunflower-seed ice cream. You couldn't top it, nutrition-wise, she said. Look it up. I did: "Canned beets and sunflower seeds," I typed into my computer. "URGENT PRODUCT RECALL," Google spat back. Everything she gave us should have been pulled from the shelves.

Sometimes when I tell these stories, I have the feeling that people think I should have done something. Well, it was difficult psychologically to piece all of this together, and as a kid I didn't understand what was going on. Before Grandma put me to bed she'd sometimes serve me this really rich hot chocolate that looked oily and thin. And when I woke up it would be twenty-four or even seventy-two hours later. Three or four times we rushed to the hospital in the middle of the night because I was having trouble breathing. But it wasn't until my thirties that I connected all this and it dawned on me that sleeping for three days is not normal or O.K., and that the only times I woke up in the middle of the night unable to breathe, I was at Grandma's.

And even when I did figure it out, so what? After Joe, Grandma's last boyfriend, died, I went to the cops and told them I thought Grandma was involved. They said, "Whaddya want us to do about it?"

And now, once again, I feel like I'm supposed to care. Like there should be closure. Either I purge my past, forgive her, and arrive at a higher vibrational state, or I find proof of what she's done over the years and expose her once and for all. I'd always planned to search her house one last time, but now the house is gone. And nobody is exhuming any bodies, and Grandma doesn't even know what Grandma did. And there's not going to be any grand finale. And as I sat there listening to Grandma sing with my children—not quite crying, I wasn't quite crying—I realized that I didn't care what had happened, that nobody cares what happened, that caring is for cops on *CSI* and doctors on *ER* and muscle-bound Marines in the movies.

Not long ago I was talking to a friend I've told about Grandma. My friend casually mentioned that Grandma could have accidentally killed me, which surprised me. That wasn't accurate, I said.

"But didn't you have trouble breathing? Didn't you rush to the hospital in the middle of the night? She wasn't trying to hurt you, she was trying to manage you, but she could have hurt you."

"I suppose that's true," I said, nodding, slowly and in disbelief, because Grandma never would have hurt me. We had a cosmic bond.

ASHRAF H. A. RUSHDY

Reflections on Indexing My Lynching Book

FROM *Michigan Quarterly Review*

I AM NOW indexing the second and final volume of my lynching trilogy.

If you are indexing your own book, you might at some point, like me, be resigned to the fact that you are going to keep your day job. Your book is not going to make a lot of money. The kind of book that is lucrative is either not going to need an index or will have one done by a professional indexer.

You have a lot of time to have thoughts like that when you are indexing your own book, since it is not particularly mindful work. Most of my thoughts, fortunately, have not been so mordant, or so obviously envious of others. I would say that they have fallen into three large categories—nostalgia, anger, and sadness.

I.

My first response has been a particular kind of nostalgia—a mixture of joy, resignation, longing. Indexing, after all, is probably the last time an author will read the book through in its entirety. We might look up particular things for future reference, to pillage our own earlier research, but most authors I know are not going to pick up and read a book on which they have been working for a number of years. It is with mixed feelings that one recognizes that here is a book that one will not read again. I remember reading a beautiful short essay, by Jorge Luis Borges, I think, in which the blind author lovingly runs his fingers over his books and nostalgically reflects on never again reading each specific volume in his library. The experience of reading for one last time a book I have read in so many different forms during the fourteen years I have been working on it is not nearly so grandiose. Writing this book cost me much, but it did not cost me my sight or sense of proportion.

It is not just a relief to know that the task is completed, that the research and writing are at an end—although there is that. There is a curious sense of reversal in indexing. You can see the logic of the composition of your book backward, as it were. As I develop a list of particular words and page numbers, I see where I made specific choices, the places I developed key connections, when I made revisions that put this section here and not there. I see, then, through the selection of key terms and page numbers, just where the book took the particular shape it ended up taking. And I remember where I might have written a specific passage, or how a set of ideas came to occupy the same page or the same series of pages. To a reader, the index is a way of navigating the book from the back. To an author, an index reveals just how this book came to be the one it is.

That nostalgia made up of remembering and relief at finishing is likely a common one for academic authors of all books. The other two feelings that I have felt pervasively as I compile this index are more personal and specific.

2.

One is a long pent-up anger that is the result of a persistent and undue restraint. As someone trying to produce a historical study of a horrible and cruel practice, I wanted to make sure that I examined the phenomenon with as much detachment as I could muster. I don't mind reading something that is polemical or indignant, dripping with righteous antipathy for injustice, but I did not believe that the study I was writing in the historical mode and moment in which I was writing it could assume that tone or stance, or that it would be the most productive way to understand what lynching means in America. I had to be measured and temperate in my assessment of what people who performed inhumane things believed themselves to be doing.

I envy and admire those historians of an earlier age who could express their opprobrium without restraint. It would be wonderful to be able to say of some people who appear in my work, as Thomas Babington Macaulay said in one of his historical essays on the English Revolution, for example, that of Archbishop Laud "we entertain a more unmitigated contempt than, for any other character in our history" (Macaulay, "Hallam"). Or as he said of Bertrand Barère in an essay on the French Revolution: "Barère approached nearer than any person mentioned in history or fiction, whether man or devil, to the idea of consummate and universal depravity" (Macaulay, "Barère").

That luxury of honest expression, however, is not generally permitted the modern historian. And so one labors under a more painful self-control. It is taxing work to be fair to people one does not believe to be fair themselves. In indexing, though, you do not have to repress your honest reactions as you do in writing.

Here is the process by which I compiled the index. I read through each chapter, highlighting key words and concepts and names of people. After I finish the chapter, I then type in those words and names and the pages where they occur. I then read the next chapter, rinse and repeat. That means that I am constantly inserting new words and concepts into an expanding list, organized alphabetically.

So I found myself proudly writing down the name of someone I admire deeply, someone who stood up for justice and righteousness, someone who performed a daring intellectual or heroic deed. Here in a history of depravity was someone who stood for decency. Here were such august names in the history of antilynching as Jessie Daniel Ames, who as a white southern woman courageously exposed the lie that lynching was an act of chivalry, or John Jay Chapman, who in 1912 revealed the undeniable responsibility borne by all Americans in the lynching of any American, and, finally, the greatest of them all, Ida B. Wells, who incisively diagnosed and tirelessly fought lynching from the time she recognized it for the racial crime it was in 1892 until her death in 1930.

Here I also recorded the names and acronyms of important groups that demanded justice and antilynching legislation, groups famous like the NAACP and not sufficiently appreciated like the Anti-Lynching Crusaders. Here, too, were heroic individuals who were not well known. In one case there was a man whom I know only as "Reverend King," who risked his life in facing down a mob of fifteen thousand in 1893 to try and prevent the immolation of Henry Smith. He was unsuccessful, but his courage strikes me as exemplary. I felt it an honor to record his name in the only way I knew it in my index. I do not think of this index as some kind of roll of honor, a hall of fame, or anything of the sort. But I did, for those moments when I recorded the heroes of my tale, think of it as an appropriate place for those whose names deserved recuperation, recovery, and celebration.

But because it is an index, it could not remain the place for only the heroes. A book on lynching is populated primarily with villains. I, like Macaulay, felt loathing for many a character in my studies.

The people whose presence in my book raised my ire the most, the ones who struck me as the most despicable of the lot, were those intellectuals who defended and apologized for lynching. The lynchers did what they did, and ought to be arraigned for the terrible things they did, but they enjoyed the benefit of anonymity, since they were constituted as masses and mobs, not individuals. But the apologists, those who defended past lynchings and incited future ones, were individuals, and moreover they possessed the power of press and pulpit at their disposal. When they proclaimed something, they had an audience and readership that took seriously what they wrote and said. The three for whom I had the most utter contempt, the most loathsome and detestable of a despicable lot, to employ the liberating language of Macaulay, were a newspaper editor (John Temple Graves), a novelist who was racist (Thomas Nelson Page), and a rabid racist who wrote novels (Thomas Dixon).

First, and most obviously, is the fact that they were racists—that is, they believed that someone's racial identity, bred in the blood, gave that person a particular kind of moral and intellectual grounding. It is perhaps unfair to expect them not to be racists at a time when it was intellectually acceptable to believe that race was such a determinant of ability, that the genetic properties of a person constituted his or her cultural possibilities. That position, challenged from the time it assumed a coherent form in the middle of the nineteenth century, and entirely upended by the 1920s, was called scientific racism. Of course, there were lots of people in the late nineteenth century who disputed that argument, who believed that race was no determinant of cultural, intellectual, or moral abilities. This trio, my personal axis of evil, did not.

But even more than being racists of that particular sort—scientific racists, as it were—these three were intent on promoting a harmful untruth about the specific way that race inflected morals. That argument, of course, was that men of African descent, freed from the fetters of slavery, had become insatiable rapists, and that it was this very epidemic of rape that called forth the chivalrous activity of lynchers. What is striking about this untruth is not only that it was statistically false (and they knew it to be false because they were familiar with the data published in mainstream venues). Newspapers reporting on lynchings, newspapers like the *Chicago Tribune* that began in 1882 annually tabulating lynchings by region, state, and alleged instigating crime, had shown that lynchers themselves alleged rape as the cause of lynching in a minority of cases (somewhere around 25 percent). Remember, these are allegations made by mobs intent on murder—not charges issued by legal and police forces. Yet even those frenzied mobs in their frenzied acts were more discriminating than their apologists, who argued, again and again, over and over, that lynchings were performed to punish rapes and prevent future rapes of white women. Rebecca Latimer Felton, for instance, who was a populist racist in 1899, and who became the first woman to serve in the United States Senate in 1922, had issued a proclamation claiming that if it took lynching to protect white women from rape, then let them lynch a thousand a week if necessary. Graves, Page, and Dixon never reached that apogee of rhetoric, but they shared Felton's belief and always implicitly, sometimes explicitly, urged their readers to follow Felton's exhortation.

Rather, what struck me was how convoluted their arguments had to become in order to stretch the facts to fit into their preconceived beliefs. After all, interracial rape as a crime on American soil had been pretty one-sided. Anyone even superficially familiar with the history of slavery in the Americas knows the extent to which masters consistently and with impunity raped the enslaved women on their plantations and on the plantations of their neighbors. Here, then, was a truth that these writers wanted to invert, just as the masters and their wives had inverted the truth of white masters' raping slave women to blame slave women for inciting them to it. In both cases—proslavery ideologues who constructed the model of the black slave seductresses and the prolynching apologists who created the type of the black beast rapist—these writers simply projected what whites had done onto the blacks to whom they had done it. It was not even imaginative racism. One might respect a racist diatribe that had the virtue of novelty, but this was as tawdry in its morality as it was in its unoriginality.

Here, then, was the dilemma of the indexer. It pained and angered me to record the names of white supremacists and apologists for lynching, people who justified criminal and genocidal behavior, and have them live forever next to the names of people who deserve better, people who fought against their evil or died because of it. So, while I tried to be fair and temperate in the text of the book in my assessment of people who justified lynching, people I thought deceitful and inhumane, people I frankly despised with a bottomless hatred, I found myself feeling a resurgent anger as I dutifully placed their names next to those who represented heroic resistance or inhumane suffering. I fought the temptation to make up a faux concept, a word starting with the appropriate letter, just so that I could separate the names of the admired from the loathed. Every now and then, a legitimate way of separating them came my way, and I cheered whenever an opportune concept or name in a later chapter allowed me in good faith to keep the names of the doers of good separate from and uninfected by the purveyors of evil. These were small victories, the only kind of victories there are in the life of an indexer. In the end, indexing teaches you that the alphabet is unforgiving.

3.

The other and possibly most powerful feeling that I have had throughout the indexing is profound sadness. I should mention that it was by no means only during the process of indexing this book that I have felt sad. More than a decade of reading about the cruelty, the savagery, the inhumanity of lynching had its toll, leaving me fatigued with something akin to melancholy. The research for this study frequently left me in bad humor, and even more frequently left me dejected and despondent. For reasons I will explain below, I felt this sadness most poignantly while I was compiling a list of names of places and names of people.

As I proceeded in the relatively routine task of indexing, I began at first to highlight all the names of places where the lynchings I mention in my book occurred. In the historiography of lynching, the facts that are most important, or at least the ones that get mentioned most frequently, are the names of the victims, and the site and the date of the lynching. In this sense, lynchings, like any historical event, are identified by where and when they happened. The "when" requires little commentary; it is a date, and acts like any historical date—to identify the exact moment when the event took place. The name of the place where the event took place is also pretty clear. Traditionally, those who have worked to identify lynchings have used either the names of cities, when lynchings took place in or on the outlying borders of cities, or the names of counties, when the lynchings were more rural and not in the vicinity of an identifiable urban space.

At some point in the indexing, I began to reconsider whether it made sense to index all the place-names in my book. I did not want an index that was unwieldy or disproportionate to the book. As I was deciding whether to continue highlighting and indexing city and county names, I began to think about what these place-names mean for the event with which they are associated. For the victim, it is not the place of birth or home, the usual markers for a historical personage, but only the place where his or her life ended. For those who ended that life, the place-name is home or close enough to home, and the place where they performed a murder. There is a difference, though. Unlike places where a simple murder happened, these are sites of a collective act, the action of a mob that, according to some of the most influential historians of lynching, necessarily has the support of the community behind it. These are cities or counties that countenanced what was performed on their land and what was done in their name. We don't generally think of indicting a place where a murder occurs, since a murder can occur anywhere and it is not representative of the place it happens. That is frequently a matter of accident. A lynching, though, has usually brought opprobrium on the town or county where it happened, because people believe, with some reason, that the lynching had the sanction of the mob gathered from that community to perform it.

So the name of a lynching site—Paris, Texas, in 1893, Newnan, Georgia, in 1899, Coatesville, Pennsylvania, in 1911, Marietta, Georgia, in 1915, Waco, Texas, in 1916—for some of us has come to represent something more sinister. Those are places that now become associated with what happened on that land. It would be odd to find someone of my generation who was not moved by the mention of particular places—Dachau, Hiroshima, My Lai, for example—to think of the horrors that occurred there. Those are now names that do not just connote the terrible things humans can do to each other; they are names that are now primarily indicators of horrors, and only secondarily actual places, for most of us with any kind of historical memory.

These are names that have become tainted by historical associations. In these cases, it is not just that many died at that place, but rather that there was something startling, revealing, in the ways they died. In the first case, they died in a drawn-out, extended, and systematic fashion that demonstrated what genocide was and how the whole world was implicated in it. In the second, they died in a single moment that showed what horrible technology humans could create and use against other humans. Here we saw a mass of people die in a single moment in a way that was, and should remain, inconceivable. In the last, we learned about how innocent villagers died in what we comforted ourselves by calling a "war crime" in order to avoid confronting what brutality in any war exacts on the victims and the people whom war and training and opportunity have made inhumane purveyors of violence.

I brought that sensitivity to place-names—that reflex action of investing meaning into what happened in a particular site—to my research, and researching the history of lynching has tried that sensitivity. Let me offer two personal anecdotes as examples.

One beautiful spring day, I took a break from writing the book and went for a long walk with my almost two-year-old son from our neighborhood to downtown New Haven, about a thirty-minute walk pushing the stroller. As I was waiting at an intersection, a large truck-trailer pulled up at the lights. For no reason at all, other than a compulsion I cannot easily control, I tend to read the information written on the side of truck-trailer cabs, information concerning the gross vehicle weight (GVW) or combined gross vehicle weight (CGW) of the truck and the place the truck is licensed—its home, as it were. This particular truck's home happened to be Marion, Indiana. Had it been another Indiana city, I might have mused on what kinds of commodities were traveling to or from Connecticut and Indiana. But this particular name happened to be the name of the city where a notorious 1931 lynching took place, and the subject of that very morning's writing session (index: 17, 60–94, 160). The beauty of the day, the pleasure of the walk, everything but the continued delight in being with my son, was in a moment lost and became as colorless as the black-and-white photograph of that lynching.

The second anecdote is similar. I compiled the index to my lynching book while I was on a sabbatical in the South of France (a fact that may temper a lot of what I have written). About halfway through the year, I began to make the preliminary arrangements for our return. That subject of ending a sabbatical and leaving France, with its quite different nostalgia, anger, and sadness (or should I say *nostalgie, colère, et tristesse*), belongs to a different essay. As I was exploring how to travel with the least amount of luggage, including bags freighted with heavy books, I consulted a website for a British company that specialized in transporting luggage internationally. As I was entering the information on the website to get a quote, I encountered a scrolling window with a list of American city names for me to identify the one to which I wanted my luggage shipped. The first name on that list was Abbeville, South Carolina. This city's preeminence on the scrolling list, like my index, is an accident of the alphabet. But this city, to me, represents a particular lynching, which I briefly discuss in my book (index: 47, 48–49, 55).

A pleasant walk interrupted, a website visit stalled, by a place-name—because these names for me have a historical burden, a shadow, a taint. These are names that have lost whatever innocence they might have had prior to the date when that community lynched someone; these are names that are now largely symbolic and representative, rather than real and referential.

What lynching sites represent, for me anyway, is a place where the taking of life was insufficient, where the crime extended to the taking of dignity. When we think that a lynching in one of its most brutal manifestations, the spectacle lynching in which thousands watched and participated, involved not only murder but torture of the person before and abuse of the body after, we can appreciate that what a lynching involves is far more than just the awful taking of life. I think the most comparable cases for me are European concentration camps, and, in this country, those defiled burial grounds of oppressed people—of enslaved Americans and of Native Americans.

In all cases, what we are dealing with is desecration—as if the taking of life alone were insufficient to satisfy blood- or land lust. These are examples of punishment beyond the death, a failure to accept mortality itself as the boundary marking what can be punished or killed. These are cases where a mob wanted more than blood, more than flesh, where it wanted the spirit itself of what it cast as a demonic force, which in the end was a demonic force only of the mob itself.

Perhaps in the end, though, marking some places as especially tainted by acts that happened there, and trying to understand why some brutal acts can taint more than others, is simply a way to avoid making ourselves too vigilantly aware of the almost daily evidence of our inhumanity to each other—the legions of homeless men and women sleeping on our streets to whom we have become habituated, the inequality and poverty we hide from ourselves or have hidden from us by city planners, and the host of other daily injustices to which we have become inured or blind.

4.

These place-names also have an additional meaning for me in that each of them is particularly associated with the name of a person whose life was the emblem the mob required and took. In the examples I gave above—in Paris, Texas, Henry Smith; in Newnan, Georgia, Sam Hose (which turned out to be not his real name); in Coatesville, Pennsylvania, Zachariah Walker; in Marietta, Georgia, Leo Frank; and in Waco, Texas, Jesse Washington. The thought of writing this essay came to me as I was highlighting and dutifully typing the names of lynch victims into my index. It is not the number of them that startles me, although there are many, always too many. It is the fact that they often get cited once, on one page. These are not household names, people who are known for their accomplishments in some field of endeavor, athletes, politicians, artists, or activists. These are people whose solitary importance is that they were tortured and killed in a particular way.

It struck me as unfair that these were individuals who had become defined as victims or as statistics simply because their life came to an end at the hands of a mob. I must confess that I could not rectify that injustice; indeed, I may have exacerbated it. In one particular instance, some of these victims were catalogued in my book not only because they were lynched but solely because they were lynched in a very specific way.

Here is the context. I had been arguing against several writers who denied that what happened to James Byrd, Jr., when he was dragged behind a truck in Jasper, Texas, in 1998 could be called a lynching. I took up each point these writers raised and attempted to reveal what was wrong with it. Because the specific mode of his lynching was relatively unknown—most people were hanged or burned—I provided a list of lynchings where the victims were dragged behind horse carriages and then automobiles from the 1890s to the 1940s. This list was meant to show that this particularly gruesome way of torturing and taking of life was not new and had in fact been frequently employed in the history of lynching. My point was to show those who denied he was lynched because of the way he was killed (by dragging) the history of that particular form of lynching.

That specific part of the argument took two paragraphs on one page (page 140) and consisted of listing the instances where people were dragged to death or dragged after they had been killed. It included Robert Lewis, Lee Walker, Rob Edwards, William Turner, John Carter, Willie Kirkland, Claude Neal, and Cleo Wright, who all suffered this brutal treatment in various parts of America. It also included Jesse Washington, George Johnson, and David Gregory, who had all been dragged behind vehicles in Texas specifically, as had Byrd. I felt that I had made my point that this was a practice that was both national and local. It was a compact part of the argument because it primarily required examples, and in this case examples that took the form of names that, for the most part, did not appear again in my book.

This moment in my indexing gave me pause. Here was a list of names of people who were connected only by virtue of the fact that they were all victims of a particular, and particularly heinous, kind of crime. Here, concentrated in two paragraphs and one page, were decades and decades of lives whose sole importance at this moment was the specific way their lives were taken from them. It was with sadness that I recorded their names in my index. I did not think I was recuperating them or celebrating them, as I had felt when I wrote down the names of the unknown antilynching heroes. It was merely to testify that they had existed, and that the most signal thing about their existence was how their fellow citizens had ended it. There is something unalterably depressing about reducing a life no doubt rich in ideas, emotions, connections, and actions to a statistical anecdote. And in a way all histories of lynching do just that, have to do it, yes, but do it in a way that perhaps should make us think about what it means to produce such catalogues, lists, tables, and, yes, paragraphs, that encapsulate and concentrate these names and crimes into a succinct form and with the intent of making a particular point in which these lives are only examples.

5.

What I have learned, then, as I completed the final part of my book, the index, the part with the least imaginative input, is that such lists contain a great deal of emotional energy that is probably not readily apparent to the reader. Indeed, it was quite late in the process of indexing my book that I came to the startling realization that the list I was making shared the form and some of the properties of precisely the kind of lists that I had been studying for over a decade—the lists of tables and charts made by antilynching activists and organizations to show how pervasive the crime of lynching was. My list was rudimentary and organized alphabetically, while theirs were more factually detailed and organized chronologically. But they were lists all the same, a cataloguing of the bare data of a lynching (names, places, allegations, mob sizes, modes of death) that attempted in the most succinct way to demonstrate just how widespread lynching as a practice was, and just how painfully intimate and personal was each lynching of an individual human being.

I have come, belatedly but profoundly, to gain an entirely new respect for those lists and an even deeper admiration for those earlier writers on lynching who produced them. During the past decade and a half of research I have read so many tables and charts and lists of lynchings without thinking in the least about how these items were composed, about what kind of emotional investment they express. Now that I have finally compiled my own such list, I know better, much better than I did during my research, how to look for what went into the composition of those tables and charts and indices.

I have come to love even more than I had the earliest antilynching advocates, who inaugurated the making of lists—especially the pioneering Ida B. Wells, on whom it must have exacted a great toll for her to write down just facts taken from mainstream newspapers and refrain from lamentation and declamation, even when one of the names she recorded was that of the father of her goddaughter. Likewise, I have come to appreciate just what courage was shown by the record-keepers of those later institutions and organizations who followed Wells's trailblazing efforts—Tuskegee, the NAACP, the Association of Southern Women for the Prevention of Lynching, the Association for the Study of Lynching—all of whom published pamphlets and books with tables of information on lynchings, tabulated and detailed, with names of victims, places, dates, allegations, and particulars. I now find myself able to imagine what anguish must have gone into this painful task of reducing lives to a single event, of tabulating a national series of horrors in a succinct form that even the most mindless reader would have no trouble following.

I now know what pain might have attended the writing of each name, the weariness that might have moved the author listing each city and county and site of horror, the anger incited at each recording of the alleged crime, the size of the mob, and the mode of killing. These lists at the backs of lynching books are not just serial or alphabetical chronologies, not just data ready for plumbing and formulating into statistics. They are rife with all the humane emotions of those of us who could not express elsewhere in the book just how hard it was, just how much it hurt.

DAVID SEDARIS

Stepping Out

FROM *The New Yorker*

I WAS AT an Italian restaurant in Melbourne, listening as a woman named Lesley talked about her housekeeper, an immigrant to Australia who earlier that day had cleaned the bathroom countertops with a bottle of very expensive acne medication: "She's afraid of the vacuum cleaner and can't read or write a word of English, but other than that she's marvelous."

Lesley works for a company that goes into developing countries and trains doctors to remove cataracts. "It's incredibly rewarding," she said as our antipasto plate arrived. "These are people who've been blind for years, and suddenly, miraculously, they can see again." She brought up a man who'd been operated on in a remote area of China. "They took off the bandages, and for the first time in two decades he saw his wife. Then he opened his mouth and said, 'You're so . . . old.'"

Lesley pushed back her shirtsleeve, and as she reached for an olive I noticed a rubber bracelet on her left wrist. "Is that a watch?" I asked.

"No," she told me. "It's a Fitbit. You synch it with your computer, and it tracks your physical activity."

I leaned closer, and as she tapped the thickest part of it a number of glowing dots rose to the surface and danced back and forth. "It's like a pedometer," she continued. "But updated, and better. The goal is to take ten thousand steps per day, and once you do, it vibrates."

I forked some salami into my mouth. "Hard?"

"No," she said. "It's just a tingle."

A few weeks later I bought a Fitbit of my own and discovered what she was talking about. Ten thousand steps, I learned, amounts to a little more than four miles for someone my size—five feet five inches. It sounds like a lot, but you can cover that distance in the course of an average day without even trying, especially if you have stairs in your house, and a steady flow of people who regularly knock, wanting you to accept a package or give them directions or just listen patiently as they talk about birds, which happens from time to time when I'm home, in West Sussex, the area of England that Hugh and I live in. One April afternoon the person at my door hoped to sell me a wooden bench. It was bought, he said, for a client whose garden he was designing. "Last week she loved it, but now she's decided to go with something else." In the bright sunlight, the fellow's hair was as orange as a Popsicle. "The company I ordered it from has a no-return policy, so I'm wondering if maybe *you'd* like to buy it." He gestured toward an unmarked van idling in front of the house, and seemed angry when I told him that I wasn't interested. "You could at least take a look before making up your mind," he said.

I closed the door a couple of inches. "That's O.K." Then, because it's an excuse that works for just about everything, I added, "I'm American."

"Meaning?" he said.

"We . . . stand up a lot," I told him.

"Oldest trick in the book," my neighbor Thelma said when I told her what had happened. "That bench was stolen from someone's garden, I guarantee it."

This was seconded by the fellow who came to empty our septic tank. "Pikeys," he said.

"Come again?"

"Tinkers," he said. "Pikeys."

"That means Gypsies," Thelma explained, adding that the politically correct word is *travelers*.

I was traveling myself when I got my Fitbit, and because the tingle feels so good, not just as a sensation but also as a mark of accomplishment, I began pacing the airport rather than doing what I normally do, which is sit in the waiting area wondering which of the many people around me will die first, and of what. I also started taking the stairs instead of the escalator, and avoiding the moving sidewalk.

"Every little bit helps," my old friend Dawn, who frequently eats lunch while hula-hooping and has been known to visit her local Y three times a day, said. She had a Fitbit as well, and swore by it. Others I met weren't quite so taken. These were people who had worn one until the battery died. Then, rather than recharging it, which couldn't be simpler, they'd stuck it in a drawer, most likely with all the other devices they'd lost interest in over the years. To people like Dawn and me, people who are obsessive to begin with, the Fitbit is a digital trainer, perpetually egging us on. During the first few weeks that I had it, I'd return to my hotel at the end of the day, and when I discovered that I'd taken a total of, say, twelve thousand steps, I'd go out for another three thousand.

"But why?" Hugh asked when I told him about it. "Why isn't twelve thousand enough?"

"Because," I told him, "my Fitbit thinks I can do better."

I look back at that time and laugh—fifteen thousand steps— Ha! That's only about seven miles! Not bad if you're on a business trip or you're just getting used to a new prosthetic leg. In Sussex, though, it's nothing. Our house is situated on the edge of a rolling downland, a perfect position if you like what the English call "rambling." I'll follow a trail every now and then, but as a rule I prefer roads, partly because it's harder to get lost on a road, but mainly because I'm afraid of snakes. The only venomous ones in England are adders, and even though they're hardly ubiquitous, I've seen three that had been run over by cars. Then I met a woman named Janine who was bitten and had to spend a week in the hospital. "It was completely my own fault," she said. "I shouldn't have been wearing sandals."

"It didn't *have* to strike you," I reminded her. "It could have just slid away."

Janine was the type who'd likely blame herself for getting mugged. "It's what I get for having anything worth taking!" she'd probably say. At first I found her attitude fascinating. Then I got vindictive on her behalf, and started carrying a snake killer, or at least something that could be used to grab one by the neck and fling it into the path of an oncoming car. It's a hand-size claw on a pole, and was originally designed for picking up litter. With it I can walk, fear snakes a little less, and satisfy my insane need for order all at the same time. I've been cleaning the roads in my area of Sussex for three years now, but before the Fitbit I did it primarily on my bike, and with my bare hands. That was fairly effective, but I wound up missing a lot. On foot, nothing escapes my attention: a potato-chip bag stuffed into the hollow of a tree, an elderly mitten caught in the embrace of a blackberry bush, a mud-coated matchbook at the bottom of a ditch. Then there's all the obvious stuff: the cans and bottles and great greasy sheets of paper that fish-and-chips comes wrapped in. You can tell where my territory ends and the rest of England begins. It's like going from the rose arbor in Sissinghurst to Fukushima after the tsunami. The difference is staggering.

Since getting my Fitbit, I've seen all kinds of things I wouldn't normally have come across. Once it was a toffee-colored cow with two feet sticking out of her. I was rambling that afternoon with my friend Maja, and as she ran to inform the farmer I marched in place, envious of the extra steps she was getting in. Given all the time I've spent in the country, you'd think I might have seen a calf being born, but this was a first for me. The biggest surprise was how unfazed the expectant mother was. For a while she lay flat on the grass, panting. Then she got up and began grazing, still with those feet sticking out.

"Really?" I said to her. "You can't go *five minutes* without eating?"

Around her were other cows, all of whom seemed blind to her condition.

"Do you think she knows there's a baby at the end of this?" I asked Maja after she'd returned. "A woman is told what's going to happen in the delivery room, but how does an animal interpret this pain?"

I thought of the first time I had a kidney stone. That was in New York, in 1991, back when I had no money or health insurance. All I knew was that I was hurting and couldn't afford to do anything about it. The night was spent moaning. Then I peed blood, followed by what looked like a piece of gravel from an aquarium. That's when I put it all together.

What might I have thought if, after seven hours of unrelenting agony, a creature the size of a full-grown cougar emerged, inch by inch, from the hole at the end of my penis and started hassling me for food? Was that what the cow was going through? Did she think she was dying, or had instinct somehow prepared her for this?

Maja and I watched for an hour. Then the sun started to set, and we trekked on, disappointed. I left for London the next day, and when I returned several weeks later and hiked back to the field, I saw mother and child standing side by side, not in the loving way that I had imagined but more like strangers waiting for the post office to open. Other animals I've seen on my walks are foxes and rabbits. I've stumbled upon deer, stoats, a hedgehog, and more pheasants than I could possibly count. All the badgers I find are dead, run over by cars and eventually feasted upon by carrion-eating slugs, which are themselves eventually flattened, and feasted upon by other slugs.

Back when Maja and I saw the cow, I was averaging twenty-five thousand steps, or around ten and a half miles per day. Trousers that had grown too snug were suddenly loose again, and I noticed that my face was looking a lot thinner. Then I upped it to thirty thousand steps and started moving farther afield. "We saw David in Arundel picking up a dead squirrel with his grabbers," the neighbors told Hugh. "We saw him outside Steyning rolling a tire down the side of the road"; ". . . in Pulborough dislodging a pair of Y-fronts from a tree branch." Before the Fitbit, once we'd eaten dinner I was in for the evening. Now, though, as soon as I'm finished with the dishes I walk to the pub and back, a distance of 3,895 steps. There are no streetlights where we live, and the houses I pass at 11 P.M. are either dark or very dimly lit. I often hear owls, and the flapping of woodcocks disturbed by the beam of my flashlight. One night I heard a creaking sound and noticed that the minivan parked a dozen or so steps ahead of me was rocking back and forth. A lot of people where we live seem to have sex in their cars. I know this because I find their used condoms, sometimes on the road but more often just off it, in little pull-over areas. In addition to spent condoms, in one of the spots that I patrol I regularly pick up empty KFC containers and a great number of soiled Handi Wipes. Do they eat fried chicken and *then* have sex, or is it the other way round? I wonder.

I look back on the days I averaged only thirty thousand steps and think, *Honestly, how lazy can you get?* When I hit thirty-five thousand steps a day, Fitbit sent me an e-badge, and then one for forty thousand, and forty-five thousand. Now I'm up to sixty thousand, which is twenty-five and a half miles. Walking that distance at the age of fifty-seven, with completely flat feet while lugging a heavy bag of garbage, takes close to nine hours—a big block of time, but hardly wasted. I listen to audiobooks and podcasts. I talk to people. I learn things: the fact, for example, that in the days of yore, peppercorns were sold individually, and because they were so valuable, to guard against theft the people who packed them had to have their pockets sewed shut.

At the end of my first sixty-thousand-step day, I staggered home with my flashlight knowing that I'd advance to sixty-five thousand and that there will be no end to it until my feet snap off at the ankles. Then it'll just be my jagged bones stabbing into the soft ground. Why is it some people can manage a thing like a Fitbit, while others go off the rails and allow it to rule, and perhaps even ruin, their lives? While marching along the roadside, I often think of a TV show that I watched a few years back—*Obsessed,* it was called. One of the episodes was devoted to a woman who owned two treadmills and walked like a hamster on a wheel from the moment she got up until she went to bed. Her family would eat dinner, and she'd observe them from her vantage point beside the table, panting as she asked her children about their day. I knew that I was supposed to scoff at this woman, to be, at the very least, entertainingly disgusted, the way I am with the people on *Hoarders,* but instead I saw something of myself in her. Of course, she did her walking on a treadmill, where it served no greater purpose. So it's not like we're *really* that much alike. Is it?

In recognition of all the rubbish I've collected since getting my Fitbit, my local council is naming a garbage truck after me. The fellow in charge emailed to ask which font I would like my name written in, and I answered Roman.

"Get it?" I said to Hugh. "*Roamin'.*"

He lost patience with me somewhere around the thirty-five-thousand mark, and responded with a heavy sigh.

Shortly after I decided on a typeface, for reasons I cannot determine, my Fitbit died. I was devastated when I tapped the broadest part of it and the little dots failed to appear. Then I felt a great sense of freedom. It seemed that my life was now my own again. But was it? Walking twenty-five miles, or even running up the stairs and back, suddenly seemed pointless, since without the steps being counted and registered, what use were they? I lasted five hours before I ordered a replacement, express delivery. It arrived the following afternoon, and my hands shook as I tore open the box. Ten minutes later, my new master strapped securely around my left wrist, I was out the door, racing, practically running, to make up for lost time.

ZADIE SMITH

Find Your Beach

FROM *The New York Review of Books*

ACROSS THE WAY from our apartment—on Houston, I guess —there's a new wall ad. The site is forty feet high, twenty feet wide. It changes once or twice a year. Whatever's on that wall is my view: I look at it more than the sky or the new World Trade Center, more than the water towers, the passing cabs. It has a subliminal effect. Last semester it was a spot for high-end vodka, and while I wrangled children into their snowsuits, chock-full of domestic resentment, I'd find myself dreaming of cold martinis.

Before that came an ad so high-end I couldn't tell what it was for. There was no text—or none that I could see—and the visual was of a yellow firebird set upon a background of hellish red. It seemed a gnomic message, deliberately placed to drive a sleepless woman mad. Once, staring at it with a newborn in my arms, I saw another mother, in the tower opposite, holding her baby. It was 4 A.M. We stood there at our respective windows, separated by a hundred feet of expensive New York air.

The tower I live in is university accommodation; so is the tower opposite. The idea occurred that it was quite likely that the woman at the window also wrote books for a living, and, like me, was not writing anything right now. Maybe she was considering antidepressants. Maybe she was already on them. It was hard to tell. Certainly she had no way of viewing the ad in question, not without opening her window, jumping, and turning as she fell. I was her view. I was the ad for what she already had.

But that was all some time ago. Now the ad says, *Find your beach.* The bottle of beer—it's an ad for beer—is very yellow and the background luxury-holiday-blue. It seems to me uniquely well placed, like a piece of commissioned public art in perfect sympathy with its urban site. The tone is pure Manhattan. Echoes can be found in the personal growth section of the bookstore ("Find your happy"), and in exercise classes ("Find your soul"), and in the therapist's office ("Find your self"). I find it significant that there exists a more expansive, national version of this ad that runs in magazines, and on television.

In those cases photographic images are used, and the beach is real and seen in full. Sometimes the tag line is expanded, too: *When life gives you limes . . . Find your beach.* But the wall I see from my window marks the entrance to SoHo, a district that is home to media moguls, entertainment lawyers, every variety of celebrity, some students, as well as a vanishingly small subset of rent-controlled artists and academics.

Collectively we, the people of SoHo, consider ourselves pretty sophisticated consumers of media. You can't put a cheesy ad like that past us. And so the ad has been reduced to its essence—a yellow undulation against a field of blue—and painted directly onto the wall, in a bright pop-art style. The mad men know that we know the SoHo being referenced here: the SoHo of Roy Lichtenstein and Ivan Karp, the SoHo that came before Foot Locker, Sephora, Prada, frozen yogurt. That SoHo no longer exists, of course, but it's part of the reason we're all here, crowded on this narrow strip of a narrow island. Whoever placed this ad knows us well.

Find your beach. The construction is odd. A faintly threatening mixture of imperative and possessive forms, the transformation of a noun into a state of mind. Perhaps I'm reading too much into it. On the one hand it means, simply, "Go out and discover what makes you happy." Pursue happiness actively, as Americans believe it their right to do. And it's an ad for beer, which makes you happy in the special way of all intoxicants, by reshaping reality around a sensation you alone are having. So, even more precisely, the ad means "Go have a beer and let it make you happy." Nothing strange there. Except beer used to be sold on the dream of communal fun: have a beer with a buddy, or lots of buddies. People crowded the frame, laughing and smiling. It was a lie about alcohol—as this ad is a lie about alcohol—but it was a different kind of lie, a wide-framed lie, including other people.

Here the focus is narrow, almost obsessive. Everything that is not absolutely necessary to your happiness has been removed from the visual horizon. The dream is not only of happiness, but of happiness conceived in perfect isolation. Find your beach in the middle of the city. Find your beach no matter what else is happening. Do not be distracted from finding your beach. Find your beach even if—as in the case of this wall painting—it is not actually there. Create this beach inside yourself. Carry it with you wherever you go. The pursuit of happiness has always seemed to me a somewhat heavy American burden, but in Manhattan it is conceived as a peculiar form of duty.

In an exercise class recently the instructor shouted at me, at all of us: "Don't let your mind set limits that aren't really there." You'll find this attitude all over the island. It is encouraged and reflected in the popular culture, especially the movies, so many of which, after all, begin their creative lives here, in Manhattan. According to the movies it's only our own limited brains that are keeping us from happiness. In the future we will take a pill to make us limitless (and ideal citizens of Manhattan), or we will, like Scarlett Johansson in *Lucy,* use 100 percent of our brain's capacity instead of the mythic 10. In these formulations the world as it is has no real claim on us. Our happiness, our miseries, our beaches, or our blasted heaths—they are all within our own power to create, or destroy. On Tina Fey's television show *30 Rock,* Jack Donaghy—the consummate citizen of this new Manhattan—deals with problems by crushing them with his "mind vise."

The beach is always there: you just have to conceive of it. It follows that those who fail to find their beach are, in the final analysis, mentally fragile; in Manhattan terms, simply weak. Jack Donaghy's verbal swordplay with Liz Lemon was a comic rendering of the various things many citizens of Manhattan have come to regard as fatal weakness: childlessness, obesity, poverty. To find your beach you have to be ruthless. Manhattan is for the hard-bodied, the hard-minded, the multitasker, the alpha mamas and papas. A perfect place for self-empowerment—as long as you're pretty empowered to begin with. As long as you're one of these people who simply do not allow anything—not even reality—to impinge upon that clear field of blue.

There is a kind of individualism so stark that it seems to dovetail with an existentialist creed: Manhattan is right at that crossroads. You are pure potential in Manhattan, limitless, you are making yourself every day. When I am in England each summer, it's the opposite: all I see are the limits of my life. The brain that puts a hairbrush in the fridge, the leg that radiates pain from the hip to the toe, the lovely children who eat all my time, the books unread and unwritten.

And casting a shadow over it all is what Philip Larkin called "extinction's alp," no longer a stable peak in a distance, finally becoming rising ground. In England even at the actual beach I cannot find my beach. I look out at the freezing forty-degree water, at the families squeezed into ill-fitting wetsuits, huddled behind windbreakers, approaching a day at the beach with the kind of stoicism once conjured for things like the Battle of Britain, and all I can think is what funny, limited creatures we are, subject to every wind and wave, building castles in the sand that will only be knocked down by the generation coming up beneath us.

When I land at JFK, everything changes. For the first few days it is a shock: I have to get used to old New York ladies beside themselves with fury that I have stopped their smooth elevator journey and got in with some children. I have to remember not to pause while walking in the street—or during any fluid-moving city interaction—unless I want to utterly exasperate the person behind me. Each man and woman in this town is in pursuit of his or her beach and God help you if you get in their way. I suppose it should follow that I am happier in pragmatic England than idealist Manhattan, but I can't honestly say that this is so. You don't come to live here unless the delusion of a reality shaped around your own desires isn't a strong aspect of your personality. "A reality shaped around your own desires"—there is something sociopathic in that ambition.

It is also a fair description of what it is to write fiction. And to live in a city where everyone has essentially the same tunnel vision and obsessive focus as a novelist is to disguise your own sociopathy among the herd. Objectively all the same limits are upon me in Manhattan as they are in England. I walk a ten-block radius every day, constrained in all the usual ways by domestic life, reduced to writing about whatever is right in front of my nose. But the fact remains that here I *do* write, the work gets done.

Even if my Manhattan productivity is powered by a sociopathic illusion of my own limitlessness, I'm thankful for it, at least when I'm writing. There's a reason so many writers once lived here, beyond the convenient laundromats and the take-out food, the libraries and cafés. We have always worked off the energy generated by this town, the moneymaking and tower-building as much as the street art and underground cultures. Now the energy is different: the underground has almost entirely disappeared. (You hope there are still young artists in Washington Heights, in the Barrio, or Stuyvesant Town, but how much longer can they hang on?) A twisted kind of energy radiates instead off the SoulCycling mothers and marathon-running octogenarians, the entertainment lawyers glued to their iPhones and the moguls building five "individualized" condo townhouses where once there was a hospital.

It's not a pretty energy, but it still runs what's left of the show. I contribute to it. I ride a stationary bike like the rest of them. And then I despair when Shakespeare and Co. closes in favor of another Foot Locker. There's no way to be in good faith on this island anymore. You have to crush so many things with your mind vise just to get through the day. Which seems to me another aspect of the ad outside of my window: willful intoxication. Or, to put it more snappily, "You don't have to be high to live here, but it helps."

Finally the greatest thing about Manhattan is the worst thing about Manhattan: self-actualization. Here you will be free to stretch yourself to your limit, to find the beach that is yours alone. But sooner or later you will be sitting on that beach wondering what comes next. I can see my own beach ahead now, as the children grow, as the practical limits fade; I see afresh the huge privilege of my position; it reclarifies itself. Under the protection of a university I live on one of the most privileged strips of built-up beach in the world, among people who believe they have no limits and who push me, by their very proximity, into the same useful delusion, now and then.

It is such a good town in which to work and work. You can find your beach here, find it falsely but convincingly, still thinking of Manhattan as an isle of writers and artists—of downtown underground wildlings and uptown intellectuals—against all evidence to the contrary. Oh, you still see them occasionally here and there, but unless they are under the protection of a university—or have sold that TV show—they are all of them, every single last one of them, in Brooklyn.

REBECCA SOLNIT

Arrival Gates

FROM *Granta*

AFTER THE LONG flight across the Pacific, after the night in the
tiny hotel room selected so that I could walk to the world's busi-
est train station in the morning, after the train north to the area
most impacted by the tsunami in the Great Tōhoku earthquake
of March 11, 2011, after the meetings among the wreckage with
people who had seen their villages and neighbors washed away, after seeing the foundations of what had once been a neighborhood
so flattened it looked like a chessboard full of shards, after hearing
from so many people with grief and rage in their voices talking
about walls of water and drownings and displacement and refuge,
but also about betrayal by the government in myriad ways, after
the Christian minister pontificated forever while the Buddhist
priests held their peace in the meeting my hosts secretly scheduled at the end of the twelve-hour workday, after I told people I
was getting sick but the meeting went on, after I left the meeting
in the hopes of getting to the hotel and stood outside in the cold
northern night for a long time as a few snowflakes fell, or was it
raindrops, I forget, after the sickness turned into a cough so fierce
I thought I might choke or come up with blood or run out of air,
after the tour continued regardless, and the speaking tour at the
universities, after the conferences where I talked about disaster
and utopia, after the trip to the conference in Hiroshima where
I walked and saw with my own eyes the bombed places I had seen
in pictures so often and met with the octogenarians who told me,
with the freshness of people who had only recently begun to tell,
the story of what they had seen and been and done and suffered
and lost on August 6, 1945, after the sight of the keloid scars from

the fallout that had drifted onto the arm of a schoolboy sixty-seven years before, so that he grew into a man who always wore long sleeves even in summer, after the long walks along the beautiful river distributaries of Hiroshima and among its willows and monuments, draped in garlands of paper cranes, to the vaporized and poisoned dead, and plum trees in bloom but not yet cherries, after the one glorious day in Kyoto when I was neither at work nor overwhelmed and alone but accompanied by a pair of kind graduate students, after a day of wandering through old Buddhist temples with them and seeing the dim hall of the thousand golden Buddhas lined up in long rows, I arrived at the orange gates.

You get off the local train from the city of Kyoto and walk through a little tourist town of shops with doorways like wide-open mouths disgorging low tables of food and crafts and souvenirs and then walk uphill, then up stairs, under a great torii gate, one of those structures with a wide horizontal beam extending beyond the pillars that hold it up, like the Greek letter π, and then a plaza of temples and buildings and vendors, and then you keep going up. There are multiple routes up the mountain, and the routes take you through thousands of further torii gates, each with a black base and a black rooflike structure atop the crosspiece, each lacquered pure, intense orange on the cylindrical pillars and crosspiece. The new ones are gleaming and glossy. Some of the old ones are dull, their lacquer cracked, or even rotting away so that the wood is visible underneath.

The orange is so vivid it is as though you have at last gone beyond things that are colored orange to the color itself, particularly in the passages where the torii gates are just a few feet apart, or in one extraordinary sequence many paces long of gates only inches apart, a tunnel of total immersion in orange (vermilion say some of the accounts, but I saw pure intense orange). Nearly every gate bears black inscriptions on one side, and if I could read Japanese I might've read individual business people and corporations expressing their gratitude, because rice and prosperity and business are all tied up together in the realm of the god Inari, but I couldn't. The place was something else to me.

I later read that the Fushimi Inari-taisha is the head shrine of thirty thousand or so Shinto shrines in Japan devoted to Inari. It is said to have been founded in 711 and burned down in 1468, during a civil war, but much of it seems to have been replaced in overlapping waves, so that the whole is ancient and the age of the parts varied, some of them very new. The gates seem designed to pass through, and the altars—platforms and enclosures of stone slabs and obelisks and stone foxes—for stillness, so that the landscape is a sort of musical score of moving and pausing. The altars looked funereal to a Western eye, with the stone slabs like tombstones, but they were something altogether different.

The foxes were everywhere, particularly at these altar zones. Moss and lichen grow on their stone or cement backs, so some are more green than gray and others are spotted with lighter gray. They often have red cloth tied around their necks, the fabric faded to dusty pink, and there are stones at the altar sites with inscriptions carved into them, and rope garlands. The foxes, hundreds of them, a few at a time, sit up, often in pairs, sometimes with smaller torii gates that were offerings arrayed around them, and then sometimes even smaller foxes with the gates, as though this might continue on beyond the visible into tinier and tinier foxes and gates. You could buy the small gates and foxes at the entrance and some places on the mountainside.

Foxes, I knew, are *kitsune* in Japan, the magical shape-shifters in folktales and woodblock prints—and manga and anime now— who pass as human for months or for years, becoming beautiful brides who run away or courtiers who serve aristocrats but serve another, unknown purpose as well. The foxes at the Inari shrine are the god's messengers, a website later told me, more beneficent than some of the foxes in the stories. Elusive, beautiful, unpredictable, *kitsune* in this cosmology represent the unexpected and mysterious and wild aspects of nature. Rain during sunshine is called a fox's wedding in Japanese.

Gates, foxes, foxes, gates. The gates lead you to gates and to foxes, the trails wind all over the slope of the steep, forested hill. Most of the literature speaks as though there is a trail you take, but there are many. If you keep going you might come to a dense bamboo forest with trunks as thick as the poles of streetlights, and a pond beyond that, or you might just keep mounting forest paths that wind and tangle, with every now and again a little pavilion selling soft drinks and snacks, notably tofu pockets—*inarizushi*—said to be the foxes' favorite food. And more gates, unpainted stone as well as lacquered wood.

Arrival implies a journey, and almost all the visitors that day arrived out of a lifetime in Japan, seeing a different place than I did, traveling mostly in small groups, seeming to know why they were there and what to expect. I came directly from the grueling tour of disaster, but with a longtime interest in how moving through space takes on meaning and how meaning can be made spatially, with church and temple designs, landscape architecture and paths, roads, stairs, ladders, bridges, labyrinths, thresholds, triumphal arches, all the grammar that inflects the meanings of our movement.

I had been invited to Japan for the one-year anniversary of the triple disaster, reporting on the aftermath and talking about my book *A Paradise Built in Hell,* which had been translated into Japanese and published just before one of the five largest recorded earthquakes hit the country and the ocean rose up to, in places, 120 feet and scoured the shore, and the six Fukushima nuclear reactors fell apart and began to spread radiation by air and by sea. But that's another story. The Inari shrine was not part of it. My encounter there wasn't the culmination of that journey but perhaps a reprieve from it, and an extension of other journeys and questions I have carried for a long time.

Arrival is the culmination of the sequence of events, the last in the list, the terminal station, the end of the line. And the idea of arrival begets questions about the journey and how long it took. Did it take the dancer two hours to dance the ballet, or two hours plus six months of rehearsals, or two hours plus six months plus a life given over to becoming the instrument that could, over and over, draw lines and circles in the air with precision and grace? Sumi-e painters painted with famous speed, but it took decades to become someone who could manage a brush that way, who had that feel for turning leaves or water into a monochromatic image. You fall in love with someone and the story might be of how you met, courted, consummated, but it might also be of how before all that, time and trouble shaped you both over the years, sanded your rough spots and wore away your vices until your scars and needs and hopes came together like halves of a broken whole.

Culminations are at least lifelong, and sometimes longer when you look at the natural and social forces that shape you, the acts of the ancestors, of illness or economics, immigration and education. We are constantly arriving; the innumerable circumstances are forever culminating in this glance, this meeting, this collision, this conversation, like the pieces in a kaleidoscope forever coming into new focus, new flowerings. But to me the gates made visible not the complicated ingredients of the journey but the triumph of arrival.

I knew I was missing things. I remember the first European cathedral I ever entered—Durham Cathedral—when I was fifteen, never a Christian, not yet taught that most churches are cruciform, or in the shape of a human body with outstretched arms, so that the altar is at what in French is called the *chevet*, or head, so that there was a coherent organization to the place. I saw other things then and I missed a lot. You come to every place with your own equipment.

I came to Japan with wonder at seeing the originals of things I had seen in imitation often, growing up in California: Japanese gardens and Buddhist temples, Mount Fuji, tea plantations and bamboo groves.

But it wasn't really what I knew about Japan but what I knew about the representation of time that seemed to matter there. I knew well the motion studies of Eadweard Muybridge in which a crane flying, a woman sweeping, is captured in a series of photographs, time itself measured in intervals, as intervals, as moments of arrival. The motion studies were the first crucial step on the road to cinema, to those strips of celluloid in which time had been broken down into twenty-four frames per second that could reconstitute a kiss, a duel, a walk across the room, a plume of smoke.

Time seemed to me, as I walked all over the mountain, more and more enraptured and depleted, a series of moments of arrival, like film frames, if film frames with their sprockets were gateways —and maybe they are: they turn by the projector, but as they go each frame briefly becomes an opening through which light travels. I was exalted by a landscape that made tangible that elusive sense of arrival, that palpable sense of time, that so often eludes us. Or rather the sense that we are arriving all the time, that the present is a house into which we always have one foot, an apple we are just biting, a face we are just glimpsing for the first time. In Zen Buddhism you talk a lot about being in the present and being present. That present is an infinitely narrow space between the past and future, the zone in which the senses experience the world, in which you act, however much your mind may be mired in the past or racing into the future.

I had the impression midway through the hours I spent wandering that time itself had become visible, that every moment of my life I was passing through orange gates, always had been, always would be passing through magnificent gates that only in this one place are visible. Their uneven spacing seemed to underscore this perception; sometimes time grows dense and seems to both slow down and speed up, when you fall in love, when you are in the thick of an emergency or a discovery; other times it flows by limpid as a stream across a meadow, each day calm and like the one before, not much to remember, or time runs dry and you're stuck, hoping for change that finally arrives in a trickle or a rush. Though all these metaphors of flow can be traded in for solid ground: time is a stroll through orange gates. Blue mountains are constantly walking, said Dōgen, the monk who brought Zen to Japan, and we are also constantly walking, through these particular Shinto pathways of orange gates. Or so it seemed to me on that day of exhaustion and epiphany.

What does it mean to arrive? The fruits of our labor, we say, the reward. The harvest, the home, the achievement, the completion, the satisfaction, the joy, the recognition, the consummation. Arrival is the reward, it's the time you aspire to on the journey, it's the end, but on the mountain south of Kyoto on a day just barely spring, on long paths whose only English guidance was a few plaques about not feeding the monkeys I never saw anyway, arrival seemed to be constant. Maybe it is.

I wandered far over the mountain that day, until I was outside the realm of the pretty little reproduction of an antique map I had purchased, and gone beyond the realm of the gates. I was getting tired after four hours or so of steady walking. The paths continued, the trees continued, the ferns and mosses under them continued, and I continued but there were no more torii gates. I came out in a manicured suburb with few people on the streets, and walked out to the valley floor and then back into the next valley over and up again through the shops to the entrance to the shrine all over again. But I could not arrive again, though I walked through a few more gates and went to see the tunnel of orange again. It was like trying to go back to before the earthquake, to before knowledge. An epiphany can be as indelible a transformation as a trauma. Once I was through those gates and through that day I would never enter them for the first time and understand what they taught me for the first time.

All you really need to know is that there is a hillside in Japan in which time is measured in irregular intervals and every moment is an orange gate, and foxes watch over it, and people wander it, and the whole is maintained by priests and by donors, so that gates crumble and gates are erected, time passes and does not, as elsewhere nuclear products decay and cultures change and people come and go, and that the place might be one at which you will arrive someday, to go through the flickering tunnels of orange, up the mountainside, into this elegant machine not for controlling or replicating time but maybe for realizing it, or blessing it. Or maybe you have your own means of being present, your own for seeing that at this very minute you are passing through an orange gate.

CHERYL STRAYED

My Uniform

FROM *Tin House*

THERE'S A PAIR of pants I wore almost every day for the first five years I knew my husband. They were what I like to call *sport pants,* which differ from all-out sweatpants (or *yoga pants,* as fancy people now like to call them) in that they were made of a sturdy cotton twill rather than jersey material. Cut comfortably loose, the elastic waistband was the only place where the pants made any contact with my body. Anything could happen inside those pants without detection. I could be fat or less fat or kind of slender. They were extraordinarily utilitarian and patently unsexy. Nuns might opt to wear them. Or park rangers. Or seventy-year-old piano teachers. Or butch lesbians who captained coed Ultimate Frisbee teams. Or me. I wore them so often my husband took to referring to them as my uniform.

I wasn't always so blasé when it came to my husband and clothes. The first time I slept with him—back when he was essentially a stranger to me, on the second night I knew him—I wore a black lace getup that's called a baby-doll nightie. It was a little handful of a thing I'd purchased at a Goodwill just before I met him, when I was twenty-seven and constantly roaming thrift stores on the hunt for something that would help me project the sexy image of myself I was hoping for. I bought it even though I've always been profoundly confused by lingerie. Isn't sex about something that clothes are the opposite of? I could never quite discern when, in the order of things, I was meant to put lingerie *on* when the whole point was ripping things *off.*

These were the questions in my mind on the second night that I knew the man who was not yet my husband, after I excused myself from the bedroom where we'd been ferociously making out and ducked into the bathroom across the hall. As I went, I grabbed the just-purchased nightie from the top drawer of my dresser, a gob of cheap black lace in my hand. Alone, before the mirror, I removed my regular clothes and put on the nightie and studied myself. The nightie had thin shoulder straps, a form-fitting see-through bodice that gently mashed my breasts upward, and a flouncy short-skirted bottom. If the outfit had a title it would be either Slutty Cowgirl or Pretty Pirate. I looked awesome but felt ridiculous. Was I really going to return to the bedroom dressed like this? It seemed desperate and dumb and yet I couldn't help myself. I wanted him to see me like this, to seem to him to be the kind of woman who nonchalantly ranged around her place in a black lace thingamajig that scarcely covered her rear, so I walked into the bedroom and stood ever so briefly before him as he gazed at me, reclining on my futon on the floor, and then I got into bed with him and he pulled the damn thing off.

I never wore that baby-doll nightie or any other piece of lingerie again. My future husband and I became lovers and then we got married and the idea of putting that nightie on became just about the last thing on this earth I would do. I'd bought it for the sole purpose of finding and fostering intimacy, but in fact I wore it on the night when we were the least intimate, when I was projecting a slightly fraudulent image of myself to him instead of the actual me. Which, for better or worse, is a woman who wears pants a nun would find appealing.

The cool thing is, my husband finds them appealing, too. We fell in love while I wore and wore and wore those pants. The pants inside of which undetectable things can happen.

The black lace nightie disappeared soon after I wore it that one time. I handed it over to the Goodwill, tossing it back into the endless thrift-store stream from which it came, into the hands of another woman with fantastical dreams about herself. The pants lasted and lasted, for five years or more, until one day I understood it was the end of them. They'd served their time. I'd worn them so long and so often they'd become threadbare. The elastic of the waist had given way; the hemline had frayed. Instead of putting them on, I put them in the garbage can.

My husband was out of town at the time, working on a project that kept him away from home for a couple of months. It didn't seem right that he wasn't there to witness the end of the pants. My uniform. Our history. So I fished them out of the garbage can and cut out the crotch with a pair of scissors. It was a neat black rectangle of fabric that only two people on the planet would recognize for what it was.

I folded it into an envelope addressed to him. I didn't include a note. I put it in the mail and sat for a long time thinking about it, imagining him. How he'd laugh when he opened the envelope and realized what he was holding. How he'd press it to his nose and inhale.

KELLY SUNDBERG

It Will Look Like a Sunset

FROM *Guernica*

I WAS TWENTY-SIX, having spent most of my twenties delaying adulthood, and he was twenty-four and enjoyed a reputation as a partier. The pregnancy was a surprise, and we married four months later.

As my belly stretched outward with the tightness of the baby, my limbs grew heavy. I napped constantly on a long hand-me-down couch, the summer heat giving me nightmares. I dreamt of a woman floating in the corner staring at me, and I woke with my heart racing. One afternoon a hummingbird flew through the open door of the apartment to the window in the corner and beat at the glass. It was panicked, trying to turn glass into sky. I wrapped my hands around it, the hummingbird heart pulsing against my palms, then released it on the stoop.

They say that a bird in the house is an omen. It can mean pregnancy. Or death. Or both.

Eight years later, the police came to our door. When the younger one asked about my foot, I said that it didn't hurt. I told him it was no big deal, but when he asked for my driver's license, I stood up and found that I couldn't walk, that my foot was the size of a football, and it was bleeding. The bowl Caleb had shattered on it wasn't a little bowl like I had described. It was a heavy ceramic serving bowl, and I would need to wear a soft boot for a month and get a tetanus shot, and there would always be a scar shot through the top of my foot like a red star.

*

In the beginning of our relationship, I slept in his cabin in the woods with no indoor plumbing. I had to pee, so I let myself out. The ground was snow-covered and cold and I didn't feel like walking to the outhouse, so I went around to the side and squatted in the moonlight. The moon turned the snow into a million stars while my gentle lover slumbered in the warmth—such happiness.

We didn't want a church wedding, but our families insisted. Faith was what made marriage sacred. Faith was what kept people together.

I had doubts about marrying him so soon. Sometimes he would disappear for a straight week and return apologetic, smelling of alcohol. His friends gave each other looks that said they knew something I did not. One friend said jokingly, "How on earth did Caleb get you to go out with him?" Coming from a friend, the question seemed odd, but I thought it was just the way they ribbed each other.

When I met him, he charmed me. My best friend said, "You'll love Caleb. He lives in a cabin in the woods that he built by himself." A former wilderness ranger, I was attracted to ruggedness and solitude. Caleb was a writer, and he was funny. One day he joked in bed about what our rapper names would be. I said mine would be "Awesome Possum." He improvised a rap song titled "Get in My Pouch!" I couldn't stop giggling. I had never met a man who could make me laugh like he could.

My love for him was real, and I didn't want to be a single mother.

The young policeman told Caleb, "Go to your parents. Get away for a couple of days. Just let things calm down."

The young policeman told me, "It's all right. My wife and I fight. Things get crazy. Sometimes you just need time apart." I nodded my head in agreement, but I wanted to ask, "Do you beat your wife, too?"

Before our son turned two, we moved to Caleb's home state of West Virginia. He wanted to be closer to his family. There would be more opportunity for work there. His parents owned a rental house that they would sell to us. There were many compelling reasons for the move, but once there, he was the only friend I had.

The loneliness was inescapable. This was common, I told myself. My parents had been married for over thirty years, and I don't remember my father ever having a close friend. I told myself that he was enough for me.

When the older policeman saw the swelling, the black-and-blue, and the toes like little sausage links, his expression turned to dismay. "That's bad. That looks broken," he said. "Ma'am, does your husband have a phone number we can reach him at? We need him to come back."

They waited outside, and I called Caleb. "I'm sorry," I said. "They are going to arrest you."

He said he already knew.

He left his phone on while they arrested him so I could listen. I didn't want to, but I couldn't stop myself. "Did she hit you?" one of the officers asked. "Because we can arrest her, too."

Caleb answered honestly. He said no.

We were together for almost two years before he was violent with me. First he pushed me against a wall. It was two more years before he hit me, and another year after that before he hit me again. It happened so slowly, then so fast.

While the older policeman arrested Caleb, the younger one waited with me for the paramedics to arrive. "Is he going to lose his job?" I asked.

"No, probably not," he said.

"Is he going to leave me?" I asked.

"You didn't do anything wrong," he said.

I wanted him to hug me so I could hide my face in the folds of his black uniform. I crumpled into the rocking chair instead.

"He's going to leave me," I said.

When our elderly neighbor developed dementia and one night thought a boy was hiding under her bed, Caleb stayed with her. When the child of an administrative assistant in Caleb's department needed a heart transplant, Caleb went to the assistant's house and helped him put down wood floors in his basement to create a playroom for the little boy. When my dad needed help installing new windows in the house, or mowing the lawn, or chopping wood, Caleb was always ready to help. I was so grateful to be married to someone so generous with his time, so loving.

The young policeman called for an ambulance. The EMTs looked at my foot. They didn't ask about what happened. They just told me it looked bad, that it could be broken. They asked me if I wanted to go to the emergency room, but I declined, so they instructed me to see a doctor and made me sign a waiver saying they weren't responsible if I didn't get follow-up care. And then I was alone in our home.

Two years after we moved, I started graduate school and finally made some friends, but it was hard to spend time with them. I had to lie: I shut my arm in the door. I tripped on a rug and hit my face on the table. I don't know where that bruise came from. I think I did it in my sleep. I think I'm anemic. I just bruise so easily.

Once Caleb said to me, "You probably wish that someone would figure out where those bruises are coming from. You probably wish someone knew, so that things could change." He said it with such sadness.

After the arrest, I hobbled around in denial for a few days until a concerned friend pushed me into getting the foot examined.

I was embarrassed at the urgent-care center. I told the nurse, "It's okay. He's already been arrested. I don't need anything. I'm safe," but he didn't seem to believe me. The nurse put me in a wheelchair even though I insisted I could walk, and the doctor touched and turned my foot with such care that, out of some sort of misguided impulse, I almost blurted out, "Mom!" But I was thirty-four years old, and the distance between my mother and me was punctuated by so many mountains that she couldn't have saved me.

Caleb wanted to change. He got therapy. He went to anger management. He did everything right. We were allies. Together we were going to fix this problem.

He started taking medication shortly after our sixth anniversary. Every time he was violent with me, he would go to a psychiatrist who increased his dosage. I thought the psychiatrist could fix him.

He wasn't supposed to drink on the medication, but he did.

One night he was in a stupor and staring at something. "What are you looking at?" I asked.

"Myself," he said. "That's me sitting in that chair." He pointed at an empty chair across the room. "That me is laughing at me." His eyes were confused, sad.

"Are you manipulating me?" I asked, worried.

"I'm not the one who manipulates you," he said. He gestured toward the chair again, his voice quickening, earnest almost. "He's the one who manipulates you. It's not me."

I was so tired. I didn't know what to say. "You should go to bed."

His eyes turned from sadness to rage. He stood up and went to the stairs, then turned back to me and said, "I hope you get chlamydia and die."

Shortly before I left him, I told a counselor that my husband was hitting me and showed her the bruises. She held me while I wept in her arms. I then told a close friend that he yelled at me and called me names, but I didn't yet tell her he was beating me.

My counselor said, "You are taking everything he says and playing it on repeat over and over again. You have to stop the tape."

But I couldn't stop the tape. I heard over and over:

You are a fucking cunt. You are a fucking cunt. You are a fucking cunt. You are a fucking cunt. You are a fucking cunt. You are a fucking cunt. You are a fucking cunt.

And then his voice became my voice:

I am a fucking cunt.

"You can't hold the things I say when I'm mad against me," he said. "That isn't fair. Those aren't the things I mean."

At the urgent care, the doctor said, "This will take a long time to heal. It will change color over time. It will look like a sunset." As I drove home, I heard the words over and over:

It will look like a sunset. It will look like a sunset. It will look like a sunset. It will look like a sunset. It will look like a sunset. It will look like a sunset. It will look like a sunset.

I could never bring myself to leave. Instead I was a regular at the Travelodge. I always returned home before morning, keeping the hotel key card just in case, then climbing into bed and wrapping my arms around Caleb's back. All of the usual suspects drew me back—concerns about our six-year-old, money, where we would live, and love. I still loved him. I told myself he would get better.

In sickness and in health. Those were my vows in that little church in Idaho where we held hands while sunlight filtered through stained glass and spring lilacs bloomed outside. Caleb was sick.

He only hit me in the face once. A red bruise bloomed across my cheek, and my eye was split and oozing. Afterward we both sat on the bathroom floor, exhausted. "You made me hit you in the face," he said mournfully. "Now everyone is going to know."

A month or so before his arrest, I thought I was losing my hair from stress. In the shower, red strands swam in the water by my feet. Chunks were stuck to my fingers. It didn't matter. I hadn't felt pretty in years.

When I rubbed the shampoo into my scalp, the skin was tender, and I realized I wasn't losing my hair. He had ripped it out, and I hadn't even felt it.

I went into a cave when he hit me. I curled into my body like a slug, then traveled into a deep darkness where I felt nothing. I heard his voice, his fists, the blasts in my ears from the blows to the side of my head. I heard my own screaming.

Deep in that cave, it wasn't real, even as it was happening.

What was real was when we lay in bed, our son between us—my head on my husband's shoulder, his head resting on mine—and our son said, "The whole family is cuddled up."

"I'm not the type of person to hit a woman," he said. "So it must be you. You are the one who brings this out in me. I would not be like this if I was with a different woman."

The same night that Caleb pulled out my hair, he punched me in the spine with such force that my body arched back as though it had been shocked with electricity. I was jolted out of my cave. He did it again. "No," I screamed. I could not protect myself.

My only protection was the darkness—the dissociation. I hadn't felt him ripping out hair, but when he hit me in the spine, the pain was too intense. That part of my body was too vulnerable. I couldn't curl up. I couldn't wrap my arms around it.

I was present for what was happening. I stopped breathing for a moment. He paused.

It was as though he, too, felt that I was present, and he stopped. I couldn't have been human to him in those moments.

He never raped me, so there's that.

I left him two days after he was arrested, but I wasn't ready. I still wasn't ready.

We were one of those couples that others liked to be around. We laughed a lot, respected each other, and supported each other's work. We loved the same things: cooking Thai food, impromptu dance parties in the living room, *Friday Night Lights* marathons. We always found time for date nights. We vacationed in Greece, New York City, and Glacier National Park. We emailed each other silly videos during the day when we were at work. He phoned me from the car, five minutes after leaving the house, just to talk.

The day that I left him, I called Rebecca, a kind and accepting friend whom I knew would help. It wasn't an easy call to make.

She lived with her partner, and they let my son and me stay with them for a month until we had our own place. She and I had only known each other for a little over a year. I told her about the beatings, how Caleb broke my phone when I tried to call for help, how he pulled me out from underneath the bed by my ankles, how I hid shaking in the closet while he raged, how he always found me, how there was no safe place for me.

When I saw the fear in her eyes, I understood the magnitude of what was happening.

Of everyone I had dated, he was the gentlest. I loved his soft hands, his embraces, his kind heart.

He wrote me love letters, rubbed my feet, took me out to lunch, got up first in the mornings with our son so that I could sleep in. He took care of me. He was more often kind to me than unkind.

Sometimes, when I'm cooking dinner by myself, I can feel the way he would lay his head on my shoulder while I stirred a pot, the way he would turn me around and kiss me, tell me how much he loved my cooking, how beautiful I was, how lucky he was.

On Thanksgiving Day, Caleb took our son to his family's annual Thanksgiving dinner. While they ate turkey and dressing around the oak table I had eaten at so many times before, I returned to my home with Rebecca and threw as many things as I could fit into laundry baskets, then stuffed them into the back seat of my car. I packed my son's Legos, enough blankets for us to sleep on the floor, and my work clothes, but I left behind anything sentimental. Our wedding photo was on a table, the glass broken. I had thrown it on the ground.

After packing, Rebecca and I ate at a Chinese buffet attached to a casino because it was the only place open in three counties. The future loomed before me like a buffet full of hungry, lonely people.

My favorite photo of Caleb and me is a self-portrait taken on a beach at Ecola State Park on the Oregon coast. We had hiked down a steep trail, stopping to lunch on smoked salmon and bagels, and ended up on a beach. The tide was low, and sand dollars dotted the shore. We scooped them up like prizes. We ran into the surf. We hugged. In the photo we are both smiling, our heads pressed together.

When I look at that photo now, I wonder, *Where are those people? Where did they go?*

Just to the right of us was a cave. I had wanted to go in it, but the tide was coming in, and I was afraid of getting trapped and drowning.

Six months after I left Caleb, I went home to Idaho for the summer. After that I was moving to another state. It was over. The counselor at the domestic violence shelter was proud of me. So many women never get out. I didn't feel proud. I didn't want to get out. I wanted to keep dancing with Caleb, keep sending funny emails to each other, keep cuddling with our son between us.

There are days when I still wish that he would beg me to take him back, promise to change, actually change. This will never happen.

Even if he never hit me again, my body will always remember that fist on my back.

In Idaho, the state where Caleb and I met, where we had our son, I drove the sun-baked streets. There was the apartment where Caleb sat next to me on the couch, nervously wiped his hand across his forehead, and said in a halting voice, "Kelly, I want to marry you."

There was the house where our baby slept in a basket by the bed. When he cried, I nursed him while Caleb draped his arm around my waist, nuzzling his head into my hair.

There was the riverside trail where we pushed the stroller and fantasized over which fancy house we would buy if we ever had any money, where our toddler threw sticks into the river, where Caleb scooped him up and held him upside down while we all giggled.

There was the river where, in winter, our dog slid out onto the ice and into the cold water. Caleb stretched out on the ice and reached his hands out to our dog while I watched, terrified. "I can't lose you both," I screamed.

I wondered if it would have happened if we had stayed in Idaho.

But then there was the house where he first pushed me up against a wall, where he backed me into the corner, where he threw our baby's bouncer. The neighbor watched, worried, from her stoop while he put the broken pieces in the trash can on the curb and I cried in the window.

The same house where my mother took me into the backyard and said, "Listen to me. I have friends who have left their husbands. I have seen it on the other side. It is not better on the other side. Try hard. Try hard before you give up."

I tried so hard.

Contributors' Notes

*Notable Essays and
Literary Nonfiction of 2014*

Contributors' Notes

HILTON ALS is a staff writer at *The New Yorker* and also contributes to *The New York Review of Books*. He is the author of *The Women* and *White Girls*.

ROGER ANGELL, a senior editor and a staff writer, has contributed to *The New Yorker* since 1944 and became a fiction editor in 1956. His writing has appeared in many anthologies, including *The Best American Sports Writing, The Best American Short Stories, The Best American Essays,* and *The Best American Magazine Writing*. His nine books include *The Stone Arbor and Other Stories, A Day in the Life of Roger Angell,* and, most recently, *Let Me Finish.* His baseball books include *The Summer Game, Five Seasons, Late Innings, Season Ticket, Once More Around the Park, A Pitcher's Story,* and *Game Time.* He has won a number of awards for his writing, including a George Polk Award for Commentary, a Kenyon Review Award for Literary Achievement, and the Michael Braude Award for Light Verse, presented by the American Academy of Arts and Letters. He is a Fellow of the American Academy of Arts and Sciences, and in 2011 he was the inaugural winner of the PEN/ ESPN Lifetime Achievement Award for Literary Sports Writing. In 2014, Angell received the J. G. Taylor Spink Award, the highest honor given to writers by the Baseball Hall of Fame. In 2015 he won the National Magazine Award for Essays and Criticism for "This Old Man."

KENDRA ATLEEWORK grew up in the eastern Sierra Nevada mountains and is currently an MFA candidate at the University of Minnesota. Her nonfiction won the AWP Intro Journals Award in 2014, and her essays can be found in *Hayden's Ferry Review, The Pinch Journal, The Morning News,* and *Guernica.* "Charade" is her first publication. She is at work on a book of nonfiction about drought and wildfire in her brazen home state of California.

ISAIAH BERLIN was born in Riga, now the capital of Latvia, in 1909. When he was six, his family moved to Russia; there, in 1917, in Petrograd, he witnessed both revolutions—Social Democratic and Bolshevik. In 1921 he and his parents went to England, and he was educated at St. Paul's School, London, and Corpus Christi College, Oxford. At Oxford he was a Fellow of All Souls, a Fellow of New College, professor of social and political theory, and founding president of Wolfson College. He also held the presidency of the British Academy. His main published works are *Karl Marx, Russian Thinkers, Concepts and Categories, Against the Current, Personal Impressions, The Crooked Timber of Humanity, The Sense of Reality, The Proper Study of Mankind, The Roots of Romanticism, The Power of Ideas, Three Critics of the Enlightenment, Freedom and Its Betrayal, Liberty, The Soviet Mind, Political Ideas in the Romantic Age,* and four volumes of letters, the final volume of which, *Affirming: Letters 1975–1997,* was published in 2015. As an exponent of the history of ideas he was awarded the Erasmus, Lippincott, and Agnelli Prizes; he also received the Jerusalem Prize for his lifelong defense of civil liberties. He died in 1997.

SVEN BIRKERTS'S most recent book, *Changing the Subject: Art and Attention in the Internet Age,* has just been published. He is director of the Bennington Writing Seminars and editor of *AGNI,* based at Boston University. He lives in Arlington, Massachusetts.

TIFFANY BRIERE has received awards from the Rona Jaffe Foundation and Bread Loaf Writers' Conference. She holds a PhD in genetics from Yale University and an MFA in fiction from Bennington College. Her work has appeared in *Tin House.*

JUSTIN CRONIN is the author of the internationally best-selling novels of the Passage Saga (*The Passage, The Twelve,* and *The City of Mirrors*), which have been translated into over forty languages. His other work includes the novels *Mary and O'Neil,* winner of the PEN/Hemingway Award and the Stephen Crane Prize, and *The Summer Guest.* A Distinguished Faculty Fellow in the Humanities at Rice University, he divides his time between Houston, Texas, and Cape Cod, Massachusetts.

MEGHAN DAUM is the author of four books, including the essay collections *My Misspent Youth* and *The Unspeakable: And Other Subjects of Discussion.* She is also the editor of *Selfish, Shallow, and Self-Absorbed: Sixteen Writers on the Decision Not to Have Kids.* Daum has been an opinion columnist at the *Los Angeles Times* since 2005 and has written for numerous magazines, including *The New Yorker,* the *New York Times Magazine, Harper's Magazine,* and

Vogue. A recipient of a 2015 Guggenheim Fellowship, she is an adjunct associate professor in the MFA Writing Program at Columbia University's School of the Arts and has taught at the Aspen Institute's Summer Words festival, the Nebraska Writers' Conference, and CalArts.

ANTHONY DOERR'S most recent book is the novel *All the Light We Cannot See,* which was a finalist for the National Book Award and won the 2015 Pulitzer Prize for fiction. His short fiction has appeared in *The Best American Short Stories,* the *O. Henry Prize Stories, New American Stories,* and *The Scribner Anthology of Contemporary Fiction.* Doerr lives in Boise, Idaho, with his wife and sons.

MALCOLM GLADWELL is a staff writer for *The New Yorker* and the author, most recently, of *David and Goliath: Underdogs, Misfits, and the Art of Battling Giants.*

MARK JACOBSON is a longtime journalist. He has written for a wide variety of magazines over the past forty years, during which time he has been employed by *New York* magazine, *Rolling Stone, Esquire,* the *Village Voice, National Geographic,* and many others. His magazine work served as the basis for the film *American Gangster* and the TV show *Taxi.* His most recent book is *The Lampshade,* the story of a strange and unsettling object found in the aftermath of Hurricane Katrina. He was born and continues to live in New York City.

MARGO JEFFERSON is a Pulitzer Prize–winning critic and the author of *Negroland: A Memoir* and *On Michael Jackson.* She has been a staff writer for the *New York Times* and *Newsweek* and has published in *The Believer, Bookforum, New York* magazine, *The Nation,* the *Washington Post, Gigantic, Grand Street,* and elsewhere. Her essays have been anthologized in *The Inevitable: Contemporary Writers Confront Death, The Best African-American Essays, The Mrs. Dalloway Reader, The Jazz Cadence of American Culture, Black Cool,* and *What My Mother Gave Me.* She teaches in the writing program at Columbia University.

PHILIP KENNICOTT is the art and architecture critic of the *Washington Post* and the winner of the 2013 Pulitzer Prize for criticism. He was a finalist for the Pulitzer for criticism in 2012 and for editorial writing in 2000, as well as a National Magazine Award finalist in 2015 in the Essays and Criticism category. He was nominated for a 2006 Emmy Award and won the CINE Golden Eagle for video work exploring the role of oil money in the politics of Azerbaijan. He is a former contributing editor at the *New Republic,* a regular reviewer for *Gramophone,* and a frequent contributor to *Opera News.*

TIM KREIDER'S first collection of essays was *We Learn Nothing* (2012). His second collection, *I Wrote This Book Because I Love You,* is due out in 2015. He is a frequent contributor to the *New York Times* and *Men's Journal,* among other publications. He was also a cartoonist for the *Baltimore City Paper* from 1997 to 2009. His cartoons are collected in three books: *The Pain—When Will It End?, Why Do They Kill Me?,* and *Twilight of the Assholes.*

KATE LEBO is the author of two cookbooks, *Pie School: Lessons in Fruit, Flour, and Butter* and *A Commonplace Book of Pie.* Her essays and poems have appeared in *New England Review, Best New Poets, Gastronomica, Willow Springs, The Rumpus, Los Angeles Review,* and other publications. She lives in Spokane, Washington, and teaches poetry and food-writing workshops nationally.

JOHN REED is the author of the novels *A Still Small Voice* (2000), *The Whole* (2005), and the SPD bestseller *Snowball's Chance* (2002); *All The World's A Grave: A New Play by William Shakespeare* (2008); and *Tales of Woe* (2010). He holds an MFA from Columbia University. His writing and multimedia have appeared in *Intercourse,* the *Brooklyn Rail, Paper Magazine, Artforum, Bomb Magazine, Playboy, Out Magazine, Art in America,* the PEN Poetry Series, the *Los Angeles Times, The Paris Review, The Believer, The Rumpus, The Daily Beast, Gawker, Slate,* the *Wall Street Journal,* and *ElectricLit,* among others, and he is a frequent contributor to *Vice.* His works have been translated into German, French, Russian, Spanish, Portuguese, Italian, and Korean. He currently teaches at the New School and the New York Arts Program. See JohnReed.org.

ASHRAF H. A. RUSHDY is the Benjamin Waite Professor at Wesleyan University and teaches in the African American Studies Program and the English Department. He is also the university's academic secretary. He is the author of *The Empty Garden* (1992), *Neo-Slave Narratives* (1999), *Remembering Generations* (2001), *American Lynching* (2012), *The End of American Lynching* (2012), and *The Guilted Age: Apologies for the Past* (2015).

DAVID SEDARIS is the author of the books *Barrel Fever, Naked, Holidays on Ice, Me Talk Pretty One Day, Dress Your Family in Corduroy and Denim, When You Are Engulfed in Flames,* and *Squirrel Seeks Chipmunk: A Modest Bestiary.* He is a regular contributor to *The New Yorker,* National Public Radio's *This American Life,* and the BBC. His most recent essay collection is *Let's Explore Diabetes with Owls.*

ZADIE SMITH was born in northwest London in 1975 and divides her time between London and New York. Her first novel, *White Teeth,* was the winner of the Whitbread First Novel Award, the Guardian First Book Award, the James Tait Black Memorial Prize for Fiction, and the Commonwealth Writers' First Book Award. Her second novel, *The Autograph Man,* won the Jewish Quarterly Wingate Literary Prize. Zadie Smith's third novel, *On Beauty,* was shortlisted for the Man Booker Prize and won the Commonwealth Writers' Best Book Award (Eurasia Section) and the Orange Prize for Fiction. Her most recent novel, *NW,* was published in 2012 and has been shortlisted for the Royal Society of Literature Ondaatje Prize and the Women's Prize for Fiction.

Writer, historian, and activist REBECCA SOLNIT is the author of eighteen books about environment, landscape, community, art, politics, hope, and feminism, including two atlases, of San Francisco in 2010 and New Orleans in 2013, *Men Explain Things to Me, The Faraway Nearby, A Paradise Built in Hell: The Extraordinary Communities That Arise in Disaster, A Field Guide to Getting Lost, Wanderlust: A History of Walking,* and *River of Shadows: Eadweard Muybridge and the Technological Wild West* (for which she received a Guggenheim Fellowship, the National Book Critics Circle Award in criticism, and the Lannan Literary Award). A product of the California public education system from kindergarten to graduate school, she is a columnist for *Harper's Magazine.*

CHERYL STRAYED is the author of *Wild, Torch,* and *Tiny Beautiful Things.* Her books have been translated into more than thirty languages around the world. Her essays have been published in *The New York Times Magazine, Vogue, Salon,* and elsewhere and have been selected for inclusion in *The Best American Essays* three times. She lives in Portland, Oregon.

KELLY SUNDBERG'S essays have appeared in *Guernica, Slice, Denver Quarterly, Mid-American Review, The Los Angeles Review, Quarterly West,* and elsewhere. She is a PhD candidate in creative nonfiction at Ohio University, where she is the managing editor of *Brevity* magazine, and she was recently named the 2015 A Room of Her Own Foundation's Courage Fellow.

Notable Essays and Literary Nonfiction of 2014

SELECTED BY ROBERT ATWAN

LAURIE ABRAHAM
    It's Complicated, *Elle*, November.
PEARL ABRAHAM
    For the Sins We Have Committed
    Before You Through Hard-
    Heartedness, *Michigan Quarterly
    Review*, Winter.
ANWAR F. ACCAWI
    Hunger, *The Sun*, October.
ANDRE ACIMAN
    Are You Listening?, *The New
    Yorker*, March 17.
JUDITH ADKINS
    Lingua Familia, *Fourth Genre*,
    Spring.
MARCIA ALDRICH
    Enough, *The Florida Review*, vol.
    38, nos. 1 & 2.
RYAN ALLEN
    Fixing Myself at Broken Kettle,
    North Dakota Quarterly, Spring.
SANDRA ALLEN
    The Sad, Strange, True Story of
    Sandy Allen, the Tallest Woman
    in the World, *BuzzFeed*, July 14.
BETH ALVARADO
    Stars and Moons and Comets, *The
    Sun*, December.
AMY AMOROSO
    Cut Wide Open, *Mount Hope*,
    Spring.

STEPHANIE ANDERSEN
    My Mother's Secret, *Brain, Child*,
    Summer.
SAM ANDERSON-RAMOS
    On Leaving Dove Springs, *Austin
    Chronicle*, August 24.
MOLLY ANTOPOL
    Conflict Resolution, *Southern
    Humanities Review*, vol. 48, no. 1
    (Winter).
JACOB M. APPEL
    Sudden Death: A Eulogy, *Kenyon
    Review Online*, Spring.
MARY ARGUELLES
    Mending Petals, *Bellevue Literary
    Review*, Spring.
CHRIS ARTHUR
    Putting Two and Two
    Together, *New Hibernia Review*,
    Summer.
JABARI ASIM
    Color Him Father:
    Three Reflections, *Solstice*,
    Winter.
ROGER ATWOOD
    Searching for a Head in Nigeria,
    Massachusetts Review, Fall.

MATTHEW JAMES BABCOCK
    My Nazi Dagger, *War, Literature,
    and the Arts*, no. 26.

NICHOLSON BAKER
Dallas Killers Club: How JFK Got Shot, *The Baffler*, no. 25.

ROSECRANS BALDWIN
Learn to Kill in Seven Days or Less, *GQ*, February.

POE BALLANTINE
Even Music and Gold, *The Sun*, November.

PAMELA BALLUCK
Parts of a Chair, *Southeast Review*, vol. 32, no. 1.

IAIN BAMFORTH
The Embodied World, *Threepenny Review*, Winter.

TONY BARNSTONE
Monkey Mind, *Southern California Review*, no. 7.

HELEN BAROLINI
The Crossing, *Southwest Review*, vol. 99, no. 3.

TIM BASCOM
My Mystical Body, *Briar Cliff Review*, no. 26.

ANN BAULEKE
Spinsters, *North American Review*, Summer.

ANN BEATTIE
On Visitors, *American Scholar*, Summer.

S. G. BELKNAP
The Tragic Diet: Food and Finitude, *The Point*, no. 9.

GARY BELSKY
Cab Share with an Infidel, *December*, Fall/Winter.

GEOFFREY BENT
Falling Out of Love with Vertigo, *Boulevard*, Spring.

STEPHEN BENZ
Liminal Wendover, *Superstition Review*, Spring.

EMILY BERNARD
Mother on Earth, *Green Mountains Review*, vol. 27, no. 2.

ANN E. BERTHOFF
Homiletic Silence and the Revival of Conversation, *Sewanee Review*, Fall.

CHELSEA BIONDOLILLO
En Memoriam, *River Teeth*, Spring.

EULA BISS
Vampires and Vaccines, *The Believer*, September.

ESTER BLOOM
One Way to Shut Her Up, *Dogwood*, no. 13.

WILL BOAST
Pain, *Virginia Quarterly Review*, Winter.

KIM CHENG BOEY
Rambling on My Mind, *Manoa*, vol. 26, no. 1.

BELLE BOGGS
Imaginary Children, *Ecotone*, Spring/Summer.

TANYA BOMSTA
Erosion, *Gettysburg Review*, Spring.

JOE BONOMO
34 of 86 stories, *Passages North*, Winter.

MARC BOOKMAN
Executed Against the Judgment of 12 Jurors, *theatlantic.com*, January 6.

BRIGITTE BOWERS
Attempted Homicide, *Under the Gum Tree*, October.

ROBERT BOYERS
My Pleasure, My Pleasures, *Normal School*, Spring.

SVETLANA BOYM
Like New: A Tale of Immigrant Objects, *Five Points*, vol. 16, no. 2.

WILLIAM BRADLEY
Marked, *Cleaver Magazine*, December.

MARK BRAZAITIS
Locked in to Life, *The Sun*, April.

CATHERINE A. BRERETON
Trance, *Slice*, no. 14.

ELLEN BROOKS
Dayenu, *Blue Lyra Review,* Spring.

FLEDA BROWN
Strong Brown God, *New Letters,*
vol. 80, no. 2.

ROBERT S. BRUNK
Selling Everything, *Iowa Review,*
Spring.

FRANK BURES
What Price Experience? *The
Rotarian,* March.

BENJAMIN BURGHOLZER
Don't Go Over Your Hipboots,
Little Patuxent Review, Summer.

STEPHEN BURT
"Like," *American Poetry Review,*
January/February.

AMY BUTCHER
Reenacting, *Iowa Review,* Winter.

HARMONY BUTTON
Dear Spider(s), *Chicago Quarterly
Review,* no. 17.

SATYA DOYLE BYOCK
Gone Astray, *Oregon Humanities,*
Fall/Winter.

GARNETTE CADOGAN
Due North, *Virginia Quarterly
Review* (online), September 30.

DREW CALVERT
A Free Life Is Made with Words,
Pleiades, Summer.

RON CAPPS
On the Ragged Edge, *American
Interest,* Summer.

H. G. CARRILLO
Splaining Yourself, *Conjunctions,*
no. 62.

DOUG PAUL CASE
The Only Boy in Indiana, *Hobart,*
no. 15.

MARCIA CAVELL
Waiting, *Chicago Quarterly Review,*
no. 17.

ALISON CHAPMAN
The Paradise Within, *PMS,* no. 13.

KELLY CHASTAIN
Diego Forever, *Isthmus,* Spring.

JAMES M. CHESBRO
The Return of the Prodigal
Father, *Spiritus,* Fall.

CAITLYN CHRISTENSEN
Sinkholes, *Columbia,* no. 52.

JILL CHRISTMAN
The Avocado, *Fourth Genre,*
Spring.

STEVEN CHURCH
Crown and Shoulder, *Passages
North,* no. 35 (Winter).

MATTHEW CLARK
Fully Automatic, *Indiana Review,*
Summer.

TA-NEHISI COATES
The Case for Reparations, *The
Atlantic,* July/August.

ANDREW D. COHEN
Looking at Sheila, *Alaska
Quarterly Review,* Spring/Summer.

GARNETT KILBERG COHEN
Scrambled, *Gettysburg Review,*
Winter.

JEREMY COLLINS
Basic Composition, *Chattahoochee
Review,* Spring.

MARY COLLINS
The Coverless Book, *Solstice,*
Summer/Fall.

AUDREY COLOMBE
Burning Down the Schoolhouse,
Main Street Rag, Winter.

JOAN CONNOR
Bloodlines, *Hotel Amerika,* Winter.

STEVEN CONNOR
Spelling Things Out, *New Literary
History,* Spring.

PATRICK CONWAY
How It's Done: A Criminal
Defense Investigator at Work, *Post
Road,* no. 27.

JOHN COTTER
Losing Music, *Open Letters
Monthly,* July.

MARIAN CROTTY
Love at a Distance, *Gettysburg Review,* Autumn.

KATIE CROUCH
To Bloom, to Bust, to Blaze, *ZYZZYVA,* Spring/Summer.

JOHN CROWLEY
Time After Time, *Lapham's Quarterly,* Fall.

JAMES CUNO
Culture War: The Case Against Repatriating Museum Art, *Foreign Affairs,* November/December.

MARC DANZIGER
Fathers and Sons, *Proud To Be,* no. 3.

RENEE E. D'AOUST
Harry & Dancer, *Notre Dame Review,* no. 37.

CHAD DAVIDSON
Not Taking Pictures, *Five Points,* vol. 16, no. 1.

DAWN DAVIES
Don't Like It Too Much, *River Styx,* Fall.

CAMAS DAVIS
Human Principles, *Ecotone,* Fall.

CAROL ANN DAVIS
On Practice, School Buses, Hummingbirds, Rumi, and Being Led, *AGNI,* no. 79.

ERIC DAY
Raised by Trees, *Catamaran,* Fall.

HILARY DEAN
Vocational Rehabilitation, *Event,* vol. 43, no. 3.

SARAH DEMING
Colorless, Odorless, Tasteless, *Threepenny Review,* Spring.

JAQUIRA DENEVI
My Mother and Mercy, *The Sun,* August.

TIMOTHY DENEVI
John the Baptist, *Gulf Coast,* Summer/Fall.

LOUIS A. DI LEO
The Polar Bear Ethic, *Journal of Environmental Law and Litigation,* vol. 28, no. 3.

CHRIS DOMBROWSKI
Three, *The Sun,* July.

KATIE DONOVAN
The Splitting, *New Hibernia Review,* Autumn.

BRIAN DOYLE
Sam & Louis, *Georgia Review,* Summer.

JACQUELINE DOYLE
Who's Your Stepdaddy? *Jabberwock Review,* Winter.

MONICA DRAKE
Where Nothing Bad Can Happen, *Rumpus,* February 17.

K. E. DUFFIN
Castle Hill, *AGNI,* no. 80.

MARTHA GRACE DUNCAN
My Father and the Hair Grafter, *Tampa Review,* no. 47/48.

LENA DUNHAM
Difficult Girl, *The New Yorker,* September 1.

MARY BESS DUNN
Window Seat, *Pembroke Magazine,* no. 46.

KATHERINE DYKSTRA
Like Held Breath, *Crab Orchard Review,* Winter/Spring.

DEREK DYSON
Letter from Ferguson, *This Land,* December 15.

LAURIE EASTER
Crack My Heart Wide Open, *Rumpus,* October 9.

XUJUN EBERLEIN
Clouds and Rain over Three Gorges, *American Literary Review,* March.

MARK EDMUNDSON
A Paint-Factory Education, *Virginia Quarterly Review,* Fall.

JOHN M. EDWARDS
Kentucky Fried Moa, *Dave's Travel Corner,* July.

DAVE EGGERS
The Dentist on the Ridge, *McSweeney's,* no. 48.

BARBARA EHRENREICH
Terror Cells, *The Baffler,* no. 26.

OKLA ELLIOTT
Cinnamon or Crocodiles, Romanticized Suffering, and the Productivity of Error: A Polymorphous Essay-in-Fragments, *Chattahoochee Review,* Spring.

EZEKIEL J. EMANUEL
Why I Hope to Die at 75, *The Atlantic,* October.

PAMELA EMIGH-MURPHY
Seizure, *Little Patuxent Review,* Winter.

JOSEPH EPSTEIN
Death Takes No Holiday, *Commentary,* June.

BRIAN EVENSON
The Particulars, *Conjunctions,* no. 63.

THOMAS FARBER
Writing from a Distance, *Catamaran,* Fall.

ANGELA FEATHERSTONE
God Said No, *Gargoyle,* no. 61.

MELISSA FEBOS
All of Me, *Kenyon Review,* Fall.
Call My Name, *Prairie Schooner,* Spring.

MATTHEW FERRENCE
Exoskeleton, *Gettysburg Review,* Spring.

MELISSA FERRONE
Touch, *The Pinch,* Spring.

GARY FINCKE
The Physics of Desire, *Kenyon Review Online,* Winter.

JONATHAN FINK
The Pursuit of D. B. Cooper, *Witness,* Spring.

NICK FLYNN
Whose Dream Is This? *Columbia,* no. 52.

TERRANCE FLYNN
Having Faith, *Southern Indiana Review,* Fall.

RICHARD FORD
Magic, *Threepenny Review,* Spring.

ROBERT LONG FOREMAN
Dirty Laundry, *Fourth Genre,* Spring.

JOSHUA FOSTER
Bring on the Spins, *Tin House,* vol. 16, no. 2.

PATRICIA FOSTER
Awakening, *Antioch Review,* Fall.

ALASTAIR FOWLER
First Phrases, *Yale Review,* April.

AMELIA FOWLER
Space and Time, *Cleaver Magazine,* September.

PAULA FOX
Summer Losses, *Yale Review,* July.

H. E. FRANCIS
Prologue to a Life of Storywriting, *Southwest Review,* vol. 99, no. 3.

JOEY FRANKLIN
Houseguest, *Mid-American Review,* vol. 35, no. 1.

STEVE FRIEDMAN
Citi Bikes Changed My Life, *Bicycling,* August.

DAVID A. FRYXELL
Selfie Control, *Desert Exposure,* January.

AJA GABEL
The Sparrows in France, *Kenyon Review,* Fall.

MONA GABLE
The Hugo Problem, *Los Angeles Magazine,* April.

NICHOLAS GAMSO
On Marjorie, *Hotel Amerika,* Winter.

J. MALCOLM GARCIA
Stabbing Johnny, *Apple Valley Review*, Fall.

KENNETH GARCIA
Diego and Our Lady of the Wilderness, *Gettysburg Review*, Summer.

NATASHA GARDNER
Walking Scarred, *5280*, May.

PHILIP GARRISON
Before Long, in a While, *Southwest Review*, vol. 99, no. 2.

ROXANE GAY
Not Here to Make Friends, *BuzzFeed*, January 3.

CHRISTINE GELINEAU
Courtesy of the Gravedigger, *New York Times Opinionator*, December 21.

LYNELL GEORGE
Lost Angelena, *Southern California Review*, no. 7.

PHILIP GERARD
The Afterlives of the Dead, *Our State*, August.

RACHEL KAADZI GHANSAH
We a Badd People, *Virginia Quarterly Review*, Summer.

GARY GILDNER
How I Married Michelle, *Southern Review*, Winter.

CHRISTINA MARSDEN GILLIS
Waiting for the Dark, *Southwest Review*, vol. 99, no. 2.

AMANDA GIRACCA
Within This Kingdom, *Fourth Genre*, Spring.

ALBERT GOLDBARTH
Two Characters in Search of an Essay, *Georgia Review*, Summer.

MICHELLE GOLDBERG
What Is a Woman? *The New Yorker*, August 4.

ANNE GOLDMAN
Travels with *Jane Eyre*, *Georgia Review*, Fall.

STEPHEN GOODWIN
Best, Tom, *Virginia Quarterly Review*, Fall.

ADAM GOPNIK
Word Magic, *The New Yorker*, May 26.

EMILY FOX GORDON
Barnacle, *Colorado Review*, Spring.

MICHAEL GRAFF
Up, and Away, *Washingtonian*, April.

CHRISTINE GRANADOS
True Colors, *Texas Monthly*, May.

ADAM GREEN
Late or Never? *Vogue*, April.

LINNIE GREENE
Our Doubles, Ourselves: *Twin Peaks* and My Summer at the Black Lodge, *Hobart Web*, December 12.

CYNTHIA B. GREER
Doris and the Dolls, *Little Patuxent Review*, Summer.

ALLISON GRUBER
A Music in the Head, *Literary Review*, Summer.

PENNY GUISINGER
Coming Out, *Fourth Genre*, Fall.

MARGARET MORGANROTH GULLETTE
Euthanasia as a Caregiving Fantasy in the Era of the New Longevity, *Age, Culture, Humanities*, no. 1.

DEBRA GWARTNEY
Didn't Get It, *Prairie Schooner*, Summer.

JOHN HALES
Seeing, and Believing, *Hudson Review*, Winter.

DONALD HALL
Dr. Dr. Dr. Dr. Dr. Dr. Dr. Dr. Dr. Dr., *Narrative*, November 10.

DAVID HAMILTON
Glenning the Thicket, Thicketing the Glen, *December*, Fall/Winter.

PATRICIA HAMPL
Montaigne's Lute, *Gulf Coast,*
Winter/Spring.

LEE HANCOCK
That Bleak Rise Near Waco,
Consequence, no. 6.

SILAS HANSEN
An Annotated Guide to My
OKCupid Profile, *Normal School,*
Spring.

HEATHER HANSMAN
Lighthouse for Sale, *Medium.com,*
December.

KERRY HARDIE
Aftermath, *New Hibernia Review,*
Spring.

KATHRIN HARRIS
The Dolphin Lady of Siesta Key,
Post Road, no. 27.

JIM HARRISON
Gramps le Fou, *Brick,* no. 92.

MILES HARVEY
At the Grave of Sadie Thorpe,
New Ohio Review, Spring.

DANNY HEITMAN
The Boyish Side of Mencken,
Humanities, November/
December.

ROBIN HEMLEY
Celebrating Russian Federation
Day with Immanuel Kant,
Conjunctions, no. 62.

DAWN HERRERA-HELPHAND
Into the Cave, *The Point,* no. 9.

HENDRIK HERTZBERG
You're Wrong, You're Wrong,
You're Definitely Wrong, and
I'm Probably Wrong, Too,
New Republic, November 24/
December 8.

JENNY GROPP HESS
Notes on Attempting to
Understand Human Hands,
Denver Quarterly, vol. 48,
no. 2.

KARRIE HIGGINS
Strange Flowers, *Manifest-Station,*
November 11.

KATHLEEN HILL
Portrait, *Ploughshares Omnibus,*
no. 2.

JEN HIRTT
Not Less than 1,000 Bottles for
Horseradish, *Ninth Letter,* Spring/
Summer.

BONNIE-SUE HITCHCOCK
Every Third Week, *Sonora Review,*
no. 64/65.

EDWARD HOAGLAND
On Loneliness, *American Scholar,*
Spring.

LINDA HOGAN
Coming Home, *Orion,* May/
June/July/August.

MING HOLDEN
Lenin, *Arts & Letters,* Spring.

EVA HOLLAND
Why We Play, *SBNation,* June 25.

B. J. HOLLARS
The Year of the Great Forgetting,
Hayden's Ferry Review, Spring/
Summer.

JENNY HOLLOWELL
The End of the End: An
Evolution of Faith, in Five Films,
Bright Wall/Dark Room, February.

JIM HOLT
The Grand Illusion, *Lapham's
Quarterly,* Fall.

ANN HOOD
Second Skin, *Chattahoochee Review,*
Fall/Winter.

PATRICIA HORVATH
Envy, *New Ohio Review,* Fall.

GAIL HOSKING
Ode to a Surrogate's Grace, *Slab,*
no. 9.

MOLLY HOWES
Home Waters, *Tampa Review,*
no. 47/48.

PAT C. HOY II
Warring with Words, *Sewanee
Review,* Spring.

STEFFAN HRUBY
New Age Atheist, *Antioch Review,*
Winter.

EWA HRYNIEWICZ-YARBROUGH
Translation, *Threepenny Review*,
Winter.
SONYA HUBER
The Lava Lamp of Pain, *Rumpus*,
December 28.
CHRISTINE HUFFARD
Octopus Lady, *Catamaran*, Winter.
ZAC HUG
Whatever It Is, *Event*, vol. 43, no. 3.
BARBARA HURD
Listening to the Same River
Twice: Theme and Variation,
Prairie Schooner, Spring.
ALLEGRA HYDE
Banjo in the Backpack, *Grist*, no. 7.

MIKE INGRAM
A Curious Indifference, *North
American Review*, Spring.
PICO IYER
The Beauty of the Package,
Granta, Spring.

LESLIE JAMISON
52 Blue, *The Atavist*, August.
MYRA JEHLEN
On How, to Become Knowledge,
Cognition Needs Beauty, *Raritan*,
Summer.
ALEXANDRA JOHNSON
Twice Eggs, *Ploughshares Omnibus*,
no. 2.
FENTON JOHNSON
Power and Obedience,
Appalachian Heritage, Winter.
ALEX R. JONES
The Big Breakfast, *Harvard
Review*, no. 45.
MARTHA S. JONES
Who Here Is a Negro, *Michigan
Quarterly Review*, Winter.
MARY JONES
The Suicide Disease, *Alaska
Quarterly Review*, Fall/Winter.
ANNA JOURNEY
The Goliath Jazz, *Prairie Schooner*,
Winter.

HEIDI JULAVITS
Diagnose This, *Harper's Magazine*,
April.
TOM JUNOD
Everything We Think We Know
About Mass Shooters Is Wrong,
Esquire, October.

PAUL KALANITHI
How Long Have I Got Left? *New
York Times*, January 26.
JILL N. KANDEL
Paying the Piper, *Missouri Review*,
Spring.
SARAH KASBEER
Is It Cancer? *Salon.com*, April 26.
SAM KEAN
How Einstein Became a Celebrity,
Humanities, May/June.
JOHN E. KEATS
Dream of the Butcher's
Daughter, *Under the Sun*, Summer.
GARRET KEIZER
Reformed, *Virginia Quarterly
Review*, Summer.
CHRISTOPHER KEMPF
Bad Faith: The Worst First
Date of an OKCupid
Moderator, *Michigan Quarterly
Review*, Spring.
THOMAS E. KENNEDY
How James Joyce Changed My
Life, *New Letters*, vol. 80, no. 2/3.
JON KERSTETTER
Learning to Breathe, *Normal
School*, Fall.
HARRISON SCOTT KEY
How I Became a Famous Writer,
Oxford American, November 20.
HEATHER KING
Save All of Yourself for the
Wedding, *Portland*, Winter.
STEPHEN KING
The Ring, *Tin House*, vol. 15,
no. 3.
PAUL KINGSNORTH
In the Black Chamber, *Orion*,
March/April.

MICHAEL KINSLEY
Have You Lost Your Mind? *The New Yorker*, April 28.

NORA KIPNIS
Survival in the Preparatory Environment: A Field Guide, *Southeast Review*, vol. 32, no. 1.

MELISSA KIRSCH
Most Helpful Critical Review, *Southwest Review*, vol. 99, no. 4.

JUDITH KITCHEN
Tenors, *Harvard Review*, no. 46.

LISA KNOPP
Still Life with Peaches, *Georgia Review*, Spring.

WAYNE KOESTENBAUM
Odd Secrets of the Line, *Tin House*, July 28.

ELIZABETH KOLBERT
Stone Soup, *The New Yorker*, July 28.

JACQUELINE KOLOSOV
Wherefore, *Under the Sun*, Summer.

CAROLYN KRAUS
A Thing with Feathers, *1966: A Journal of Creative Nonfiction*, vol. 2, no. 1.

JIM KRUSOE
Traffic, *ZYZZYVA*, Fall.

KATYA KULIK
Annihilation Tango, *Cut Bank*, no. 81.

ALLEN KURZWEIL
Whipping Boy, *The New Yorker*, November 17.

AVIYA KUSHNER
A Duck with One Leg, *Gettysburg Review*, Spring.

OLIVIA LAING
The Magic Box, *Granta*, no. 126 (Winter).

HAFEEZ LAKHANI
If We Show That We Like They Make More Mainga, *Southern Review*, Autumn.

RICK LAMPLUGH
How Death Feeds Life, *Gold Man Review*, no. 3.

JOHN LANCASTER
Shut Up and Eat, *The New Yorker*, November 3.

ERICA LANGSTON
Landfall, *Appalachian Heritage*, Fall.

LISA LANSER-ROSE
Turnpike Psycho, *Florida Review*, vol. 38, nos. 1 & 2.

LANCE LARSEN
I Am Thinking of Pablo Casals, *Southern Review*, Spring.

JONATHAN V. LAST
Virtues, Past & Present, *Weekly Standard*, November 10.

JENNIFER LATSON
Anatomy of a Murderer, *Briar Cliff Review*, no. 26.

SYDNEY LEA
Black Marks, *River Teeth*, Fall.

BRITT LEACH
An Inability to Control Objects Around Me, *River Teeth*, Fall.

JEFFREY B. LEAK
Memories of Brooklyn, *Charlotte*, September.

CHRISTOPHER J. LEE
Mourning Mandela, *Transition*, December.

FRANCES LEFKOWITZ
Dry Season, *Catamaran*, Summer.

DAVID LEGAULT
On Bridges, *Wake: Great Lakes Thought and Culture*, April 9.

LAWRENCE LENHART
Give Me That for Nothing, Now I Am Going Away, *Wag's Review*, no. 19.

SARAH K. LENZ
Dad's Kitchen Table, *South Dakota Review*, Summer.

HENRY W. LEUNG
Quitting the Box, *Crab Orchard Review*, Winter/Spring.

PHILLIS LEVIN
Four Tesserae, *Southwest Review,*
vol. 99, no. 3.

E. J. LEVY
Bread, *Normal School,* Spring.

J. D. LEWIS
Heat, *Hayden's Ferry Review,*
Spring/Summer.

S. LI
Criticism and Self-Criticism,
Kenyon Review Online, Fall.

TAO LIN
Final Fantasy III, *Granta,* no. 127.

ALPHONSO LINGIS
Being Seen, Being Faced, *Denver
Quarterly,* vol. 48, no. 4.

BRANDON LINGLE
Keeping Pace, *Guernica,* August 1.

GORDON LISH
The Boys on the Block, *Harper's
Magazine,* January.

MEL LIVATINO
The Lost Friend, *Under the Sun,*
Summer.

SANDRA TSING LOH
After the Affair, *Harper's Bazaar,*
May.

PRISCILLA LONG
What Killed My Sister, *American
Scholar,* Spring.

ARTHUR LONGWORTH
Wheeled Fortress, *PEN America,*
no. 17.

PHILLIP LOPATE
Early Memories of a Class Traitor,
Tin House, vol. 15, no. 3.

JOE MACKALL
Reflections of a Moderately
Disturbed Grandfather, *River
Teeth,* Spring.

PATRICK MADDEN
Aborted Essay on Nostalgia,
Tusculum, no. 10.

BETHANY MAILE
Anything Will Be Easy After This,
Normal School, Fall.

PATRICK MAINELLI
But We Loved It All the Same,
Fourth Genre, Fall.

ANTONIA MALCHIK
Reclaimed Ambition, *Full Grown
People,* July 15.

EMILY ST. JOHN MANDEL
Notes on Sontag, *Humanities,*
September/October.

SARAH MANGUSO
Short Days, *Paris Review,* Winter.

VYSHALI MANIVANNAN
The Meaning of a Machete,
Consequence, no. 6.

ALEX MAR
Sky Burial, *Oxford American,*
Fall.

CLANCY MARTIN
The Marriage Paradox, *The
Chronicle,* February 28.

LEE MARTIN
Heart Sounds, *River Teeth,* Fall.

BOBBIE ANN MASON
Reading Between the Lines,
Virginia Quarterly Review,
Spring.

PATRICIA MARX
A Tale of a Tub, *The New Yorker,*
February 3.

ALEXANDRIA MARZANO-LESNEVICH
The Trouble with Knives, *Iowa
Review,* Fall.

DAVID MASELLO
Reasons for Looking, *Fine Art
Connoisseur,* April.

HILARY MASTERS
My Father's Mistress, *Sewanee
Review,* Winter.

KHALED MATTAWA
Repatriation: A Libya Memoir,
Massachusetts Review, Winter.

JOYCE MAYNARD
We Regret to Inform You . . . ,
New York Observer, April 7.

COLIN MCADAM
The OA, *Harper's Magazine,*
February.

JOSH MCCALL
A Love of Food, *Southern Review,*
Winter.

J. B. MCCRAY
Blue Magic, *The Sun,* April.

GARY L. MCDOWELL
An Eye That Never Closes in
Sleep: A Nightbook, *Green
Mountains Review,* vol. 27, no. 2.

DAVID MCGLYNN
On Wisconsin, *Yale Review,*
October.

HEAL MCKNIGHT
Traffic, *PMS,* no. 13.

JOHN MCPHEE
Elicitation, *The New Yorker,* April 7.

LA TANYA MCQUEEN
Violin Dreams, *Grist,* no. 7.

SUKETU MEHTA
Nina, *Harper's Magazine,*
December.

EDIE MEIDAV
The Dead Ones, *ZYZZYVA,*
Spring/Summer.

MARISA MELTZER
The Last Feminist Taboo, *Elle,*
January.

SARAH MENKEDICK
Living on the Hyphen, *Oxford
American,* Fall.

MORTON A. MEYERS
Lifelong Lessons, *Mayo Clinic
Proceedings,* September.

BILLY MIDDLETON
The Fear of Secondhand Guilt,
River Styx, no. 91/92.

JACK MILES
Why God Will Not Die, *The
Atlantic,* December.

MIKE MILEY
Reading Wallace Reading, *Smart
Set,* August 17.

MICHAEL MILBURN
Home Grown, *Chicago Quarterly
Review,* no. 17.

BEN MILLER
Village Bakery, *New England
Review,* vol. 35, no. 2.

JIM MINICK
Drowning Dear, *Oxford American,*
Spring.

THOMAS MIRA Y LOPEZ
Etiology, *Cut Bank,* no. 81.

RYAN MITCHELL
Ashley and I, *Under the Gum Tree,*
April.

HAROON MOGHUL
The Late Great Mosque of
Cordoba, *Tikkun,* Winter.

DAVE MONDY
How Things Break, *Iowa Review,*
Winter.

DEBRA MONROE
On the Down-Low, *Florida Review,*
vol. 38, nos. 1 & 2.

ANDER MONSON
The Problem with Memory,
Denver Quarterly, vol. 48, no. 3.

SARAH FAWN MONTGOMERY
Syndicated Silence, *Southeast
Review,* vol. 32, no. 1.

ANGELA MORALES
Bloodyfeathers, *Chattahoochee
Review,* Fall/Winter.

DIONISIA MORALES
Homing Instincts, *Hunger
Mountain,* no. 18.

SUSAN MOREHOUSE
What You Said; What I Meant,
New Ohio Review, Fall.

C. E. MORGAN
My Friend, Nothing Is in Vain,
Oxford American, Spring.

JAN MORRIS
Keep Smiling, *American Scholar,*
Summer.

MERRITT MOSELEY
Evening, All, *New England Review,*
vol. 34, no. 3/4.

ELIZABETH MOSIER
Believers, *Cleaver Magazine,* June.

LAURA MULLEN
Ghost Story, *Witness,* Spring.

ALEX MYERS
Just Like . . . , *Hobart Web,*
January 9.

ODED NA'AMAN
Mortal Risks, *Boston Review,*
March/April.
DAVID NAIMON
Third Ear, *Fourth Genre,* Spring.
MARA NASELLI
On Being a Mother, *Kenyon Review,* Summer.
NICK NEELY
Slow Flame, *Harvard Review Online,* April 22.
CHRISTINA NETTLES
Death of an Independent Bookstore, *PMS,* no. 13.
MAUD NEWTON
America's Ancestry Craze, *Harper's Magazine,* June.
CHRISTINA NICHOL
Infinite Village, *Subtropics,* Fall/Winter.
JAY BARON NICORVO
Jesus Was a Surfer, *Ploughshares,* Fall.
The Miracle of Mentors, *Poets & Writers,* January/February.
AMY NOLAN
My Mother's Hips, *Ruminate,* Summer.
JAMES NOLAN
I'll Be Watching You, *Boulevard,* Spring.
NANCY J. NORDENSON
Two-Part Invention, *Harvard Divinity Bulletin,* Summer/Autumn.

JOYCE CAROL OATES
The Childhood of the Reader, *Conjunctions,* no. 63.
PEGGY O'BRIEN
Telling the Time with Emily Dickinson, *Massachusetts Review,* Fall.
COLETTE O'CONNOR
Bruno in the Afternoon, *Iron Horse Literary Review,* vol. 16, no. 6.
JOE OESTREICH
The Botch Job, *Creative Nonfiction,* Fall.

MEGAN O'GIEBLYN
Hell: The New Strategy for Dealing with Damnation, *The Point,* no. 9.
KEN OLSEN
Pain's Addiction, *American Legion,* April.
STEPHEN ORNES
Archimedes on the Fence, *The Last Word on Nothing,* May 23.
RANDY OSBORNE
All Sorts of Things and Weather, Taken in Together, *Full Grown People,* February 27.

GEORGE PACKER
Cheap Words, *The New Yorker,* February 17/24.
LARRY I. PALMER
The Haircut, *New England Review,* vol. 35, no. 1.
ADRIANA PARAMO
Un Cabron in Kuwait, *Columbia,* no. 52.
PATRICIA PARK
How to Run a Supermarket, *Fourth Genre,* Spring.
LEE PATTON
Howling Grounds and Scorched Earth, *Under the Sun,* Summer.
ALEXANDRIA PEARY
Holes and Walls, *New England Review,* vol. 35, no. 3.
RACHEL PECKHAM
Graven Images, *Southern Indiana Review,* Fall.
APRIL BLEVINS PEJIC
A History We Can Live With, *Arcadia,* Fall.
DANNY PENNY
A Model Camp, *Slice,* no. 15.
JED PERL
Liberals Against Art, *New Republic,* August 25.
ANNE HELEN PETERSEN
Confidently Yours, *The Believer,* May.
PAMELA PETRO
Flow, *Slab,* no. 9.

CARL PHILLIPS
Foliage, *Kenyon Review,* Fall.
CLAIRE PHILLIPS
Hanging from the Chandeliers, *Black Clock,* no. 19.
MARK PHILLIPS
Songs, *Notre Dame Magazine,* Autumn.
JOHN PICARD
At the Creation Museum, *North Dakota Quarterly,* Winter.
CECILIA PINTO
Cups, *New Ohio Review,* Spring.
MIYA PLEINES
These Orbits, Crossing, *1996: A Journal of Creative Nonfiction,* vol. 2, no. 1.
ARTHUR PLOTNIK
Wrong Turn, *Creative Nonfiction,* Fall.
JAY PONTERI
In Defense of Navel-Gazing, *Oregon Humanities Review,* Spring.
LIZA PORTER
Labyrinth, *Passages North,* no. 35.
NICK FRANCIS POTTER
Debbie, *Parcel,* Fall/Winter.
MELISSA PRITCHARD
On Bibliomancy, Anthropodermic Bibliopegy, and the Eating Papers; or Proust's Porridge, *Conjunctions,* no. 63.
JOHN PROCTOR
The Question of Influence, *Normal School,* Fall.
JEDEDIAH PURDY
The Accidental Neoliberal, *n+1,* no. 19.
LIA PURPURA
Metaphor Studies, *Harvard Review,* no. 45.

JONATHAN RAUCH
The Real Roots of Midlife Crisis, *The Atlantic,* December.
ROBERT REBEIN
A Fire on the Moon, *Ruminate,* Summer.

DEE REDFEARN
Paper Cut, *North Dakota Quarterly,* Winter.
JOHN JULIUS REEL
My Darlings: An Autobiographical Essay, *Human Life Review,* Spring.
ARNOLD RELMAN
On Breaking One's Neck, *New York Review of Books,* February 6.
EMILY RICH
Jailbait, *The Pinch,* Fall.
FRANK RICH
Nothing You Think Matters Today Will Matter the Same Way Tomorrow, *New York,* October 20/November 2.
DAN RILEY
I'm Only into Jean-George's Early Stuff, *GQ.com,* April.
SUZANNE ROBERTS
The Same Story, *Creative Nonfiction,* Fall.
TARA ROBERTS
The Smallest of the Small, *Bayou,* no. 61.
ROXANA ROBINSON
The Warrior and the Writer, *War, Literature, and the Arts,* no. 26.
JOHN G. RODWAN, JR.
Greetings from Detroit, *Belt Magazine,* April 4.
JAMES SILAS ROGERS
Speed Graphic: November 2013, *Still Point Arts Quarterly,* Winter.
LEE ANN RORIPAUGH
Loop-de-Loop, *South Dakota Review,* Summer.
DANIEL ASA ROSE
Am I Hurting You, Dear? *New York Observer,* November 21.
JOANNA ROSE
The Thing with Feathers, *Oregon Humanities Review,* Spring.
NATANIA ROSENFELD
On Being Ashamed; Or, Shit, Race, and Death, *Michigan Quarterly Review,* Winter.

JIM ROSS
This Is How I Post, *Morning News,*
May 28.
ALLIE ROWBOTTON
World of Blue, *Hunger Mountain,*
no. 18.
ELIZABETH ROYTE
The Remains of the Night,
Medium.com, January.
NORMAN RUSH
On Nudity, *Granta,* no. 126.
KENT RUSSELL
Enforcers, *n+1,* no. 20.
KATIE RYDER
Indian Lake, *The Believer,*
January.

OLIVER SACKS
The Mental Life of Plants and
Worms, Among Others, *New York
Review of Books,* April 24.
DAVID SAMUELS
Justin Timberlake Has a Cold,
n+1, no. 20.
SCOTT LORING SANDERS
My Father, *Creative Nonfiction,*
Fall.
SCOTT RUSSELL SANDERS
Hooks Baited with Darkness,
Daedalus, Winter.
ANDREW SANTELLA
All in Due Time, *Notre Dame
Magazine,* Autumn.
MARIN SARDY
A Shapeless Thief, *Missouri
Review,* Summer.
EVA SAULITIS
Wild Darkness, *Orion,* March/
April.
ANITA SAWYER
Good Humor, *Southern Humanities
Review,* vol. 48, no. 1 (Winter).
ROGER SCHMIDT
To What Shall I Compare This
Life? *Raritan,* Spring.
RICHARD SCHMITT
Crossroads, *North American
Review,* Summer.

JL SCHNEIDER
Unculting Ayn Rand, *Boulevard,*
Fall.
CANDY SCHULMAN
Opening the Family's Vaults, *The
Forward,* July 4.
KATHRYN SCHULZ
Final Forms, *The New Yorker,*
April 7.
A. O. SCHWARTZ
You Must Remember This,
New York Times Magazine,
December 14.
LYNNE SHARON SCHWARTZ
Letters from Robben Island,
Denver Quarterly, vol. 48, no. 2.
STEVEN SCHWARTZ
Principal's Office, *Normal School,*
Fall.
RION AMILCAR SCOTT
The Etiquette of Police Brutality:
An Autopsy, *As It Ought to Be,*
August 14.
ROY SCRANTON
The Terror of the New, *Sierra
Nevada Review,* no. 25.
ANDREW D. SCRIMGEOUR
Scribbling in the Margins, *New
York Times,* February 2.
MOLLY SEALE
Illness, *Hotel Amerika,* Winter.
DAVID SEARCY
Still Life Painting, *Paris Review,*
Fall.
ROBERT SEIDMAN
Sports Fanaticism: An Insider's
Report, *Southwest Review,* vol. 99,
no. 2.
FRANCES STEAD SELLERS
The Long Way Home, *Washington
Post Magazine,* September 14.
HEATHER SELLERS
Breathless, *Brevity,* January.
LYNDA SEXSON
Implicit Tree, *Image,* no. 81.
DAN SHANAHAN
To Be Unfathered: An Ode, *North
Dakota Quarterly,* Winter.

ANIS SHIVANI
A Manifesto Against Authors Writing for Free, *Boulevard,* Fall.

JAN SHOEMAKER
Tenebrae, *Colorado Review,* Summer.

DAVID SHRIBMAN
Why We Love Sports, *Notre Dame Magazine,* Summer.

JASON SHULTS
Finer Than Prayer, *Carolina Quarterly,* Summer.

GREG SIEGEL
A Decent Interval, *Cabinet,* November.

CHARLES SIMIC
The Prisoner of History, *New York Review of Books,* August 14.

WILLIAM H. SIMON
Rethinking Privacy, *Boston Review,* September/October.

PATSY SIMS
No Twang of Conscience Whatever, *Oxford American,* Fall.

PAUL SKENAZY
The World Left Behind, *Chicago Quarterly Review,* no. 17.

R. D. SKILLINGS
M'Dear, *Notre Dame Review,* no. 37.

DAVID SKINNER
The Rise of Cool, *Humanities,* July/August.

JEFFREY SKINNER
Religio Scriptor, *Yale Review,* July.

FLOYD SKLOOT
Let the Dark Come Upon You, *Boulevard,* Fall.

SARAH SMARSH
Poor Teeth, *Aeon,* October 23.

JODY SMILING
Through the Rockies, *Prism,* Winter.

ALI SMITH
The Hour and the Woman, *Brick,* no. 92.

GERALD L. SMITH
Whittling at the Edges of Childhood, *Sewanee Review,* Fall.

MIKE SMITH
My Two Emilys, *Notre Dame Magazine,* Winter.

MIKE SMITH
Place Names of 501 Filomeno, *Tin House,* vol. 16, no. 1.

RON CLINTON SMITH
A Pilgrimage to Dennis Hopper, *River Teeth,* Fall.

ROBERT F. SOMMER
Leavenworth, *Rathalla Review,* January.

ALYSSA GRACE SORRESSO
Don't Borrow Trouble, *Creative Nonfiction,* Summer.

DIANA SPECHLER
The Matchmaker's Mouth, *Southern Review,* Spring.

MATTHEW SPELLBERG
The Chimeric Element in Perception: A First Exploration, *Southwest Review,* vol. 99, no. 1.

WILLARD SPIEGELMAN
Proust Goes to the Country Club, *American Scholar,* Summer.

SUSAN M. STABILE
Bestiary, *Iowa Review,* Fall.

JEFF STAIGER
Kindle 451, *New England Review,* vol. 34, no. 3/4.

BRIAN JAY STANLEY
Taxonomy of Disorder, *North American Review,* Winter.

TIFFANY STANLEY
Jackie's Goodbye, *National Journal,* October 4.

M. D. STEIN
Remains, *Southwest Review,* vol. 99, no. 3.

ADAM STERNBERGH
Smile, You're Speaking Emoji, *New York Magazine,* November 17/23.

SEBASTIAN STOCKMAN
This Fan's Notes: A Football Elegy, *Los Angeles Review,* January 31.

ANDREA STUART
Tourist, *Granta,* no. 129 (Autumn).

JODIE VINSON
Sleeping in on Sundays, *Minerva Rising*, Spring.
ROBERT VIVIAN
Mother Forever, *Upstreet*, no. 10.
MATTHEW VOLLMER
Music of the Spheres: A Meditation on NASA's Symphonies of the Planets, *Normal School*, Spring.

JULIE MARIE WADE
The Big Picture, *Southern Indiana Review*, Spring.
NICOLA WALDRON
My Thick Waist, *Sonora Review*, no. 64/65.
DONNA WALKER
The Stone God's Daughter, *Prick of the Spindle*, no. 7.
NICOLE WALKER
On Anger, *Passages North*, no. 5.
THEODORE WALTHER
Homeless in the City, *American Scholar*, Winter.
MOIRA WEIGEL
Searching for Shanghai, *The Point*, no. 8.
EMILY MEG WEINSTEIN
Mating Habits of the Asterisk, *Morning News*, June 25.
SARAH M. WELLS
Human Resources Training, *The Pinch*, Fall.
TONY WHEDON
Belvidere, *Green Mountains Review*, vol. 27, no. 1.
SUSAN WHITE
Crazy Legs, *The Labletter*, no. 16.
JOEL WHITNEY
Poetry and Action: Octavio Paz at 100, *Dissent*, March 25.
DOUGLAS WHYNOTT
The Extent of the Shock Is Equivalent to the Rate of the Flow, *Massachusetts Review*, Spring.

LEON WIESELTIER
The Mental Odyssey of the Ordinary Citizen, *New Republic*, November 24/December 8.
PATRICIA WILLIAMS
The Luminance of Guilt, *Transition*, no. 113.
ALAN WILLIAMSON
The Trouble with "Theory," *Yale Review*, July.
WENDY WILLIS
Boxed In, *Oregon Humanities*, Fall/Winter.
S. L. WISENBERG
The Jew in the Body, *Ars Medica*, vol. 10, no. 1.
LAURA ESTHER WOLFSON
Infelicities of Style, *ZYZZYVA*, Winter.
SAINT JAMES WOOD
The Smuggling Humans Affair, *Boulevard*, Fall.

AMY YEE
"This Will All Be Under Water," *Roads and Kingdoms*, July 30.
MAKO YOSHIKAWA
Tokyo Monsoon, *Harvard Review*, no. 45.

ANDI ZEISLER
Feel-Good Feminism, *Oregon Humanities*, Fall/Winter.

Notable Special Issues of 2014

Aperture, Fashion, guest ed. Inez & Vinoodh, Fall.

The Believer, The 2014 Film Issue, ed. Heidi Julavits, Andrew Leland, Vendla Vida, March/April.

Brain, Child, Special Issue: Teens, ed. Marcelle Soviero, vol. 16, no. 2.

Chattahoochee Review, Skin, ed. Anna Schachner, Fall/Winter.

Chicago Quarterly Review, The Chicago Issue, ed. S. Afzal Haider and Elizabeth McKenzie.

Conjunctions, Speaking Volumes, ed. Bradford Marrow, no. 63.

Creative Nonfiction, Telling Stories That Matter, ed. Lee Gutkind, Summer.

Daedalus, What Humanists Do, guest ed. Denis Donoghue, Winter.

Denver Quarterly, 150th Anniversary of the Sand Creek Massacre, ed. Billy J. Stratton and Eleni Sikelianos, vol. 49, no. 1.

Ecotone, The Sustenance Issue, ed. David Gessner and Anna Lena Phillips, Fall.

Georgia Review, Strange and Wondrous Pairings, ed. Stephen Corey, Summer.

Hobart, Hotel Culture, ed. Aaron Burch and Elizabeth Ellen, no. 15.

Lapham's Quarterly, Comedy, ed. Lewis Lapham, Winter.

Massachusetts Review, Celebrating 50 Years of the Master of Fine Arts for Poets and Writers, ed. John

Emil Vincent and Pamela Glaven, Spring.

Minerva Rising, Turning Points, ed. Kimberly Brown, Spring.

New Literary History, Interpretation and Its Rivals, ed. Rita Felski, Spring.

New Republic, One Hundredth Anniversary Issue, ed. Franklin Foer, November 24/December 8.

North Dakota Quarterly, Tribute to Robert W. Lewis, ed. Donald Junkins, Linda Patterson Miller, and Richard A. Davison, Summer/Fall.

Oregon Humanities, Me, ed. Kathleen Holt, Spring.

Oxford American, The Music Issue, ed. Roger D. Hodge, Winter.

Seneca Review, We Might as Well Call It the Lyric Essay, ed. John D'Agata and the graduate students of the Nonfiction Writing Program at the University of Iowa, vols. 44, no. 2 and 45, no. 1.

Sewanee Review, War—That Devil's Madness, ed. George Core, Spring.

Threepenny Review, A Symposium on Libraries, ed. Wendy Lesser, Fall.

Transition, What Is Africa to Me Now? ed. Alejandro de la Fuente, no. 113.

Witness, Ghosts, ed. Maile Chapman, Spring.

...

Correction: The following essays should have appeared in *Notable Essays of 2013:*

DEVORAH FREUND, My Father's Death, *Ami,* December 4.

TYLER C. GORE, My Life of Crime, *The American,* December.

CHRIS WIEWIORA, M-I-S-S-I-S-S-I-P-P-I, *Slice,* Fall/Winter.

THE BEST AMERICAN SERIES®

FIRST, BEST, AND BEST-SELLING

The Best American series is the premier annual showcase for the country's finest short fiction and nonfiction. Each volume's series editor selects notable works from hundreds of periodicals. A special guest editor, a leading writer in the field, then chooses the best twenty or so pieces to publish. This unique system has made the Best American series the most respected—and most popular—of its kind.

Look for these best-selling titles in the Best American series:

The Best American Comics

The Best American Essays

The Best American Infographics

The Best American Mystery Stories

The Best American Nonrequired Reading

The Best American Science and Nature Writing

The Best American Science Fiction and Fantasy

The Best American Short Stories

The Best American Sports Writing

The Best American Travel Writing

Available in print and e-book wherever books are sold.
Visit our website: *www.hmhco.com/popular-reading/general-interest-books/by-category/best-american*